GAME OF CAPTIVES

FIRE AND FANG
BOOK 3

LINDSAY BUROKER

1

Newly coronated Queen Syla Moonmark grinned like a little girl as she rode upon the great red dragon Wreylith, who wheeled and dipped and dove above the croplands and pastures of Castle Island. Oh, Syla was occasionally terrified she might fall and constantly worried the wind would rip off her spectacles, but she kept her hands flattened to the dragon's scaled back and used her gods-gifted power to create tendrils of magic that anchored her in place. Whenever Wreylith dove, the grin returned, and Syla relished the breeze whipping about her auburn locks and flapping the hem of her dress. Usually, only stormer dragon riders knew such exhilaration.

Thinking of them reminded Syla of her mission, and she tapped Wreylith. "You're still heading toward Harvest Island so we can observe what our enemies are up to, right? While General Dolok has been polite and obedient in carrying out my orders—almost oddly so—he's been palpably reluctant to keep me informed about the war. The only thing he's admitted is that our warships dare not go near the island because dragons attack them every time. It's also not safe to sail to *other* islands to deliver messages and supplies right now."

Though her military leaders had assured Syla in a meeting that morning that they had numerous plans poised to launch, she believed it would be up to her to return a shielder to Harvest Island. That was the only certain way to deny their enemies a base within the waters of the Garden Kingdom. Too bad she'd lost the magical components needed to repair the broken shielder from Castle Island. Those were currently nestled in a stormer base somewhere.

"Fortunately, I have another plan," she murmured. "Assuming my dragon ally can assist me with it."

Wreylith responded telepathically. *I am indeed flying toward the island that, without the protection of a magical barrier, is exposed to dragons who are denuding the forests of elioks and other delicious prey.*

Syla glanced at the new dragon-shaped tattoo on the back of her left hand, an outward sign of the bond that Wreylith had magically granted her. During the ceremony, they'd promised to assist each other as needed, but Wreylith might also have been motivated by a desire to hunt on shielded Castle Island, something the link allowed as long as Syla was present. Wreylith had suggested she would enjoy it if Syla journeyed to other protected islands in the Garden Kingdom as well, islands that dragons, wyverns, and other aerial predators usually could not access. And denude. The hunting, Wreylith assured her, would be exquisite.

"I only ask because we're flying around the western end of Castle Island, and you keep eyeing the forests edging the pastures, instead of south to Harvest Island."

Many domesticated stormer dragons lurk on Harvest Island, and they will have the ability to see and sense me as I approach. It will be ideal if we wait until twilight to gather your intelligence.

"Won't they sense your powerful approach no matter what time of day it is?"

We need not get that close to observe their activities. Dragon eyes are keen. Twilight will be best.

"Isn't that about the time that your favored horn hogs are most active?" Syla waved toward the woodlands along a pasture they were flying over. "And come out of the trees to drink from the irrigation canals?"

Maybe Wreylith wanted to hunt on *multiple* islands this evening.

Many delicious prey are active at that time of day, yes. The stormer dragons will be more likely to be hunting than lurking around the population centers that you desire to visit.

"Not visit. Check on them from afar to determine if my plan would be possible."

At twilight, checking will be easier.

"Are you sure you don't just want to hunt then yourself? I—"

Wreylith must have spotted something moving in the trees or the pasture because she dove abruptly. Startled, Syla leaned forward and flattened her hands to the dragon's back again.

Wreylith's wings folded to her sides, and her head pointed downward. Syla's weight threatened to send her tumbling forward, her spectacles shifting on her nose despite the strap around her head, but she willed more power into her anchors. The quarter-moon birthmark on her right hand flared silver as she drew upon her magic.

At top speed, Wreylith descended so rapidly that Syla feared they would crash into the pasture. But the dragon's wings extended at the last instant, and her head came up on her long neck. They skimmed over high grass, yellow as summer transitioned into autumn, and rustled the seed heads as Wreylith chased a bristle-backed hog with two horns protruding from the top of its head.

The creature raced through the pasture toward what it believed was the safety of the trees, but it wasn't fast enough.

Wreylith caught up, flew above its back for a moment, then snapped her powerful jaws downward, catching the animal behind the skull. With a loud crunching of bone, she broke the hog's neck. Wings flapping again, she lifted the dying creature from the ground and carried it to a stone wall that divided the pasture from a well-tended garden and farmhouse.

After Wreylith perched, biting and chewing sounds drifted up to Syla.

"Uhm, do you want me to get off?" Syla looked skyward, uncomfortably reminded of the wyverns that had descended upon the castle after the stormer invasion. Like giant scaled vultures, they'd feasted on the dead in the courtyard.

Do you wish to join me in this meal? Though you did not contribute to the slaying of the horn hog, I am not ravenous and would allow you to partake in a small and less desirable portion. The intestines are often stuffed with the remains of partially digested vegetation and are not as appealing as the delicious heart, liver, and tongue. I do love tongue meat. It is hearty and delectable.

"I… Being bonded isn't exactly like what I expected. I wish I'd been able to have more chats with Vorik so I could have asked him about his relationship with Agrevlari."

Wreylith issued a noise between a grunt and grumble at the reminder of the green dragon that she'd mated with while under the influence of magical cactus flowers that had inspired randiness in their entire party. Surprisingly, she didn't say anything insulting about him, but that was probably only because she was busy noshing on delectable tongue meat.

While the dragon ate, Syla thought of Vorik, preferring to picture his handsome face and brilliant smile in her mind over vulturous wyverns or the images that discussing Wreylith's culinary preferences brought up. Syla *shouldn't* have been thinking about Vorik, since he and his lieutenant had been the ones to steal the rare magical shielder components. But… she'd mostly lost them due to her own foolish choice, so she couldn't entirely blame him. Besides, she intended to get them back. These past few days, she'd been scheming up ways to retrieve them. Vorik figured more prominently in those schemes than he probably should have as she envisioned seducing him and questioning him to learn their location. Even if he was her enemy, she struggled to think of him that way, and he remained a fixture in her dreams at night. An active fixture with *very* skilled hands that could make her body—

Wreylith flicked her neck, and something splatted onto the stone wall beside her. Were those... intestines?

"Thanks," Syla said, "but I ate before leaving. I'm fine."

The door to the farmhouse opened, and Syla's instinct was to duck low or even jump behind the stone wall to hide. Horn hogs were wild, not domesticated livestock raised by farmers, but they'd landed on someone's property, and she promptly felt guilty of trespassing.

A man stepped outside with a lit dragonspark match and lifted it toward a lantern mounted on the wall beside the door, but he spotted Wreylith and gaped, stumbling back. The match dropped to the stone pavers at his feet and went out.

"It's all right," Syla called, lifting a hand, not certain if the man had noticed her or only the huge, powerful, and terrifying dragon. "We'll leave momentarily."

He glanced at her but continued to gape at Wreylith.

Perhaps he does not recognize you, the dragon said as she continued to nosh on her meal, the man's appearance not disturbing her enjoyment of the tongue or whatever other favored horn-hog part she was eating now. *You should have worn your crown.*

"It's for ceremonies, diplomatic negotiations, and public appearances," Syla whispered, willing the dragon to finish so they could continue on with their mission.

Are you not currently appearing in public?

"I hadn't *planned* to." Syla hadn't even told her bodyguard, Sergeant Fel, that she was leaving the castle. He wouldn't have approved of her departing, even with a powerful dragon ally, without him. He wouldn't approve of this self-appointed mission at *all.* "Besides, the crown fits awkwardly when I'm wearing the strap to keep my spectacles on."

She touched the rims of the new crimson-framed pair that she wore, the color a match for Wreylith's gleaming red scales. When Syla had finally caught up with her optometrist, he'd been awestruck by the dragon but inspired as well. He'd not only made her the spectacles she'd ordered but two spare sets as well. She would, he'd assured her, require myriad options now that she was the queen and didn't always wear a drab dark-blue healer's robe. She'd accepted the extras, but she wanted spares less for fashion and more because encounters with assassins, dragons, and enemy riders were likely to break her spectacles regularly.

Wreylith emitted a noise like a belch. Maybe it *was* a belch. Something else that Vorik hadn't mentioned to Syla that dragons did.

The heads of two children peeked out of the door behind the man.

"It's Queen Syla!" one blurted.

"She's come to bless our farm!"

Syla eyed the intestines draped over the wall. That had to be the opposite of *blessing.* Before she could do more than wave at the children, Wreylith finished her meal and sprang into the air.

We will depart before your minions suggest that you have tamed *me*, Wreylith said.

"They're my subjects, and I'm composing an article for the newspaper that will explain your independence, fearsomeness, and magnanimity in assisting me with defending the Kingdom." Syla had already written it, but she hadn't yet figured out how to get it printed without her cousin, Relvin, the editor of the *Kingdom*

Journal, altering it into something scandalous and untrue—if he allowed it to be distributed at all.

I should think my fearsome independence would be evident to all. As the setting sun burnished her scales, Wreylith soared over the remaining croplands and pastures and headed south toward the Sea of Storms and Harvest Island, its outline soon visible on the horizon.

"It should be, yes."

In minutes, dragons could fly the miles that it took ships many hours to sail, and twilight wasn't yet deep when they neared the shallower waters around Harvest Island. Fires burned inland, the flames bright against the encroaching darkness, and Syla grimaced. They weren't campfires or anything that had been started by humans. More likely, stormer-allied dragons had wantonly lit the forest and farmlands on fire. Maybe their riders had even *encouraged* them to, though why they wanted to damage the island they were trying to claim for their people, Syla didn't know.

"Trying to?" she murmured.

The stormers had successfully taken over Harvest Island, driving out or killing the Kingdom troops, and pillaging vineyards, bogs, and croplands for food. Thus far, her attempts to get messages to and receive reports from the island lord, Ravoran, had failed. Only rumors from refugees suggested he was still alive and directing the local populace.

Unfortunately, Syla wouldn't likely be able to find and speak with him this evening. Wreylith would have to keep her distance. What Syla hoped to learn was how many dragons were in the area and if she might successfully sail over with the ancient gods-created weapons platform that she'd recovered from the Dire Desert. At the moment, it rested in the castle courtyard where Wreylith's allies had dropped it, the magical marble proving heavy and difficult to move. But it would be worth the effort to do so if it could be transported here until a shielder could be returned to the island.

I sense wild dragons and also stormer dragons, Wreylith said, though Syla couldn't see any winged creatures in the sky.

"Near Hazel Harbor or farther inland?"

Based on a couple of tests Syla had done with the weapons platform, she believed it could send its magical projectiles about five miles. Since Harvest Island, only a little smaller than Castle Island, was more than thirty miles across in places, she would only be able to protect a portion of it. But if she could sail the weapons platform to the island's capital, the city wrapped around Hazel Harbor, she could defend a good portion of the population. More, people currently hiding on their farmsteads and in their homes on other parts of the island could flee there for protection.

Most hunt inland, but I sense a couple of stormer dragons among the dwellings in the city. They may be perched on rooftops as scouts, watching the skies for spies even as we seek to observe them.

"Right. Let's not get close."

Had you more dragon allies, you might drive them away.

"Sadly, only one dragon has seen my worth and offered to align with me."

Few are as perspicacious as I am.

"That's a good word. I'll see if I can work it into your newspaper article."

Yes. Wreylith banked before reaching the harbor and flapped her wings to head back north.

In the distance, in the direction of the volcano Syla had visited weeks earlier, a couple more dragons flew into view, their winged silhouettes visible against the darkening sky. She chewed on her lip, having a feeling that openly sailing over here with ships would be difficult. There were probably enough dragons in the area that they could keep the fleet from getting close. Since it had lost many ships during the initial invasion of Castle Island, she wouldn't be able to bring as many as she wished.

Could she launch weapons from the platform while it was on the moving deck of a vessel? She would have to experiment.

Before deciding on that mission, Syla would speak again with General Dolok to see if his intelligence officers had learned the location of the stormer headquarters. If she could retrieve the stolen components and bring a repaired shielder to Harvest Island, *that* would be ideal.

Before they'd turned fully away from the harbor, Syla glimpsed a dragon flying up from the city. One of the ones that had been skulking about on a rooftop down there? It flew after them but not at top speed.

That one desires to make certain we are departing, Wreylith said.

"Did he or she speak to you?"

No. I've had few telepathic conversations with stormer dragons or even my wild kin since our bonding.

Syla digested that as she gazed back at the dragon. It flew out over the sea, following them. "Is it because... Are you being ostracized? Because of me?"

It hadn't occurred to her that Wreylith might be lowered in status with the wild dragons because she was now bonded to a human and allowing herself to be ridden. And the stormer dragons might be irked with Wreylith too since she was helping someone from the Garden Kingdom. Even though the gods had been responsible for long ago placing the shields over the twelve islands, the shields that kept dragons and other aerial predators out, Syla could imagine that their winged kind believed her people at the heart of the problem, their inability to hunt on those islands.

I go where I wish and do what I wish with whom I wish.

"That's a yes, isn't it?" Syla patted Wreylith's back. "I'm sorry. I appreciate your help."

Yes. One of Wreylith's eyes rotated to consider the dragon behind them. It hadn't gained on them, but it also wasn't veering away, and it was undoubtedly following them, not coincidentally flying in the same direction.

Abruptly, Wreylith's attention swung forward. Beyond her horns, Castle Island was visible. At first, Syla didn't see anything that could have drawn Wreylith's attention. Then, a blue dragon and a yellow dragon flew up from the northern side of the island —they'd been hidden by the bluff on which Garden Castle perched.

Syla sucked in a startled breath as the dragons headed in their direction. "Are they under the shield?"

The barrier couldn't have fallen. Not in the short time that Syla and Wreylith had been gone.

They fly just above it, their bellies nearly skimming the translucent surface.

Syla would have found that a relief—the dragons couldn't have been threatening her people—but they were flying straight toward her.

Wreylith beat her wings faster. *They intend to cut us off and prevent us from reaching the protection of the shield.*

"You mean they're going to attack us?"

A growl emanated from Wreylith's throat and reverberated through her body. *That is the only way they could prevent me from reaching my destination.*

Unlike the dragon following them, the two heading toward them had riders. One was a woman with two long braids of silver hair, and Syla's gut clenched. From this distance, she couldn't make out facial features, but Captain Lesva, the vile rider who'd magically tortured her, had silver hair and rode a blue dragon.

Hold on tight, Wreylith warned.

Hands planted on scales, Syla willed more power into the dragon through their link, anchoring herself in place. The effort drained her, especially since, until recently, she'd only used her gods-gift for healing, but falling a thousand feet into the ocean would drain her even more. Likely by killing her.

As the yellow and blue dragons flew closer, they spread apart. Intending to catch Wreylith between them so they could bite and slash at her flanks from either side?

Wreylith flew to a higher altitude and angled away. As the dragons attempted to follow, to cut her off and engage her, the riders drew weapons. A male stormer that Syla hadn't seen before rode the yellow, and he hefted a gargoyle-bone bow, the arrows also carved from the magical material.

On the blue dragon, the rider lifted a gargoyle-bone sword. Yes, that was Lesva. Her blue eyes locked on Syla with cold determination, and she waved the blade threateningly.

"Looks like she wants to kill me this time, not question me," Syla said.

Wreylith, wings beating hard, sought to outfly the dragons and maneuver around them. Or at least, Syla *thought* that was what an outnumbered dragon would do. But after Wreylith had half-circled around the pair, she banked hard, angling toward the yellow dragon, and tilted alarmingly. Syla flattened herself to Wreylith's back while applying more of her magic.

It was luck and desperation more than skill that saved her, for the archer, though surprised by the dragon turning on him, loosed an arrow. It whizzed past scant inches above Syla's head.

Wreylith opened her maw, roared, and launched a gout of fire at the yellow dragon. But Lesva's blue was coming around its ally, opening its own maw. Lesva leaned forward on its back, almost quivering in her eagerness to get close enough to lop Syla's head off with her sword.

Perhaps you should learn to use a weapon, Wreylith suggested, her telepathic voice calm even though she was in the middle of twisting to parry jaws snapping toward her head.

I'm not bad at throwing books at things.

That is unlikely to deter a determined enemy.

Unfortunately, I've found that to be true. This time, Syla spotted the archer firing. She had to duck and dip halfway off Wreylith's back to avoid the arrow, but it buzzed past without hitting her.

In the mayhem, the two dragons managed to surround Wreylith briefly. Her wings bumped against those of the blue dragon, and she tilted to get away but also raked the air with her forelimbs, talons slashing toward their enemies. But only for an instant. Without the steady wingbeats, gravity caught up to Wreylith, and she fell away from the other dragons.

Syla's heart tried to spring out of her throat. The strap of her spectacles threatened to fly off her head, and she smashed her frames to her face to keep them on.

Once she'd fallen well below the other dragons, Wreylith started flapping her wings again. Maybe all along she'd intended the move as a way to escape them.

Booms came from below, startling Syla. Thanks to the deepening darkness and all the gyrating they'd done, it took her a moment to realize they were over Sky Torn Harbor and Garden Castle. Home.

A familiar warm buzz against her skin made her sag with relief. They'd passed through the barrier. Wreylith clearly felt it too, for her flying turned into something of a smug sashay.

One more arrow flew after them—no, straight at *Syla*—but Wreylith turned, snapped her jaws, and caught it before it struck.

Thank the gods. No, thank *Wreylith*.

The stormer dragons were unable to follow her. They flew back and forth above the barrier, their version of pacing in agitation.

Again, cannons fired from castle walls. The mundane iron balls lacked the oomph of the magical projectiles the weapons platform could send out, but they reached beyond the shielder, and the blue and yellow dragons had to fly apart to avoid them.

Their riders glared down at Syla for a moment, but Wreylith flew farther from them, descending toward the castle without looking back. Syla also turned her back but not before spotting Lesva glaring after her.

"Coward!" the woman called, the wind not quite muffling the word.

Syla clenched her jaw in irritation. She didn't have a weapon, and they'd been outnumbered.

"Fleeing was prudent, not cowardly," she said, though Lesva and her allies were flying off and couldn't hear.

Is that another word that you will incorporate in your newspaper article? Wreylith asked.

"Probably not. People aren't tantalized to read about prudence."

Alas. As a queen, wasn't that a quality Syla should seek to achieve?

As Wreylith spread her wings to slow their descent toward the courtyard, Syla looked back at their enemies again, wondering if the dragons would linger in the area. No, they were flying south, back to Harvest Island.

Syla grimaced at the knowledge that she would have to deal with the captain to get that territory back for the Kingdom. And Lesva was going to make it personal.

2

AFTER PACKING, CAPTAIN VORIK HEADED TO THE BACK OF THE LARGE cave that housed the Wingborn Tribe and currently acted as the Sixteen Talons headquarters. Soon, they would all head to a new camp, the stormers never staying in one place long enough for Garden Kingdom intelligence officers to figure out their location.

Vorik wrinkled his nose. Unlike in the front of the cave, where the salty breeze swept past the wide ledge overlooking the Sea of Storms and cleared the air, smoke and the scents of past meals and body odor hung thickly. He looked forward to a change. Or... would he soon have a new mission?

In a nook, Vorik's brother and the commander of the Sixteen Talons, General Jhiton, stood with Chieftess Shi and General Amalia, their heads bowed as they spoke around a campfire. Highlighted by the dancing flames, their lean faces were determined, their eyes intent.

Jhiton shook his head, and Shi frowned, pointing a finger at his chest and then toward the front of the cave. In the direction of the Kingdom? The sprawling chain of a dozen islands lay many hours of travel by dragon to the southwest, but they were a likely topic of discussion. And Jhiton, who frowned and shook his head again, didn't like something that he was hearing. Amalia, who commanded the Storm Guard, also wore a bleak expression, but she didn't make any negative gestures.

Usually, Vorik would avoid meetings among the tribe leaders and highest-ranking military officers, instead waiting for his superiors to hand down orders for him and his squadron of riders, but something Lieutenant Wise had said on their last mission had been niggling at him. No, *disturbing* him.

Apparently, some of the chiefs had spoken of, "Ruling over the gardeners and keeping our existing life while they farm for us."

A couple of months ago, before Vorik had crossed paths with —no, had orders to seduce and question—then-princess-and-now-queen Syla Moonmark, he had been indifferent to the Kingdom. Countless times over the years, following orders from above, he'd battled their soldiers as they sailed between their islands. He'd never minded, since the goal had been to obtain food from their bounteous lands, food that could sustain his people during the harsh winters and storm seasons. But now… he cared deeply about at least *one* gardener, as his people called the agricultural people, and that made him want to find a peaceful way forward, or at least one that wouldn't result in eternal hostilities and war. He also didn't think his freedom-loving people should enslave others, as Chief Tenilor had suggested. That wasn't *honorable*.

"Captain Vorik." Jhiton, who'd seen him coming, inclined his head toward him instead of shooing him away. He'd smoothed his frown, his expression now neutral, his scarred face and green eyes hard to read, as usual.

Also nodding at Vorik, General Amalia seemed receptive of him joining the meeting. Shi's gaze was less welcoming, her eyes slitting slightly as she regarded him, and her thin lips pinching together.

"Evening, generals and chieftess," Vorik drawled. "It's a fine night to pack one's loincloths, sword oil, and dragon bribes, isn't it?"

Shi mouthed *loincloths* as she retied a thong binding back her graying brown hair.

The ever-deadpan Jhiton, who, when they were in public, never responded in kind to Vorik's jokes, gazed impassively at him.

Amalia, a handsome woman despite weathered brown skin and close-shorn gray hair, had a touch more humor in her dark eyes as she mouthed, "Dragon bribes?"

"I've smoked up some salmon for Agrevlari," Vorik said. "He performs best if I feed him delicacies while singing ballads pronouncing the magnificence of dragons."

"Did you give him salmon before he attacked Ozlemar above a whaling ship full of enemies?" Jhiton asked.

"No, I didn't, and I think that's why his behavior was substandard. That and his perennial aching and pining for the beauteous wild dragon Wreylith."

"My teenage daughters would assure you that salmon can't cure aching and pining," Amalia said.

"That dragon isn't *wild* anymore, is she?" Shi asked without humor. "She has a rider."

"Ah." When all three gazes fixated on him—*accusingly* fixated? —Vorik didn't know what to say. "I do believe she's decided to allow the Garden Kingdom queen to ride her."

Saying *the queen* instead of mentioning Syla by name, probably while showing aching and pining in his own eyes, seemed wise when dealing with the chieftess. With anyone who might be concerned about Vorik's allegiance these days. To remind them he always did his duty and was loyal to the tribe, he waved toward another nook in the back of the cave. It contained the three magical components that he and Wise had stolen from Syla's team. He hadn't admitted to anyone that the ignoble act had bothered him or that, more than once, he'd thought about slipping out of camp with the components and taking them to Syla while imagining how delighted and grateful she would be. He'd acquired them. That ought to be all that mattered.

"There are rumors that the new queen now has a dragon tattoo," Shi said, "and is bonded with Wreylith. Do you know anything about that, Captain Vorik?"

"I wasn't there to witness that, no." Vorik pulled his gaze from the components in time to see Shi frowning at him. With suspicion? "I came over here because I'd like to know what our people plan for the Garden Kingdom. What's being done to the subjects who live on Harvest Island? Will they be kicked out to find homes in the rest of the Kingdom, or will they be forced to work to feed our people? And what of the subjects on future islands we may capture?"

Jhiton raised his eyebrows, probably surprised that Vorik was asking and not simply waiting for someone to give him orders.

"I assume we're still planning to capture more islands," Vorik added.

"We are." Jhiton looked to Shi, as if to say she could answer the rest.

Capturing as many of the islands as possible had always been his goal, so Vorik wondered what he'd been disagreeing with her about.

"Why do you want that information, Captain?" Shi asked softly, her eyes locked on Vorik. Was that suspicion again? What, did she think he would turn traitor and report everything he learned to the Kingdom? To *Syla*?

Vorik lifted his chin. "For my own edification. I don't believe we should include enslaving people as part of our plans, and I understand that's been discussed. The tribes aren't united enough to rule over a nation. We don't even officially have our *own* nation. Even if we were and we did, we don't have a large enough population to keep the gardeners under our thumbs. It would be dangerous in the long term. Besides, it's not honorable to enslave other human beings. We should take the islands, drive the subjects away to whatever others the Kingdom will retain, and gather and hunt food there ourselves. The islands can be our new homes and headquarters so we don't have to spend time scurrying from temporary camp to camp while always living in dark, dank caves to avoid aerial predators."

"Nobody has said anything of enslaving anyone," Shi said.

Jhiton's eyelids flickered, but he didn't contradict her. Vorik believed Wise had accurately relayed what he'd heard the chiefs speaking about; he'd had no reason to lie about that.

"That's good then." Vorik opted out of calling Shi a liar. Instead, he smiled and bowed. "After all, if you put a leash on something, the other end attaches to you, and you're as bound as your captive."

"You will have a new mission soon, Captain," Shi said. "I suggest you focus on it and leave the leadership and command of the tribes to others who are more dedicated and capable."

Vorik's jaw tightened. Just because he'd never butted into meetings before didn't mean he wasn't dedicated to serving his people. It certainly didn't mean he wasn't *capable*.

Shi stepped closer and gazed into his eyes. She was a couple of inches shorter than he, but she, like most of the tribal leaders, was bound to a dragon and radiated power granted to her via their magical link. Though she was twenty years older than Vorik, he wouldn't assume that he could defeat her without trouble in a battle. It hadn't been that many years since she'd won her place as chieftess by defeating the previous tribal leader in a duel.

"Your interest in the queen makes your motivations suspect," Shi said softly, "and you're not acting like your usual self, Captain. These aren't the kinds of questions you typically ask."

Vorik didn't back up or look away. "In the past, I haven't had reason for concern over the choices being made. We should be careful about the future we're trying to create. We all know we need to do something new to survive the changing climate and scarcity of food it's bringing, but if we stray too far from our origins, we may lose our way and become something we don't wish."

"I will note your concern," Shi said without sincerity. "And *you*, Captain, will engage in your next mission and follow your orders. Should you one day rise in the ranks, you may have a place among the elders and leaders of the tribes and military, but you are yet young. And impulsive. And occasionally ruled by elements other than your *brain*." She glanced toward his groin before lifting her chin and walking away.

General Amalia, who'd watched the exchange without much expression, raised her eyebrows toward Jhiton, then clasped her hands behind her back and also strolled away.

Vorik eyed his brother warily. He didn't *think* he'd given Jhiton a reason to doubt his loyalty, but, as he'd many times noted, Jhiton could be hard to read.

"There's a new mission?" Vorik asked to change the subject. That topic seemed safer.

"Why are you pulling on wyvern tails, Vorik?" Jhiton asked.

"It sounds like some of the older and more crotchety wyverns have a future planned that would *not* be good for our people. And would ensure the gardeners are enemies for all eternity."

"That's ensured anyway."

"Why?"

"We've killed almost all of their royal family, slain many members of their military, captured their high-ranking leaders on Harvest Island, and delivered damage to two of their major cities. So far."

"Yes, I realize that. I *was* there." For the Castle Island attack, he had been. Thus far, Jhiton had Captain Lesva leading the troops on Harvest Island, and he hadn't sent Vorik over there since its shield had fallen. "But war is war. That's how things go. If we can establish a treaty with their people after we've claimed enough islands to nourish the tribes going forward, we wouldn't have to constantly watch our backs in the years and generations to come."

"You've a naive belief in that regard. Or did Queen Syla suggest that?"

"She doesn't talk politics with me and is evasive about answering my questions on most subjects. This is my own opinion. I don't think enslaving a population should be a part of our plans."

"Our goal is to obtain *all* of the Garden Kingdom islands for our people. There will be no place else for the gardeners to live except under our rule."

"We don't have enough people to establish *rule* over twelve islands. Unless you plan to kill most of their population—which would not be honorable and I *hope* is not your plan..." Vorik watched his brother's face for a reaction but didn't get much. "Unless their population got a lot smaller, we'd never rule successfully over so many."

"History tells us that it takes very few people to reign over a population. Before the storm god's mad tinkerings, there were many human civilizations, and an elite few always ruled over the masses. There are ways to keep people in line."

"That's not *really* our goal, is it? Your goal? I know you spoke of taking all their islands, but don't you really just want there to be a food supply and safe place for our people to live in the future? A world where children can be raised safely without being killed by the storm god's creations?" Vorik raised his eyebrows, certain Jhiton's lost son, Jebrosh, was never far from his mind.

"I do want that. As to the rest, I'm a soldier, Vorik. As are you. I may have some sway with the chiefs, but I'm not in charge of our people."

"How many of our leaders want to enslave the gardeners? I know Shi was lying to me."

"Not all of them. It's being contested at the tribe meetings. Chief Tenilor is the one pushing for that. Swordhawk and Sunchaser speak as you do and have no interest in ruling over others. Chieftess Marvola of the Starlion Tribe just wants hazelnuts and pears."

"I knew it. She's my favorite of our tribal leaders. I wish she were in charge of Wingborn."

"Because her loyalty might also be won with a berry cobbler?"

"You *know* my loyalty is to our people."

Jhiton smiled slightly and waved to a couple of troops who'd walked their way but hesitated to approach while they were speaking. He pointed them toward the three components.

"Be careful with the urn," Jhiton said. "The contents are magical, but I don't believe the container itself is."

"Yes, sir."

"I'm told it's an amphora," Vorik said. "Not an urn."

"By the queen?" Jhiton asked.

"She was a princess at the time, but yes."

The two men wrapped the components in hides and carried them off.

Aware of Jhiton watching him, Vorik didn't ask where they would be taken. He'd already issued enough questions that his superiors didn't care for, and he didn't want Jhiton to suspect that he'd been contemplating taking the components to Syla. Besides, it wasn't as if Vorik had *seriously* considered that. He'd mostly daydreamed about Syla's potential gratitude and how she might physically reward him if he showed up with them, but it had been a fantasy, nothing more.

"What's the new mission?" Vorik asked again.

"I'm considering if you're the right person to lead it."

Vorik fought the urge to bristle and grow indignant. "Does that mean it has to do with Queen Syla?"

Eyes of the moon, what were his people contemplating now? He already worried that Captain Lesva, who'd requested the mission of assassinating Syla to ensure she was no longer a threat, would find a way to slip away from Harvest Island and make her desire a reality.

"It shouldn't," Jhiton said. "Harvest Island is fully under our control. While the Kingdom is trying to figure out how they'll get it back, it's the perfect time to take control of *another* island. As long as the queen stays on Castle Island, she shouldn't appear in your flight path."

"She has a dragon and wants those components back. I wouldn't assume she'll stay put."

"Perhaps not, but she shouldn't have a reason to visit Bogberry Island anytime soon. If she's scheming ways to get the components, she shouldn't be looking in that direction."

"That's probably true, unless their intelligence officers figure out that we'll strike there next. Since it's the other of the three northernmost islands that are clumped relatively close together, it makes sense as a target. Wouldn't it be wiser to strike at one farther down the chain?"

"As we've discussed before, our chiefs believe that if we ultimately can only acquire three islands, it would be easiest for us to defend the ones together at one end of the chain." Jhiton hitched a shoulder, as if indifferent. He wanted *all* the islands and probably believed they could get them. "As to the Kingdom's ability to obtain information on our plans, we've been careful about finding and ostracizing Freeborn Faction spies. And the intelligence officers that the Kingdom itself sends out are hard-pressed to even find our camps. Without dragons of their own, they can rely only on their slow-moving naval ships. Ships we regularly attack at various locations around the Sea of Storms so that their crews are confused about where our people originate."

"Yes." Over the years, Vorik had been a part of many of those attacks. He'd also watched as his people hid and did nothing while enemy ships sailed past within sight of their camps. "What do you want me to do on Bogberry Island?"

Jhiton didn't answer right away. Did he doubt that Vorik was the right officer for the job?

"Jhiton, you can trust me to competently lead a military mission. Even if I have doubts about what some of the tribal leaders want to do in a hypothetical future in which we've been successful at all our aspirations, I wouldn't act against your wishes. You're—we're... With Mother and Father and our brother gone, you're all I have left. And I owe you for... a lot."

"I believe you, but I would like you to give me your word about something."

Vorik tensed, worried this would be about Syla. "What?"

"If you *do* decide that you disagree with the tribal leaders and the direction they want to take the tribes, fight them in the way of our people, not through covert sabotage."

"What, by challenging Shi to a duel for the leadership of the tribe?"

"Exactly that. If you want to effect change..." Jhiton spread his palm toward the roof of the cave.

"I don't want to be a tribe leader. I'm not even— You know I'm not ambitious. All I want is to be a dutiful warrior and to continue flying into battle with Agrevlari. Maybe I also want a few strawberries every summer."

Jhiton gazed at him.

"*You* could challenge Shi," Vorik suggested. "You'd win that duel—I have no doubt—and such a maneuver wouldn't be without precedent. It's rare, but there *have* been chiefs who also commanded the Storm Guard or Sixteen Talons."

"Not for long," Jhiton said softly. "It's never been encouraged, and it's been during desperate times when it's happened. Remember the warlord Avidrak from our own history? And how a dagger in his back ended his life? People want their government, even a government as simple as ours, and their military separated so that the tribes don't turn into dictatorships. Besides, commanding soldiers is more appealing to me than leading civilians. Soldiers are disciplined." He gave Vorik a sidelong look. "Most of them."

"My discipline is excellent."

"Until someone drops a strawberry in your path."

"Please. It would take a handful of strawberries and a peach to deter me from a task."

"I'll keep that in mind."

"While I'm away on the mission you're going to assign me?" Vorik didn't yet know what the mission *was* and mostly longed for it because... to have been considered for it and not given it would mean he'd lost his brother's faith. Maybe some of his trust. The idea stung, and when Jhiton hesitated again, Vorik closed his eyes. As difficult as it would be, he needed to get all thoughts of Syla out of his mind so there wouldn't be conflicts of interest going forward.

"You should have kidnapped her," Jhiton said gently, as if he knew exactly what Vorik was thinking and wasn't completely without sympathy.

"To use her against her people and keep her prisoner for her moon-mark forever forward?"

"To be your mate," Jhiton said dryly. "We discussed that."

"That was before she became the queen. Even as a princess, she wouldn't have come to live a nomadic life full of danger and hard conditions."

"That is *not* how our future will be." Jhiton gripped his shoulder. "We've already acquired one island. We will have more. Lord

Oyenar, who governs over Bogberry Island, greatly loves his wife, Lady Abrya, who has a moon-mark. Our spies believe that she also loves him and is loyal to her people but may have a soft spot for stormers. Decades ago, her older sister lived with one of the tribes for years, until her stormer lover died, and she brought back many romantic tales that she relayed to the lady. We don't believe Abrya would openly betray her people, but she may be easier to influence than others. Our spies believe she is the one entrusted with the location of the Bogberry Island shielder."

"Please tell me you don't want me to kidnap her and seduce her." Vorik grimaced.

"That *was* suggested, since your supposedly devastating smile has occasionally appealed to even elders, but I assured the chiefs that you wouldn't mate with a sixty-five-year-old married woman."

"I wouldn't *mate* with a married woman of any age."

Jhiton acknowledged that with a palm tilted upward.

"I will, however, point out that my devastating smile *especially* works on elders. They're flattered when I flirt with them. But Jhiton, I don't want to kidnap anyone else." Technically, he hadn't kidnapped Syla. He'd pretended to want to protect her and gone along on her mission, but he'd *lied* to her the whole time, and his intent had been to use her to his own ends. It had *not* appealed to his honor. Or to him. "And, as wondrous as my smile is, I doubt it would prompt a loyal Kingdom subject to betray her island."

"You only need to retrieve the woman. We've a plan for the rest."

Vorik rubbed his face. "Do you really approve of such tactics? Kidnapping old women?"

"No. That was part of our disagreement." Jhiton nodded in the direction Shi had gone. "I wanted to have you kidnap the husband."

"That's not all that honorable either."

"Perhaps not, but he is the one who stepped forward to rule

the island on behalf of the crown. When you enter into a position of leadership, you must accept that you might be a target of machinations. And he's reputedly a former military officer and a warrior. I didn't think it would be as objectionable to you." His voice softened. "It wouldn't have been as objectionable to me."

"I wish we didn't have to use such tactics at all. I prefer facing my enemies openly in battle, not skulking around and *kidnapping* them."

"I know, but, as you pointed out, even though we are strong warriors, our population is much, much smaller than that of the Kingdom. We must sometimes use equivocal tactics to achieve our goals. In the end, it will be worth it." Jhiton nodded firmly.

Vorik wished he were that certain, but he had long ago sworn to do his duty as a member of the Sixteen Talons, which meant taking orders from the chiefs and his superior officers.

"I'm not going to torture the lady to get the information out of her," Vorik said.

"That shouldn't be necessary. Our people went back to investigate the storm god's laboratory that you revealed, and Healer Yavaron found a container of rare hydra-scale powder." Jhiton delved into a pocket and withdrew a small blue jar.

"Hydras are extinct."

"Hence the rarity of the powder."

"What does it do?"

"It makes people susceptible to telling the truth. Very susceptible. Especially if they feel camaraderie toward the person applying the drug and asking the questions. If Lady Abrya is already inclined to think favorably of stormers, and she likes your smile..."

Vorik sighed. It would still be an interrogation, just not physically painful. "Are you sure you don't want me to lead a squadron of riders to attack some nice military ships?"

"You did ask for this mission. Besides, it's important. We need to act while we can. I don't know if you heard, but we lost several of our warships two days ago. We had them anchored in the bay protected by the Sunchaser Tribe, but, after a volcano erupted inland, the wyverns, cloud strikers, and other predators in the area were particularly aggressive. They swept in and attacked the camp and destroyed several of our vessels in addition to killing a number of our people and injuring the two dragons on guard there."

"One might take that as a sign that the gods don't want us to make war."

"I did consider that," Jhiton surprised him by saying. "That volcano hasn't erupted in centuries. You know I'm not overly religious, but I don't deny that the gods exist and were heavily involved in our world at one time. Perhaps one or more has returned. I brought the notion up with Shi and Tenilor."

"And they scoffed?"

"They accused me of being superstitious."

"You're about as superstitious as a boot."

"I'm not sure if I should take that as a compliment or not."

"Good." Vorik smiled but only briefly. On their earlier mission, he and Wise had considered if Syla was being assisted by one of the gods. Vorik believed it was possible and didn't like the idea that he might be going against the wishes of the deities that the stormers and gardeners shared.

"These are the orders I've been given," Jhiton said, "and I'm sworn to obey our leaders. Just as you are."

"I am, yes."

"Once we find the Bogberry Island shielder, we won't destroy it. As you, I believe, pointed out, leaving the islands undefended isn't ideal, as part of the reason they're bountiful is that aerial predators can't harass the livestock and wild animals there, and we'll only be able to protect limited land area with our dragon allies. Instead of destroying further shielders, we'll aim to take control of them. For that, we'll need someone with a moon-mark on our side."

Vorik stepped back. "Is *that* why you suggested I bring Syla here and convince her to become my mate?"

"It is one of the reasons. She would, as I said, birth strong children with you, and a healer with the gods-gift would be an asset to our people."

"Her coming here and staying isn't going to happen."

"I agree that's unlikely now that she's queen."

"It was unlikely before."

"I thought your smile ensured the adoration of women."

"Oh, she might adore me, but she's not leaving her people."

Unfortunately, Vorik didn't know if even the first part of that sentence was likely. He hadn't been there when Syla had woken from her daze after using the weapons platform, but he suspected she'd cursed his name after he and Wise had absconded with the shielder components. For all he knew, she'd drawn a picture of him and was having her troops use it for axe-throwing practice in her castle courtyard.

"She's loyal to them and bound by her duty," Vorik added softly, respecting her for that even as he lamented those traits.

"I know," Jhiton said, and maybe he did. Syla had been willing to give up her life to protect the shielder, and he'd witnessed that. "After all, she tried to blow me up twice."

"Yeah, but any woman with sense would do that." Vorik smiled though he wasn't in a mood for humor.

"Perhaps so." Jhiton briefly returned the smile. "Retrieve the island lord's wife, Vorik. Since she also has a moon-mark, we can use her while we have her to access the island's shielder. If you don't want to question her under the influence of the hydra-scale powder, I will."

Such determination filled his eyes, that Vorik didn't dare argue further.

Jhiton shifted his cloak aside to withdraw a folded piece of paper from his pocket, then handed it to Vorik. "A portrait of the husband and wife to help you identify them."

As Vorik considered the bespectacled woman in the ink sketch, his stomach sank. Many people in the Kingdom wore spectacles, so it didn't mean there was a link to Syla, but...

"She looks like a cross between Syla and her aunt Tibby," Vorik said. "Is she related to them?"

"All of those with a moon-mark are related, if distantly after so many generations since the gods first branded their ancestors. I believe Lady Abrya is one of the queen's aunt's cousins."

Vorik sighed. He hadn't liked the kidnapping plan before, but now it felt like it would be a direct betrayal to Syla. *Another* one.

"You leave in the morning to retrieve the lady," Jhiton stated, then clasped his hands behind his back and started to walk away.

"Is this really the path forward that you want to take, Jhiton?"

"No," came his brother's soft reply over his shoulder.

"But orders?"

"Orders." Jhiton walked away without looking back.

Vorik wished he hadn't argued to have this mission. The chiefs were turning noble riders into brigands. But what choice did he have but to obey?

3

Lanterns burned all along the walls of the courtyard when Wreylith landed near the weapons platform and Syla slid off her back. Among the usual soldiers that guarded the castle from the towers, gatehouse, and walls, Sergeant Fel stood in the area, and he strode toward her with a scowl that could have withered the wings off a wyvern. Given his six-and-a-half-feet in height, broad shoulders, scars, and muscles that men half his age would have envied, he was an intimidating figure.

"Good evening, Sergeant," Syla hurried to say before he could lecture her on departing without a bodyguard—and the entourage of troops he'd said a queen should have to defend her. "Is Aunt Tibby around? Have she and my cousin Teyla made any progress in figuring out how to make the weapons platform operable to more people than me? One would think that anyone with a moon-mark should be able to use it to defend the castle."

Since Syla had only been gone an hour, she doubted her aunt and cousin had figured out anything, but she'd learned long ago that tirades could sometimes be diverted by a tangent or three. *Usually,* she'd employed that tactic in the temple, hoping to distract patients from their discomfort until she could fully heal them, but she'd also had opportunities of late to practice on the military officers who hadn't wanted to see her return from her last mission. She still didn't know if General Dolok had been the one to send the Royal Fleet—and handpicked assassins—after her or if that had been someone else's scheme. He, of course, denied it, and, without proof, she hadn't attempted to remove him from his position. Not *yet*. Once she got a shield back in place around Harvest Island, she would deal with internal affairs—like ferreting out all the people who wanted her dead so they could have the throne.

"Your aunt called me a troglodyte three times, then grumbled under her breath as she took your cousin to the library to search for more reference materials." Fel waved to the weapons platform resting atop cracked flagstones in the center of the courtyard—the place where the dragons had dropped it. Looking somewhat like a giant marble four-poster bed with a canopy on top, it was a strange adornment for the royal castle, but it had proven capable of harming dragons, so Syla would never object to its presence. "She did not seem enlightened," he added.

"It doesn't sound like it, no. As I recall, the runes carved into it roughly translate to: *one blessed by the gods and sworn to protect her people might call upon its power.* Others with similar intent and a moon-mark should be able to operate it."

"From what I gathered, she's irritated that *she* hasn't been able to do so."

"Is that why she insulted you? Misdirected frustration?"

"She insulted me because I was distracting her by stalking around the courtyard, thumping my fist against walls in irritation because the charge I'm sworn to protect took off on a dragon without me."

"That was rude of that charge."

"*Yes.*" There was the scowl again. "While you were gone,

Colonel Mosworth came by looking for you and suggested that a bodyguard who can't keep up with his charge should retire."

Syla grimaced, even though she knew Fel, who neared sixty, *wanted* to retire. He'd served twenty years in the military and then another twenty years as a bodyguard for the royal family. He *deserved* to retire, and he'd been on the verge of it when the stormers had invaded. But he was also one of her few trustworthy allies.

"Colonel Mosworth might replace you with someone who has orders to assassinate me at the first opportunity," she said, though he, like General Dolok, had been polite since her return with Wreylith. Polite, respectful, and even obedient. She didn't trust either of them.

Fel chewed on the statement for a moment. Since she'd spent the last ten years of her life serving in the temple and only occasionally visiting the castle and never attending meetings with the military officers, Fel probably knew far better than she the various senior officers and their tendencies. She waited to hear what he would say. She wished it would be that Mosworth was loyal to the crown, not individuals, and she could count on him.

"I don't mistrust him specifically," Fel said, "but you're wise to be wary of the military in general right now."

"That's what I thought."

"And *un*wise to leave without a bodyguard."

"I had a dragon."

"A dragon isn't *dependable.* And other dragons chased you back here." Fel pointed skyward to indicate he'd seen the skirmish. "What were you doing?"

"A brief survey of Harvest Island. I'm trying to figure out the best way to get it back. Do you think I should focus on trying to reclaim the magical components to repair its shielder from the stormers? Or sail to Harvest Island with the weapons platform and attempt to drive the dragons away from the harbor so we can take it back whether there's a shield in place or not?"

Fel squinted at her. "I think you should send a *team* to retrieve the components. Your place as queen is here, commanding people and ruling over your subjects, not risking your life on missions that take you from the safety of Castle Island." He waved upward to indicate the shield protecting it.

"That is a wise place for a queen, but it won't be that safe here until I can figure out who sent assassins after me—and if they'll try again. Did you ever learn who the officer was who launched those ships after us?" When they'd returned from their last mission, Syla had requested that Fel snoop around and ask questions of old military contacts in the harbor, but everyone knew he was her bodyguard, and he'd met evasiveness when he'd made inquiries.

"I did try. Those who were good friends and superior officers when I served have since retired." The wistful look in his eyes was brief before he went on. "The answer I got when I questioned the younger men serving now was simply *orders*. That's all anyone said. Orders."

"I would suspect General Dolok, but when we left, he only wanted to put me in a dungeon cell, not have me killed."

"*Only*."

Syla spread her arms. The whole situation had her daunted and at a loss as to where to start. Maybe that was why she was having fantasies about sneaking into the stormer headquarters and finding and seducing Vorik to get back the components. Funny how many of her fantasies involved her getting horizontal with him to achieve her goal. Too bad she didn't know where the stormer headquarters were. If she did...

"It is your prerogative as the ruler of the Kingdom to relieve military officers of duty and promote new men into leadership positions over the Royal Fleet, Protectors, and Enforcers," Fel said.

"Your mother didn't when she took the throne after your father's passing, but *he* made a number of changes when he became king. As I recall, he got rid of some corrupt figures and promoted a captain all the way up to general."

"That was before I was born, but I'm glad to know my father couldn't abide corruption." She wasn't surprised in the least.

Fel's expression turned wry. "I'd already served many years when it happened and remember it well." He rubbed his hip, probably an old injury.

Fel had many that bothered him chronically, and Syla wished she *could* allow him to retire. But she needed him, at least for a time.

"I am aware that it's my right to do that," she said, "but I don't have any familiarity with the officers who would be logical choices. I suppose I can start talking to some of them, but..." She waved toward the weapons platform and vaguely in the direction of Harvest Island. "I'm not sure when there will be time to conduct interviews or if that's even a good way to go about finding people worthy of promotions."

"You'd typically want to be aware of their records and if they're respected as leaders, but it might be wisest, at this point, to pick from those you're certain are loyal instead of the most capable. Sometimes, the most capable are also the most ambitious."

"How do I find those who would be loyal to me?" Syla spread her arms.

"You need spies," Fel replied without hesitation, "to keep their ears open and let you know what gossip is going around in the military offices and barracks. You can trust that the general has spies in the castle."

"Maybe I should... give it some time and attempt to take actions that inspire loyalty in people. If I could prove myself *worthy* of their regard, surely that would be ideal."

"I'm not going to call that naive, but..."

"That's the word that popped promptly into your mind?" Syla smiled sadly.

"I don't know if those who aspire to control the throne and are conspiring as we speak will give you *time* to prove yourself."

"I guess I could visit the brothel where I healed that woman—Celena. She mentioned that high-ranking officers and minor lords visit regularly, and she volunteered to report on them for me." Syla longed to be above employing spies but accepted that she alone couldn't gather the information she needed.

"I agree that you should use her, but summon her to visit you here or at a neutral location. Queens don't visit brothels."

"I visited two weeks ago."

"You were a princess then."

"So it was all right?"

"No, it wasn't, but you were determined."

"I'm determined now, but I'll concede your point that more people are watching my every move now than before." That didn't keep Syla from fantasizing about having Wreylith carry her to the brothel for a quick meeting, but the entire town would see a dragon flying over the city. It was *not* a discreet mode of transportation. "Maybe I'll visit one of the temples in town and ask the woman to come by while I'm there. If I'm to recruit spies, utilizing the city's network of healers—my old colleagues—would be a logical place to start. Unfortunately, a number of them were killed when Moon Watch Temple was destroyed." Her throat tightened at the reminder of the home and friends that she'd lost, in addition to her family, and Syla had to pause to blink away tears. "Others survived and have started working at different temples in the city and the surrounding countryside. They frequently get soldiers for patients and might hear things."

Fel nodded. "A good idea."

Syla removed her spectacles to wipe a smudge that was distorting the light of a nearby lantern. When she returned them to her face, Fel was looking toward a side gate. Her cousin Relvin walked into the courtyard with several military officers and a minor lord Syla recognized as a landowner from the western end of the island. Zlargard. That was his name. She also recognized another older man with the group and groped for his name. Well-dressed and impeccably groomed, he wasn't a military man. Lord Fograth. His family had owned land on the islands since before the gods had established the shields and the Kingdom.

Relvin blinked in surprise when he spotted Syla but recovered and smiled and waved to her. He held up a blue-velvet bag with a silver moon and dice embroidered on the front, and it jangled with game pieces. "Come join us later if you're free, Syla."

She lifted a hand in acknowledgment, though she knew the invitation hadn't been in earnest.

"Brazen of them to scheme so openly," Fel murmured as the group disappeared into the barracks instead of the keep. "Get your spies in order swiftly, Your Majesty."

"You don't think I could show up at the dice game, and they would tell me all their plans?"

"No." Fel hesitated, then added, "For them to be this open about everything suggests… They may believe that events that you can't stop have already been set into motion."

"I can stop a lot. I have a dragon." Syla looked around, but Wreylith hadn't lingered. Maybe she was off to look for her next meal. "Somewhat part-time, admittedly. Did you know how much time dragons need to spend hunting to keep themselves full and fit?"

When Fel shook his head, it probably had nothing to do with dragon hunting schedules.

Syla's spectacles didn't need another cleaning, but she removed them to wipe anyway. "I don't have a lot of time, do I?"

"I don't think so."

"I will do my best to get spies employed, but… while people are listening to others on my behalf, I'm going to give the order to have warships prepared, the weapons platform loaded onto one, and, unless Tibby and Teyla are able to find someone else who can operate it, I'll plan to go along and reclaim Harvest Island."

Fel's wyvern-withering glower returned in an instant. "That's *not* a good idea."

"Trying to take back the island or—"

"You being involved with it."

"You can come along with me on this trip." Syla *knew* that wasn't his objection but smiled anyway, as if she were solving his only problem.

His scowl didn't lighten. "Exactly what happened before could happen again. Whoever created the *orders* for fleet ships to follow you and attack—and for assassins to board your vessel—might not fail a second time."

"This time, we'll leave *with* the fleet, and I'll write the orders to hand to the captains myself."

"It would still be an opportunity for your enemies to strike against you."

Syla lamented that she *had* enemies. Never as a healer would she have considered any Kingdom subjects to be foes. She'd saved the lives of countless soldiers during her years at the temple. Why couldn't their senior officers shift their allegiance to her without a fight?

"Wreylith will fly along with us and perch on the wheelhouse." Syla hadn't checked with the red dragon yet but believed she would do so, though Syla might have to arrange a large offering of delicious livestock as part of the deal.

Fel opened his mouth, likely with an objection on his lips, but he didn't utter it. "That *might* deter assassins, but I still don't think you should risk yourself. Even if our own people don't strike against you, your plan is to engage with the stormers and their winged allies. And they have many more dragons than you do." He waved toward the sky where the yellow and blue dragons had tried to get her.

"I know." Syla wished she could reach out to the Freeborn Faction for help. *They* had dragons. But, even though she'd spoken recently to Chieftess Atilya, and the woman had promised assistance, she hadn't stuck around, and Syla didn't know how to get in contact with her. "Nonetheless, we have to take back Harvest Island, and I don't know where the shielder components are. Maybe if we capture one of the high-ranking dragon riders, we can question him or her for that information." She couldn't imagine capturing Captain Lesva or successfully getting her to share intelligence even if she did, but there had to be less powerful individuals who knew where the components were. After all, not all riders were bound to—and received magic from—their dragon allies. "This is the logical way to achieve that." She waved to the weapons platform again.

"Wait until your aunt finds someone else who can operate it," Fel said.

"I would be open to handing the duty to someone else. It's draining, and I agree that I'd be vulnerable to attack while using it."

"*Yes.* Vorik knocked you off there, and you barely reacted. You're lucky he didn't thrust a dagger into your heart."

"You know he wouldn't do that."

Fel narrowed his eyes, looking like he wanted to object, but he'd been with her the numerous times that Vorik had risked his life on her behalf, and the two men had even fought together against gargoyles. "You're lucky his *lieutenant* didn't thrust a dagger into your heart."

"True. But he was busy stealing our components." Syla sighed, lamenting for at least the twentieth time that she'd allowed herself to be distracted by her desire to use the weapons platform to end General Jhiton's life. He *deserved* death after ordering his troops to slay almost everyone in the royal family—*her* family. Of course, she'd been thinking more about how he was Vorik's superior officer and that if Jhiton disappeared, Vorik might...

What? Renounce his loyalty to his people and stand by her side? To spend his nights with her and help her stave off assassins, manipulative lords, and scheming relatives during the days?

If only. But he was as loyal to his people as she was to hers. It had been a foolish impulse, and she'd deserved defeat.

"I'm open to someone else operating it," Syla said again, "but I also want to send it and the fleet to Harvest Island soon. *Tomorrow*, if the ships can be readied that quickly. As long as the stormers and their dragons have control there, more people will die and more property will be destroyed." She remembered the fires that had burned throughout the countryside. "And we have to assume that they're coming up with other schemes as we speak. They want *all* of our islands, not one."

"I'm aware," Fel said grimly, then looked across the courtyard.

Carrying lanterns and armfuls of books, Aunt Tibby and Teyla were walking out of the keep and toward the weapons platform. In addition to what they held, Teyla had a pack slung over her shoulder. She set it down by one of the marble posts of the platform.

"Have you learned anything new?" Syla asked, joining them.

"Have you figured out how to have someone *else* operate it so that Queen Syla may stay safely in the castle?" Fel asked.

"We've not learned that, exactly," Tibby said, speaking to Syla and ignoring Fel, other than to slant him a brief peeved look, no doubt for his troglodyte ways.

Teyla, who was usually chatty when discussing her archaeological passions, didn't answer at all, instead glancing at Fel and blushing. Syla, reminded that they'd had a sexual encounter in the canyon of randiness-inspiring cactuses, wondered if she should ask Fel to step away. She didn't think either of them had wanted that joining, nor had they figured out how to interact with each other in the aftermath. Fel had a tendency to look *over* Teyla's head instead of at her.

"We haven't found anything about weapons platforms at all," Tibby continued, not noticing the silent exchange, "but we did translate a text that talks about how a moon-marked individual might activate artifacts left behind by the gods. Once activated, those artifacts stay in that state for a time before falling into a dormancy that preserves their magical power. I'm surmising that if you activate the weapons platform, it might be easier for someone else to use afterward."

"Would it stay active long enough for a trip to Harvest Island?" Syla asked.

"I don't know. We would have to experiment."

Teyla climbed onto the platform and peered at a couple of runes under the handprint mark on one of the marble posts. "You pressed your palms against the marks on these two columns to activate it before, didn't you, Syla?"

"Activate it? It was more than that. Those magical projectiles shot out to hit that black dragon, and then they targeted the weapons built into the laboratory that were firing at all the other dragons, friend and foe."

"Yeah, that was amazing." Fingers tracing a rune, Teyla brightened, seeming to forget her discomfort.

Of his own accord, Fel had stepped away, remaining in the area so that he could protect Syla but not insisting on being a part of the conversation. Syla thought he gave good counsel, even if he was as protective as a nanny with a squadron of five-year-olds, and wouldn't have minded including him, but she didn't want her cousin to feel stifled. With time, they would hopefully work things out.

"You were directing those, right? Telepathically?" Teyla looked at her. "The projectiles struck with great precision."

"I was, uhm, *willing* them where to go, I guess you'd say. There wasn't any means of targeting things other than that."

"It was effective. What an amazing gift from the gods. I'm so glad we found it."

"Me too."

A book open in her hand, Tibby walked around the platform, holding her lantern up to various runes and murmuring to herself.

Teyla waved for Syla to join her on the platform, then whispered, "My menses came."

Syla blinked. Even though she and her female colleagues at the temple had shared such information from time to time, she couldn't remember discussing such things with her cousin, who was usually so busy studying, writing papers, and practicing swordsmanship that she could hardly be bothered with noticing. But the relief in Teyla's voice clued Syla in that more than a desire for commiseration about cramps prompted the statement.

"I trusted the yerathma root you gave me would take care of it," Teyla said, still whispering, "but I wasn't *entirely* certain." She sent the briefest of glances toward Fel.

"Oh," Syla said with new understanding.

"I would like to be a mother one day, but not because of weird *cactus* flowers. And not with—" Teyla waved toward Fel. "I mean, there's nothing wrong with your bodyguard—he seems very qualified and dedicated—but you know."

"Yes."

"I like muscles and don't mind an older man, but, er, *you know*." Teyla's cheeks reddened, and she looked away from Fel and Syla as well. "Not *that* much older, even if he was, er, *decent*. I mean, kind of good, all things considering." Teyla bit her lip.

"I'm glad it wasn't an entirely loathsome experience," Syla said, though the last thing she wanted to discuss was her bodyguard's sexual prowess.

"It was surprisingly not, but I'd want the father of my children to be..."

"Married to you? Of the proper station?"

"More likely to read books than eat them."

"I haven't observed Fel noshing on the pages of my tomes," Syla said dryly.

"I suppose not, but he's not the scholarly type. Anyway, I'm not looking, regardless. I'd love to be a mother *someday* and take my children on digs and teach them all about ancient civilizations, but I'm not ready yet. So thank you for the root."

"You're welcome. I've taken to carrying it in my first-aid kit as well as consuming vynglar tea regularly since I'm not ready for motherhood either. I'd like for there *not* to be assassins after me before I consider that."

"Once things settle down, I hope you will consider it though. Have *lots* of children. Then I won't have to worry about being an heir and what would happen if you died. Relvin would probably assassinate me to make sure I don't make moves on the throne. As if I want that. It sounds *awful*."

"I always thought so," Syla murmured, still numb from the loss of her mother and siblings and being in a position she'd never expected nor wanted. It was so strange that she was fighting to be queen and rule the Kingdom. Already, she missed the days of being a simple healer. No, a *good* healer. Thanks to her godsgift, she'd brought people back from the brink of death and healed others of illnesses that wouldn't have been curable without magic.

"Oh, I have something for you." Teyla snapped her fingers and dug into the pack she'd brought out. It had appeared to contain mostly books, but jars clinked when she rummaged. "You remember that I foraged a few items from the laboratory before we left, right?"

"I think when you're removing items from shelves, it's called pillaging, not foraging."

"Not when the items were left there centuries ago by a mad

god who created beasts that like to eat humans. Really, the term should be *liberating*."

"Archaeologists have a unique way of looking at the world, don't they?"

"We're fascinating people. Some of the jars contain medicinal substances that are hard to find. Are you interested?"

"Yes, please." Syla leaned forward with curiosity.

"This one has a substance that I don't believe is medicinal, but you'd probably know more about all the various uses than I. I just know that hydras are extinct."

"Hydras?" Syla peered at a dusty blue jar not much larger than a vial, runes carved into the front to label its contents. "Oh, hydra-scale powder?"

"That's what it says, yes. I translated the runes on several of these. That one is interesting because—"

"It induces a desire to tell the truth. People in ancient civilizations wrote much about how handy it was for questioning enemies."

"Yes. I thought you might use it for the same purpose." Teyla handed it and several other jars to her, then waved vaguely toward the city and the island beyond the castle walls, probably suggesting the greatest danger came from ambitious Kingdom subjects rather than the stormers or other distant enemies.

"It might come in handy. Thank you."

"I think to activate the weapons platform," Tibby said, a book open as she stopped beside them, "you press your hands to those marks. They're the right shape and invite touching, do they not?"

"Yes." Syla set the jars aside in a safe spot. "That's what I did before to prompt it to hurl projectiles at enemies."

"Well, don't hurl anything *here*." Tibby pointed her book toward the courtyard walls. "Think about establishing a connection, such as when you mind-link with someone, and will the platform to come out of dormancy."

Syla had only mind-linked once, and Tibby had initiated it, but she nodded, believing she understood the gist. Teyla scooted off the platform to make room, and Syla took a deep breath and stood, stretching her arms between two posts and resting her palms against the cool marble.

Immediately, magic buzzed appealingly against her skin, as if the marble had been eager and waiting for her touch. A silver glow flared around the edges of her hands and fingers.

"Is that all I needed to do to activate it?" Syla asked.

Tibby responded, but surges of power swept from the posts and up Syla's arms, making her gasp. The energy went through her shoulders to her spine and up into her head, and blackness blanketed her eyes as it overwhelmed her. The last thing she was aware of was crumpling onto the platform.

4

SOMETHING AWAKENED VORIK FROM HIS SLEEP AROUND THE campfire he shared with a few other unmarried officers from his squadron. Earlier, he'd sparred with them for a couple of hours, exercise always ensuring good rest for him, but he sensed that it was still early in the night. The embers in the fire hadn't yet burned low. He listened intently in case he'd been woken by the distant screech of wyverns or other predators that could threaten them in their cave.

A woman walked toward his campfire, a faint silver glow limning her, as if the moon shone upon her from behind. Vorik blinked in confusion. She wore spectacles, a dress that hugged voluptuous curves, and had a cute nose and full lips. He would recognize Syla anywhere, but how had she gotten here?

In the dim light, she paused and peered around the cave.

Vorik sat up, his first thought that she'd come to steal back the components and that he had to stop her. But his movement drew her attention, and her face brightened when she saw him, pleasure filling her eyes.

"Vorik," she said with the same pleasure in her voice, and her gaze dropped to his chest.

He hadn't put his tunic back on after sparring, and his sleeping fur had drooped to his waist when he sat up. His bare muscled chest sparked interest in her eyes—no, *lust*—and his body responded instantly, aroused by her perusal.

"Syla," he said, his voice already husky with anticipation. "Come to me."

Her gaze lifted to his face. "I don't think that's why I'm here."

Despite the words, she walked past other burning fires and headed straight toward him. The silver light provided enough illumination for him to appreciate her curves, which he did, but he also glanced at her hand. Not the one with the quarter-moon birthmark on the back but the other. As Jhiton's spies had reported, it was now tattooed with a red dragon. Syla and Wreylith were indeed bonded.

"Do queens not visit handsome dragon riders who pine for their company?" Vorik lifted his gaze to her face as she neared.

"Well, I would, but your people would shoot me if I did."

Strangely, the scouts always at the mouth of the cave hadn't called alerts about her presence, and nobody was waking up and looking over at the sound of Vorik's voice. A haziness had settled about the camp everywhere except between him and Syla, and he suspected he was dreaming. That made sense, and it wouldn't be the first time he'd dreamed about her. He adjusted his fur to make room and patted the spot next to him. He was *tempted* to pat his lap, inviting her to sit there.

She smiled, settling beside him, but her weight didn't rustle the fur, and when he reached for her, his hand met only air. Disappointment swept through him as he realized they couldn't touch. The silver moonlight that continued to limn her, even here, in the back of the cave, should have clued him in that this wasn't real.

Syla blinked, seeming surprised that she hadn't felt his fingers, and reached for him. Her hand swept through his shoulder, and he didn't feel anything except a faint draft. He touched his chest, half-expecting to find his body also incorporeal, but it was solid. Did that mean that *he* was real and she was a vision? Or only that he couldn't expect his unconscious mind to conjure up a world that fully made sense?

"Is it a dream?" Syla wondered aloud and looked around again. "Or...?"

There was a question in that *or,* but she didn't finish it aloud.

"Usually, when you're in my dreams, we can touch. With great physical vigor." Vorik smiled. "It always seems real until I wake up alone and..." Remembering that she was a queen now, he hesitated. Maybe it wouldn't be respectful to speak bluntly about the state of his penis in the mornings. "Is there a word that's polite and acceptable to use around royalty that means, er, stiff?"

Her mouth twisted. "I'm the same as I've always been, Vorik. Besides, I always spent more time in temples than at court. I'm more familiar with medical terms than what's polite and acceptable."

"Ah, is there a *medical* term appropriate for lower-extremity stiffness?"

"Well, I suppose we're talking about rigidity. Probably not spasticity. And arthralgia refers more to joint stiffness."

"My joints are fine. Due to my youthful vigor."

"Vigor comes up a lot with you."

"When I'm with you, yes."

"Hm." Though she sat next to him, Syla looked thoughtfully around the cave again. "I may have been sent to spy. Do you think it believes I should find the shielder components? There weren't instructions, so I'm not sure."

"What is *it*?" Vorik scratched his jaw. She wouldn't refer to Wreylith that way.

Syla hesitated. Were they, even in their dreams, to be evasive with each other and avoid answering questions? He supposed he should be wary about giving her information about the components, but it wouldn't truly matter, would it? Not if he was dreaming. It wasn't as if she, halfway across the Sea of Storms, could be having the same dream.

"I shouldn't tell you," she said.

"No? I'm curious."

"I have no doubt."

"I could reward you." Vorik waggled his eyebrows and gave her chest a leer. Too bad *she* hadn't come to him without a top on. Though that might have made matters worse since they couldn't touch. How disappointing would it be to have her here—to *seem* to have her here—and only be able to touch himself? That, he supposed, was also something one shouldn't do in front of royalty.

Wistfulness crept into her eyes. "Without touching?"

"It would have to be a promise to do so the next time we meet." Vorik gave her a sultry, half-lidded look. "Like in the wheelhouse."

"That was amazing."

"Good."

"So amazing that I forgot the crew was standing outside and your dragon's belly was visible through the hole."

"I enjoy thoroughly distracting women with my abilities. Especially one woman." He lifted his hand, wanting to trace his fingers along her jaw, and then trail them lower, but again found her incorporeal. He sighed.

"Do you think we'll meet again soon?"

Vorik opened his mouth, but this time *he* paused. Was she asking because she longed to see him and be with him? Or because she hoped to learn about his next mission? In case this *was* more than a dream, he dared not share any intelligence with her.

"Unfortunately, I don't think our paths will cross again soon. You're on Castle Island, right? I can't visit you there." Technically, he could swim or kayak through the barrier and reach the castle. After all, that was what he would have to do at Bogberry Island to implement the kidnapping. A brief fantasy of visiting *her* island first came to him, but he doubted he could sneak past all the troops defending her castle to reach her suite. Even if he had the skill to avoid human detection, Wreylith might be perched on her roof, and she would sense him.

"I am. It's where queens belong, I'm told. At least by Sergeant Fel. There are those who would appreciate the opportunities presented by me traveling." A furrow creased her brow.

"Queens should be able to go wherever they wish," Vorik said before realizing what kind of *opportunities* she might be referring to.

"You'd think, but there are assassins about, and your Captain Lesva is out there too."

"Have you encountered her?"

"Earlier this evening, yes."

Vorik blinked. "On Castle Island?"

"Above it. I went with Wreylith on a hunt."

"A hunt outside your shield?"

"Hm."

"Were you spying on our troops on Harvest Island?" Vorik guessed.

"Maybe a little. From a distance." Syla shrugged without apology, as if to say it was her duty.

And it was. He couldn't blame her.

"I'm trying to help my people," she whispered, then drew her knees up to her chest, wrapped her arms around them, and gazed toward the mouth of the cave and the night sky beyond it.

She looked cold. Or maybe... vulnerable. Having assassins—and Captain Lesva—waiting for an opportunity to kill her couldn't leave her resting easily.

"I understand." Vorik wished he could wrap an arm around

her shoulders and pull her close to him, to offer his support. "The next time our dragons presume to fly close to your castle, you should use that weapons platform to knock them out of the sky."

Maybe he shouldn't have suggested that since it would be an attack against his own people, but Lesva shouldn't have been near Castle Island anyway. If her ambition and desire to slay Syla got her killed, she would deserve it.

"You heard we have that now?"

Maybe he shouldn't have admitted that; she would know that Jhiton had spies in her city, maybe even among the staff or soldiers in her castle. But she had to suspect that already, didn't she?

"I heard," was all he said.

"My people would *love* to use it against enemy dragons, but, so far, I'm the only one who's been able to activate it."

"Ah." That was something she shouldn't have told him. But if this was a dream, he couldn't rely upon what she said, anyway, right? But *was* it a dream? That *it* she'd spoken of… "Is the weapons platform what you were talking about when you said *it* sent you here?"

Still looking out to the sea, Syla didn't glance at him or answer. But she also didn't promptly say *no*.

"Does it have the power to do such things?" Vorik asked. "More than sending out magical projectiles?"

"It was made by the gods, so I can only guess at its powers. Back in the desert laboratory when we were trying to figure it out, a voice spoke into my mind. It said to protect humanity."

"That's fascinating." Vorik remembered his conversation about the possibility that the gods were helping Syla, and he shifted, again uneasy at the idea. "Could it have sent you here to spy?"

"I don't know. But if it *can* send me places, in a manner of speaking, and did for that reason… I suppose I shouldn't be telling you everything about it."

"No," he agreed. "Evasiveness and mendacity are recommended for spies."

"I've little practice at the job."

"I don't think those are traits you naturally possess."

"I prefer to be honest and help people."

"You'll be a good queen."

"Thank you."

"If it eases your mind, we're moving camps, so the components have been packed away and won't be here long anyway. Even if you'd seen them..." He hitched a shoulder.

"I don't suppose you'd like to tell me where you're moving?" She smiled wryly at him. "In case I want to send you a housewarming gift."

"We call them cave-warming gifts, and I can't tell you, no. I'm not sure myself. I'm being sent on a new mission." After the words came out, Vorik realized he shouldn't have admitted that. Maybe *neither* of them had the traits needed to be good spies.

"Is it at cross-purposes with mine?"

"Most of them seem to be. I'm surprised you're not angry with me after we took the components from you."

"I *am* perturbed about that."

"You weren't so perturbed that you didn't ogle my chest when you arrived."

"Maybe your chest is irresistible to women."

"Oh, it undoubtedly is." Vorik returned her wry smile, then ogled *her* chest for a moment. "I wish I could hug you."

"Is hugging really what you have in mind?"

"Vigorous hugging, absolutely."

"Vigor is involved in all your activities, isn't it?"

"I keep myself fit so that it comes naturally to me. Maybe after our vigorous hugging, there could be more sedate and cozy snuggling."

"I'd like that."

"I would ensure you did."

"I believe you."

Syla lay back beside him, the silver light still limning her, though it was faint. Just enough that he could see a hint of moisture in her eyes.

"I'm sorry," Vorik said quietly, even though she hadn't said anything to suggest she wanted an apology from him. It didn't matter. He and his people were the reason for all the horrors in her life, past and ongoing. As much as he would have liked to pretend that *he* hadn't done anything to her, that wasn't true.

"I want to find a way ahead, Vorik," she said, "that doesn't pit our nations in eternal war or leave more of my people dead and our islands lost. Why do the stormers insist on this course of action? I know you need food, and, as I told your chiefs, I'd be willing to trade our surplus in exchange for goods that your people could provide from the world beyond our islands. I'd even be willing to *give* our surplus to the stormers, though I doubt your proud people would accept charity, and after the invasion and murders of my family… I might struggle to convince my people to gift you anything but cannonballs and sword blades." She lowered her voice and looked at him as she continued. "Do *you* personally want our islands? How many of your people truly desire that? And how much of this is because of your leaders? You don't elect them to serve the needs of the many, do you? It's the strongest and fittest who win duels against the old leaders to take charge?"

Vorik shifted uneasily, wanting to speak with her about the future and to comfort her but also increasingly doubtful that he was dreaming. What he offered her here she might remember, and he couldn't say anything treasonous or that would give away his people's plans.

"It's something like that," he said. "The chiefs are there to serve us though. If the people aren't satisfied with their leadership, someone new inevitably challenges them, and the duels, though they're *supposed* to be fair, sometimes reflect the desires of more than the challenger." That was a vague way to say they were sometimes rigged. "As to the rest... I don't know. *I* have no desire for an island or even to be chained to one location, but the food you can grow in your protected environments *is* a draw. And not to have to constantly watch the sky for threats... That's a dream that appeals to many of my people."

"What if those who want to live in such a manner were allowed to return to the Kingdom?"

"And be forced to exist under your rules and laws and adopt your customs?"

Syla hesitated. "I... suppose they'd have to do that and integrate into the existing culture, yes."

"That would not appeal to many of my people, though there would be some who would agree. Wouldn't you always wonder about them though? If they were honest or if they were spies?"

"We already *have* your spies living among us, don't we?" Syla asked.

"Hm."

"You already knew I was the queen. And about this." She lifted her dragon-tattooed hand.

"I'm perspicacious."

She turned her face toward the roof of the cave. "Earlier, I discussed with Wreylith that I like that word."

"How are you getting along with her?"

"Dragons are interesting. Her least favorite dish is intestines. She loves tongue."

"Dragons *are* interesting." This seemed a safer topic than discussing the future, one he, unfortunately, couldn't help her with. He was destined to work *against* her, a thought that made him frown. "My brother said that if I have a problem with our leadership, I should challenge Chieftess Shi for her position."

Syla looked at him. "*Do* you have a problem with it?"

"I… have some concerns about the choices that are being made." Vorik didn't mention the hypothetical enslavement. What his people had done that Syla already knew about was bad enough. "I never envisioned myself as a chief though. I wasn't even sure I wanted to be promoted to captain. I think I'm doing all right as a leader of a squadron of riders, but leading an entire tribe…" Realizing she'd had the position of leading an entire *kingdom* thrust onto her, Vorik reconsidered how to end the thought. "It doesn't seem in line with my natural aptitudes."

"You don't believe your people would appreciate your vigor?"

"Only the women."

"There are a lot of our kind in the world." She gazed toward the roof of the cave again.

"There are, and they control more than we men sometimes think." Vorik lay back in a similar pose and rested his hand next to hers, wishing again that they could touch. "There are a lot of tribes, so leading one probably wouldn't make a difference in our people's overall plans, and I… even if I was interested in challenging Shi and succeeded in becoming chief, I don't think I'd live long. My people have figured out that I have some… feelings and conflicts of interest when it comes to the Garden Kingdom queen."

"You're not so conflicted that you didn't take the shielder components."

"Technically, my lieutenant did that, but you're right that I didn't stop him. My duty compels me to obey orders. And my superiors and leaders."

"I know."

Vorik shrugged apologetically. "Anyway, as I said, our people tend to correct the situation if someone they don't approve of takes the position of chief."

"Are you saying we'd *both* have to watch our backs for assassins?"

"Yes. And, don't take this as an insult to the skills of your people, but I think I'd be dead a lot sooner than you."

"Your people are effective at killing," she murmured.

He sighed, certain she was thinking of her slain family—maybe all those who'd died during his people's invasion.

"I can't give away any of our islands, Vorik. After the atrocities, my people would never forgive me for conceding them to your chiefs. For conceding *anything.* I'm going to fight for Harvest Island. For *all* of our islands."

"You should."

"Even if it pits us against each other?"

He blinked a couple of times, moisture threatening his own eyes, but he nodded firmly. "Yes."

A shake to her shoulder woke Syla from her sleep. And that vision. Was that what it had been? She didn't think it had been a dream. Her visit with Vorik had been too real. She remembered every word.

"Syla?" Teyla asked. "Are you waking up?"

"She'd better be," Fel grumbled from somewhere nearby. "She's got the healer mystified."

"I'm not *mystified,*" a familiar voice said. Was that Emmie, one of her old colleagues from Moon Watch Temple? "I told you that the power of the gods has entered her."

"That sounded like superstitious hokum," Fel said.

"To a heathen barbarian who worships only his weapons," Aunt Tibby said.

Fel growled.

Afraid she needed to stop an incipient fight, Syla rubbed grit from her eyes and sat up. Light from nearby lanterns made her blink, especially one held close to her face. Yes, that *was* Emerzela.

With half her graying hair falling out of a loose bun, she looked like she'd been dragged out of bed. How long had Syla been knocked out?

"You came all the way up to the castle to see me, Emmie?" Syla asked. "Last winter, I had to bribe you with hot chocolate to get you to walk down the hallway to my room to rub your secret-recipe, cure-all tincture on my back after I fell on the ice."

"You're a queen now. My husband assured me I'm honored to serve you. I wouldn't object to hot chocolate though. There's a hint of fall in the air." Emmie pulled a shawl tighter around her narrow shoulders.

"I'll see if any is available. Thanks to all the dragons out there attacking cargo ships right now, we haven't had any shipments from the southern islands in weeks."

Her last words with Vorik came to mind, her promise that she would take back Harvest Island. She'd inadvertently given him far too much information, but he'd probably shared more than he'd intended as well. They were dangerous to each other.

She would have to act fast before Vorik thought to inform his general and have more troops sent to Harvest Island. She needed not only to drive out the stormers but to ensure their dragons didn't have anywhere within the Kingdom to perch. Having a landmass with food and fresh water made it far too easy for them to indefinitely remain in the area.

"Your pupils look normal." Emmie was peering into her face. "Teyla said you crumpled and hit your head."

"It's all right." Syla probed her skull and found a tender bump on the left side but nothing that could have been responsible for her unconsciousness. That had to have been... She eyed the marble posts and canopy of the bed-like weapons platform. The runes and hand marks were dark, no magic emanating from them. If she'd succeeded in activating it, as her aunt had suggested, that state must not have lasted long. "I think the magic of this is what caused me to lose consciousness, though that's not *exactly* what happened. It's more that my mind left my body for a while."

"Where did it go?" Teyla asked curiously.

"To spy on a stormer camp."

"That sounds useful." Tibby patted one of the posts.

"Was it a camp on Harvest Island?" Fel asked.

"No. A cave overlooking the sea. I couldn't tell anything from the stars when I glanced out other than that the camp was in the same hemisphere as we are." She waved to the sky. "It probably doesn't matter anyway. Vorik said they're moving it, so there wouldn't be any point in sending ships, even if I'd gotten the exact location."

"*Vorik* said," Fel blurted. "The gods sent you to see him? He's your—"

"Enemy," Syla interrupted, glancing at Emmie. She had few delusions about her relationship with Vorik remaining a secret from her allies, but she would prefer if the entire Kingdom didn't learn about it.

"The enemy you have sex with," Fel grumbled, less concerned about her secret getting out.

Syla's cheeks warmed, especially when Emmie's eyebrows flew up.

"I gain intelligence from him when we're together," Syla said.

Fel made a sour face. "That's *not* why you do it."

"No. I… like his vigor."

Fel groaned. "I should have accepted Dolok's offer to retire."

"Probably."

"If your dragon were more reliably around, I might have been tempted."

"As I mentioned, she needs to hunt frequently," Syla said. "Due to their size and the effort required to fly, dragons need a lot of food."

"Someone might assassinate you while she's pilfering goats from pastures."

"Why would the gods have sent you to see Vorik?" Tibby asked.

"I doubt *they* did." Syla couldn't imagine that scenario. As far as she knew, the gods weren't present in their world and hadn't been for centuries. Though she did wonder about the voice she'd heard in the storm god's laboratory. "I must have inadvertently activated another defensive power this has." She waved to indicate the weapons platform. "It was helping me gather intelligence. It was probably my desire to find the shielder components that guided the, er, vision, not that I wanted to chat with my… enemy."

Fel grunted but didn't contradict her classification of Vorik again.

"I would like to have those components," Tibby said. "I've done a lot of reading and am itching to apply my engineering skills to making a new shielder with them."

"And Harvest Island is itching to be protected by that shielder," Syla said.

"I have no doubt."

"Did you learn where the components are?" Fel asked. "Or where the new camp will be?"

"No, but I *will* learn where they are." Remembering her vow to capture and question a stormer at Harvest Island, Syla nodded to herself. This convinced her more than ever that she couldn't hesitate to put her plan into action. She slid off the platform, momentarily dizzy when she stood, but she used the post for support. "I have another duty for you, Sergeant."

"What?" Did Fel sound wary?

Syla hated to rely upon him for so much, but until she could gather more loyal men, she had little choice. "I need you to arrange for the weapons platform to be carried down to the sturdiest and most weapon-filled warship in the harbor and, as I was talking about earlier, for an entourage of other warships to accompany it. Tonight. We'll leave at dawn to attack the stormers and take back Harvest Island."

"Dawn?" Fel mouthed.

"We have to act quickly. Vorik has a new mission."

"Does that mean there's going to be another attack on the Kingdom?"

"I'm afraid it does."

5

Rain fell as the warship *Stormslicer* sailed out of Sky Torn Harbor, accompanied by eight more warships and loaded with the weapons platform. The marble structure was strapped down so that it wouldn't slide across the deck.

It was three hours past dawn, but Syla didn't complain about the late start. The ships had needed to be loaded with weapons, supplies, and dozens and dozens of uniformed men to crew the cannons and harpoon launchers. It must have taken a great feat of organization to get everything together so quickly. But would it be enough?

Before the stormer invasion had delivered so much destruction, Castle Island could have sent thirty warships on a mission. Syla worried this wouldn't be enough firepower, not to battle dragons. She was counting on the weapons platform to tilt the odds in their favor, but since it had a limited range, she had doubts. She had also ordered small fast-sailing ships to head to Bogberry, Frost, Orchard, and Vineyard Islands to request the governing lords send ships to help.

Fortunately, Wreylith was in the area, and whenever she flew past, her presence bolstered Syla. She would be an invaluable ally during this endeavor.

In a cabin that had hastily been converted to suitable *royal quarters*, Fel waited for Syla to instruct soldiers on where to put the trunks she'd brought along. They mostly carried medical supplies, but, not knowing how long this would take, she'd packed several changes of clothing and a few books too.

"You shouldn't have brought *her* along," Fel said as they returned to the open deck. He glowered at Aunt Tibby sitting on the weapons platform as if it were a park bench. Protected from the rain by the marble canopy, a book lay open in her lap, and others nestled in a pack next to her.

Cloak wrapped around her shoulders, Syla stopped near the structure, and a man in a blue uniform with gold piping nodded at her. He was one of six Royal Protectors that were also following her about the ship. The castle steward had sent them along as further protection beyond Fel's mace. She recognized him as someone who'd held the position for many years and had often been in her mother's wake. Hopefully, he was content transferring his loyalty to her. The Royal Protectors also seemed to be keeping an eye on Tibby. Syla hadn't asked for that, but she appreciated it.

"Tibby is still studying the weapons platform and trying to figure out how someone besides me can activate it and launch the projectiles. In case..." Syla tilted her palm toward the cloudy sky, not wanting to bring up the possibility that she could die, either in combat or because an assassin got to her. "In case."

Fel grumbled under his breath.

Syla looked toward the capital before it disappeared from view, to a few red-tile-roofed temples around the city, those that hadn't been destroyed during the invasion. That morning, in addition to sending messages to a few healer colleagues, asking them to keep an eye—and an ear—out for her, she'd sent bags of coins from the castle coffers. As she'd shared in letters to the temple leaders, the money was to pay for the healing of anyone who came in wounded or injured and would struggle to pay. Syla genuinely wanted to help her people, but she also wanted to give them a reason to think kindly of her. Thus far, the general populace hadn't opposed her coronation—they'd even cheered for it when she'd arrived riding Wreylith's back—but she wanted to make sure she had their support while she figured out how to gain the regard of the military and the various minor lords and ladies with land and influential positions around Castle and other islands. At some point, she would have to visit each of the island lords and assure them she would be a reasonable and capable ruler that they should support.

But first... Harvest Island. Surely, kicking out the stormers was the most significant thing she could accomplish right now to win the regard of the Kingdom subjects.

"Is that an enemy?" Fel pointed toward the east.

An orange dragon had flown into view, scales gleaming with dampness from the rain. Syla's first reaction was to grimace, but it —she—lacked a rider and had a distinctly youthful sashay to her flight.

"No," Fel said, answering his own question. "That's the little orange one that helped us, isn't it?"

"Igliana."

Syla looked toward the wheelhouse where Wreylith now perched, the crew often glancing toward her. They must have heard that the red dragon was associated with their new queen because nobody lifted a weapon.

Wreylith? Syla asked silently. *Did you invite Igliana to join us? And help us battle the stormer dragons?*

I did not.

So, she's here because she misses your jovial personality?

Wreylith regarded Syla with her golden eyes, irises slitted like those of a lizard, a faint glow emanating from them. *Is my new rider being snarky with me?*

If she were, that would be a foolish choice.

Undoubtedly.

Greetings, humans! Igliana's gleeful voice sounded in Syla's mind. No, in *everyone's* minds, if the dozens of sets of wide eyes that swung in her direction were an indicator.

Wreylith exhaled slowly, a trickle of smoke wafting from one nostril. Was that a dragon sigh?

Greetings, Igliana. For the most part, Syla didn't yet know what kind of power she might develop as a result of her new bond with Wreylith, but she *had* learned that she could communicate telepathically not only with her but with other dragons in the area. *What brings you for a visit?*

The sheep was delicious!

And you want more? Syla recalled that Wreylith had grudgingly parted with one of the herbivores that she'd earned for toting Syla and her allies around on the mainland.

Naturally! But I came to give you a warning.

From the Freeborn Faction?

From Chieftess Atilya, yes. Igliana alighted on a cannon, startling the two-man crew poised to use it when enemies appeared, and they skittered back. Even though she was a younger and smaller dragon, she dwarfed the weapon—and the men. Her tail dangled over the side of the ship, skimming the surface of water that was growing more turbulent as they left the sheltered harbor. *She has people and dragons keeping an eye on the stormers, both because they may seek to attack us again and because she desires to assist you.*

I appreciate any and all assistance.

You should know that dragon ships and also stormer-aligned dragons are departing the mainland and heading toward your kingdom.

I did not see them on my way here, so they may intend to visit—or attack—an island farther south.

I see. Syla had worried Vorik's people would send reinforcements to Harvest Island, but it wouldn't surprise her if they meant to attack on another front while the Royal Fleet was occupied there. Each island had its own defenses but perhaps not enough to drive off so many, especially if… *Do the stormers have a plan to bring down another shielder?*

She groaned at the thought. What if Vorik or another handsome rider was being sent to seduce one of the island lords' moon-marked daughters? The thought of him playing the same game he'd tried to play on her with another woman made her clench her fists, imagining him kissing one of her distant relatives as he sought to extract information on a shielder location.

I do not have that information, Igliana said. *We are only observing their movements from afar. Chieftess Atilya has lost the spies she had placed among the tribes.*

Yes, I remember. That's unfortunate for all. Syla unclenched her fists, recognizing that her indignation was more at the idea of Vorik spending time with another woman than because of a genuine belief that he had such a plan. Few of the island lords even knew the locations of their own shielders. The royal family had always guarded that information closely.

It is. If you wish, I can fly along your chain and see if I can spot the ships and dragons myself.

Would that endanger you?

No, Igliana said at the same time as Wreylith said, *Yes.*

I am young and fast. Even if they saw me, they would not catch me.

Even a fast dragon might be surprised and surrounded. Wreylith looked toward the sky above the eastern end of Castle Island—the spot where the yellow and blue dragons had waylaid them.

Since they'd gotten away, and Wreylith hadn't been that threatened, Syla didn't blame her for the incident. If anything, she'd kept Syla alive with her rapid maneuvers.

I will go with you, Wreylith told Igliana, then swung her big head down to the deck to gaze into Syla's eyes. *Do not attack the island until we return. You will require the assistance of a powerful ally.*

Probably true, but Syla intended to attack as soon as she arrived. With luck, she could catch the stormers before they had time to ponder the weapons platform, learn its limits and capabilities, and come up with a plan.

It'll take us several hours to sail over there. You can probably scout the entire Garden Kingdom island chain in that time and be back.

The glow of Wreylith's eyes intensified. *A dragon cannot be rushed when it comes to scouting. There may be enemies to fly around.*

And hunting to do?

Perhaps fishing. But we will not dally.

Thank you. I'm sure I will *need the assistance of a powerful ally. Many of them.*

Wreylith sprang into the air, and Igliana followed her.

"Where are they going?" Fel asked.

Igliana must not have shared her words after the greeting. Syla summed up the conversation.

"Do you want to delay the attack on Harvest Island?" he asked.

"Not unless or until we know where the rest of the stormer forces are heading. And if they have a way to get through another island's shield. They may simply seek to pull us away from this mission."

"They shouldn't yet *know* about this mission," Fel said.

"They could easily guess that we would soon make an attempt to get Harvest Island back." She pointed toward the distant shoreline that was visible whenever the *Stormslicer* crested a wave.

The rain had stopped, but dark clouds on the northern horizon suggested more would come. A storm might rage as they were engaging in battle. Syla didn't know if that would be more advantageous for their enemies or for them. Most likely, it would inconvenience both sides, but only she had to worry about waves capsizing ships.

Fel frowned at an officer walking up in a black Royal Fleet uniform. A fit woman of about thirty with keen brown eyes and raven-colored hair pulled back in a bun, she wore the insignia of a captain.

She dropped to one knee and bowed her head to Syla. "May I have permission to speak, Your Majesty?"

Fel lifted a hand, as if to shoo the officer away, or maybe tell her to go through her superiors if she wanted to get word to the queen.

But Syla hurried to say, "Of course," before he could insist on proper protocol. Besides, the captain was being respectful. Few of the castle staff and none of the higher-ranking officers she'd interacted with since her coronation had been dropping to a knee, and she'd almost forgotten that was the proper etiquette and that her mother had insisted it be observed.

Still kneeling, the captain lifted her head. "Might it be in private, Your Majesty?"

"No," Fel said promptly.

"Perhaps by the railing?" Syla offered, thoughts of assassins coming to her mind as readily as they doubtless came to Fel's.

She couldn't count on the military to protect her, not when scant weeks had passed since several Royal Fleet ships had sailed after and attacked the whaling ship she'd ridden aboard. Not only that, but they'd sent a team of assassins, men recruited from within her own military. Even though nobody had tried to kill Syla since she'd returned with Wreylith and had been coronated, the back of her neck itched at the mere thought of being alone with a soldier.

The captain rose and nodded, extending her hand toward a spot between two cannons. Syla headed in that direction and caught Fel striding right behind her. The captain looked at him, opened her mouth, but when the tall, strong, and scarred Fel scowled, it was an intimidating sight.

"No, you're right," the captain decided, addressing Fel, though he hadn't said anything. "You should hear this too."

Fel grunted.

Syla rested her hand on the railing, water droplets from the rain moistening her palm. The captain glanced at it—or maybe the dragon tattoo.

"That's beautiful, Your Majesty," she said. "And the dragon is too. She's wondrous."

"She would be the first to agree." Syla raised her eyebrows, certain this wasn't the reason the officer had drawn her aside.

The captain licked her lips and glanced around the deck. Her gaze lingered briefly on a fellow officer standing at the bow and watching them. A major.

"What are you doing?" the senior officer mouthed to her and jerked his head to the side.

"Nothing," the captain mouthed back and smiled innocently, then saw something out at sea—or *pretended* to see something?—and pointed for Syla to look in that direction.

She might not have if not for Fel watching her back, but she was curious about what the captain had to say.

"I'll have to come up with an excuse for why I'm over here," the officer said, looking out to sea instead of at Syla. "I'm Captain Vonla, by the way. I, uhm. I want to give you a warning."

"Another one?" Syla sighed.

The captain glanced at her, her brow furrowed. She wouldn't have heard Igliana's words of trouble brewing.

"Go ahead, Captain Vonla." Syla forced a smile. If someone wanted to offer a warning, she ought to accept it.

"Yes, Your Majesty. My superior officer told me—told all of us—not to interfere if we heard you, uhm... if something happened that seemed like it had nothing to do with us." Again, Vonla's brow furrowed, and she glanced at Syla. "The vague order struck me as strange. I think..." She lowered her voice so that Syla barely heard her over the waves smacking against the hull. "There's a lot of chatter going around right now, and it's hard to know the truth from lies and whether rumors mean anything, but I think there might be assassins onboard."

"Ah. Yes. Thank you for letting me know."

Vonla blinked. "You're not surprised?"

"It wouldn't be the first time assassins from within the military have gone after me. It's not even the first time this month."

Vonla opened her mouth but seemed too stunned to say anything. Finally, she blurted, "But you're the queen."

"Last week, I was only a princess."

"That doesn't make it all right to assassinate you! We're sworn —" Vonla's voice had risen, and she cut herself off and glanced at the major again. The man continued to watch them. Vonla pointed to the fin of a shark swimming parallel to the ship. "We're all sworn to protect the royal family. And you're... you're a healer!"

"Yes, I'm affronted by the situation too."

"You're so calm about it." Vonla looked at her with what seemed like genuine awe.

At this point, Syla didn't feel she could trust anyone from the military, but the captain's warning and expression touched her nonetheless. She hoped Vonla *was* genuine.

"I will keep an eye out for assassins. Thank you for the warning and risking going against your superior's wishes. Is that major the one who gave you your dubious order?"

Vonla licked her lips again. Nervous about betraying her superior officer? Probably. But she nodded. "I think *he's* just following orders from above, though, Your Majesty. He shouldn't be if they're immoral and criminal, but... we're all trained to obey our superiors. It's hard to go against them and risk your career."

"I understand. Thank you." Syla didn't know if there would be time to talk to that major before the engagement began, but she would if she got a chance. What she would say, she didn't know. She didn't want Captain Vonla to be punished for circumventing him to speak with her. Maybe she would have a simple chat with the major and see if he gave anything away.

"You're welcome, Your Majesty." The captain dropped to one knee again before departing. She hurried belowdecks, pretending not to see when the major lifted a hand toward her.

Syla wondered if she should start wearing armor instead of dresses. Fel was right. She needed to assign people to do research for her—to *spy* for her—and figure out who she could rely upon and who was scheming against her. But right now, with little to no relationship with the military personnel, she was as apt to recruit someone who was against her as someone who supported her.

A thought crossed her mind, one she didn't like but had to consider anyway. During the battle ahead, there would likely be injured soldiers. If they allowed it, she could use her healing power and possibly gain at least temporary allies among troops who felt obliged as a side effect of her applying her magic to them. That hadn't worked on General Dolok, but it had on many others over the years, and she could use a few soldiers who felt compelled to report schemes to her.

"I just need to stay alive and uninjured myself," she murmured.

Since she would be on the open deck, firing the weapon that the dragons would target as soon as they realized its power... that would be far easier said than done.

~

Wind gusted, bringing the first raindrops of a storm, and ominous gray clouds darkened the northern horizon.

"Lovely day to kayak through roiling waves to reach an unwelcoming island," Vorik said, though the storm would ensure few people were out on the coastline to notice his approach.

You could swim, came his brother's dry telepathic commentary.

Vorik flew on Agrevlari beside General Jhiton, who rode on his great black dragon, Ozlemar. More than a dozen dragons and riders were strung out in the sky behind them. Once the squadron reached the Kingdom, it would head off on its own mission, leaving Vorik to breach Bogberry Island solo.

Are you monitoring my thoughts, Jhiton? I didn't know your ability to speak telepathically with others gave you that gift.

Agrevlari has been sharing your mutterings with me.

Has he? One would expect one's bonded dragon to hold his rider's mutterings in confidence. Vorik made sure to direct the words to Agrevlari as well as Jhiton.

I was merely observing to your general, Agrevlari said, *that the midst of a storm might not be the ideal time to engage with the enemy—or attempt to infiltrate a protected island, leaving one's fine and most agreeable dragon ally outside of its barrier, forced to fly about in pelting rain and wind. There aren't rock formations around The Island of Bogs on which a dragon might perch and relax.*

Those sound like your *mutterings,* Vorik said, *not mine.*

He shared yours to add weight to his argument that we should return to the mainland and wait for a sunny day for this endeavor, Jhiton said. *You have a hedonistic dragon, Vorik.*

You're not giving me new information.

Wanting to fly in less treacherous conditions isn't hedonistic. Agrevlari flapped his wings harder, melodramatically harder, a couple of times to send rain droplets flying. *It's practical. You should be pleased I did not tell the general that earlier you were composing a ballad about Queen Syla.*

I am pleased. And hush. Vorik swatted the dragon's scaled back. That was not information he needed shared with his brother.

Perhaps, as a learned and experienced general, he can come up with a rhyme for spectacles.

I told you I'm going to use sentinels, Vorik said.

Is that a full rhyme?

It's close enough.

We don't have the luxury of waiting, Jhiton said, ignoring and interrupting the banter. *Captain Lesva sent back word that the Garden Kingdom queen was spying on Harvest Island yesterday and that their people might intend to attack soon.* Jhiton gave Vorik a long look across the wings of their dragons.

Vorik hadn't mentioned his dream from the night before. No, he didn't think it *had* been a dream. If it had been, he wouldn't have contemplated telling his brother or anyone else about it. But the gods-created weapons platform might truly have the ability to send an incorporeal form of Syla across the sea to spy. Whether she'd commanded it to do so or the deities themselves had played a role, Vorik didn't know, but he probably *should* have told his brother that she'd gained that ability. Such power was disturbing. If she could draw upon it repeatedly, she might be able to learn the location of their next camp and many more things.

But, even if Jhiton had known about the new ability, their people couldn't defend against it. Other than the power that bonded riders received from their dragons—largely gifts of strength, agility, fast healing, and stamina—the stormers didn't have a way to combat divine magic.

At least Vorik hadn't shared much information with Syla. Oh, he'd said more than he should have, but she'd lain next to him and chatted instead of poking all around the cave, trying to find advantages. If they'd been able to touch, he might have distracted her from asking questions, and they could have instead enjoyed themselves in his furs.

It's inconvenient that she's acquired a dragon, Jhiton said, still looking at Vorik.

Had he expected a response to his other comment? Or had he asked something else while Vorik had been daydreaming? Fantasizing...

Yes, Vorik said, *it's tedious when one's enemies gather allies and weapons so they can put up a real fight.*

Is that snark, Captain?

Of course not. My respect for you is so vast that I haven't made a comment about how the wind is making your cloak flap with villainous flair behind you.

I shouldn't have given you a collapsible kayak for your penetration of Bogberry Island, Jhiton said. *You should swim.*

As much as I enjoy stroking miles through storm-driven waves, swimming back with a sixty-five-year-old lady in tow might have been challenging.

You like challenges.

I do. And you should too. It should tickle your honor that the Garden Kingdom is making itself a more challenging opponent. When we defeat them, the victory will be sweeter. Vorik tried not to think about his doubts about the future and their chiefs' plans. Instead, he smiled and kept his words light. *The* strawberries *will be sweeter,* he added.

Too bad the season for such had passed, but Vorik knew they would be able to find apples and pears yet, and wouldn't all those fascinating gourds and winter squashes be ready soon? He'd once had a treat called pumpkin bread and had found it delectable.

I don't mind challenges, Jhiton said. *You know I never have. But it's only your* queen *who's making herself a more challenging opponent.*

That's why I adore her. Maybe Vorik shouldn't have admitted that, but it wasn't as if his brother hadn't figured it out. *You have to admit that she's a worthy opponent.*

If only she could be worthy on *their* side.

She is a vexing opponent.

You're only saying that because she tried to kill you.

Twice. No, three *times.* Jhiton's expression grew exasperated. *Twice with explosives and once with that gods-crafted marble device.*

I didn't know you were keeping track.

There are things that stick in a man's mind. I almost agreed to Captain Lesva's third *request for permission to sneak onto Castle Island and assassinate the queen.*

A chill went through Vorik that had nothing to do with the northern wind whipping at his clothing. *When did Lesva make that?*

Just last night, with the report that the queen was spying on them. She reiterated how dangerous the woman is.

Syla. Her name is Syla.

Jhiton's eyes narrowed. *She also reiterated that your feelings for* Syla *could be problematic going forward.*

I had no idea Lesva sent back such detailed and chatty *reports. Isn't she busy defending that island and rounding up all the high-ranking military officers and lords and ladies there who might cause trouble?*

Those are her orders, yes. Jhiton turned his gaze forward. The approaching storm had dropped visibility, but they could make out Castle Island on the horizon. *I told her to leave the queen alone for now, but we may have to deal with her one day, Vorik. As I've heard from others and seen with my own eyes, she's quickly becoming far more than a healer.*

That cold chill lingered, and Vorik wanted to argue that they could achieve their goals without killing or *dealing with* Syla in any way. But was that true? He didn't know. Since Jhiton had said he hadn't agreed to an assassination attempt, Vorik kept his telepathic tongue from flapping further on the matter.

Veer off, and head to Bogberry Island for your mission, Vorik. I'll be in the area with the rest of our dragons and riders. Jhiton tilted his thumb over his shoulder toward the squadron stretched out behind them. *While we're waiting for you to kidnap the lady so we can question her under the influence of the hydra-scale powder, we'll check on Harvest Island. We'll also fly over the rest of the Garden Kingdom chain to make sure Freeborn Faction dragons aren't lurking. Lesva's report mentioned that one of their young dragons had been spotted in the area. If Queen Syla lures* them *over as allies...*

Vorik didn't like the significant look that Jhiton sent him. *Think of the challenge, Jhiton. The sweetness of the strawberries!*

Just get Lady Abrya, and— Jhiton broke off and frowned toward Castle Island. Or was he looking at the back of Ozlemar's horned head?

The Garden Kingdom is sending a fleet toward Harvest Island, Agrevlari told Vorik. *We're close enough that our kin there can report to us.*

Their fleet is going to attack dragons with their warships? Vorik asked. *That'll be a quick victory unless they've gained a new advantage.*

Agrevlari shudder-flapped his wings again to send water flying. *The queen sails on one of the ships, and it is loaded with the weapons platform of the gods.*

Vorik leaned back and groaned. When Jhiton's spies had reported that the massive marble thing had been delivered to the Castle Island courtyard, he hadn't imagined the Kingdom *moving* it anywhere. He certainly hadn't envisioned it on the deck of a ship.

Jhiton, who had to be getting the same report through Ozlemar, looked over at Vorik, his expression cool. *Change of plans.*

Vorik groaned again, dread creeping into him. What would he do if his brother ordered everyone to attack that ship? To attack *Syla*?

We're all flying to Harvest Island to ensure that fleet fails to drive our forces away, Jhiton said. *And we're going to sink that ship—and the weapons platform.*

Syla will be on *the weapons platform,* Vorik replied with far more distress than he should have shown.

So be it.

Damn it, Jhiton.

Vorik, she's declared herself our enemy. We have to—

No, we declared ourselves her *enemies. She never wanted this. She's a healer, damn it. We slew her entire family, and now we're trying to take over her kingdom. None of this is her fault. She doesn't deserve to be* killed. Vorik clenched his fist, fury flushing his face with heat. He couldn't let more than a dozen dragons, not to mention the ones already protecting Harvest Island, descend on Syla. Even if she had Wreylith's help and that weapons platform, she couldn't survive against so many.

Break away, and go on your mission to Bogberry Island, Captain. Jhiton's face remained cool, his telepathic tone unyielding as the dragons flew inexorably closer to the islands—and Syla's fleet. *We'll handle this.*

No, Vorik said.

Are you disobeying a direct order?

Vorik closed his eyes, torn. Was he? Even if he made the choice to do so, what could he do to stop this? Stand at Syla's side and fight his own people while she used that weapons platform to kill his friends and the dragons allied with them? He'd known some of those riders all of his life and loved them like brothers.

Vorik cursed with frustration. *I don't want to disobey you, Jhiton, but let me help you find another way. We don't need to kill Syla. We just need to remove her as a threat, right? What if we— Oh.* Vorik sat straighter. *Let me kidnap* Syla *instead of Lady What's-it. We aren't even certain that she or her husband knows the location of their shielder, are we? But Syla would.*

It is believed that Lady Abrya does know its location. Besides, Syla did not give you that information the last time you tried to wheedle it from her.

We didn't have that powder before. Vorik brightened with that realization. It was true—and a good argument. *Syla knows the location of* all *the shielders. And now we have the means to coerce her to tell us.*

Vorik didn't like the idea of coercing Syla to do anything—or *kidnapping* her—but both were better than the only alternative Jhiton was offering. Her death.

Jhiton didn't knock the idea down right away. Was he considering it?

I can get her, Vorik said. *Unlike with the rest of our people and dragons, she won't attack me if Agrevlari flies close.*

Another truth. Vorik hated to use that against Syla, but to save her life, he would. He had to.

Jhiton looked toward the island again. *Islands.* Harvest was now visible on the horizon in the misty distance, and soon the Kingdom fleet would be too.

Very well. You may make an attempt to capture her, but if you aren't able to get her quickly... Jhiton looked over again, his face chiseled from granite. *If she succeeds in killing even* one *of our people or dragons with that thing, I will assassinate her myself.*

I'll get her, Vorik said.

He had to.

6

Nervous as the ships sailed closer to Harvest Island, Syla wiped water droplets from her spectacles. Though the rain was picking up, she remained on deck, standing at the railing and watching the sky as the wind tugged at her cloak. Maybe she should have been chatting with the major who'd scowled at his captain throughout their conversation, but he'd disappeared belowdecks. It had crossed her mind to have him arrested, but the fleet commander might well be in on the special *orders* too. If she locked up all the senior officers, who would lead the ships into battle? Thus far, no dragons had flown overhead, but they had to be aware of the fleet's approach, and they might attack at any moment.

Tibby joined Syla at the railing, a book tucked under her arm, her cloak arranged to protect it from the elements. Her thick spectacles were also dotted with water droplets. She'd been determinedly sitting on the weapons platform and reading, trying to find a way to allow someone besides Syla to employ the device. But it hardly mattered. It would still take someone with a moon-mark, and she and Tibby were the only ones onboard. Syla wouldn't let a relative risk herself while she hid belowdecks.

"I was close enough to catch the gist of your discussion with that captain," Tibby said.

"Are you here to advise me on the situation?"

"You might want to fire the weapons platform at all the barracks around Castle Island and start over with the military."

"That's not an option," Syla said.

"Maybe not, but you can't have people who are supposed to defend you and the Kingdom more likely to spin toward you and plant a dagger in your back."

"I know. When there's time, I need to talk individually with all the senior officers and figure out who's giving the orders to get rid of me." But when would there *be* time? As long as the stormers were threatening the Kingdom, Syla had to prioritize dealing with them.

"Only someone who stands to gain a lot would risk it."

"The throne itself."

"Or a lordship and lands granted by whoever takes the throne next," Tibby said. "You already know Relvin is angling for it. I would start there."

"It's hard to believe he could entice the Royal Fleet to back him." Syla thought of General Dolok and how she'd heard rumors of people—officers—proposing military leaderships for the Kingdom. But did he aspire to that? For the past few weeks, she'd believed he merely objected to *her* leadership, perhaps believing she might fall for a stormer and inadvertently betray their people, as her sister Venia had done.

Vorik's face floated through Syla's mind, but she wouldn't let her feelings for him get in the way of her duty.

"Maybe, maybe not. Relvin's father backs him, and he has sway with the aristocrats. Oh, Syla." Tibby pushed a hand through her damp hair. "This all gives me a headache. I do prefer dealing with machinery rather than people. *Machines* don't plot against you."

"Except by breaking down when you need them."

"If you take good care of them, that doesn't happen. Unlike with people, some of whom would betray you for an ounce of gold and an opportunity to gain prestige."

"Fel thinks I should cultivate a spy network."

"That's an excellent idea." Tibby blinked and looked back at the sergeant. "*He* came up with it?"

"He's not dull, my aunt."

"One wouldn't know it from the way he grunts and fondles his weapons."

"Smart men can like swordsmanship. *Mace*manship." Syla waved to indicate Fel's favored weapon hanging from his belt.

"Hm."

"It's too bad you weren't along on the trip to the storm god's laboratory. You and Fel could have walked side-by-side together among the cactus flowers." Syla smiled, thinking that would have been a better match than Fel and Teyla.

Tibby squinted at her. "He's not the kind of person I would consider walking through a garden with."

"It was wild and thorny, hardly garden-like. Among such dangerous flora, someone who can protect you with a weapon is a boon."

"Dragons ahead!" a lookout called.

"Man the cannons!" the fleet commander called through a megaphone, and the order was relayed by the captains on the decks of the other ships.

The fleet was nearing Hazel Harbor, the city built in tiers up the slope around the water before stretching inland. Syla picked out four dragons perched upon rooftops, riders on their backs. All sets of eyes were toward the approaching ships.

"We'd better attack before they come up with a plan to deal

with our fleet." Syla kneaded the hem of a sleeve and wished she had somewhere dry to wipe her hands. As the moment of battle approached, more than rainwater moistened her palms.

"I wish *you* didn't have to be the one using that thing." Tibby glanced at the weapons platform, then turned a sour expression on her book, as if it had betrayed her by not providing an answer to her question. "You're a healer, not a killer. A soldier should have that job. Worse, you'll be a target as soon as the stormers figure out what it can do."

"The whole ship will be a target." Syla worried about that. If their enemies managed to sink the *Stormslicer*, she would lose the only weapon they had that could effectively slay dragons. "We might lose everything," she murmured.

Tibby looked at her, but someone yelled that two dragons were flying toward the fleet.

"Guard me," Syla told Fel and strode toward the weapons platform.

"I always do." He took up a position beside one of the marble posts.

"I know. Thank you."

Wind gusted across the ship, and Syla wobbled as she climbed onto the platform. The waves were getting rougher as well. With luck, the dragons would be as hindered as the fleet, the wind battering their wings as they maneuvered in the air.

As Syla stood on the platform, the rest of the Royal Protectors circled it to lend their swords to its defense. To *her* defense, she hoped. She couldn't help but eye the backs of their heads, aware that an assassin could come from any direction. And, as draining as using the weapon was, she wouldn't be able to defend herself from enemies nearby.

She looked in the direction that Wreylith and Igliana had flown off, hoping her winged allies would return soon. Instead, a pair of gray dragons with riders approached from the island. Without a doubt, *they* were not allies.

Wreylith, Syla called silently, *we're engaging in battle. I could use your help.*

Since the red dragon had warned her *not* to engage until she returned, Syla wasn't surprised when she didn't receive an answer. By now, Wreylith could be at the far end of the hundreds-of-miles-long Garden Kingdom chain of islands. But the battle was coming to Syla, so she had no choice but to engage.

After taking a deep breath, she placed her hands on the marks on the posts. Magic tingled against her palms, promising the weapon's readiness.

The fleet fired its cannons, but the dragons tilted their wings or dove, fast enough to track the trajectories of the cannonballs and avoid them. Their flightpaths weren't deterred for long, and they kept coming. Both dragons angled toward the lead ship—Syla's ship.

Since many of their kind had been at the battle over the storm god's laboratory, she had a feeling they'd all learned about the threat the weapons platform represented. They would go after it—after *her*—first.

Syla closed her eyes and let her own power mingle with the magical energy humming within the marble posts. She didn't have any choice but to make herself vulnerable to defend her people. Tension knotted her shoulders as she attempted to will the posts, with their cannon-like openings in the top, to fire magical projectiles, as they'd done in the desert laboratory.

But, with cannons booming and dragons trying to reach her, their riders raising swords as they stared down at her, Syla struggled to focus her thoughts. Terror and doubt stampeded into her. The success of this mission was predicated on her being able to launch projectiles from the weapons platform.

"This wasn't hard before." She stared alternately at her hands while willing the power within the posts to flare to life. All the while, she sensed more dragons launching from Harvest Island, arrowing toward the fleet. Toward *her*.

The two gray dragons tucked their wings in to dive. They would arrive in seconds, and were their maws already opening to breathe fire?

Cannons fired from all ships. One dragon lurched in its dive as a cannonball clipped its shoulder. Another twisted to avoid two more whizzing past. But the dragons were undeterred. As their riders loosed arrows at the crewmen, their aerial allies banked to come around and try again to reach the weapons platform. Four more enemy dragons flew toward the fleet. Inevitably, some would get through.

Again, Syla willed her power into the posts, but panic tightened her chest and scattered her concentration. What if she couldn't do this? She would have doomed her fleet—her *people*—to failure. To destruction and death. Sweat trickled down her tense muscles as roars sounded over the increasing wind from the storm.

A blue dragon dodged cannonballs and streaked over the deck of a neighboring ship. Its maw opened, and fire streamed into the sails and rigging, a mast bursting into flame, the dampness from the rain not enough to prevent it.

From the deck beside the weapons platform, Fel looked at Syla, concern furrowing his brow, expectation in his eyes. Maybe Vorik would have said something supportive and encouraging.

She snorted. He would have told her to be aware of her peripheral vision since that supposedly calmed a person down.

It couldn't hurt to try...

As she wiped sweat from her damp palms, she looked through the posts toward the wheelhouse but also tried to be aware of the men on the deck to either side of her. The sea was visible at the edges of her vision, the cloudy sky slanting rain at dragons as they wheeled and dodged cannonballs. Those dragons were *not* calming to look at. Instead, she kept her peripheral vision on the men, the men reloading cannons and archers firing at enemies flying close. They were all blurry when she wasn't peering at them through her lenses, but maybe her heartbeat slowed a touch? With her central vision unfocused and her awareness to the sides, she groped for and found the posts, her palms sliding onto the hand-shaped marks.

To one side, the dragon that had lit the neighboring ship on fire arrowed toward the *Stormslicer*, a blue blur descending rapidly. Without looking directly at the creature, Syla willed the weapons platform to launch a projectile at it. She imagined Vorik giving her an encouraging nod, even though he wouldn't have if he'd been there. Her enemies were his people.

"Ever a problem," she whispered.

A soft *thwump* came from above. A moonlight-silver ball of energy launched from one of the posts and sped toward the blue dragon and its rider. Faster and brighter than the cannonballs, it blazed through the dark sky. The dragon saw it coming and tried to dodge, but the projectile altered course and slammed into the creature's side. The rider flew off its back as his mount screeched and wobbled.

Two more projectiles streaked out, one coming under the dragon and striking it in the belly. The other hit it squarely in the head, its horns briefly glowing silver, as if they were conducting the energy, the power. The dragon's wingbeats halted, and it plummeted into the choppy waves below.

Dead? Syla couldn't spend the time to check, but it crossed her mind that Vorik would be disappointed that she was using his advice against his people. It couldn't be helped. They were attacking *her* people.

Determined, Syla found another target. An orange dragon. It wasn't Igliana. This was a big female that screeched as she descended, dodging cannon fire to stretch her talons toward the weapons platform.

Continuing to be aware of the world visible in her periphery, and willing herself to remain calm, Syla launched projectiles at the dragon. The weapons platform drew upon her energy to aid it, its tremendous magic coming at a cost, but there were more than a dozen dragons in the air now. She would have to continue to fight, to lend it her power, for much longer. If she didn't...

"I will," she vowed.

As it fired again, four more dragons flew toward the ship, two from each side. The orange was fast and dipped, only clipped by the projectile. It veered left, then down, then up, zigzagging about as it continued downward. It was buying time, Syla realized, drawing her attention and willing to sacrifice itself so that the others could attack her.

Fel and the Royal Protectors stood their ground, weapons raised to keep the dragons from reaching Syla, but all it would take was one well-aimed gout of fire to incinerate them all.

Since the weapons platform had multiple posts, Syla willed it to send out more than a single ball of energy at once. Two launched, with a third and fourth following in rapid succession, but the rush to fire made her aim imprecise. Only one projectile reached its target, blasting into the flank of a green dragon. The projectile knocked it from its course, and the dragon screeched in pain as its wings beat erratically. Its rider had a bow and, though he was being jerked about as he tried to stay on the dragon's back, he managed to loose an arrow at Syla.

She ducked as Fel leaped up, trying to time his swing to deflect the attack. He clipped the arrow, and it ricocheted off one of the marble posts.

Syla had lost her grip on the others and rose to place her hands on the marks again.

"Look out!" Fel barked, pointing toward the opposite side of the ship.

Two blue dragons angled toward them, dodging cannonballs as they flew close enough to attack with fire. Thunder rumbled from the clouds, but it wasn't loud enough to drown out the roars of the Kingdom's enemies.

One of the blue dragons opened its maw, flames roiling in its throat. Syla had seen that dragon before—and its silver-haired rider. Captain Lesva.

"More dragons are coming in from the back half of the island!" someone yelled.

As her mount flew closer, Lesva aimed a bow at Syla.

Syla launched a projectile, tempted to aim at the rider instead of the dragon, but fire spewed from the blue's throat, close enough to engulf the side of the *Stormslicer*. Even as Lesva loosed her arrow, balls of energy streaked straight at her mount. Syla ducked behind one of the posts as her projectiles landed, one taking the blue dragon in the shoulder and the other in its chest.

A gargoyle-bone arrow streaked between the posts, grazing Syla's shoulder and raising fiery pain, but she kept from crying out. The blue dragon's wings had stopped beating, and it plummeted toward the sea. Unlike the other rider, Lesva remained on her mount, even twisting to shoot two more arrows as it fell.

Shoulder burning, Syla ducked lower, but lightning flashed in the dark sky, and she glimpsed more dragons coming from the other side of the ship. Arms stretched up, hands on the marks, Syla willed two more projectiles to race toward their enemies and protect the *Stormslicer*.

Lesva's last arrow sped toward her head, and, with weariness sapping her energy, Syla couldn't dive away. The projectiles shot out of the weapons platform, deterring the dragons, but the arrow—

One of the Royal Protectors leaped in front of Syla. The arrow pierced his chest and he cried out, tumbling below the edge of the weapons platform. He landed on his back within her view, face twisted in pain, but he met her eyes.

"Defend us, my queen," he whispered.

"I will," she managed, though she was stunned that he'd sacrificed himself for her.

Determined not to waste his life, she rose up again and summoned more of her flagging energy to fire further projectiles. Lesva's blue dragon floated in the waves, not moving. Syla didn't see Lesva and hoped she'd landed under the dragon and was dead too, but she doubted it. That woman had fallen off a cliff and survived.

We are coming, Wreylith spoke into Syla's mind. *With allies.*

Thank you! Syla replied, relieved.

With dragons everywhere now, she felt overwhelmed, but she kept firing, keeping them away from her ship and the fleet the best that she could. In the distance, more dragons appeared, flying from the east, the mainland. Since Wreylith had gone in the opposite direction, those wouldn't be her allies.

She spotted a green dragon at the lead. Was that Agrevlari? And Vorik?

Before she could feel any relief at seeing him, she realized a black dragon flew at his side. The general's big beast. With his brother watching, Vorik wouldn't be able to help her. And all those dragons and riders flying behind Vorik? They had to be his allies, his fellow stormers. They must have heard that Harvest Island was under attack and had come to help.

Fel saw them too and swore vehemently. He wasn't the only one. As the crewmen fired cannons and tried to put out flames, they groaned and cursed.

"Sail toward the harbor!" the fleet commander called.

Thunder crashed overhead. Lightning flashed, but no

branches arched down to strike the riders. The gods, it seemed, would only help so much.

With exhaustion making her legs leaden, Syla struggled to remain upright and launching projectiles. Each burst streaked inevitably toward an enemy, but each also sapped more of her strength.

"*More* dragons?" someone demanded, pointing toward the southwest.

"The red one is at the lead!" another man cried. "Is that the queen's dragon?"

Syla peered in that direction, struggling to see detail through her spectacles, the lenses dotted with water, rain spattering the side of her face with each gust of wind. A red dragon *was* leading several others and coming from the direction of the rest of the island chain, and a small orange dragon flew at her side.

Wreylith, Syla said with certainty.

You have made a mess in my absence.

The mess came to me.

Keep blasting that contraption at them. I've found dragons to assist us but not nearly as many as you've *found.*

We should have spied more thoroughly last night.

Clearly.

Six dragons trailed behind Wreylith and Igliana, but Syla feared they wouldn't be enough to combat General Jhiton's forces, especially with her energy flagging.

Still, as she willed more of her waning power into the weapons platform, she realized there were only a few dragons flying in the air above the fleet. With the help of the gods' device, she'd brought down many of their attackers. A half-dozen dragons floated in the waves, and had more disappeared beneath them? Sinking dead below the choppy surface?

If Jhiton hadn't been coming, the battle might have been theirs. Storm-cursed luck. She hated that man.

Her hatred renewed her strength, and she willed all four posts to send out projectiles. If she could finish off the dragons around the fleet, maybe her people could regroup in time to meet the new threat.

But Jhiton's dragons, wings beating hard, were almost there. Wreylith flew overhead, not slowing down but streaking out to meet them. That would help, but there were too many enemies for her to deal with alone. And her allies—were those Freeborn Faction dragons?—hesitated to fly straight toward the oncoming forces. They knew they were outnumbered.

Hoping to hearten them, Syla willed all of her projectiles toward Jhiton's dragons. The silver balls streaked much farther than cannons could have reached, and one sped toward the great black dragon carrying the general. Syla clenched her jaw, willing it to take the creature in the chest—and bring its rider down with it.

Lightning flashed in the sky, branches streaking down from the black clouds. At first, Syla thought the gods would help her, that one might knock the general from his dragon. But a branch streaked into her projectile, brilliant white light meeting the glowing silver sphere with a blinding flash that stunned her.

She blinked furiously, trying to recover her vision as the light faded, her projectile gone from the sky. Had it *exploded*?

Before she could see if it had affected Jhiton and his dragon—probably not, as the lightning had caught the projectile before it got close—a clash of metal on the deck between the railing and the weapons platform pulled her attention downward. Though she was still blinking to clear her vision, she made out someone leaping down from the railing and into the Royal Protectors and several soldiers running toward him. No, toward *her*.

Dripping water from her black riding leathers, Captain Lesva wielded a dagger and a sword, her gargoyle-bone weapons almost glowing white as they deflected attacks from numerous angles.

Though many men sprang for her and archers aimed, trying to get a shot over the heads of their allies, Lesva didn't appear daunted in the least. She wasn't even focused on her attackers, somehow dodging and parrying while glowering at Syla.

The memory of her last encounter with the captain flashed in Syla's mind, and, for the first time during the battle, she longed to flee, to run belowdecks and barricade herself behind a door.

As if that would be enough to deter the magically enhanced rider captain. One of Lesva's blades darted through the defenses of a Royal Protector and sliced into his jugular. He stumbled back, dropping his weapons as blood spattered the deck. An archer fired through the opening his absence created, but with uncanny speed and accuracy, Lesva batted the arrow away. It deflected into the shoulder of one of the men at the cannons.

Even as she battled the Kingdom men, Lesva took step after step toward Syla.

Hands still on the posts, Syla thought about trying to strike her with one of the projectiles, but, even if it landed accurately, it would crash through Lesva and into the deck and hull of the ship. She might sink her own vessel and lose the weapons platform to the bottom of the sea.

"Get more men over here!" Fel barked, though he couldn't reach Lesva through the troops trying to surround her. The captain should have been overwhelmed, but she moved so quickly, even anticipating attacks from behind.

Wreylith? Syla glanced toward the sky as lightning flashed again.

This time, it didn't strike anything, but it highlighted the enemy forces, including a red dragon battling a black dragon. Wreylith and Ozlemar.

The Freeborn Faction dragons were flying to help Wreylith, but they were still outnumbered. Though Lesva would inevitably reach Syla and kill her if she didn't run, Syla willed two more projectiles toward the stormer dragons, afraid for Wreylith. She also worried she wouldn't have many more opportunities to attack their enemies. Once the forces mingled, Syla wouldn't be able to tell friendly dragons from enemy dragons, not from such a great distance.

Defeat the human foe! Wreylith ordered.

If only Syla could. Lesva was far from human, and now she was only a few steps from the weapons platform.

"Get that storm-cursed mutant of a woman!" someone yelled.

"Excellent idea." Again, Syla contemplated sending a projectile toward Lesva, the risk to the ship be damned.

As if she sensed the threat, Lesva spun, slashing rapidly, driving men back, and then she took two running steps and leaped in Syla's direction, somersaulting over the heads of the defenders. Syla scrambled back, intending to jump off the other side of the weapons platform, but she'd used too much of her energy firing the weapons. Utterly drained, her knees buckled, her legs giving out.

An instant before Lesva would have landed atop Syla, something crashed into the woman from above. Vorik.

Surprise flashed across Lesva's face before she disappeared from Syla's view, flattened to the deck. The arrival of Vorik startled the men who'd been trying to get to Lesva's back. If they'd been quicker to react, they might have driven weapons into her, but, even startled, Lesva recovered with eerie rapidity. She sprang to her feet with her weapons still in her hands.

But Vorik now stood between her and the weapons platform. He glanced back at Syla but only for an instant before Lesva, not hesitating in the least, leaped at him.

Their weapons came together in blurs, clangs sounding more like the meeting of metal than of bone, and sparks flew from those magical blades. Two remaining Royal Protectors and a handful of crewmen not busy loading cannons and loosing arrows at dragons backed away from the fight. Blood ran from many of their faces, mingling with sweat and rain, and they glanced at Syla. An archer raised his bow with uncertainty, the two riders *both* enemies as far as he was concerned.

"Don't fire!" Syla yelled. "Stay back!"

Vorik had defeated Lesva before, and Syla believed he could do so again—as long as none of her people *shot him*. Recognition sparked in the archer's eyes—he'd figured out who Vorik was and knew he was an enemy. But Lesva was even *more* of an enemy.

Syla tried to stand as the archer drew back his bowstring, aiming at Vorik. "No!"

Her legs couldn't hold her. She crawled across the weapons platform, but she couldn't reach the archer in time.

Embroiled in their own battle, Vorik and Lesva didn't glance at the man. Did they even know he was there? They were such dangerous opponents that neither dared glance away from the other.

A second before the man would have fired, Fel stepped up to the archer and pushed the bow aside. He pointed toward the sky at a dragon heading their way.

"Your Majesty." A soldier jogged up to the weapons platform from the other side. "We need to get you to safety."

"We need her to shoot down more dragons!" That was the fleet commander.

Syla pulled her arm away from the soldier reaching for her. Though she struggled to find strength, she agreed that her place was at the weapons platform, firing at their enemies.

Screeches and roars sounded over the thunder and the booms of cannons. The aerial battle had grown closer, the Freeborn Faction dragons combatting the stormer dragons, wheeling and diving in the dark sky. A gray dragon had joined the black in battling Wreylith. She was magnificent, biting and slashing and keeping them from flanking her, but there were too many foes, even for her.

Syla gripped one of the posts and used it to pull herself up. Leaning heavily on it, she managed to plant her hand on the mark.

Ozlemar was no longer fighting Wreylith—where had Jhiton and his mount gone?—but two green dragons had joined the gray to gang up on her. Indignant and afraid for her ally, Syla managed to summon another projectile, sending it toward the fray.

The silvery sphere blazed across the sky and struck one of the green dragons attacking Wreylith, knocking it away from her. Blackness edged Syla's vision after the effort. Bloody daggers, would she pass out if she tried to call upon more projectiles?

Lesva cried out, stumbling back. Blood flowed from a fresh gash in the side of her neck. Determined, Vorik strode after her. For the first time, uncertainty crept into Lesva's eyes.

"Vorik, you're betraying your people," she yelled, glancing past him toward Syla.

"You're not killing her." Vorik sprang after Lesva.

She scrambled back to the railing and glanced overboard. He raised his sword, slashing so that she wouldn't have the time to turn and jump over, if that was what she intended.

"Traitor!" she screamed at him as his blade knocked hers aside and dove for her neck.

Lightning flashed, and the shadow of a dragon grew visible on the deck an instant before taloned feet lowered. They snatched up Lesva before Vorik could land a killing blow.

Syla peered out from under the canopy of the weapons platform, hoping that was an ally dragon and that it would slay her enemy. But it was the black dragon, with General Jhiton on his back, his short hair plastered to his skull, his face as hard as stone as they flew away. Captain Lesva dangled from the black dragon's grip as they flew over the ship and toward the far side of Harvest Island.

Vorik lowered his sword, his mouth drooping. He looked as surprised as Syla by his brother's intervention.

A pained screech came from the aerial battle. Wreylith?

Frustrated, Syla risked falling unconscious and used the last vestiges of her strength to fire two more projectiles into the air. They sped away from the platform, striking one of Wreylith's enemies as she clamped onto the neck of another. It was too far away for Syla to hear bone crunch, but as she sank to her knees, she saw Wreylith's foe go rigid, and then very limp. Wreylith released her enemy and flew about, searching for more threats, but the remaining stormer dragons were flying away, heading in the same direction as the general.

On the deck of the warship, several archers who'd paused while Vorik and Lesva battled, stepped forward now with their bows raised and determination in their eyes. Vorik stood alone, a single stormer surrounded by enemies.

Undeterred, he raised his sword, as if to say he would parry a dozen arrows flying at his chest if he needed to. Syla didn't think that even he could manage such a feat.

She struggled to find the strength to call out an order, but the blackness threatened all of her vision now, not only the edges.

Fel opened his mouth, as if he might try to call off the archers, but he looked toward her. Undecided? A part of him had to wonder if it would be better to let Vorik be killed.

But he'd saved Syla's life. She couldn't allow that.

"Prisoner, Fel," Syla rasped. "To question," she managed to add, hoping the logic would sway Fel and the soldiers.

Vorik didn't look like he would *allow* himself to be taken prisoner. He glanced toward the railing. Thinking of jumping over?

Before he could, Wreylith landed on that railing, her huge

body denying him an escape route. Her golden eyes pinned him, and her maw opened.

Prisoner! Syla blurted telepathically to the dragon. *Take him prisoner.*

The effort was the last she could manage, and she lost consciousness before she saw what happened next.

7

I would cheerfully rescue you, Agrevlari spoke into Vorik's mind, his voice distant, *but the weapons platform remains in place on that vessel, and the corpses of my kin are floating in the waves.*

What's the status of our forces? Vorik lay on the floor of a cell, his ankles and wrists shackled. The occasional bump against the door and a loud sneeze earlier suggested he had at least one guard.

Outside, wind railed against the hull of the ship, and creaks and groans came from within, but the craft wasn't rocking as much as he would have expected if it were in the open sea. The Kingdom fleet must have sailed into the harbor for protection from the storm—and to ensure his people and dragon allies didn't return to the city around it.

The storm rages, so we are hunkering in caves in the volcano on the far end of the Island of Eliok while the human leaders decide what to do next. The dragons are discussing that weapons platform. We believe it has a limited range.

How limited?

Perhaps five miles.

That's not very limited.

No cannonball had ever sailed that far. With the unerring accuracy of the magical projectiles, and their ability to twist and turn to chase a target, Vorik wouldn't want to test them at even the edge of that range.

No, Agrevlari agreed, *but the ship carrying it would have to sail in this direction to reach us here. We may still hunt on this end of the island.*

Does that mean the dragons aren't that concerned?

As I said, we lost kin to that contraption, Agrevlari said with atypical grim seriousness. *We* are *concerned. We are joining with the general in contemplating how it might be destroyed or sunk and rendered inoperable.*

I understand. I'm sorry you lost kin. Vorik closed his eyes, questioning his decision to volunteer to capture Syla. If he hadn't argued to take her alive, and his people hadn't been worried about hitting him, might they have succeeded in sinking the ship?

Maybe, maybe not. The arrival of Wreylith and the Freeborn Faction dragons had made everything more difficult.

If it makes you feel better, Vorik added, *I'm shackled in a cell. When I was thinking of trying to leap overboard, Wreylith blocked me, knocked me to the deck, and planted a taloned foot on my back while the gardeners disarmed me. It was humiliating.*

"To think, I claimed to like challenges," he said aloud to himself.

I would have enjoyed having Wreylith touch me in any manner, Agrevlari said.

Her talons aren't as appealing as you might think. In the next ballad you compose to screech at her, I would not suggest highlighting their magnificence.

All of her is magnificent. I'd hoped that our romantic time together would have left her pining for me and eager to join again, but when, after your queen fell unconscious and no longer manned the weapons platform, I flew close... Wreylith snarled at me.

Didn't she do that while you were joining too? I remember a lot of activity up there. For the most part, Vorik had been distracted by his own joining with Syla, but having the dragons overhead with rocks falling off the platform they'd used as a bed—a *nest*—had distracted him a couple of times.

Yes, but, in that context, I believed they were affectionate snarls of arousal. She was not *affectionate when she was keeping me from reaching you.*

Wasn't she fighting with Ozlemar earlier? That probably made her crabby.

That is a good point. Encounters with Ozlemar make everyone *crabby.*

My brother doesn't mind him.

Your brother is a rare human and not easily perturbed.

Vorik wagered Jhiton was perturbed now and didn't look forward to meeting up with him again. He *especially* didn't look forward to seeing Lesva again and grimaced as he imagined the two of them standing shoulder to shoulder and facing him.

Perhaps Wreylith is not *displeased with me and was only expressing her ire which was naturally roused after her encounter with Ozlemar. Now that you mention it, that does seem likely. While I wait for you to extricate yourself from your predicament, I may see if I can hunt down an eliok or other tasty morsel that I might offer to share with Wreylith. After her battle, she is undoubtedly hungry.*

Undoubtedly.

Do you know what her favorite meals are? Perhaps I should have asked. An offering is always welcomed by a dragon. Perhaps a delicacy would win her regard more effectively than a ballad.

I think that's likely. Syla mentioned that Wreylith likes tongue but did not say which creature's tongue she was consuming.

Hm. Tongues are quite ubiquitous among herbivores. I should not think that slinging one toward her from a less favored prey would be effective.

Probably not. From what I've observed, women don't care to have tongues slung at them, regardless. Now, if the tongue was attached to an appealing mate and used in an evocative way, that might be different.

Do you refer to acts of coitus?

Among humans, yes.

Tongues are involved? How strange. Would you perhaps speak to your queen and see if she knows Wreylith's favorite prey? I am certain she enjoys eliok, but they've been hunted extensively these past weeks and may be difficult to find on this island.

I can ask her the next time I see her, yes.

Someone spoke in the corridor, words muffled by the thick walls and doors. In case someone was coming to question him—or torture him?—Vorik rolled into a crouch, ready to spring, though the shackles would hinder him.

Syla wouldn't order him tortured, but if she hadn't yet recovered from using the weapons platform, some overly assertive military officer would be in charge. It was bad enough that several of the soldiers had slammed punches into Vorik's sides as they'd dragged him down here. With Wreylith looming nearby, Vorik hadn't even been resisting them.

A key turned in a lock, and the door opened.

Sergeant Fel ducked his shaven head to enter the cell, his mace *and* a dagger in his hands. Vorik straightened to face him, their eyes meeting.

Earlier, Fel had kept the soldiers from killing Vorik, instead giving orders to have him locked up, but he didn't look pleased about the situation. More men lurked in the corridor. Wearing the blue uniforms of Royal Protectors, they all gripped swords or crossbows. They didn't step into the cell behind Fel, however. Syla did.

Clad in a blue dress damp at the hem and neckline, with her equally damp hair fallen from the bun it had been in earlier, she had bags under her eyes and stood with a weary slump. That didn't keep Vorik from looking at her with appreciation, admiring everything from her engaging curves to her full lips to the warmth in her gray eyes when she looked at him through her spectacles. She wore new ones, the red frames bright against her auburn hair. Someone must have crafted them to match Wreylith's scales.

Syla looked at Fel, as if she wanted to ask him to leave, but she must have known he wouldn't. Instead, she closed the door, stepped around him, and hugged Vorik.

He hadn't expected that and lamented that he hadn't tried to free his wrists so that he could return the embrace. He could feel not only the warmth of her body through their clothing but the energy of her power, more noticeable than it had been before when he'd been with her. The dragon bond must have added to the magic she already possessed.

"Thank you for coming," she whispered into his neck, brushing her lips over his skin.

A thrum of heat coursed through Vorik, and he wished she *had* sent her bodyguard outside. He shouldn't want to be with her after she'd killed his allies, but they'd attacked her, so how could he blame her for the result?

"I would say you're welcome, but I would feel guilty if I did." As he so often was with her, Vorik felt compelled to honesty—far more than was wise. "I came to kidnap you."

Syla leaned back to look at his face, though she left her hands on his shoulders. "I thought you saw Lesva attacking and decided to rescue me from her again."

"When I flew down, I had no idea she would pop out of the water like a hyperactive dolphin."

She snorted softly. "Is kidnapping me what your general ordered?"

"No, he wants..." Vorik looked away. "Since you are the one who can control that weapons platform, he wanted another fate for you."

"My death?"

Vorik shrugged vaguely. Since she hated Jhiton already, he didn't want to make it worse by voicing his brother's desires.

"He's loathsome," Syla said.

"You've stated that opinion before."

"It's not an opinion. It's a fact."

"He's not overly fond of you either, if it helps. He's keeping track of all the times you've tried to kill him."

"Can he count that high without using his thumbs?"

"He's rather bright, actually."

"Uh-huh. I hate him."

"I know." Vorik shrugged again, not blaming her but wishing the situation were different. Wishing... He sighed. He didn't even know what to wish.

"Did you volunteer to attempt to kidnap me as an alternative to killing me?" Syla asked.

"Yes. I knew you would hate me as well if I succeeded, but... I didn't think there was any other way you would survive the battle."

"I doubt I *would* have survived if your general had come after me. He would have *helped* Lesva."

Vorik closed his eyes, hating to imagine that situation, but he agreed that it could have played out that way. It almost had.

"I think you're right that I would have resented you for kidnapping me. I probably would have railed at you and not understood your sacrifice." Syla smiled wryly, her evocative lips drawing his eye. "I guess it's a good thing we captured you instead."

"Calling this situation *good* is overly optimistic, at least from my point of view, but if you don't resent me, I am pleased about that."

"I should, but I don't. You saved my life, Vorik."

Syla stepped forward and hugged him again. This time, instead of brushing her lips along his neck, she kissed him on the mouth. Hard.

Pleasure and arousal flared within him, and he tried to pull his wrists apart so that he could touch her. The chain linking his shackles clinked, restraining him. A burst of fury at being denied the ability to embrace her made him flex muscles enhanced by dragon magic, and he jerked his arms apart with a snapping of iron.

As Vorik succeeded in wrapping his arms around Syla and pulling her close, Fel swore and stepped forward, raising his mace.

Syla turned her mouth from Vorik and lifted a hand toward her bodyguard, even as she molded her body to Vorik's. "It's all right, Sergeant."

"He snapped his *chains*," Fel barked, his fist clenched around the haft of his mace. Before, he hadn't looked like he wanted to brain Vorik, but he seemed to be reevaluating that.

"It's his dragon magic," Syla explained.

"He's not *human*."

"He's amazing." Syla turned her mouth back to Vorik, and he leaned forward, capturing her lips with his. *She* was amazing. And he wanted her.

Fel groaned with disgust.

Vorik didn't care. With his wrists free, he had no trouble lowering his arms and cupping her ass, pulling Syla tightly against him. Maybe he should have been worried about Fel, but all he could think about was the heat of her body, the adoration in her eyes when she looked at him, and the fiery passion in her kiss. If he had to be a prisoner, Vorik could think of no captor he'd want more.

And by all the gods, he wanted her. As he deepened his kiss, tongue sliding between her eager lips, he slid his hands along her body, relishing in her full curves, growing harder as she pressed into him. The chains clanked, but he scarcely noticed, other than to make sure he didn't let them hit her. Though she might not have noticed. She moaned hungrily as their tongues stroked each other, and her hands slid over Vorik's shoulders and chest.

"Queen Syla," Fel whispered, his back to them as he pointedly looked at the door. "This isn't appropriate. *He* isn't appropriate."

"Send your bodyguard away," Vorik said against her mouth. "I want you."

"Prisoners don't get what they want," she whispered even as she rubbed against him, pushing against his cock, making him harder by the second.

"Captors do. And you want me too." Vorik crushed his mouth against hers, stealing further words, but she moaned what could only be agreement.

A knock sounded at the door before she could send away the bodyguard.

At first, Syla ignored it, and Vorik stroked and kissed her in approval, but it came again. Insistent.

"Your Majesty?" someone called from the corridor. "There's a wounded soldier badly in need of your gift, and others who aren't doing that well either. The temple healer asked if we could get you to help."

Syla drew back. Vorik didn't want to release her—his penis *especially* didn't want him to release her—but he knew that her duty would call her away from her own pleasure. He had some small satisfaction in seeing her panting from their exertions, her spectacles drooping down her nose. Gods, when had he started to find that sight so arousing?

"All right," she said, her voice raspy before she cleared her throat, her gaze still locked on Vorik. She swallowed and managed a louder, "All right," that the man might hear through the door, then nodded toward Fel.

With palpable relief, he sprang to open the door and step out of the cell.

"I don't think your bodyguard enjoys our encounters as much as I do," Vorik murmured softly enough that those in the corridor wouldn't hear.

"Strange."

As Syla stepped toward the door, it occurred to him that he hadn't asked her what Wreylith's favorite foods were.

"He is," Vorik said. "How odd that he accused *me* of being inhuman."

"He was awed by your strength."

"Alarmed by it, I'd think."

"I need to do what I was trained to do." Syla nodded toward the waiting men. "But I'd like to... speak further with you later."

"Speak?" Vorik twitched an eyebrow, wondering if she'd come down to question him before being distracted. But, by now, she knew he wouldn't answer inquiries about the plans and movements of his people.

"Vigorously." Her own eyebrows twitched. Or maybe that was a seductive waggle.

Whatever her intent, it made his aroused body want to spring to the door, slam it shut, and return to what they'd been doing.

"What is Wreylith's favorite meal?" Vorik blurted, less because he was worried about satisfying Agrevlari's curiosity and more because he didn't want Syla to leave. He knew she had to help her wounded troops, but she looked so tired. Shouldn't she rest first? Perhaps while cuddled in his arms in the aftermath of...

Syla looked back at him. "I'm not sure about her favorite, but she enjoys elioks and horn hogs."

"Thank you. Agrevlari wondered. He has offerings in mind. He enjoyed their cactus-flower-induced dalliance."

"Ah." Syla stepped into the doorway, no suggestion on her face that *she* would dally. "May I have your word that you won't escape?" She waved at his broken shackles. "I suspect there's nothing I could do to hold you if you wanted to leave."

"I..." Vorik's penis wanted him to give his word without hesitation, but his brain managed to hold rein over his tongue. He was a prisoner, and his people were at war with hers. If an opportunity presented itself, he had to escape. More, he should try to complete his mission and kidnap her. If he voluntarily stayed here, it would be a betrayal of his orders, his duty. By the eyes of the moon, why was it all so complicated? "I don't think I can give my word on that."

"Ah." Syla looked disappointed but not confused or surprised. "I would promise to reward you for staying, but that would be manipulative."

Contemplating what *kind* of reward she had in mind excited his groin all over again, but he tried not to let eagerness show in his eyes. "I think you're supposed to be manipulative with enemies. And conniving."

"I don't want to win a war that way." Syla lifted a hand, then stepped into the corridor, letting the soldier and Sergeant Fel lead her away.

Vorik closed his eyes, glad she *hadn't* promised a reward. That would have left him even more conflicted if the opportunity to escape arose.

Long after the door thudded shut, the lock turning with a thunk, he stood with his broken shackles dangling from his wrists and debated what to do next.

~

Syla woke when someone prodded her shoulder. She blinked a few times before remembering where she was. She half-sat, half-slumped across a stool and the lower half of one of the narrow bunks in the warship's infirmary. A couple of bumps under the blanket confused her until she realized they were someone's legs. After healing five people, she'd fallen asleep, utterly exhausted, before finishing the sixth.

"Sorry," she murmured to her patient, her eyes gritty and achy.

Her entire *body* ached. Her back and neck were stiff, the arrow gouge she'd received stung, and her hip throbbed when she shifted upright. She'd been exhausted when she'd stumbled off the weapons platform, and she hadn't gotten an opportunity to rest after that. Before going to check on Vorik, she'd been drawn into a meeting with the fleet commander. Surprisingly, he'd consulted her for direction, wanting to know if their ships should only occupy the harbor or if he should send troops into the city to search for wounded and free prisoners. Not sure how long they would have before the stormers retaliated, Syla had told him to send as many men as he dared and that they could take anyone who wanted to go back to Castle Island. Unfortunately, she still didn't have a shielder to make the reclaiming of this island permanent. And, she reminded herself, they only had *part* of it.

"It's all right, ma'am," came the amused voice of the soldier she'd fallen asleep on. "Er, Your Majesty."

Sunlight beamed through the porthole behind his bunk. Was it dawn already? *Past* dawn? It had been early nightfall when she'd gone to visit Vorik.

"How long was I out?" she wondered.

"All night," came a dry voice from behind her. Aunt Tibby. Was she who'd woken Syla?

Tibby set a mug of coffee and a muffin on a small table for her. Sergeant Fel stood by the door behind her, bags under his eyes. The poor man must have stayed up all night watching over Syla. He needed a break. She wished she could give him the retirement he deserved so he could truly rest.

"Was I sleeping on..." Syla looked back to the soldier. "I'm sorry. I didn't get your name."

"Corporal Genlikar, Your Majesty. I was unconscious when you started healing me, or I would have properly introduced myself." He glanced to the side, as if wondering if he should get out of bed so he could drop to one knee.

Syla lifted a hand to stave off any such effort, especially since she hadn't finished healing him.

"And it's all right," he added. "You sleeping on my legs, I mean. It'll be a story I can tell my kids someday."

"As if someone as reckless as you will live long enough to have children," a grumpy male voice said.

The major that Captain Vonla had been avoiding stepped into view. Syla barely kept from grimacing.

Was he here to lecture her about her *prisoner*? Or to assassinate her while she was in a groggy and weakened state? Maybe both.

Having delivered breakfast, Aunt Tibby left as the man removed his uniform cap and stepped up to the bed. The corporal raised his eyebrows and looked around, as if wondering if he should leave. The major lifted a staying hand toward him.

"Your Majesty." Black uniform rumpled, short black hair sticking out in all directions, the major touched a fresh scar cutting across his cheek. Had a dragon talon done that? Or maybe Lesva's sword. The officer surprised her by dropping to one knee and bowing his head. "I failed to introduce myself yesterday, but I'm Major Hixun. On behalf of all the men who survived the battle against overpowering numbers, I thank you for fighting with us and using that strange cannonball launcher on our enemies."

"I... You're welcome, Major." Syla hadn't expected anything except veiled hostility from the man, not after the looks he'd given the captain who'd warned her about assassins.

Was it possible he was being polite so she would lower her guard? She waved for him to rise, doubting she would get used to people dropping to a knee in front of her.

"You were brave to come along on this journey, Your Majesty, and I didn't expect..." Hixun glanced at the corporal, as if the young soldier might have input. "I don't think any of us, well, quite knew how that big marble cannon worked or thought you would stand on it in the middle of a battleground. In the middle of *dragons* trying to kill you."

"Well, the platform is somewhat protected by the overhead canopy."

"An *arrow* hit you," the corporal said. "And that dragon-rider woman tried to *kill* you."

Adoration shone in the young man's eyes. That wasn't surprising since Syla had been healing him, but the major nodded as well. His gaze wasn't one of adoration, but it also wasn't the distant and cold contemplation of an enemy plotting one's demise. It was... respectful. The fleet commander's had been too, she realized. At the time, she hadn't known how to interpret his regard. Huh.

"The sides of the weapons platform *could* use more protection," she said. "It should be more like an armored carriage, don't you think? With a few shatter-proof windows. I wonder if my Aunt Tibby—she's an engineer, you know—could make some adjustments. Do you think it's permissible to adjust a gift from the gods?"

"Isn't she an agricultural engineer?" Hixun asked.

"Yes, but I'm certain she could handle armoring a platform. She might even have thoughts about adding axles and wheels, maybe a whole wagon frame so it could be more easily transported."

"It would end up looking like one of her vile man-eating tractors," Fel said.

"A weapons platform *should* be vile," Syla said. "We could paint a scary face with fangs on the top of it."

"To answer your question, no," Fel said, "I don't think it's permissible to adjust gifts from the gods. Not like *that*."

"But wheels and armor would be okay?"

"I'd think so."

Hixun stepped back from the bed. "I'll leave you to your work and rest, Your Majesty, but we would be honored if you would attend a short ceremony we're having for the fallen later."

"Of course." Syla swallowed a lump that formed in her throat at the memory of the Royal Protector who'd taken an arrow for her. How many others had died during the engagement?

"Thank you. And thank you for healing the men and also helping during the battle—you're the only reason we *survived* that. Oh." Hixun lifted a finger as if he'd remembered something. "You should also know that the fleet commander took teams ashore now that the storm is past, and they're searching for the island lord and other high-status individuals and military leaders. Before departing, he asked me to find out what your plans are for… the prisoner."

"Captain Vorik."

"Yes. We know who he is. And we're uncertain why you want him held instead of executed."

"He saved my life by fighting off Captain Lesva."

"We were confused by that, Your Majesty. We understand that thanks to you and your dragon—" Hixun gave her another respectful nod, "—members of a rogue stormer faction assisted us, but Vorik can't be affiliated with them. He's General Jhiton's right-hand man."

"Yes, he is. From what I've gathered, it's actually Captain Lesva who went rogue, in a manner of speaking. She was trying to kill me."

"Isn't that in line with their goals?" Hixun asked.

"Their horrible and *odious* goals," the corporal said. "Queen Syla is a *healer.* You don't kill healers."

He sounded affronted on her behalf, and Syla decided that he, like the captain, probably hadn't been on board with the assassination plot. She hoped other troops felt as they did—and that the major's apparent change of opinion of her was in earnest.

"The queen single-handedly brought down several riders and dragons," Hixun pointed out.

"But she removed the arrowhead in my hip and healed the puncture." The corporal touched his side. "Even my groin pull feels better."

"That may be because a pretty girl fell asleep sprawled across your lap." A soldier who'd been pretending not to listen in from a nearby bunk couldn't resist making that comment.

The corporal rolled his eyes. "She was sleeping on my *legs*, Froggie. Not my, you know."

"Whatever makes you warm and tingly."

Hixun cleared his throat. "The prisoner, Your Majesty. I'm hoping to get a little clarity. Captain Vorik is very dangerous, and I'd rather have him dead than in a cell and wearing shackles that can't hold him. At the least, I would prefer he be sedated if you're keeping him alive for some future plan. Are there Candles of Serenity in here?" Hixun looked toward cabinets along one wall. "I'll have one of the medics look for some."

"Ah, yes." Syla didn't want to sedate Vorik, but she also didn't want her military officers to execute him while she was busy healing people. "That's a practical suggestion, Major, but I… want to question him." Yes, she remembered that had been what she'd told Fel to keep Vorik alive, and it was a practical thing to do with a prisoner. "He's high-ranking enough that he should know all about the stormers' plans."

It occurred to her that this could also be an opportunity to learn where the shielder components had been taken. Vorik wouldn't voluntarily answer questions related to that, and he would be upset if he betrayed his people, but she might have to coerce him, regardless. For the moment, her fleet had Hazel Harbor and this part of Harvest Island, but until she found the missing components and Aunt Tibby made a working shielder, the Kingdom would be vulnerable to more attacks by the stormers. Didn't she owe it to her people to get what information she could out of Vorik? Even if it meant manipulating him?

The thought held no appeal, and he would resent her for it, but she had to consider it.

"We have someone who specializes in interrogation, Your Majesty," Hixun said. "There's no need for you to bother yourself with him."

But she *liked* bothering herself with Vorik. Words she did not voice to the officer.

"I have some tinctures and powders that I can apply to make him more amenable to questioning." As soon as the words came out, she realized they were truer than she'd intended. In her trunks, she'd brought along Teyla's finds from the storm god's laboratory, including the hydra-scale powder. If the medical history texts were accurate, it could be quite effective at lowering a prisoner's mental guards. "Have him taken from his cell and up to my cabin, please."

"Your… what?" Hixun stared at her.

"My potions will work better to convince him to answer honestly if he's in a relaxed environment and doesn't feel threatened."

"A relaxed environment? Your Majesty, we're not in the habit of giving dangerous prisoners pillows and blankets and apple cotlets."

"No? I think apple cotlets would help loosen his tongue. Vorik likes sweets."

Hixun's mouth opened, but he didn't seem to know what to say. He looked stunned. She herself had been bemused to learn that the fearsome and deadly Captain Vorik had a sweet tooth. A *fruit* tooth, as she'd called it before.

"Put him in my cabin," Syla said again. "As you suggested, I'll prepare Candles of Serenity."

"Your cabin isn't *secure*, Your Majesty," Hixun protested. "It has *portholes*."

"Yes, they're delightful. Put him in there with shackles and guards, please. Remember, I've also got Wreylith onboard to help me. She'll pluck open the portlight and snatch Vorik up in her talons if he tries to do anything to me or jump overboard and escape." Syla pointed upward.

"I don't know, Your Majesty." Hixun rubbed the back of his neck.

Agrevlari is attempting to seduce me by promising to retrieve horn hogs or offering to show me an excellent hunting spot on this island that he's discovered, Wreylith said, as if she'd been listening in on the conversation from her position perched above decks. Maybe she had been.

Are his seduction attempts likely to work?

No, I told him that if he comes close, I'd bite his tail off while you pummel him with the death launcher.

Is that... what you're calling the weapons platform?

It is what he is calling it now. It is an appropriate name.

I suppose it is. Syla regretted that she'd used it to kill. With every death, human and dragon, it seemed her people were driven further and further away from a potential future treaty with the stormers, but maybe she was foolish to have ever believed one might be possible. When they'd first invaded, murdering her siblings and mother, hadn't that turned what had been a rift into an uncrossable chasm? If not for Vorik, she might not have an iota of sympathy for any of them.

They will seek to destroy it, Wreylith said.

Good luck to them. When your allies delivered it, they dropped it a thousand feet, and it didn't so much as chip a corner.

It is sturdy, but nothing is indestructible. They will seek a method to render it inoperable.

After we restore the shielder to this island, we'll return the weapons platform to the protection of Castle Island. We just need to find those components. And I intend to do so. Soon.

She meant the words but wondered if there was any way to achieve the goal without drugging Vorik. She didn't want to betray him, nor did she want him to betray his people. Why was everything she wanted with him so difficult?

8

Morning found Vorik sitting against the wall, his chin to his chest as he dozed. Before going to sleep, he'd snapped the chain between his ankle irons, the same as the one between his wrist shackles. He hadn't attempted to break the hinges or lock on the door to escape, but he'd contemplated it.

He sensed Wreylith on the ship and doubted he could swim away under her vigilant eye. And he dared not call Agrevlari to try to collect him, not with the weapons platform on the deck. Besides, Vorik wasn't that eager to return empty-handed to his people. He was *supposed* to be kidnapping Syla, not spending time as her captive.

Oh, he didn't want to capture her at this point, but he felt bound to try. It was the only reason Jhiton had allowed him to fly ahead and try to get to her. Jhiton could have denied that request and helped Lesva kill Syla. Their combined might would have been too much for Vorik to overcome. He'd never even bested his brother in a one-on-one fight. Jhiton had taught him everything he knew about combat. And, though he was older, with grays creeping into his dark hair, Jhiton was *very* fit and capable.

Further, he derived as much power from Ozlemar as Vorik did from Agrevlari. Maybe more. Ozlemar was equal in size, power, and prowess to Wreylith.

How is the kidnapping going? a dry voice spoke into his mind from the distance.

Jhiton. It was as if he'd known Vorik was contemplating him.

I've allowed myself to be captured and am lulling Syla and her troops into believing I'm a subdued prisoner. Meanwhile, I'm planning a way to kidnap her, keep the weapons platform from being used again, and rejoin our troops with my prisoner slung triumphantly over my shoulder. Vorik eyed his cell door while waiting for a sarcastic retort.

If you capture her, the weapons platform wouldn't be able *to be used, would it?* Jhiton mused.

I don't know. It's possible anyone with a moon-mark can operate it. In fact, I would think that likely.

If that were true, someone else would have been sent along. Queens *don't lead fleets into battle.*

Vorik scratched his cheek. *She's a willful and determined queen.*

I gathered that when she was trying to kill me.

All three times?

It's four *times now. One of those glowing balls almost knocked me back to the mainland.*

I'm sure you would have dodged it if it had gotten close.

Unlikely. Did you not notice that they adjust their flightpaths to track their targets? They're far deadlier to dragons—to all of us—than cannonballs.

Yes, Vorik *had* noticed they had that ability. *How did you avoid being hit?*

I did nothing. A lightning bolt struck it before it reached me. It was great luck.

Either that, or you're being protected by the gods. Vorik thought of their musings that *Syla* was being protected by their deities. Never before had he seen anything to suggest that *Jhiton* held divine favor. Of course, Jhiton was still alive, despite countless battles with dangerous enemies. One might argue that all stormers who survived for decades in their ruthless world had the favor of some god, but this was more of a sign than Vorik had ever experienced.

It would be nice if they supported me, Jhiton said, *but I think it's more likely the magical energy or something in the projectiles attracts lightning.*

That's possible. Vorik recalled that swords had first been crafted from gargoyle bone because his ancestors had learned the hard way that steel conducted lightning, and a man riding high in the sky on a dragon while holding a pointy metal object could attract a strike.

Let me know when you're able to escape with the queen. I'll order Agrevlari or another dragon to pick you up, and we will test my hypothesis.

That she's the only one that can use the weapons platform?

Yes, Jhiton said. *If she's gone, and it cannot be operated, we will sink the ship on which it rides, destroy the rest of the fleet, and retake that half of Harvest Island.*

You sound determined.

I am determined. We lost Cith and Tarvoran, and several dragons. Lesva lost Verikloth and is furious.

Vorik had seen the blue dragon go down and had been afraid of that. Lesva had already hated Syla. Before, it had been unreasonable—as far as Vorik had been able to tell, Lesva had simply disliked Syla because she'd dared hold her tongue when Lesva had questioned her under magical duress. Under *torture*.

Now, she would have a more legitimate reason to loathe Syla. Not that hatred needed to be legitimate or reasonable. Sometimes, it just was.

Vorik rubbed his face, wondering if he would have to kill Lesva to keep Syla safe. The idea of doing so made him grimace, not only because they'd once been lovers but because she was on his side of this war. And Syla was...

"A problem," Vorik said with a sigh.

Kidnap her, Vorik, Jhiton said firmly. *I want her away from the weapons platform, and I want what you suggested yesterday, her drugged and questioned until she draws us a map to each shielder.*

Does this mean you don't need me to kidnap Lady Abrya anymore? Why did Vorik keep getting orders to capture women? He felt like the villain he so often teased his brother of being. Why couldn't they come up with another more *honorable* way to win this war?

We yet have plans to take Bogberry Island while the majority of the Kingdom forces are occupied with Harvest.

Did that mean Jhiton had already sent troops in that direction? Would someone else kayak in and try to capture the lady?

If you're not available to kidnap the lord's wife, Jhiton added, *I will.*

Be careful. Between your nefariously flapping cloak and scarred face, you might not be able to win her favor. Vorik doubted his brother would try any such thing, but Jhiton had pointed out that the lady supposedly had a soft spot for stormers—or had before all this had begun.

The hydra-scale powder should ensure I don't need *her favor to get what I want, but if you retrieve the queen and join us at Bogberry Island, I'll let you attempt to smile at Lady Abrya and charm her.*

The way you entice me, General.

I'll also give you whatever fruits and berries we're able to find in the lord's palace.

That's more likely to tempt me.

I'm aware. Get the queen, Vorik. Jhiton's telepathic voice sounded more distant, like he was flying away as they conversed. Maybe he was already on his way to Bogberry Island, leaving behind only part of his forces to take back the harbor if Vorik succeeded in getting Syla away from the weapons platform.

I'll capture her, but I need your word on something. Vorik didn't feel right extracting promises from his brother, but Lesva might now be flying at Jhiton's side, maybe even astride Ozlemar with him, and able to influence him. Against his wishes, the memory of Lesva resting her hand on Jhiton's chest and flirting with him came to Vorik's mind. *If I bring Syla to join you and the others...*

She won't be harmed.

Vorik trusted his brother would do what he said, but Jhiton wasn't the only obstacle.

If you give that order, Vorik said, *Lesva might disobey it.*

I will see to it that she doesn't. As long as the queen knows the locations of all the shielders, she has value to us.

She has value to me for more reasons than that.

I'm aware. As are others.

Like Chieftess Shi?

Yes.

Vorik bristled, but he had made choices that could call his loyalty into question. After he'd openly defended Syla from Lesva on the deck of a Kingdom warship, even more people than the chieftess would question his motivations. The riders in his own squadron, men and women he'd worked with for years, might doubt him. The notion stung almost as much as the thought of losing his brother's respect.

If you can also sabotage or destroy that weapons platform while you're aboard their ship, Jhiton said, *that might still some wagging tongues.*

I sense Wreylith near the device, Vorik said, *but if I get an opportunity to take a closer look, I will.*

Take that look while holding explosives. Perhaps your queen can supply you with the ones they booby-trapped their shielder with during our last incursion.

Oh, yes. I believe captors regularly give explosives to captives. It's sound war policy.

Use your smile on her. She likes you.

Not enough to give me explosives. She might bake me a blackberry cobbler. Vorik smiled wistfully.

Maybe you can stuff it in one of the column-barrels to gum up the works.

A solid military tactic. Vorik imagined blackberries flying out of the weapons platform instead of deadly projectiles. *I'll at least get Syla. As to the rest, I acknowledge that destroying that device would be a boon to our people, and if I get an opportunity, I will.*

Destroying Syla's means of defending the island in the absence of a shield struck him as terrible, but one wasn't supposed to be *nice* during war. And the thing could kill *dragons*. At least the shielders only kept dragons out. That weapons platform was dreadful.

Bring her to our new camp, Jhiton said, *and I'll ensure she's kept alive.*

His back still to the wall, Vorik propped his arms on his knees and laced his fingers together to rest his chin on them. He didn't like the idea of taking Syla anywhere near Lesva. But what was the alternative? To stay here in this cell? To escape but not return to his people? To walk away from his tribe and his family and friends? All that he was?

Somewhere along the way, that thought had become less undesirable than the thought of hurting Syla. Or causing her to be hurt—or killed. But he couldn't...

Clanks and voices sounded in the corridor.

Undecided about what he would do, Vorik rose to his feet. The lock turned, and the door opened. Two soldiers he didn't recognize stepped inside, and more filled the corridor. Numerous weapons were pointed in Vorik's direction. He peered hopefully through the doorway, wanting to see Syla, even though she was at the center of his conflict.

"Step outside, stormer." One guard jerked his chin toward the corridor. "You're to be questioned."

"By Queen Syla? Or a master interrogator?"

"*Queens* don't question prisoners." The soldier noticed the broken chains. "Storm-cursed bastard, what happened to your shackles?"

"Oh, these?" Vorik held up his wrists so the broken chains clanked. "They fell apart. Shoddy workmanship. You'll probably want to have the smith who forged them flogged."

The soldier licked his lips, eyeing Vorik more nervously, but he pointed his chin toward the corridor again. "Come on."

Eight armed men accompanied Vorik through the bowels of the ship. He didn't try to escape, more because of Wreylith's ongoing presence than because of the troops. Besides, he wanted to see Syla again before he decided what to do. As silly as it was, he wished he could speak with her about his conundrum and that she could be a confidante instead of an enemy, instead of the woman he was supposed to kidnap.

"Go get some more shackles, Uzarik," one of the soldiers said. "Ones with thicker chains."

"Yes, sir."

Vorik's escort deposited him in a large cabin, one that had to belong to an officer. It had two portholes, a spacious bunk, and a desk that held—

He halted by the doorway, groaning as a familiar scent wafted over him. The thick green wax pillars weren't *lit*, but after his last experience with Candles of Serenity, he recognized them immediately. Even unlit, he could pick up the scents of eucalyptus and whatever was in there that had the power to knock a man unconscious.

Beside the candles rested several vials and a couple of small ceramic jars, all secured in a holder attached to the desk so they wouldn't slide off. With a start, Vorik stared at one of the smaller jars. He couldn't read the runes labeling it, but it appeared identical to the one that Jhiton had pulled from a pocket and that held hydra-scale powder. Dread crept into him.

Could Syla also have brought back *souvenirs* from the storm god's laboratory? Of course. More than once, she'd mentioned her collections of items related to medicine and herbalism. A truth drug from a past era would qualify as an intriguing find.

Was her plan to semi-sedate him, hoping that would render him more susceptible to imbibing the hydra-scale powder in a beverage? That… might work.

Vorik frowned. He would prefer torture to being drugged. He'd been injured often enough in his life to have learned to endure physical pain and grit his teeth through questioning. But Syla wouldn't order him hurt. She cared for him. And he appreciated that. But this… this would be painful too. Maybe *more* painful. If he betrayed his people, it wouldn't matter how it had been accomplished.

Vorik sorted through the information in his head. Did he *know* enough to betray his people?

He knew about the plan to take over Bogberry Island next. He also knew the location of the new camp where the shielder components had been taken. Most likely, that was what Syla wanted to know, but his entire tribe would be in that camp. If she sent ships full of military men to it, women and children could be in danger, especially if the Sixteen Talons squadrons and all their dragon allies were busy hundreds of miles away on Bogberry Island.

Vorik shook his head bleakly. Yes, he knew enough to be a threat to his people. He couldn't babble.

He eyed the candles, then a porthole, and was on the verge of seeing if the glass would open so he could chuck everything into the sea. But the door creaked, and he swung about. A barrage of troops entered, one man carrying fresh wrist shackles. Vorik glimpsed the side of someone in a yellow dress. Syla? That looked like the curve of her hip, but another woman's voice floated in from the corridor.

"Use the powder to find out what his people are up to next and where they're lurking right now," the speaker whispered. It sounded like the aunt. Tibby. Had she come along on a military mission? That was surprising, but Syla also shouldn't have put herself into such a dangerous situation. They must have both come to ensure the storm-cursed weapons platform would work. "Where are the components for the shielder? He'll know. I'm ready to get to work on that as soon as I have them. And are there stormers still on Harvest Island?" Tibby added. "Are they plotting something else? Get what you can out of him, then knock him out so he can't break any more shackles."

"Knock him out and throw him overboard," the gruff Sergeant Fel added from somewhere out of sight.

The soldier with the shackles left the broken bands on Vorik's wrists and ankles, pinching skin as he tried to maneuver the new set of irons into place. It didn't work, and he was forced to unlock the others. Feeling quite patient and accommodating, Vorik stood with his arms out while he listened to the conversation, wanting to hear Syla chime in with her thoughts on what should be done to him.

In the cell, she'd thanked him for saving her life and had wanted to have sex with him. He had little doubt about that. But time had passed, and if this was her cabin… she'd clearly chosen items for his interrogation.

He couldn't blame her. They were at war. It would be far wiser for her to interrogate him than have sex with him. But if he got an opportunity to seduce her and distract her from questioning him, he would do his best to do so.

"Wreylith says the stormers and their dragons are in caves by the volcano," Syla said. "Only Agrevlari is closer to us, probably hoping for a chance to rescue Vorik."

"Out from underneath your dragon?" Fel asked. "And the weapons platform? We'll shoot him down if he comes close."

We'll?

Jhiton assumed that only Syla could operate that device. Maybe that was an incorrect assumption.

"I think Wreylith intimidates Agrevlari enough that he won't approach while she's here," Syla said. "Though I understand there have been promises of horn-hog meat."

"Just see what your captain will reveal while he's drugged," Aunt Tibby said.

"And *don't* have sex with him." Fel groaned.

Was the bodyguard planning to stand in the room again while Vorik and Syla spoke? That would make engaging in a seduction plan challenging.

"You don't think that would prompt him to babble secrets?" Syla asked wryly.

"*No*," Fel said.

"Maybe," Tibby offered. "Did it before?"

"No," Syla said.

"Then stick with the drug. There's no need to... Goodness, Syla." Tibby had already been whispering, but she lowered her voice even further. If not for Vorik's magically enhanced hearing, he wouldn't have caught any of the conversation. "What if you were impregnated? With *stormer* offspring?"

"I'm taking a contraceptive." Syla sounded uncomfortable, like this wasn't a topic she wished to discuss.

Vorik didn't blame her, though he did find himself curious if the thought of having children with him was as appalling to Syla as to her aunt. Oh, he knew they never could, not when they were at war, but... he remembered Jhiton offering a place in the tribe for Syla if she wanted to live with them. If only...

"Such methods aren't foolproof," Tibby said. "You of all people know that. Can you imagine the scandal? Normally, *I* wouldn't care about such things—and given that none of your siblings were able to have children, I'd consider it a blessed event if you became a mother, but not of *his* child. It would be one more reason for your political opponents to try to oust you."

"I'll keep that in mind," Syla murmured, then called into the cabin, "Corporal, is he ready?" with a tinge of desperation in her voice.

She hadn't *said* she loathed the idea of having children with Vorik, but she wanted to escape that conversation. He didn't blame her.

The man who'd been shackling Vorik stepped back. "Uhm."

He looked toward another soldier holding a long chain that could be hooked to the shackles and attached to a ring mounted in a cell, but his perusal of the cabin didn't reveal any eyelets bolted to the walls. This was someone's sleeping quarters, not a proper dungeon.

"He's not very secured, Your Majesty, but he is shackled again."

"For all the good it'll do," a soldier with a fresh scar down the side of his neck muttered.

During the battle, Vorik hadn't attacked any of the fleet troops —he'd been focused on Lesva—but it was possible he'd encountered the man before.

"Good. Thank you." Syla stepped inside, Fel walking in behind her.

The bodyguard immediately glowered at Vorik. It probably had more to do with the earlier kiss than a desire to throttle him. Vorik wouldn't go so far as to say Fel was on his side now, but he *could* have ordered Vorik slain while Syla had been unconscious.

Vorik bowed to them, his chains rattling. "I'm distressed that seeing my face still prompts such dyspeptic expressions from you, Sergeant Fel."

The glower turned into a growl. Maybe there *were* some fantasies of throttling.

"You can go, Corporal," Syla told the man who'd shackled Vorik. "And leave the keys here, please."

The soldier blinked. "We can't leave the keys in the cabin with him, Your Majesty. He would easily overpower you, take them, and unlock himself."

"My bodyguard is here with me."

The soldier looked at Fel. "Your bodyguard is sixty years old."

Fel growled again. This time, it wasn't directed at Vorik.

"And very capable." Syla stepped forward, plucked the keys from the corporal, then shooed him toward the door.

"Your Majesty," the soldier protested without moving. "This is highly unorthodox. And dangerous."

"It'll be fine, Corporal." Syla walked to the table and picked up a dragonspark match resting in the holder with one of the odious green Candles of Serenity.

What a ridiculous name. Candles of Knock You on Your Ass was what they should have been named.

The soldier looked like he would protest further, but a major stepped into the doorway and cleared his throat. "Come out, men. You won't want to stay in there once that's lit. Not unless you'd like to take a nap." He gave Vorik a pointed look.

"I like naps," someone whispered, sounding wistful.

Under the major's eye, the soldiers trooped out, though many frowned back with concern, looking between Syla and Vorik.

"You'll want to wait in the corridor too, Fel. And don't stand too close to the door. The vapors of the candle may waft out through the gap." Syla waved toward the bottom of the door. "I'll yell if anything goes awry, but I have all the tools I need to question Vorik." She pointed to the jars, candles, and was that her medical kit on the desk as well?

"*That* I don't doubt," Fel said, not moving.

"You question if I'll use them?"

"On someone you have *feelings* for, yes." People said curse words with less loathing.

Syla hesitated, but then used the match to light the candle. "I'll put the good of the Kingdom ahead of my feelings."

Vorik grimaced. She sounded sincere.

Fel also grimaced, but then grunted and turned to leave.

"I like naps too," he grumbled, but he stepped out and closed the door.

Syla locked it after him, then returned to the desk, the first hint of eucalyptus and another pungent scent mingling in the air. Last time, it had taken Vorik some time to pass out, but the cave had been much better ventilated than a cabin with the door and portholes closed.

He eyed her with wariness but a part of him remembered what had happened the last time those scents hung in the air. Long before he'd passed out, they'd enjoyed magnificent sex. And now... they were alone again. She stood before him with her lush auburn hair around her shoulders, drawing the eye toward her chest, especially the curve of her breasts under a dress that hugged her body in a most appealing manner. Snug over her hips, it trailed down past her knees, but it would be easy enough to lift her hem to see more of her legs, to let his hand slide along her smooth thigh, relishing in the soft warmth of her skin...

Vorik swallowed and lifted his eyes toward the ceiling, trying to tamp down his arousal. Even if *seduction* had crossed his mind, it was foolish to think of sex with someone about to drug him.

But it wasn't just *someone*, he admitted. It was Syla. And he always longed for her. Even when he shouldn't.

Unaware of his thoughts—or how sexy he found her—she sat down at the desk. For a long moment, she studied his face before shaking her head and surprising him by snuffing out the candle.

"You're not going to knock me out?" Vorik asked.

"I should, but no."

"That was... a ruse to get rid of your men?"

"Fel especially, yes."

"So we can enjoy a private and exquisitely pleasurable sexual encounter?" Vorik doubted she had that on her mind, but his groin tightened anyway, excited by the possibility. Once more, the word *seduction* floated through his mind, and a surge of desire almost made him draw upon his power to break his shackles again so that he could spring to her and carry her to the bed.

Her gaze slid to the jars on the desk, especially the small blue one that likely held the hydra-scale powder. She hadn't said yet that *it* was a ruse. Was it something Vorik had to ingest? Or a substance she could blow into the air that he might inhale?

Had Vorik envisioned it being used on him, he would have asked Jhiton—or maybe the tribe healer—for more details. But how could he have known that Syla had also recovered some from the laboratory?

"My advisors believe wholeheartedly that I should question you," Syla said, following his gaze, "under the influence of hydra-scale powder. We know you won't otherwise betray your people."

"Your advisors? Your aunt or your bodyguard?" Vorik tilted his head toward the corridor, though he'd caught the gist of their conversation—their *advisement*.

"They're in rare agreement on this matter." Instead of grabbing the jar of powder, Syla removed her spectacles, set them on the table, and rubbed her eyes. "I admit it crossed my mind independent of them. I proposed it, in fact. And I'm... torn, Vorik. I don't suppose you'd like to *tell* me where the shielder components are? It's not like they rightfully belong to your people."

"Since they were all foraged from the wilds, they don't rightfully *belong* to anyone, do they?" Vorik asked, though he *did* feel like he'd stolen them. Without Syla, he wouldn't have been able to acquire any of them.

Surprisingly, she didn't argue that, merely sighing again and leaning back in the chair. Weary? Emotionally wrought? The responsibility of protecting her people had to weigh heavily upon her shoulders. If she *didn't* question him and get the information she sought, would she feel she'd failed her kingdom?

Even though she'd attacked Vorik's people—attacked and *killed* some of them—with the weapons platform, he struggled to think of her as a true enemy. He longed to walk over and rub her shoulders, to lend her his support. How could someone so powerful look so vulnerable and… appealing?

It would be so easy to take her in his arms, to kiss her and more. He tried to remind himself that he not only couldn't allow himself to be questioned but he needed to kidnap her. How he would do that with her dragon perched on the wheelhouse above them, he didn't know.

Have you figured out a way to lure Wreylith away from this ship, Agrevlari? Vorik asked, trusting his dragon remained within telepathic range.

Is that supposed to be my goal? I've simply been trying to entice her to hunt with me. Or accept an offering of meat.

If you could do those things about five miles inland, that would be great.

She's not proved amenable to my suggestions, thus far. It's possible she even suspects me of working with you to try to trick her into leaving.

I can't imagine where she'd get that idea. Let me know if you do *get her to go off with you for a romantic interlude.*

Should I succeed at that, I'll be too distracted by my ardor to discuss the matter with you, but you ought to be able to sense when she leaves. Her aura of magnificence is difficult to miss when she's nearby, and her absence leaves a gaping emptiness in the world.

Yeah, I've observed that about her too.

Syla put her spectacles back on.

"*Are* you going to question me under the influence of that drug?" Vorik waved at the jar.

"If I were, I would have had to put it into a fruity dessert to convince you to consume it."

"I wondered if it was something that has to be ingested."

She shrugged. "It has to get into the bloodstream and eventually pass into the brain somehow."

"As a good captive on the lookout for ways to escape, I shouldn't wish that you *had* brought me a fruity dessert."

"Probably not."

"I am disappointed, however. I was recently discussing blackberry cobblers with my brother."

Syla gazed at him. "*How* recently?"

Vorik opened his mouth but paused, realizing she probably didn't know that Jhiton's link with Ozlemar had given him the power to speak telepathically across many miles to other humans. Vorik could only speak telepathically to Agrevlari and other dragons if they were nearby.

"I don't recall," Vorik said.

"In your cell? Did he reach out to you through Agrevlari? I know your dragon is close enough to flirt with Wreylith."

"Agrevlari is here to rescue me if an opportunity arises." Vorik wasn't giving anything away with that statement—she'd already guessed as much—and wanted to deter her from musing upon Jhiton's magical abilities.

"Unless he succeeds in wooing Wreylith?"

"Well, naturally that would take precedence over my welfare."

"Naturally." Syla joined him in a smile.

Ah, that smile. So beautiful. The desire to offer her a shoulder rub returned.

"Is your general angry that you stepped in front of Captain Lesva and protected me?" Syla asked.

"Jhiton is rarely angry. *Lesva* is pissed. Not just at me. You killed her dragon." Again, he didn't think he was telling Syla anything she didn't know, but he second-guessed himself. He shouldn't say anything at all on these matters. But it was so easy to speak with Syla, to answer her questions. Maybe he needed to distract her from asking them.

"She was trying to kill me at the time," Syla pointed out. "Your people have invaded the Kingdom that I'm blood-bound to protect."

She was right—and he wouldn't argue with her on the matter—but a hint of doubt entered her eyes. Probably because she was a healer and conflicted about using that weapons platform to kill. He'd come to know her well enough to believe that guess correct.

"I understand," he said quietly. "But you'll want to watch the sky above even more assiduously than before if she's around."

"The sky? She came out of the water like a sea serpent."

"The oceans are dangerous too. You'll also want to watch them."

"I need to watch everything."

She looked toward the door, and he wondered if her own people were still after her. Did assassins lurk among the uniformed men on the ship? He wouldn't be surprised. Syla being crowned probably hadn't done anything to squelch the ambitions of others who sought the throne for themselves.

"I'm sorry, Syla." Vorik came to her chair and lifted his arms so that he could drape them around her, but the chain linking his shackles made that hard. She ended up as bound as he, but she didn't move away from his embrace. Instead, she leaned her head against his chest. "I wish I could stand with you against all who threaten you," he said. "You deserve loyal allies."

He rested his face against the top of her head and inhaled her scent. She must have found a moment to wash since the stormy battle, for her hair smelled lovely. A lush floral and fruity scent that was far more appealing than what lingered in the air from the candle.

"I wish you could stand with me too. I'd like that a lot. Instead, you're here to kidnap me."

"I'm not doing a good job of it."

"You do have me trapped in your embrace." She poked at the chain.

"How trapped do you truly feel, given that there's a powerful dragon perched ten feet above us? Close enough that she could swing her head down, smash her snout through that porthole, pluck me up, and snap me in two?"

"Her snout wouldn't fit through the porthole."

"She could smash through the entire *hull*."

"That is true. She once extricated me from my room via the roof."

"And thus you don't feel trapped at all."

"Not by you. By my duty perhaps. But I'm alive when others aren't, so I guess I can't whine."

"It's all right to whine a little when the world is unfair." Vorik kissed the top of her head as he enjoyed the warmth of her body—of *her*—in his arms.

"I'll keep that in mind." Syla tilted her head back to gaze up at him. Her expression was more contemplative than adoring, though she wasn't trying to escape his embrace, so he trusted she enjoyed having him close. "Since you saved my life, I'm struggling with what my duty dictates I should do."

"Question me under the influence of that drug?"

"Yes. I know you would feel it a betrayal to your people if you let anything important slip."

"I would." Vorik smiled. She had also come to know *him* well.

"How would you feel if I tried to trade you to them in exchange for the shielder components?"

"The shielder components that would, if turned into a shielder, effectively end our ability to attack your islands?"

"Yes, wouldn't that be delightful?"

Vorik snorted, certain *Jhiton* wouldn't agree. Nor would any of the chiefs. But all Vorik had ever wanted was a way to feed his people. If that could be achieved by other means, would *he* object to a cessation of hostilities?

The problem was that, once all the islands were protected again, the Kingdom wouldn't have any reason to concede to demands—or even polite requests—made by the stormers. More, they would undoubtedly hold a grudge. He was amazed that *Syla* wasn't holding a grudge. Oh, she hated Jhiton and kept trying to kill *him*, but, even though she should, she didn't hate Vorik. He couldn't help but wonder if a deal might be struck if he were involved. But his people wouldn't let him make deals—he wasn't even as trusted as he should be right now. And Syla... There wasn't a guarantee that she would remain queen, not with so many plotting against her.

"If our people could get food to see them through the harsh winters," Vorik said carefully, aware that she was still watching him, her words perhaps not as much of a joke as they'd seemed, "*I* wouldn't care if your islands had all their shields back. But my people wouldn't trade much for me."

Especially now, he thought grimly. At that very moment, Lesva was probably explaining in great detail to everyone who would listen how he'd betrayed her. Betrayed all of them.

"Your brother would," Syla said. "He brought all those dragons and riders a thousand miles to get you back from the Freeborn Faction."

"He had superior numbers and wouldn't have believed there was much risk in coming for me. He would also be the first to sacrifice me if it would lead to a victory for our people. He's sworn to put his duty as the leader of the Sixteen Talons ahead of personal wishes, and I'm a lowly captain anyway, not anyone worth risking the military or the tribes over."

"You could be a chief if you dueled yours for the position. Right?"

Vorik gazed at her, remembering that they'd spoken of that in the middle of the night in his cave. When she'd been limned in silver and appeared like someone in a dream. This was confirmation that it *hadn't* been a dream. He'd already suspected, but he made a note of her new power.

"I'm not qualified for the job of chief," he said.

"Not being *qualified* doesn't mean that you can't lead," she said with a smirk, waving at herself. "Sometimes, when the gods place you in a position where you're needed, you have to figure out how to qualify yourself along the way."

"You're doing a good job of that yourself." Vorik kissed her, in part to end what seemed a dangerous discussion and in part because her lips were so close, so appealing.

She sank against his chest and let him. With a fumbling hand, she pushed the key on the desk toward him.

"What will we do with the next few hours?" he murmured against her lips, not yet picking it up. "If you don't drug me and interrogate me?"

"This is nice." Syla raised her hands to his shoulders, then slid them up the side of his neck to thread them through his tousled hair. "Or did you want to instruct me on how to juggle? Someone gave me balls, and I've longed for a teacher."

Vorik snorted softly, leaning his head slightly into her touch, and she kneaded his scalp. "Maybe later. I do enjoy participating in safe discussions and hobbies with you."

"Those where neither of us betray our people?"

"Quite." Smiling, he deepened their kiss.

9

I am getting updates from Igliana, Wreylith spoke into Syla's mind as she leaned against Vorik, returning his kiss while he stroked her hair. She longed to do more with him. *Much* more.

Could she? She'd told Fel and the major that she would be in here interrogating Vorik, something that might take hours. That dishonesty disturbed her but not as much as the thought of an exuberant stormer-hating military officer *actually* interrogating him. With knives, not hydra-scale powder.

Eventually, her people would check on her, but the threat of succumbing to Candles of Serenity ought to keep them away for a time. She could have a few hours with Vorik. She was sure of it.

But what would she say when she didn't walk out with any information? She needed to find those shielder components, and someone who knew their location stood in her arms, kissing her and making her forget that need.

Drugging and questioning him would be a poor way to reward him for saving her life—again—but wouldn't it be a betrayal to her people not to learn everything she could from him? The fleet had driven the stormers away from the harbor but not the entire island. The Kingdom was far from safe.

As you may have observed, Wreylith continued as Syla enjoyed kissing Vorik while mentally wrestling with herself, *the Freeborn Faction dragons are resting on this end of the island, within range of the weapons platform. They've informed me that the stormer dragons are perching and scheming on the other end of the island, occasionally slinging telepathic threats at them. Meanwhile, Igliana and one of her kin have been scouting the rest of your island chain, suspecting your enemies are up to something else.*

Are they? Syla slid her hands over Vorik's shoulders as he trailed his down her arms, fingers grazing her waist through her dress, waking her nerves—her entire body.

Though he stood in shackles, there was nothing *prisoner*-like about him. No, he radiated the power of a great predator, as he always did, danger coiled beneath the calm. He could flex his magically enhanced muscles and break those shackles at any moment.

The stormers, Wreylith said, *were in the process of bringing many more dragons to the Island of Eliok—or perhaps another destination within the Kingdom—when they saw your ships and attacked.*

I assumed their scouts relayed to them that we were coming with the weapons platform, and that was why they sent reinforcements.

A dragon would not be able to speak telepathically all the way from here to either of the mainlands. A scout would have had to fly much of the way there before sharing that information, and then numerous wings of dragons would need to have been gathered and fly all the way back to the islands.

Something that would have taken longer than our sailing from Castle to Harbor Island. Syla assumed that was what Wreylith was saying. Jhiton and his squadrons had been heading this way *before* they'd known the weapons platform was on the move.

Yes. They were prepared for another incursion.

They may simply have intended to bolster their forces here. I'm sure they'd heard about the weapons platform. But would they have guessed that she would carry it to another island on a ship? She was less certain about that.

Vorik's hand brushed the side of her breast, and a zing of pleasure swept through her body. Syla didn't want to be ungrateful to her dragon ally, but couldn't she have a couple of hours before musing about what the stormers were up to? As Vorik's capable hands stroked her, one sliding past her hip and down her thigh to lift the hem of her dress and graze bare skin, thoughts of enemy plots slipped from her mind.

Two dragons have left the western end of the Island of Eliok, Wreylith said.

Syla didn't answer. She was too busy relishing the feel of Vorik's warm calloused hand trailing up her thigh and the delicious taste of his lips against hers, teasing, stroking, nibbling. Eyes of the moon, that was arousing.

He lifted his arms over her head long enough to pick up the key to his shackles. With scarcely a pause in their kissing, he unlocked himself. Maybe she should have second-guessed her decision to give him the key, but she didn't. She wanted him to be unrestrained, fully capable of using his hands to touch her.

"I was waiting for you to break those," she murmured.

"You kept the key and even pushed it toward me. I assumed you wanted me to use it, not rudely destroy another set of shackles."

"Seeing you rudely destroy the first was kind of..."

"Hot?" Vorik smirked and flexed his muscles.

"A little."

"I can break something else for you later, if you wish." Wrists free, he lifted his hands to either side of her face, tracing her jaw as he lowered his mouth to kiss her again.

Yes, that was wonderful, and she leaned forward, enjoying his touch, his taste, and not saying anything else to Wreylith. Even if Syla *hadn't* wanted to spend this time with Vorik, what could she have done about the comings and goings of enemy dragons? Fly over and try to scout with Wreylith? That hadn't gone well the last time. Besides, her people were collecting refugees from Hazel Harbor. They would need time before the fleet could go anywhere else, and she didn't even know where she would go. If she left with the weapons platform, the dragons would return. And until she knew where the shielder components were, she couldn't venture off to collect them.

"We have to be quiet," she whispered even as stimulating sensations swept through her body. Already, she wanted to groan her pleasure. "I'm interrogating you."

Vorik's eyes gleamed with humor as he stroked her. "I understand."

Syla slid her hands down his chest to the hem of his shirt, pushing it up so she could run her fingers over his muscled abdomen. He obliged her by pausing his ministrations long enough to tug the garment over his head and toss it onto the desk. She reveled in his taut contours as she traced her fingers over them, nails brushing him, raising gooseflesh on his skin as he shifted into her touch.

The lamplight and shadows created hills and valleys out of his musculature, and the urge to explore that terrain with her tongue swept over her. Anticipation and heat coiled within her, and, lips leaving his, she brought her mouth lower. Tongue venturing out, she tasted the curve of his pectoral, aroused by exploring his lithe athletic form.

She remembered him fighting on the deck, striking with lightning-fast power as he deflected Lesva's attacks while keeping the captain from reaching Syla. Everyone aboard would have happily shot him, but he'd been fearless, defying his people's wishes on her behalf.

And now he was here with her, breathing in her scent and stroking her as she explored his body. He leaned into her tastes, her touches, as if he wanted nothing more than to be with her.

Maybe she should have been plotting and scheming and trying to wheedle information out of him, but she hated the idea of betraying him. She wanted to support him and to appreciate him, not to trick him into revealing anything he held dear. It was the wrong choice for her people and her kingdom, but she couldn't do anything else. Not with Vorik. He deserved to be more than a prisoner, to be honored as the loyal warrior he was and that she longed to be with.

"Syla," Vorik whispered hoarsely as her tongue trailed lower, and she reached for his belt.

She dropped to her knees, and he kneaded her shoulders, her neck, and her scalp, his deft fingers lighting her nerves on fire, awakening pleasure in her whole body. Pleasure and anticipation.

As she unfastened his belt and lowered his trousers, she looked up at his face and caught lust burning in his eyes. When she brought her lips to his hard cock, his head lolled back, taut abdomen flexing. She ran one hand over the ridges of his muscles, nails scraping to arouse *his* pleasure, then curled the other around his shaft to hold him as she kissed along its length.

"Syla," Vorik said again, a groan of desire this time.

"Quiet," she murmured even as she teased him with her lips and grew more aroused herself.

Hearing her name spoken with such feeling and need excited her, and she slid her mouth around his shaft, tongue stroking and teeth grazing ever so lightly as she took him in and out. He stiffened, almost thrusting into her, but he made himself stand still, desire and tension radiating from him. Holding and touching him aroused her, as did his taste, his heady scent. Feeling her own need building, she quickened her pace.

Vorik looked down at her again, drinking her in as she worked him, and he kept rubbing her scalp, the hot tingles driving down to her core, intensifying her desire even as she focused on pleasing him. Just being near him always made her long for him, and being able to stroke him and taste him… it made her hot and wet with desire of her own. She envisioned him lifting her and striding to the bed, pinning her down and plunging deeply into her to satisfy her. She almost begged him to do exactly that.

But he liked this. His body quivered as his need built, and his breathing quickened as his hands lowered to grip her shoulders. She smiled around his cock, satisfied that she could affect him so.

"You're wearing too many clothes," he said at one point, his words almost pants.

Mouth full, she mumbled an agreement but didn't stop. Later, they could amend her clothing situation, but now…

He couldn't hold still any longer, and he rocked into her ministrations, words turning into eager grunts and groans that he kept soft but couldn't quite stifle. She gripped his ass with both hands, taking him as deeply as she could, and he touched her face in warning, shifting away from her mouth before exploding with a gasp of pure ecstasy. Sweat glistened on his magnificent body as she gazed at him, enraptured and hungry with her own need.

"Incredible," he panted, his eyes locking on her again, full of satisfaction and almost awe. As if she'd accomplished a great achievement. "You're incredible," he whispered again.

"People may doubt the efficacy of my candles if they heard your grunts," she said, glad he'd been satisfied, never wanting to disappoint him.

"What a scholarly word." Vorik laughed softly and picked her up, carrying her to the bed, just as she'd wanted. Perfect. "Nobody has ever spoken of efficacy during my climactic moment before."

"It was after," she informed him, shifting to press herself against him, wanting to wrap her legs around him. He'd had his moment, but she longed for hers.

"Two seconds after, maybe."

As he lay her down on the bed, kneeling beside her, she let her hands trail over his naked form. It was such a delight to touch him. Though his earlier taut tension had faded, he remained firm and fit. So appealing. She kissed the curve of his pectoral as he untied the laces of her dress and shifted it up. His hands brushed her bare skin along the way, and her core throbbed in anticipation of her turn.

"Ah," he murmured after he'd peeled away her clothes and lay propped beside her, hand roaming, his gaze lingering on the curves of her breasts, her pert nipples. His perusal excited her, knowing that he *wanted* to look at her body. "You are beautiful, Syla."

She groped for a response—*thank you* seemed an inane thing to say—but when he cupped her breast, thumb brushing the sensitive flesh of her nipple, she could only gasp, the pleasure almost startling in its intensity.

It must have been the right response, because his eyes flared with interest. He bent his head to slide his tongue along her breast, then take her nipple in his mouth. He licked, then sucked, and she arched toward him, grabbing the back of his neck.

Shivers of need and pleasure coursed through her, making her squirm against the blanket. Almost languid, his tongue trailed across the valley between her breasts to find her other nipple. His hand remained on the first, tracing the curve of her skin. Already, she throbbed with need and caught herself squirming and thrusting herself toward him.

When his tongue left her breast, she thought that brilliant mouth might delve lower—she *wanted* it to—but he was in no hurry and brought his lips back to hers. She kissed him hard, feeling urgency that he did not, and she rubbed and stroked, pulling him closer, wanting his heated form against hers. He obliged, his tongue teasing hers as they kissed, and his fingers slid over her abdomen and lower. Already hot and throbbing, she shifted toward him, legs parting in anticipation of his touch.

He smiled against her mouth, probably smug that she was so eager for him. She hardly cared. He was amazing; let him be smug. As long as he gave her the pleasure she so badly needed.

When his fingers slipped between her legs, she knew he would. He wouldn't disappoint her. Maybe he wouldn't betray his people for her, but he would give his heart to their joining, to her.

She kissed him and rubbed him to show her appreciation. And maybe a part of her hoped that if she pleased him enough in bed, he would walk away from his kin, from his orders, from everything that pitted them against each other, and be hers. Always.

As his deft fingers slid in and out, rubbing her exquisitely from within, she bucked and twisted, the delicious stimulation leaving her breathless.

"Quiet," he murmured, echoing her earlier order, smiling and teasing her.

It was hard to obey when his touch built such intense need within her. Every rub, every brush brought pleasure and promised greater ecstasy. She didn't cry out, but, almost frenetic, she rocked her lower half into him even as she ran her hands over his muscled form, kissing him hard, needing him like she'd needed none before.

She assumed Vorik would bring her to a climax and wouldn't grow aroused himself for a time, but her eagerness must have renewed a spark of interest—of *lust*—in him. When his cock brushed her leg, he was hard again, and growing harder by the second.

"By all the stars in the sky," he said huskily, pulling away from their kiss to look at her body, glistening from her efforts, from her need, "you're so hot."

"You too," she panted, barely able to articulate anything as he found the center of all her desire and rubbed her exquisitely.

"How can you want me this much, Syla?" he wondered, watching her thrash.

She couldn't get anything articulate out, only arching toward him, craving the release that only he could give her. Maybe she should have been embarrassed to want him so much, to writhe and twist at his every touch, to be so raw and naked about what she needed, but she trusted him not to tease her later. And the lust in his eyes grew and grew, her display making him growl with increasing need of his own.

She glimpsed his swollen shaft and gripped him. "Take me, Vorik. Hard."

"Oh, I will." As if a floodgate had opened, he shifted over her, bringing his lips back to hers as his fingers shifted aside, making room for his cock. "I'm making you mine."

"Yes," she agreed.

Like the powerful predator she'd envisioned earlier claiming his prey, he plunged into her without holding anything back, filling her to the brim. And she relished it, satisfaction and longing for more mingling within her. She gripped him, arching and matching his eager thrusts as he drove into her again. She barely stifled a cry of enthusiasm as she grew closer and closer to ecstasy. He pounded his own desire and need into her, soon as frenzied and frantic as she. They panted and thrust, coming together again and again. So primed it was almost painful, Syla came with such explosive satisfaction that she threw her head back and clunked the wall as he poured himself into her. At least she kept from screaming out her brilliant satisfaction for all on the ship to hear.

Finally, he collapsed atop her, and she pulled him close, wanting their chests mashed together, wanting him to stay with her forever.

He kissed her neck and nuzzled her ear, then stroked her head where she'd hit it. "Every time I'm with you, it's even better than in my dreams."

Tears sprang to her eyes, and she wrapped her arms around his back and turned her face to kiss him. "Do you dream of me often?" she whispered, hoping the answer was yes.

"Every night. Days too." He laughed softly and shifted, not pulling out of her but drawing her over so that her weight lay atop him, and his hand found and cupped her ass, holding her to him. "Never has a woman so enraptured me, Syla. My queen."

"I wish I *was* your queen. Then we could be… we could be."

His eyes sharpened. "We will be. We'll find a way."

"There is no way." She smiled sadly. "You're my prisoner."

He laughed again. "A moment ago, you were begging for me. And here you are, deep in my embrace." He lowered his eyelashes in a sultry gaze. "I think you're *my* prisoner."

"I…" She didn't have a response for that.

"And I'm your captor," he murmured, stroking her while holding her possessively.

In that moment, she couldn't deny the truth of his words. And as his touch sent new tingles of pleasure through her, she didn't want to be anywhere else. She even caught herself turning so he could more fully hold her.

"You're my captor," she whispered.

"I thought so," he said, that smugness in his eyes again. "And you like it. You *want* to be mine."

"You're cocky, Vorik."

"You like that too."

Yes, she did. She kissed him and didn't try to escape his grip. She didn't ever want to escape his grip.

~

After her joining with Vorik, Syla lay, deliciously sated and snuggled with her back to his chest, his arm over hers, and their hands touching. By the gods, why couldn't they stay together forever? Never had she known sex could be so glorious and satisfying, nor had she ever felt as safe as she did in Vorik's arms.

The arms of her enemy. It was such a struggle to remember he was that after all the times he'd saved her life. And after their intimacy.

She threaded her fingers through his, thinking nothing of the gesture, but a faint silver light glowed from the hand pressed against his dragon tattoo. Her moon-mark. It didn't buzz or tingle or suggest it was doing anything magical—or drawing upon her power. It merely glowed warmly, like a gentle beacon. As if it were... content?

At the moment, *she* was content, but she didn't know what to make of the glow. She worried Vorik would open his eyes, see it, and think she was calling upon her magic, that she meant to use her power on him in some way.

She released his fingers and shifted her hand up to his wrist. The light from the moon-mark, as if it had been activated by the proximity of his tattoo, faded. Good. But what had it meant?

She remembered their passionate joining against the rock formation in the cactus-flower canyon, the way she hadn't been able to activate the rune that had revealed the storm god's laboratory, not when she alone had touched it. Only when their hands had both pressed against it had the way shown itself to them.

At the time, she'd been too distracted by the revelation—and her steamy climax to Vorik's lovemaking—to consider it fully. But it had to mean *something*. Didn't it?

Syla turned her head to consider Vorik's face. Eyes closed and breathing even, he didn't seem to have noticed the glow.

By the light of the lantern, she admired his profile, the strong line of his jaw, and she let her gaze roam over the rest of him. Old scars marked his body, signaling all the battles he'd survived. He wasn't that much older than she, but he'd lived a hard life and endured much. That he could smile and joke so easily—and find pleasure in the little things like a fruity dessert—was a testament to his resilience and his steady and agreeable attitude. All of him was agreeable, and her heart ached at the thought that the world would soon force them to part again.

"If you wanted to become a leader of your tribe, you'd do a better job than you think," she murmured, though she believed him asleep.

He wasn't entirely and emitted a muzzy, "Hm?"

"You're capable in a lot of ways, and you want what's best for your tribe. For all your people, I'm sure. You'd be a good leader."

"Are you suggesting this because you'd prefer to negotiate with me over Chieftess Shi?"

"Anyone would prefer you over her. She's insulting and difficult. I doubt her loyalty could be won by a blueberry cobbler."

He snorted softly and patted her hand. "I doubt that too."

"I suppose my words are motivated by what I want for my people. I said I wouldn't try to connive or manipulate you, and urging you to duel for the chieftainship of your tribe might count."

"I don't think that's conniving."

"Manipulative?"

"Well, maybe a little. Especially if you start stroking my ego and telling me how magnificent I would look wearing the ceremonial headdress."

"What if I stroke other things?" She shifted so that she faced him and rested a hand on his chest.

His lashes drooped, but some of the sleepiness left his eyes as she trailed her fingers over his muscles.

"I do enjoy that," he murmured. "It might work. I must warn you, however, that we have almost twenty tribes in our loose coalition. Even if I was willing to duel Shi and attempt to take control over ours, it wouldn't change anything for the Kingdom."

"You'd have a stronger voice, though, wouldn't you? They'd have to listen to you, at least, right?"

"A month or two ago, they would have, but given my current questionable status with my people… I doubt I'd survive long as chief. As I mentioned, our people have a tendency to fix leadership situations they do not find palatable."

"Meaning you'd get a dagger in the back because you might speak fondly of the Garden Kingdom queen?"

"Most assuredly. And I've made the mistake of speaking more than fondly. I'm composing a ballad, you know."

"I didn't know, but I doubt you're unwise enough to sing about my glory or how wondrously the sunlight glints off my spectacles to your people."

"So far, I've only shared a few lines with Agrevlari. As it so happens, I *have* consulted him on rhymes for spectacles. We came up with sentinels as being fairly close, but I'm mulling over how to fit that in."

"That's better than the words that popped into my mind."

"Such as?" Vorik raised his eyebrows.

"Tentacles and testicles, neither of which I'd care to share lines of a ballad with."

"No? I might be able to make those work logically into the tale. I'm creative."

"To think, you don't believe you have the talent to lead a tribe."

"You know what I *do* have talent for?" Vorik drew his fingers along her arm and then down her side, stirring heat and gooseflesh, and making her body tighten with anticipation.

"Are rhymes with spectacles involved?"

"You'll find out."

He lowered his mouth to hers, and for a while longer, she let herself forget her duties.

~

Vorik?

The telepathic inquiry woke Vorik from sleep, the glorious and exhausted sleep of a man who'd enjoyed a *wonderful* time with a woman. And not just any woman. Queen Syla, healer, defiant adventurer, and blackberry-cobbler-maker. His Syla.

Full darkness enshrouded the cabin when he opened his eyes, night pressing against the portholes, the lanterns having burned out. Syla lay breathing evenly in his arms, and he wished the world hadn't intruded. He wanted to enjoy the feel of her warm skin, her full curves pressed against him, the appealing way her hair lay tousled about her shoulders and breasts.

Ah, those glorious breasts. How he loved their shape, their weight in his hands, the taste of their skin under his tongue. The line of thinking made his groin stiffen, and the last thing he wanted was to answer a telepathic summons. Maybe if he didn't respond...

Vorik?

It was Jhiton, his voice sounding distant but insistent. Was he leaving Harvest Island on a new mission?

I'm here, Vorik answered, though he didn't want to. He wished his brother and all his plans to take over the Kingdom would disappear, at least for a time. Vorik wanted to stay where he was, not mull over ways to kidnap Syla or whatever else the general had in mind. Since Vorik could still sense Wreylith up above, he wouldn't be tempted to try that, even if Jhiton wished it. Getting past the soldiers onboard might not be that hard, but a dragon could fly much faster than he could swim, especially with a captive in tow.

Do you know where the queen is? Jhiton asked.

I have a notion.

Are you in her bed?

In her bed as he contemplated her breasts and remembered the way she'd thrashed at his ministrations and groaned his name. Gods, that had been hot. *She'd* been hot.

Cheeks warming, he looked at the wall and willed himself to focus on satisfactorily finishing the conversation so that his brother would leave him alone. How under the eyes of the moon had Jhiton known where he was? Had Agrevlari said something? The dragon had an undesirable knack for knowing what Vorik was up to even from a distance.

I remain a captive, he answered.

A captive in her bed? You took much longer to wake than is typical for you.

He smiled, remembering his discussion with Syla of who was the captive and who the captor. All he replied to Jhiton was, *I'm tired.*

Thus my assumption. That ship is still in the harbor, right? That's what the dragons report.

I think so. From the bed, Vorik couldn't see anything but the night sky through the porthole, but the gentleness of the waves suggested the ship remained in protected waters.

Are the fleet officers taking orders from the queen, or is she only along to operate that device?

We didn't discuss the fleet's chain of command.

Did you discuss anything *of importance?*

Vorik thought about summing up his conversation with Syla, and offering to be an earnest spy, especially since he would need to do a lot to redeem himself when he returned to his people. But Syla hadn't drugged and questioned him when her people had wanted her to—when, by all rights, she should have. In all their meetings, she'd never hurt him when she had the opportunity, never betrayed him. His honor kept him from knowingly sharing anything that might be used against her.

Testicles came up, he answered.

Jhiton sighed into his mind.

You can't deny their *importance.*

If she is *in charge, do your best to keep her in bed until morning, eh?*

I don't think that will be difficult.

Since she was breathing evenly, probably exhausted by all that the previous day had involved, Vorik doubted she would wake until well after dawn.

Should I ask why? Vorik added when Jhiton didn't respond.

No.

Vorik gazed bleakly into the darkness of the cabin, realizing his brother had been checking on the location of the ship—of that weapon—and the queen because he was up to something. Of course he was. *He* wouldn't let his feelings for a woman deter him from the future he wanted for their people.

Maybe Vorik shouldn't have either, but he couldn't help it. He wanted his future to involve Syla. But how could he possibly make that happen?

10

SYLA HADN'T MEANT TO FALL INTO A DEEP SLEEP AFTER HER SECOND joining with Vorik, but she'd already been drained from healing people earlier, and also hadn't fully recovered from the exhaustion induced by the weapons platform. Their multiple encounters that night had been exhausting as well, though in a delightful way. When she woke, she felt relaxed after their wonderful time together and longed to stay in his arms, even though daylight brightened the sky beyond her porthole.

Vorik lay on his side behind her, her back snuggled into his chest, his arm draped around her. Freed of his shackles, he could have slipped away and escaped, especially if Wreylith had also chosen to doze during the night, but Vorik appeared to be sleeping. Relaxed and comfortable. Something neither of them should have been.

Igliana approaches, Wreylith stated. She sounded like she was a few miles away on the island instead of on the ship above—she'd probably gone to hunt for breakfast. *Your Island of Bogs is under attack.*

Bogberry Island? Syla stiffened, memories of Wreylith's warning from the night before flooding her mind.

They were prepared for another incursion, the dragon had said.

Was Bogberry Island what had brought General Jhiton and his squadrons of dragons? With the shield up, winged predators couldn't have reached its shores.

What happened? Syla asked.

Stormer-allied dragons attacked two warships that were leaving the protection of its shield.

Syla closed her eyes, grimacing. She'd sent word, requesting aid from the Royal Fleet stationed on other islands. Had those two ships left their safe harbor because of her request? They must have.

Further, Wreylith continued, *humans must have sneaked onto the island because numerous fires burn in its capital city at the mouth of the river. Many buildings have been damaged. Also, a large fire is burning in the walled compound of what Igliana believes is the dwelling of its island chief.*

Island lord, Syla thought but didn't correct the dragon. The Kingdom terminology hardly mattered now.

Distressed, Syla sat up in bed. She had to get the fleet over there to help. *Are there a lot of stormer dragons still by the volcano on the other end of Harvest Island, Wreylith?*

There are.

At Syla's movement, Vorik opened his eyes and glanced toward the porthole. "Everything all right?"

"No." She struggled to keep her tone calm, but she wanted to rail at him—and at herself. If she'd drugged him and questioned him, she might have learned of the attack before it had happened. She might have headed toward Bogberry Island with the fleet and *kept* it from happening. "Damn it, Vorik."

"Was my performance that poor? Women don't usually curse

me in the aftermath." He smiled at her, but his eyes were serious—or were they *wary*?—as he studied her face.

"Your people are attacking Bogberry Island." Syla rolled out of bed and snatched her dress up from the floor.

"Ah." He didn't look surprised, and that lack of reaction was like a spear to her heart, a piercing confirmation that she'd made the wrong choice.

"You knew."

Vorik sat up. "I didn't know they would attack last night when we were having sex, no, but I knew Jhiton had plans to obtain Bogberry Island."

"Are you *sure* you didn't know it would be last night?" Syla demanded as she yanked on her dress. "And distract me on purpose? To deliberately keep the fleet—the weapons platform—here and out of the way for your people's incursion? Your brother can communicate with you from afar, right? Did he *order* you to do this?" She flung her hand at the bed, at their tousled blankets and Vorik's naked form among them.

"No. I just wanted..." He spread a hand toward her. "You. I always want you."

"Damn it, Vorik," she said again, though she was more angry and frustrated with herself. She *knew* he was her enemy—and loyal to his people. He might care for her, but that didn't change that he was a stormer dragon rider through and through.

After dressing, Syla ran to the door and flung it open, finding a Royal Protector standing nearby in the corridor. Fel must have finally succumbed to his weariness and allowed a replacement to stand in for him.

"Tell the fleet commander—" She caught herself and stopped, aware of Vorik in the cabin.

He'd climbed out of bed and was bent over, peering about. Looking for his underwear? Even if he was distracted, she had no doubt he would hear her every word. Even if he wasn't in direct contact with his brother, he would be with Agrevlari, and the dragon could relay messages. Relay *intelligence.*

"I'll tell him." Syla didn't even know if the commander was back on board. "Take Vorik back to his cell."

"Ah, yes, Your Majesty." The Royal Protector peered into her cabin. "Where are his shackles?"

"Probably with his underwear," she muttered and jogged toward the ship's ladder at the end of the corridor. She felt bad leaving the Royal Protector to round up men and deal with moving Vorik, who might well escape now that he'd suitably delayed her. Maybe that would be for the best. Since she apparently couldn't stand to interrogate him.

As she climbed the steps, she regretted not delegating that duty to someone else. If they'd used the hydra-scale powder, they wouldn't have needed to physically torture him, and she would have received warning about Bogberry Island.

Maybe. Vorik might have told the truth when he'd said he hadn't known about the attack.

But what of the shielder components? She hadn't learned where they were yet either. All he'd admitted was that they were being taken to his people's next camp.

"I should have let him kidnap me," she said, then stumbled, the thought making her miss a step. Was that... "Maybe that's not a bad idea."

If he took her to the camp, she would be in the same place as the components. If she could figure out how not to be tied up and interrogated herself—or have her moon-mark used against her people—then she could escape and slip away with them...

But how? The stormers wouldn't let Wreylith get close, and Syla would be surrounded by powerful riders and dragons if she was in their camp. Escaping would be next to impossible unless she thought of something clever.

Suborning Vorik? Suborning someone else in his camp? By

healing them, perhaps? The stormers had been in battle. Some would surely be injured. But healing people didn't always leave them kindly inclined toward her. Assuming she could suborn any of the stormers would be foolish. She hadn't even gotten Vorik to choose her over them.

No, intentionally being kidnapped wouldn't work. Not unless she could think of something brilliant to ensure she could achieve what she wanted. Even if she could... since she was, so far, the only person capable of firing the weapons platform, she needed to stay with it, not let a stormer steal her away.

"Your Majesty?" A fleet officer near the door was looking curiously at her. "Are you all right?"

After coming out on deck, Syla had halted mid-step. The officer wasn't the only person looking curiously at her. Many men were out, working on repairs from the battle, and Aunt Tibby sat with her books on the weapons platform, though she hadn't yet noticed Syla.

Beyond the railing, the city of Hazel Harbor stood, most of the buildings still intact, though a few blocks had been destroyed since the last time she'd visited—before the stormer invasion. And here and there, other buildings had been flattened without devastating those around them. Of those still standing, many showed signs of fire damage. How many inhabitants—Kingdom subjects—had died to stormers and their dragons?

"I'm fine," Syla said, though she wasn't. She was letting her feelings get in the way of her duty. "Is the fleet commander here?"

She spotted two dinghies full of men, women, and children being rowed toward one of the warships. Refugees. Another dinghy headed toward the *Stormslicer*, and she frowned when she recognized a stern-faced white-haired man standing while crewmen rowed and other refugees sat. Lord Ravoran. He would have cross words for her when he arrived. And she would deserve them.

"He's on the *Spry Shark*, Your Majesty. Major Hixun is in charge at the moment." The officer pointed her toward the wheelhouse.

"Thank you." Syla strode toward the door, wanting to get underway as soon as possible. Maybe she could put off dealing with Ravoran if he knew other fires burned in the Kingdom and needed to be dealt with first.

"Syla." Aunt Tibby had spotted her and beckoned.

"Just a moment."

"It's important." Book in hand, finger marking a page, Tibby scooted off the platform.

Syla held up a finger of her own, opened the wheelhouse door, and leaned in. "Our Freeborn Faction dragon allies have been relaying information," she told the major and the helmsmen when they faced her. "Bogberry Island is under attack."

Hixun's eyebrows flew up. "Did the shield drop?"

"No. At least not yet." Syla winced, suspecting the stormers had a plan for finding the shielder and sabotaging it. "Men sneaked in via ships and attacked the capital city."

Hixun cursed. "You're sure? How reliable are the allies that reported to you?"

"They helped us yesterday against greater numbers."

"It was hard to tell what exactly was going on yesterday with all those dragons and riders." Hixun waved toward the weapons platform, probably indicating the confusion of Lesva and Vorik fighting in the middle of the deck.

Seeing the spot reminded Syla that Vorik had risked his life and probably the hatred of his people to help her. It wasn't his fault that she had been too polite to drug and question him. But if Jhiton was still talking to him, Vorik couldn't be *too* hated.

"Dragon!" someone called from the crow's nest, the alarm in his voice suggesting it wasn't their familiar red dragon ally.

Syla spotted Tibby walking toward her with the book but also a green dragon flying toward the ship. "I think that one is from the Freeborn Faction."

She peered at the rider, wishing her eyesight were better. Was that Chieftess Atilya's gray hair?

"You can ask the faction leader herself how dependable the intelligence is," Syla said when Hixun joined her in the doorway.

His grunt suggested he didn't find the notion appealing.

"I need you for a moment, Syla." Tibby lay a hand on her arm and tilted her head toward the weapons platform.

"Get some of the ships underway for Bogberry Island, Major," Syla said. "As soon as possible."

"I'll have to speak with the fleet commander first," he said, "but I'll urge him to follow that direction."

"Thank you."

The dragon landed on the deck, Chieftess Atilya lifting her hand toward Syla before sliding off.

Tibby *harrumphed* as her news was delayed a moment more.

"Thank you for your help yesterday, Chieftess," Syla said. "I appreciated it immeasurably."

"I'm glad. There was some debate about whether we should approach while you were casting magical cannonballs with that... device." The side-eye Atilya leveled at the weapons platform suggested she hadn't valued its contributions as much as Syla had. Maybe because she and her people were also allied to dragons, Atilya didn't like seeing them slain. "Some were concerned that it —did *you* control it?—wouldn't differentiate faction dragons from those who've declared themselves your enemies."

"I was controlling it, yes."

"Ah. That is somewhat reassuring, though that is a lot of power for a human to wield."

"Especially one trained to be a healer." Syla smiled sadly.

Atilya considered her answer for a moment. "Perhaps, a healer, as long as she has the wherewithal to use deadly force, is a better person to wield such a weapon than one who longs for the power to slay others."

"I wish nobody needed to use it."

"That would be ideal. We of the Freeborn Faction do seek peace rather than hostility. Also an opportunity to earn food yielded from your bountiful islands. *We* have not taken any, though it has not always been possible to keep our dragons from coming here to hunt. They've minds of their own."

"Yes, the minds of predators. I've noticed." Syla smiled toward the northern coast of the island, sensing through her link with Wreylith that she was hunting near the cliffs by Lavaperch Temple.

"Of course. You're linked with a dragon now." Atilya looked at her hand. "I'd forgotten. I could sense power from you even before the wild red dragon marked you."

"From my moon-mark, I assume."

"I suppose it must be." Atilya considered her hand, as if she wasn't sure, but didn't suggest anything else. "Have you developed new abilities from your bond yet?"

"Not that I've noticed."

"Sometimes, it takes a while, but you may notice soon that you're faster and stronger in battle."

"I go into battle less often than you might think. My cousin, Teyla, may have been a better bet to link with a dragon. She takes sword-fighting lessons, at least."

"Dragons choose those they've an affinity for. You must have proven yourself to Wreylith."

"Oh, yes."

"I believe," Atilya said, "that Igliana may have already warned you that your Bogberry Island defenses have been breached. Someone, presumably General Jhiton's riders, set fire to several buildings in the main city."

"Yes. I'm thankful that she brought the news. We're going to head that way soon."

"We could fly along to assist you or stay here and attempt to stave off stormer dragons. In case Jhiton splits his forces and sends some to reclaim this area. I would expect him to."

"It's my concern that he will, yes. But even if his forces are split..." Syla held her palm toward the sky.

"They would outnumber us? That is likely, yes."

"As I said, I appreciate any help you can offer, and we'll surely invite you to a feast in your honor as soon as we're able to drive the stormers out of the Kingdom. We'll send you home with many pounds of fruit, vegetables, and grains, but I don't expect you to lose people on our behalf."

"We'll assess the situation when their dragons are in the sky."

"All right. Thank you."

Even at fifty-something years of age, Atilya was strong enough and agile enough to leap upon her dragon's back when she departed. When Syla had time, she would have to explore whether she had developed any special abilities from her bond.

Tibby cleared her throat, but, before Syla could join her at the weapons platform, someone called from the railing. The dinghy carrying Lord Ravoran had arrived.

He climbed aboard before any of his escort and strode straight toward Syla. "You!"

"It's Your Majesty," Syla said, bracing herself. Normally, she wouldn't care about pomp, as Fel had once called it, but more than a dozen witnesses were close enough to observe them, and it would demean her authority if the island lord treated her like a wayward child instead of his monarch. Never mind that he was thirty years her senior and probably *thought* of her like a child.

"You stole our shielder!" he said without correction. Red-faced with jowls that waggled when he yelled, he pointed a stout finger at her face. "You've caused this carnage. All of this." He flung his arm toward the charred and missing buildings in the city hugging the harbor. "Hundreds have been killed, the crops that are to see our people through the winter have been stolen, and those flying vultures have *eaten* our livestock and wild animals."

"I'm aware, Lord Ravoran." Syla made herself politely and respectfully use *his* appropriate title, though she kept her back straight and her chin up as she faced him. "As I wrote to you in my letter, we suffered the same fate on Castle Island."

"For a couple of *days*. Until you stole our shielder. *Weeks* ago."

"I told you the reason why, and I promise we're actively researching how to repair your shielder or build a new one." She nodded toward Tibby, hoping the book in her aunt's hands made her look like someone on the verge of a solution. If only Syla hadn't thus far failed to get those shielder components.

"As if you can hammer one into existence like a horseshoe!"

"We know a new one can be made, and doing so is my priority."

At that moment, the major called to his crew to ready the ship to sail to Bogberry Island.

"We're not a priority at all," Ravoran snapped. "You're already preparing to leave."

"Not for long."

"Those stormer *animals* have not only been stealing but have been killing our people. Gleefully. And their dragons enjoy hunting them down. I demand you return our shielder. Your sister is the one who let yours be sabotaged, isn't she? That's not *our* fault. Your family screwed up. You and your island need to deal with the consequences."

"Do you know how many dragons and stormer ships we might face, Your Majesty?" Hixun called—he'd waved the fleet commander on board and was speaking to him now. "Should we take all of our ships or only some?"

Ravoran reached for Syla. "You're not going anywhere until you return our shielder."

Had Fel been at her side, he would have blocked Ravoran, but she'd left her interim bodyguard figuring out how to get Vorik back in his cell, and there was nobody nearby to spring to her defense. Syla lifted her hand and gripped Ravoran's wrist as he reached for her shoulder. Despite his age, he was bigger and stronger and didn't hesitate to grab her. But she hadn't been trying to deflect the blow, just touch him. She didn't want to hurt him—not when he was right to defend his people and understandably felt betrayed—but she willed her power to come to her, to warn him that she wasn't defenseless, that he couldn't hurt her or throw her overboard. Who knew what the red-faced man had in mind?

The moon-mark on the back of her hand thrummed and glowed silver, and power slid easily out of her and into him, a tendril that locked around his wrist but also shot down through his body to his legs, to the nerves that instructed his muscles on how to ambulate him. He halted abruptly, anchored, and his eyes widened.

The moon-mark on the back of *his* hand also glowed, a reminder that he was also descended from those early people that the gods had shared their gift with, and she braced herself in case he could use his power to counter hers. But his flare died down as quickly as it had come. Her hand flared brighter, and he glanced at it.

"You're more than a healer," he whispered.

"I've had to become more."

Releasing him from her power, Syla stepped back. She didn't want to threaten a man who had, for a decade, loyally served her mother and her father before that. All she needed was his cooperation, or at least for him not to fight her.

"Major Hixun," Syla called without looking away from Ravoran. "Take the island lord to a private cabin where I can talk to him later." She had no desire to do that but felt compelled to hear him out fully. Once the fleet was underway and she learned what Aunt Tibby wanted.

"Yes, Your Majesty." Hixun saluted her, then ordered a couple of men to escort Ravoran and the refugees below.

Syla let out a slow breath, trying to will some of the tension out of her shoulders, but there was too much to be tense about. Her muscles wouldn't unwind.

"What did you do?" Tibby waved to Syla's hand and watched as the lord headed below.

Since Tibby hadn't been around on the previous occasions when Syla had used her power to attack enemies, she didn't know that Syla had learned to use her healing magic to hurt people. Even to kill a man. That had been an assassin, and Syla had acted to defend her own life, but her action that day haunted her. She'd never wanted the power to kill a man.

"I've been forced to pick up a few new ways to use my magic," was all she said, then pointed to Tibby's book, hoping to distract her from asking further questions on the topic. "What did you learn?"

Before Tibby could answer, Major Hixun jogged up. "The fleet commander believes all the warships should stay together, Your Majesty. Unless you disagree? We're worried that if we leave some of our forces here, without the protection of the weapons platform, that stormer dragons will return to sink the ships. Even though we'd prefer to keep Harvest Island from falling again to them... we don't feel that we have a choice. That's the *only* thing that's been effective against their kind."

"I understand, and I don't disagree." Syla almost asked him not to tell Ravoran that they would be leaving his island defenseless, but she would feel duty-bound to report that to him herself. Even if she dreaded it. She had to face the consequences of her choices —the anger of people hurt by them. Her parents had never mentioned how emotionally difficult it was to lead, how much she would long for her simple life in the temple.

The major saluted her again, then jogged away.

"When did the military men start deferring to you?" Tibby asked. "And including you in the decision making?"

"I..." Syla thought of the discussion she'd had with Hixun in the infirmary. "I guess some of them liked that I stayed on deck and fought with them yesterday."

"That was foolish. You could have been killed. *I* went belowdecks, like a sane woman."

"That's where engineers are supposed to go. But queens have different obligations. Especially a queen who is the only person who can operate an invaluable weapon."

"You might not be for long. That's what I wanted to talk about."

"Oh?"

The small fleet set sail as Tibby led Syla to the weapons platform and stopped in front of the runes on the frame that Teyla had first pointed out back in the storm god's laboratory.

"You're able to read these, I trust," Tibby said.

"Yes." By now, Syla had them memorized. "One blessed by the gods and sworn to protect her people might call upon its power."

"And this." Tibby turned to a page she had marked with her finger.

"That's in Kingdom Standard, not carved in ancient temple runes," Syla said dryly.

"I trust it won't challenge you then."

Humoring her aunt, Syla read aloud. "'Many artifacts created by the gods are attuned to respond to the first moon-marked descendant of the gods-chosen to wake them from dormancy, so long as the individual is worthy. Upon achieving a state of activation, control of an artifact may be passed to another who is deemed worthy through a conscious choice to establish a new link while the two potential users are themselves moon-linked.' Oh." Syla brightened at the first good news of the day. "We've moon-linked before. If that's all it takes, I can appoint you to use the weapons platform right now."

Tibby made a face. "I'm your engineer, not a warrior or protector of the people."

"I'm not a warrior either, but it let me wield it."

"You're... something."

"An enigma?"

"Special."

"You are too, my aunt. Trust me. Anyway, you're the only other moon-marked person onboard except our angry island lord, and I'm not trusting him with a super powerful weapon right now. Let's try to pass the ability to use it to you. I know you don't object to slaying dragons. Just imagine they've ravaged a treasured magical machine that you've made."

"They *have* done that. Your boyfriend's odious green dragon destroyed one of my tractors. He's as loathsome as Fel."

"But you give Fel a much harder time than you gave Agrevlari." Syla didn't point out that whatever Vorik was to her, he wasn't her boyfriend.

"It seems unwise to insult a dragon."

"But six-and-a-half-foot-tall bodyguards with maces are appropriate targets for teasing?"

"I think he likes abuse."

"That *must* be true." Syla spotted Fel approaching, his jaw and head freshly shaven and a clean uniform on. She was glad he'd finally gotten some rest and lifted a hand. If he watched over them, Syla and Tibby could try the moon-link now. "Let's see if this will work. If you can wield the weapons platform, I can fly into battle on Wreylith."

"I don't condone that. Besides, you don't have a weapon to wield from her back. What could you do besides risk your life? She doesn't need you."

"Of course she needs me. I can heal any gouges that she receives, and if I'm on her back, she can fly through an island's shield. We may need that. All right, do you touch that post and I this one?" Since Syla didn't know how long this would take, she didn't want to delay further.

"We can try." Tibby eyed the hand-shaped mark on the closest post without stepping closer. "We should have brought Teyla along. *She* has the heart of a warrior."

"She tried to activate it when we first found it and had to fetch me." Syla waved for her aunt to touch the mark, but Tibby continued to hesitate.

Because she didn't believe herself capable? Or because she didn't want to step onto the platform and potentially kill people and dragons? Syla wouldn't blame her for that but believed her aunt—her aunt who'd recommended she poison Vorik back in her farmhouse—was more likely daunted. Or skeptical this would work.

"What is the problem?" Fel asked.

"I need you to tell Aunt Tibby that she has the capacity to be a fearsome warrior if she desires," Syla said.

Tibby's face twisted dubiously, and she adjusted her spectacles.

"She is a mighty scroll warrior," Fel stated dryly.

"But she has the *heart* of a warrior and could fight for her people with more than scrolls if necessary," Syla said, suspecting the weapons platform desired heart more than sword skills, which she surely did not have.

Fel eyed Tibby. "Yes. She has heart."

Her eyebrows rose in surprise.

"When we met," Fel said, "you were aiming a hand cannon out a loft window at us."

"Mostly at the dragon," Tibby said.

"With heart."

"That is somewhat true. I had to defend the farm. And my machines."

Syla nodded toward the mark on the post, her own hand on the adjacent one. Tibby stepped closer and lifted her fingers but continued to hesitate. Fel took her hand and pressed it against the post. She bared her teeth at him like a vexed guard dog.

"You do like abuse, don't you, Fel?" Syla murmured.

"I, too, have the heart of a warrior." He managed to smile slightly while glaring defiantly at Tibby and holding her hand in place.

She didn't try to yank it back, instead sighing, then looking at Syla.

With the passage from the book in mind, Syla reached out to clasp Tibby's free hand, then closed her eyes. The mark hummed under her hand, and she sensed the power of the platform. Also, a hint of awareness. The same awareness that had swept her mind across the sea to visit Vorik in his cave?

As Syla was debating how to convince the platform to allow Tibby to use it, she sensed something for the first time. Almost like a vision, an image of the inside of the thick platform between the four posts came to her. The mattress, Syla had thought of it when they'd first discovered the device and she'd likened it to a bed with a canopy.

Magical energy occupied a hollow space within the marble, as if it were a liquid in a tank. It appeared about two-thirds of the way full. The image lingered in Syla's mind, as if the gods-crafted device wanted her to grasp something. If that was a tank—or maybe a reservoir?—could the energy be what the weapons platform drew upon to create the silver balls that it hurled? If so, did this indicate that Syla had depleted it one-third of the way? Would it cease working if she depleted it *all* the way?

She grimaced at the thought that it had only limited magic

with which to drive the dragons and their riders out of the Kingdom.

"Better to know than not to know," Syla murmured.

"Yes," Tibby said. Was she also seeing the reservoir? "It's possible the energy within might recharge with time, but… it's also possible that what magic was given to it upon creation is all we have."

"We'll have to use it carefully."

Syla attempted to convey understanding to the platform before directing the awareness embedded in it toward her aunt. *Tibby needs to be able to use you in case I'm needed elsewhere.*

A hint of acknowledgment came from the weapons platform, but then Vorik's face floated into Syla's mind. It floated there and stayed there. At first, she thought the platform intended to send her to spy on him again, but, unless he was in the midst of escaping, she knew where he was. She would happily send her mind across the sea to visit his new camp, to learn where the components were, but the device didn't offer that, only holding Vorik's face in her mind.

What did it want? He was a warrior, but certainly not the right kind of warrior for this.

"We're not going to let *him* use the weapons platform," Tibby said. "He's not on our side."

Through the moon-link, Syla sensed her aunt's disapproval that she continued to have a relationship with Vorik and her belief that Syla hadn't interrogated him the night before. Syla didn't have a defense for that and pretended she hadn't caught the thought.

"Not him," Syla said in agreement, willing the platform to accept Tibby.

Vorik's face lingered, as if it was still trying to convey something, but it eventually faded. Tibby's face replaced his in Syla's mind. Silver light emanated from the weapons platform, and nearby crewmen murmured and pointed. The light flowed out of the device, and energy crackled all around Syla and Tibby.

Fel removed his hand from Tibby's and stepped back. The silver light faded, and Syla looked at her aunt to see if she felt anything had changed.

She nodded. "I think I can use it now."

"Do you want to test it?" Syla asked.

They were sailing past the volcano on the far end of Harvest Island, about to head across the sea toward Bogberry Island, and Syla wondered if any stormer dragons lurked among the rocks, close enough to target.

"We'd better not waste any of its reserves," Tibby said quietly, then looked to the southwest, the direction of Bogberry Island. "We'll get an opportunity to find out soon enough if I can operate it."

"All right."

A Royal Protector jogged out on deck, blood from a split lip trickling down his chin, and his eyes locked immediately on Syla. Before he spoke, she knew something was wrong, and she could guess what.

"The prisoner has escaped, Your Majesty." He pointed at the deck. "He escaped your cabin, overpowered us, and is on the ship somewhere."

"He didn't go overboard?" Syla glanced toward the wheelhouse, but Wreylith hadn't yet returned from her hunt. If Vorik wanted to swim to land where Agrevlari could pick him up, this would have been an opportunity for him to do so.

"We don't know for sure, Your Majesty, but we think someone would have seen him swimming away." The man waved around to the open space and all the crewmen at work or stationed near the weapons. There was also someone in the crow's nest. "We're afraid he's sticking around to sabotage something." His gaze went to the weapons platform.

Syla sighed. She thought Vorik had stuck around to try to kidnap her at an inopportune time, but if his brother ordered him to destroy the weapons platform or sink the ship, Vorik would try.

"Keep a team up here to guard this." Syla believed the weapons platform nearly indestructible, but she had seen the stormer gargoyle-bone blades damage magical and supposedly indestructible things, including the shielder on Castle Island. "Then get every available man together, and search the ship. We've only got a few hours until we reach Bogberry Island, and we'd better find him before then."

"Not *every* available man." Fel pointed at Syla. "Leave a team to guard the queen."

"We will." Judging by the relieved nod the man gave to Fel, he'd wanted to do exactly that.

Syla didn't object, but she did add, "When you find Vorik, get me. *I'll* deal with him."

She didn't know how, and expected the man to scoff, but he looked from the weapons platform to her and nodded, as if he believed she could handle a powerful dragon rider. Then he added, "It's too bad the Candles of Serenity didn't keep him knocked out for longer."

Syla managed not to wince, though her cheeks did flush red at the reminder that she'd been dishonest with her people, leading them to believe she'd been questioning Vorik, not having *sex* with him.

"I have more of them," she said.

If they caught Vorik again, she would use the candles and drugs this time.

11

Belowdecks, Vorik crouched in a dark nook near the armory, his forearms still burning after spending the first couple hours of his escape hiding by clinging to the outside of the ship, well below the railing and anyone's view. Once the search had grown more half-hearted, he'd slipped back aboard, finding a spot where the Kingdom men had already looked.

A guard stood outside the stout wooden door of the armory, and Vorik was contemplating overpowering and subduing him so he could help himself to the contents within. Too bad that would clue the crew in on where Vorik was—and what he intended. Earlier, he'd managed to find his sword and pluck it up without anyone noticing. His plans would be easier to implement if he could remain hidden until the last moment.

He didn't sense Wreylith, which was why he'd dared escape, but if she returned, he would have to reconsider those plans. Unlike the soldiers poking around the ship, a dragon would have no trouble sensing him and locating him. He wasn't positive that Syla, who ought to have gained power from her new link to the red dragon, wouldn't be able to sense him, but he didn't worry as much about her snapping him in half.

What is your status? Jhiton spoke into his mind from a distance. Bogberry Island, most likely.

I'm free and on the ship, dodging search parties.

Our dragons have spotted the Kingdom fleet on its way here. We will soon keep that vessel too busy for its crew to search for you.

Oh, good. It's always a joy to be on the ship that our forces are attacking.

I trust you can find a way overboard at any time, Jhiton said.

Having to get Syla will make that more complicated, but, yes. I'm waiting until we're not in the middle of the sea and Agrevlari can pluck us up.

He could retrieve you any time if you destroyed that weapons platform.

That's... been on my mind. Vorik eyed the door of the armory. He'd been wondering if it contained explosives similar to those Syla had used to booby-trap the shielder chamber under the castle. They had detonated on impact.

Whether you destroy it or not, bring the queen and join us, Jhiton said.

I will.

We'll soon have the Lady Abrya as well. We will extract the information on the Bogberry Island shielder from one *of them. I don't care which.*

Vorik cared, but he didn't say so. *You should like Syla and want to treat her well. She agrees with you that I should challenge Shi for leadership of the tribe.*

I didn't say you should do that, only that it would be the appropriate way to have an impact on decisions being made on a tribal level. Jhiton managed to convey dryness through their telepathic link. *But I have no doubt that your queen would prefer to negotiate with* you *than Chieftess Shi.*

I don't think she was impressed with Shi's suggestion that they engage in girl chat over their menses.

Chieftess Shi was being sarcastic about that. I doubt she's ever engaged in girl chat with anyone in her life.

I suppose that's true. And I know Syla wasn't merely thinking of my goals and aspirations when she suggested I have the ability to lead.

Certainly not.

But I also don't think she was being deliberately manipulative. Just... supportive.

Kidnap her, convince her to let someone else rule, and have her join the tribe and become your mate. Then she can support you all you like.

Unfortunately, as I said before, that's not going to happen. She's especially not going to be pleased if I kidnap her.

We are at war, Vorik.

I know. He kept himself from saying *unfortunately* again. Barely. Instead, he resolved to get into the armory and look for explosives. Then he would hope that the gods wouldn't consider it blasphemous if he managed to destroy an artifact they'd crafted. Admittedly, he was more worried about what Syla would do to him if he succeeded. No, not what she would do. How she would *feel.*

He kept thinking about how she hadn't drugged him and questioned him. She *should* have, but she hadn't. Every time he acted against her, it felt like a betrayal and left him more conflicted than ever.

Why did it feel like whatever choices he made going forward would betray someone?

A part of him was tempted to talk Agrevlari into picking him up, flying him away, and leaving his people and the Kingdom to figure things out for themselves. But if he weren't here... Syla might already be dead. Lesva was still alive and angrier than ever. By helping Syla, Vorik had made things worse. For her and for himself.

~

With the ship less than an hour from Bogberry Island, its verdant shoreline visible on the horizon, Syla jogged down to her cabin. The Royal Protectors and Fel tramped after her. Despite several hours of searching, nobody had found Vorik.

Earlier, Wreylith had flown past, saying she could sense him within the bowels of the ship, but hadn't been able to give a pinpoint location. Should Syla wish her to tear apart the *Stormslicer*, the dragon had informed her, Wreylith had been certain she could pluck him out of the wreckage. Syla had politely thanked her for the offer before declining it and asking Wreylith to scout ahead.

Fel strode into the cabin ahead of Syla to search and make sure Vorik wasn't skulking in a cabinet or under the bunk, not that there was copious storage space in which to hide. The cabin was fine for her needs, but this was a warship, not the spacious royal yacht which, Syla had heard, hadn't survived the initial invasion.

"He's not in here," Syla said with amusement after Fel peeked under the desk and looked in a waste bin hooked to the side.

"He was."

Yes, everyone doubtless knew he'd spent the night.

Fel pointed with significance at the desk. "Unless you were the one who put those candles and jars away."

Syla stared. Her observant bodyguard had noticed what she hadn't. The Candles of Serenity, as well as the powder and other drugs one might use in an interrogation, were gone. The Royal Protector who'd taken Vorik from the cabin that morning wouldn't have allowed him to shop for souvenirs. Since escaping, Vorik had come back. Specifically for them? Or because he'd been hoping to catch her in here? Maybe both.

She shifted uneasily. "I didn't. You're right. He took them."

"Maybe he's planning to interrogate *you*." Fel scowled.

"I'm immune to the Candles of Serenity, but..." She didn't have a defense against hydra-scale powder. The thought of Vorik forcing her to take it and use her moon-mark to give his people access to a shielder chilled her.

Would he do that? Even if he would hesitate to drug her, his brother wouldn't.

"You'd better stay in here until..." Fel looked like he wanted to say *forever* or maybe *until the stormer threat is past.* "Until we're sure he's off the ship," was what he opted for.

"I need to be up on deck when we reach Bogberry Island. Aunt Tibby may need help the first time she uses the weapons platform. For that matter, there's no reason for her to be the one to do so if I'm available."

"*You're* more likely to be a target than she is."

"We both have moon-marks."

"Yeah, but the stormers *like* you." Fel looked sourly at her.

"Just one," Syla murmured. "Others loathe me."

"All of which makes you a more likely target. And, remember, there could also be assassins recruited from within the Kingdom aboard." Yes, he'd probably caught the gist of the captain's warning. "Further, you brought Lord Ravoran aboard. *He* might kill you, as well."

Syla wished she could deny that, but the meeting she'd made herself give the island lord hadn't gone well. She'd tried to bring him around to her way of thinking, but he'd refused to believe Castle Island was more important to defend than Harvest. She'd promised she would get a shielder back there as soon as possible and had tried not to feel like a dog fleeing with its tail clenched between its legs when she'd departed.

"I'll stay in here until I'm needed," she said.

Fel's squint suggested that answer hadn't pleased him, but maybe he knew it was the best she could give. After nodding curtly, he walked out to join the Royal Protectors in the corridor. The door thumped firmly shut.

Syla looked around the cabin, a little uneasy now that she knew Vorik had been back and taken things. Was his brother communicating with him? Giving him orders? Telling him he had to make up for fighting Lesva and not capturing Syla earlier?

She exhaled slowly, walked to the trunks she'd brought along, and pulled out her medical kit and a case with pharmacological offerings. Fortunately, Vorik hadn't rummaged through her luggage and found and taken items from within. Most of the bottles and jars were only labeled with their contents, not what they did. Such information was stored in her memory.

She opened the case to mull over options she could use if Vorik succeeded in kidnapping her. Though she'd dismissed the idea of *trying* to be kidnapped, so that she could be taken to where the shielder components were, it might happen, whether she cooperated or not. Of course, he would be suspicious if he caught her wandering around the ship toting a pack with changes of clothing and a toothbrush, clearly prepared for a journey, but he might not think anything of her carrying her medical kit. And he might let her take it along. After all, his people could need a healer's touch.

"Too bad I don't have anything that could knock out an entire cave of stormers," she mused as she rummaged through the case.

A few candelabras loaded with Candles of Serenity might, but he'd taken the only ones she'd seen in the infirmary. She tucked a couple of vials of margroth tree oil into her kit, the astringent liquid she'd spattered onto the face of one of the giant bug-creatures in the laboratory. With luck, she wouldn't have to knock out an entire *cave* of stormers, maybe only a couple of guards charged with watching her during the night. She did have ground dayvak buds, which could be mixed into food or wine to sedate someone. It was what Atilya had used on Vorik and his lieutenant in her cave. The stormers wouldn't let Syla prepare them a meal, but she took all the powder she had.

"Just in case." Syla slung the strap of her medical kit over her shoulder and across her body so it wouldn't fall off if someone grabbed her.

My return is blocked, Wreylith stated into her mind.

By enemy dragons? Syla guessed.

Yes, I was unable to get close to the Island of Bogs earlier since stormer-allied dragons lurk there. I returned to the Island of Eliok to fish and fill my belly before our inevitable battle, but, now, the stormer dragons have placed themselves in my flightpath to deter me from reaching you. They do not answer me when I question them. I am contemplating attacking them and reaching you regardless of the threat. Wreylith growled into her mind. *They are overly arrogant because they have greater numbers.*

If you can get within five miles of the ship, I ought to be able to target them with the weapons platform. Syla wondered if Wreylith might be that close now.

Agrevlari has just joined them. Wreylith growled again. *He seeks to impede me. The gall!*

Maybe he'll help you against the others if they attack.

That was my first thought, but he has informed me that he has orders to keep me away from your ship and the Island of Bogs.

A knock sounded at the door, and Syla walked over.

"You shouldn't open that with so many enemies on board," Fel told her, though he stood to the side. Major Hixun had been the one to knock.

"I should make visitors yell through it?" Syla asked.

"Yes."

Ignoring their exchange, Hixun said, "I regret to inform you that we're still looking for Captain Vorik, Your Majesty."

Syla nodded, having assumed Vorik could remain hidden if he so chose.

"We also, ah." Hixun grimaced. "I have to report that he got into the armory. He didn't kill the men guarding it, fortunately, but we believe he took a few things."

"Like... explosives?"

"We don't carry explosives beyond the black powder for the cannons, but..." Hixun cleared his throat, and were his cheeks pink?

Maybe he was embarrassed that his men hadn't been able to find Vorik. The ship wasn't that large. But Vorik... Syla wouldn't blame anyone for not being able to find him. She wouldn't be surprised if he'd hung from the ceiling while men walked under him, or maybe he'd been outside the ship, clinging from barnacles on the hull like a spider.

"Lady Tibaytha," Hixun continued, "reported that her cabin was broken into and someone stole a booby trap."

"An *explosive* booby trap?"

"Apparently, she'd started making some this morning, using black powder and some of her magic. She said she'd only completed one but that it's missing."

Syla shook her head bleakly.

"We're worried he'll blow a hole in the hull of the ship to sabotage us as soon as we enter battle," Hixun said.

Syla glanced upward, certain of what Vorik would target. "He'll go after the weapons platform."

Hixun opened his mouth, paused, then rocked back. "Of course, Your Majesty. It's out in the open, but—"

"Put more guards up there. Don't let anyone get close."

"Yes, Your Majesty."

As he hurried away, Syla asked Fel, "Do you think my aunt's booby traps could damage something made by the gods? Of marble and magic?"

"Questions on that topic weren't discussed in my basic Fleet training," Fel said.

"It didn't come up in your twenty years as a bodyguard for the royal family either?"

"Your parents and siblings didn't acquire any magical marble artifacts that I was aware of."

Syla didn't truly expect Fel to know the answer to her question but wished someone did. "I'm going up there."

Fel dropped an arm to block the door. "It's been less than ten minutes since you agreed to stay in your cabin."

"My dragon ally is being deterred, and my weapons platform is in danger. Things have changed."

Exasperation stamping his face, Fel didn't lift his arm.

"Let me go, Sergeant," Syla said. "Vorik won't blow it up if I'm *sitting* on it."

"If someone in his chain of command orders it, he will." Fel tapped his temple to indicate the possibility of telepathic communication.

Since Syla already knew General Jhiton could talk to Vorik that way, she didn't argue that part. "No, he won't. If he wanted me dead, he could have broken my neck any number of times, including last night."

Fel's eyebrow twitched. "While he was drugged and sedated by your Candles of Serenity?"

"His sedation wasn't as complete as you would have liked."

Fel did not appear surprised. "I don't believe he *wants* you dead, but if General Jhiton commands it... are you certain he would disobey a direct order?"

The memory of Vorik standing between her and his brother in the shielder chamber under the castle came to mind. "Regarding my life, yes."

Syla ducked under Fel's arm and jogged for the ship's ladder. Her long-legged bodyguard could have caught her, but he sighed and strode after her to protect her instead of slinging her over his shoulder and locking her in her cabin. He would have *preferred* that, she was certain. But he was ever loyal. Someday, she hoped she could reward him for that.

When Syla stepped out onto the deck, distant screeches reached her ears.

Wreylith? she asked telepathically, afraid a battle had already started.

Bogberry Island filled the horizon now, the landmass dotted with lakes, bogs, and forests, with a single sprawling hill rising miles inland. Unlike the volcanos at the core of many of the Kingdom islands, the high ground had been formed by an underground salt dome. A mine within it provided the Kingdom with all the salt its people needed to preserve their food, with surplus left for trade. It would be a valuable resource for the stormers to claim.

Syla frowned at the thought, eyeing the hill as they sailed toward the mouth of the Prominence River, a waterway that flowed down from the inland lakes and springs. The main city of Seaward lay along both sides of the river, the bridge over it visible beyond docks along its banks. Close to the mouth of the Prominence, those docks were in deep enough water for ocean-going vessels to sail to them.

Inland from the river and uphill lay the island lord's palace. As promised, smoke wafted from the structure, and numerous other buildings in the city burned, as well.

To each side of the mouth of the river, wide stone towers with multiple platforms supported cannons that were currently pointed toward four stormer ships anchored out of range. Archers and crossbowmen stood upon the platforms, facing the threat.

With dragon figureheads, the stormer ships were nearly identical to the one that had brought the supposed diplomatic party to Castle Island weeks earlier. They were laden with cannons aimed toward the city. More concerning than the ships, six dragons flew back and forth just outside the island's barrier, as if they were waiting for something.

The screeches, however, came from the opposite direction, back toward Harvest Island.

The oaf is singing *to me while he and his allies obstruct my flight-path,* Wreylith said.

Are you within five miles? Syla couldn't yet pick out a red dragon in the sky.

After glancing around the deck to make sure Vorik wasn't crouched somewhere with an explosive in hand, Syla strode toward the weapons platform. There were enough crewmen about —each cannon was manned, and the fleet commander and major stood outside near the wheelhouse—that she trusted he couldn't have approached it without being seen. In addition, four Royal Protectors surrounded the weapons platform. Aunt Tibby sat on it, a book open in her lap, though she was looking pensively toward the stormer ships.

I am uncertain of the precise distance, Wreylith said.

I can hear *his screeching. You can't be that far, right?*

A dragon's cries may travel a great distance.

More than five miles?

Many more. A wolf's howl can carry ten, and dragons are, naturally, superior to lupines.

Vocally superior too?

Certainly.

Another screech floated to Syla's ears, and she winced as she stepped past the Royal Protectors to climb onto the platform. *I'm not sure vocally superior is the right adjective to describe that particular dragon.*

I will agree on that matter. Are you going to engage in battle? I will attempt to get past these presumptuous dragons who block my way.

Do you want help? Syla placed herself between two posts and rested her hands on the marks, though, now that she believed the weapons platform could only fire a certain number of rounds before being depleted, she was loath to send them off carelessly.

To stop Agrevlari's caterwauling?

A magical silver energy ball down his throat may achieve that, Syla replied, though she couldn't imagine attacking Vorik's dragon. Even if Vorik was skulking around the ship, plotting ways to kidnap her and destroy her weapons platform, she struggled to think of him as an enemy. "Which is a problem," she admitted softly.

Tibby glanced at her. "Are we going to attack the dragons?" She touched her chest, then pointed at Syla.

"Unless they leave of their own accord," Syla said.

"You should blast them whether they show signs of leaving or not," Fel said. "The stormers have already sneaked into the city and burned buildings. There may be Kingdom subjects lying dead in the streets. And we don't know if the island lord or someone else who knows where the shielder is might have been kidnapped."

Syla didn't explain the possibly limited reservoir in the weapons platform, saying only, "That is something we need to determine. It looks like we're angling to head up the river toward the docks. We'll see if the stormers oppose us."

"We have to attack them, not sail *past* them."

Syla waved toward the fleet commander and major—they were stepping into the wheelhouse. They hadn't consulted her, but it wasn't as if she had vast military experience, so she didn't fault them for that. She was here to man the weapons platform.

"It's such a beautiful island." Tibby gazed toward the lush green landscape. "It's a shame the stormers are targeting it."

"All of our islands are beautiful in one way or another," Syla said.

"True, but this one has the salt mine too. That's an important resource for the Kingdom, and it's full of history and something of a national treasure."

"I remember the ancient carvings from my family's visit years ago."

"The mine itself is magnificent. An engineering marvel. I worked there for several months during an internship. Before I decided to specialize in agricultural engineering, I helped ensorcel some of the large drills, borers, and excavators."

"So, the mine has significance because there are machines you touched down there." Syla smiled faintly.

"I designed and *built* a couple of them."

"Which involved touching."

"A lot of it, yes."

As the fleet sailed closer, the dragons circling in the area glanced toward the weapons platform, then flew farther out to sea. They didn't leave entirely, however, and more dragons were visible in the distance. Was that green one Agrevlari? And, yes, there was Wreylith's red-scaled form beyond him. Agrevlari and other dragons were flying toward her. To intercept her.

Syla clenched her fist, wanting to urge Wreylith to come but also worried about her. As great and powerful as she was, she couldn't fight so many.

Unlike the dragons, the stormer ships moved closer to the Kingdom fleet.

"Are they going to barricade the river?" Tibby wondered.

The stormer ships weren't positioning themselves to block the way but to ensure the fleet would have to pass well within their cannon range to reach the docks.

"Looks like they want a fight." Fel pointed at the weapons platform. "That thing'll work as well on ships as on dragons, right?"

"I would think so." Syla had used it to blow up the storm god's laboratory defenses without trouble.

"Cheeky of them to get in our way," Tibby said.

"Maybe they expect something to happen to distract us. Or distract *you*." Fel pointed at Syla.

"Yes," Tibby said. "They won't yet know that I'm able to operate the weapons platform, so they might believe if Syla is busy, they'll be safe from it."

"Maybe they think Vorik has already kidnapped me," Syla mused, her gaze toward the stormer ships.

"He's planning to do that?" Tibby asked.

"And he *told* you?" Fel asked.

Syla realized she shouldn't have voiced that out loud. "We… don't have as many secrets from each other as we should."

"That relationship is going to be the death of the Kingdom," Fel told Tibby.

"That's my concern as well," she replied.

"Maybe *we* should kidnap her," Fel said.

"And lock her up for her own good." Tibby nodded with approval.

"I liked it better when you two were sniping at each other," Syla said, "instead of in agreement over my failings."

More screeches sounded, not so distant now. Wreylith flapped her wings, heading toward the *Stormslicer* with three dragons on her tail. Another arrowed in from ahead and to the side of her. She wasn't going to make it.

12

POWERFUL WINGS BEATING, WREYLITH SPED TOWARD THE *Stormslicer*, but a gray dragon intercepted her, roaring and snapping for her neck with its fangs. Wreylith twisted to avoid the bite while raking with her talons. Tail lashing out like a whip, she contorted herself to breathe fire at her enemy. The gray wheeled away, but the other dragons had caught up. Agrevlari flew at the back of the group, hanging back slightly, but he didn't look like he would help her, not this time.

"*I'll* help her." Syla wiped her palms, already nervous for the battle, then planted her hands on the posts of the weapons platform.

"Do you want me to assist?" Tibby asked uncertainly.

Syla started to shake her head but realized this would be the time to test her aunt's ability to do so. "Yes, try shooting a sphere from one of the back posts."

"Take out the stormer ships too," Fel suggested, standing on the deck where he could keep an eye on Syla and Tibby and waving the Royal Protectors closer to the platform.

More worried about her winged ally at the moment, Syla

targeted the gray dragon. Thus far, Wreylith had sped past two others, flying so fast that they hadn't been able to stop her, but the powerful gray flapped its great wings and kept up.

Syla willed a ball of magical energy to launch. With a soft *thwump* reverberating through the platform, one shot out from her corner. As the gray dragon opened its maw to breathe fire at Wreylith, it noticed the silvery ball speeding toward it. With a quick barrel roll in the air, it tried to escape, but the projectile curved to follow, then slammed into its side. The screech that came from the dragon had nothing to do with singing.

Booms erupted from the stormer ships.

"They're firing at us!" came Major Hixun's call. "Fire back! Blow them out of the seas!"

Though Syla worried she hadn't done enough to help Wreylith, she turned her attention to the enemy vessels. A cannonball splashed into the water a few feet from the bow of the *Stormslicer* as their enemies sought to find their range. Another soared overhead, so close that it clipped the corner of the wheelhouse before streaking through the railing and splashing down on the far side.

As the *Stormslicer* returned fire, cannonballs blasting toward the enemy vessels, Syla launched two more projectiles. With the targets so near, they landed quickly, one crashing into the hull of a stormer ship. Shards of wood flew hundreds of feet, and what remained burst into flame. The other magical sphere slammed into a cannon, blowing it across the ship to land in the water on the far side and hurling its crew in all directions.

Syla grimaced, telling herself to pick her targets more carefully. She needed to use her precious magical ammunition to sink the ships, not blow up single weapons mounted on them.

Behind her, Tibby cursed. So far, she'd been unsuccessful in her attempts to launch an attack. Maybe the weapons platform would only respond to one wielder at a time?

The dragons that had scattered when the *Stormslicer* arrived returned now that the battle had begun. Flying as one cohesive unit, they arrowed toward the Kingdom fleet. No, toward Syla's ship specifically. They had riders, and she spotted a black dragon in the lead. Was that General Jhiton and Ozlemar?

With so many cannonballs flying, and the *Stormslicer* maneuvering, trying to pass the enemy vessels and reach the barrier, Syla struggled to keep the wheeling and diving dragons in sight, but she knew they were coming at her. And on the other side, the dragons harrying Wreylith were also closer than they had been, their battle sweeping toward the island.

As if Wreylith had noticed her checking, she reported, *He is attacking me!*

Agrevlari? Syla asked.

Numerous dragons were attacking Wreylith, but that had been a singular *he*.

Yes! I will tear his horns off and shove them into his cloaca.

That sounds painful.

It will be!

Though sinking the stormer ships would keep them from sending more people to the island to attack, the dragons were more dangerous to everyone's lives. Syla shifted her focus to them. She wanted to help Wreylith, but the closer dragons were a greater threat to the fleet—and the weapons platform.

Jhiton's great winged beast flew past, the general riding on his back and gripping a bow, shooting down at the deck of the *Stormslicer*. A closer yellow dragon was diving toward the weapons platform, talons outstretched.

Though Syla doubted a single dragon could lift what had taken four of their kind to deliver, she had to focus on it. The next magical spheres she launched sped toward the yellow creature. It had almost reached them when the projectiles slammed into its chest. Silver light flared, and it screeched—no, *shrieked* as its wingbeats faltered. Its momentum carried it into the ship, and men scattered as it slammed onto the deck, snapping wood, then bounced off and splashed into the water on the far side.

Another silver projectile sped away, and it wasn't Syla's doing.

Tibby blurted, "Yes!" as it zipped across the water and toward a stormer ship. It blew through one of the vessel's masts and sped toward the city. Tibby's next cry was, "No!" as it struck a waterfront building, blowing it to pieces.

"You'll get it down!" Syla promised, hoping nobody had been inside.

She launched a projectile at the other stormer ship, careful to angle it so that it wouldn't hit anything important if it went all the way through the vessel. It landed low enough on the hull to ensure the ship would take on water.

Nearby, an arrow pierced one of the Royal Protectors in the throat, and he crumpled to the deck.

Syla gaped, horrified. That would be a fatal wound.

Swearing, she searched the sky for the riders with bows. Cannons boomed from the deck of the *Stormslicer*, but the enemy dragons didn't have trouble evading them. The ones targeting the ships were more effective.

An arrow clinked off a marble post less than a foot from Syla's head, and she stumbled back. Cold eyes, face chiseled from granite, General Jhiton stared down at her from his dragon's back as he nocked another arrow. The bastard was trying to kill her. He'd already killed one of the men defending her.

Syla sprang back to the post, planting her sweaty palm on the mark, determined to get Jhiton. But Fel moved abruptly, startling her. Vorik was running across the deck toward them. Where had he come from?

Men charged at Vorik, but he sprang over their heads, jumping so high that the swings of their weapons didn't reach him. For an instant, he met Syla's eyes, shouting, "Move!" before he landed on top of the weapons platform with a soft thud.

Even as archers on deck turned bows toward him, and Fel and the Royal Protectors spun to climb up after him, Vorik raised something above one of the hollow tops of the posts—the barrels that the projectiles fired from. The stolen booby trap.

"Don't shoot!" Syla yelled to her aunt, imagining the weapon exploding like a blocked cannon.

Before Fel and the Royal Protectors reached the top of the canopy, Vorik dropped the explosive and leaped off. He twisted in the air, anticipating and dodging an arrow speeding toward him.

Magic flared within the post, and the booby trap didn't go off right away.

Roars above the *Stormslicer* made Syla flinch. She ducked low, not wanting to leave the weapons platform but also feeling vulnerable. Her instincts were right. Jhiton loosed another arrow. It zipped between the platform and its canopy, then clipped the ship's railing as it sailed away on the far side. By the gods, if she hadn't ducked at the right moment... it would have pierced her throat.

Vorik had landed, his sword in hand, and clangs erupted as he parried a barrage of blows from men charging at him.

Two types of magic mingled within the post, and Syla thought the weapons platform might have a way to nullify Tibby's booby trap, but then a thunderous boom came from right above. Though the canopy somewhat protected Syla and Tibby, they wobbled, and Syla lost her grip on the post again. She scrambled back toward it, knowing they would never win if she couldn't take down more enemy dragons, but she didn't know if that explosion had damaged the platform. The frame seemed to be intact, but she couldn't see the opening at the top of the post.

Even as she wondered if she dared try to fire, willing the weapon to use one of the other posts, Vorik battled his way toward her, determination in the set of his jaw. Fel moved to block him, and she scowled, afraid Vorik would slay him to get to her.

"I'm not going with you!" Syla shouted.

More dragons flew closer, one diving for the weapons platform again. Syla leaped up beside Tibby, and they launched weapons at the same time, using the back posts in case the other was destroyed.

Relief flooded into Syla when two projectiles zipped away. Their dragon target tried to veer off but wasn't fast enough to dodge the gods-gifted magic. Both projectiles struck, knocking it back dozens of yards. It splashed into the water and didn't move again.

"We're almost to the barrier!" Hixun called. "Keep firing, everyone. We'll pummel those dragons from behind its protection!"

"Look out!" Vorik yelled.

Syla reacted, ducking low with speed that startled her, almost making her tumble off the platform, but she managed to pull Tibby down with her. Another arrow zipped between the posts, another projectile that had been meant to slay Syla. Tibby stumbled against her, and this time Syla couldn't keep her balance. She fell off the platform and hit the deck, glimpsing the black dragon flying low overhead as she did. Jhiton looked down at her without expression.

That bastard wanted her *dead*, not kidnapped. As clangs and booms and roars filled the air all around, Syla pushed herself to her feet, almost as afraid of being trampled as shot.

"Get under the platform!" Tibby yelled to her. Wisely, she'd already done so.

Syla shook her head, intending to climb back on to keep launching weapons, but she hesitated. Vorik had fought aside several men and faced Fel now.

She yelled an inarticulate garble, half-warning, half threat. If Vorik killed her bodyguard...

But he was forced to spin and duck as an archer standing on top of the wheelhouse almost took him out. The arrow sped over his head, and Fel jerked his mace up as *he* had to dodge. The projectile grazed his shoulder, then clipped a marble post and sped away.

Brace yourself, Wreylith warned as Syla started to climb back onto the platform.

Guilt blasted her because she'd forgotten that her dragon ally had been under attack. A shadow crossed the sun, and Syla looked up. With blood dripping from gouges in her flank and teeth marks in her tail, Wreylith plucked up Syla, sweeping her from the ship and into the air.

"Wait, I have to—" Syla started, but fire blasted the spot where she'd been.

Two dragons had dived down from the opposite side of the ship, and one poured flames onto the weapons platform.

"Aunt Tibby!" Syla cried as Wreylith carried her away from the ship.

Vorik and the men defending the platform scattered. One Royal Protector dropped to the deck, rolling to put out fire burning the back of his uniform. Vorik gaped at Syla being carried away.

The pair of dragons wheeled to attack again—though fire burned on the ship, the marble weapons platform stood unscathed—but they pulled up abruptly. Sparks lit the air all around one of them as it bounced off something. The barrier. The *Stormslicer* had sailed through it.

"Get him!" Hixun called.

Vorik was still fighting, defending himself from the men all about him, but he'd lost the determined set of his jaw. The weapons platform still stood. In the air, dangling from Wreylith's talons, Syla could see the top of it and didn't think the explosion had damaged it. Further, *she* was out of Vorik's reach.

Probably seeing no reason to stay, Vorik parried a few more attacks as he backed toward the railing, then spun and leaped over it and into the sea.

"What happened to Agrevlari and the other dragons after you? And where are you taking me?" Syla saw Jhiton's black dragon still flying, dodging cannonballs as its rider tracked her.

I do not have a destination in mind. I sought only to retrieve you from incineration.

"That's always appreciated. Thank you."

Because he had many allies, I did not get a chance to de-horn Agrevlari. I did *bite him on the back of the neck.*

I can't believe he attacked you.

He was faster and stronger than I expected based on his singing and overall goofiness. I evaded two of his allies, but he was the one who raked my side with his talons.

Was her telepathic tone the slightest bit *admiring*? Maybe that was Syla's imagination, but Wreylith didn't sound as angry as Syla would have expected after having a dragon she'd mated with turn on her. Admittedly, that had been magical-cactus-flower-induced mating, but still. Agrevlari sang to her regularly.

His superiors must have given him orders to attack you, Syla said.

Possibly. I believe he felt the pressure of his peers. Also, I did bite him on the neck first.

I suppose that'll get a rise out of even a goofy dragon.

Quite.

On the ship, Tibby crawled out from underneath the weapons platform and climbed onto it again. The fire hadn't gotten her; thank the moon god. She peered toward the dragons, but Fel shouted something and pointed toward the water.

Vorik was swimming toward one of the stormer ships. None of them appeared seaworthy, and the one that had lost its mast listed so far sideways that the crew struggled to keep from sliding off the deck, but the tenacious stormers kept loosing arrows at the Kingdom crewmen, and more than one of their cannons continued to fire.

Syla thought Tibby might aim at one of the ships since, with the dragons beyond the barrier, they were no longer a threat to the fleet, but when she planted her palm against a post, her face resolute, Syla realized what her target was. Since she still dangled from Wreylith's talons, the dragon circling while waiting for a suggestion on a destination, Syla couldn't do anything to stop her aunt.

Vorik was swimming fast, his sword sheathed so he could use both arms, but he had to navigate around wreckage from the ships, and she didn't think his speed would be great enough.

"Look out!" Syla yelled, but with cannons still booming and dragons roaring their frustrations, he wouldn't hear her. Trying to use telepathy, she also called, *Look out!* with her mind.

She feared it was fruitless, since she could only speak telepathically with dragons, and blurted a distressed, "No!" as Tibby fired a single silvery ball.

It sped straight toward Vorik, but he was already diving. He couldn't have seen the attack coming as he swam away, but had he somehow sensed Syla's warning? And would it even matter? Or would the magical sphere follow him through water as easily as it did through air and strike its target?

The projectile dove into the waves, and she groaned, certain it would hit him. A silvery flash came from the sea, then a strange bubble rose up, almost as if the water were boiling. Maybe it was.

Had the weapon struck Vorik? Syla worried it had, but he was so capable of avoiding death that she watched, hoping to see him surface, to keep swimming.

Long seconds passed, and she caught herself holding her breath as she searched. Though she spotted a few injured and some perhaps dead men floating on the waves, she didn't see Vorik come up. Had her aunt succeeded where so many others had failed?

A lump formed in Syla's throat. She told herself that between the waves, the lingering chaos of the battle, and the awkwardness of searching while dangling from a flying dragon's talons, she might have missed Vorik. But dread settled into her as she worried he hadn't survived.

It is not safe out here, Wreylith said. *Now that your fleet is out of dragon reach, they will turn all their attention on us. Do you wish me to take you to your vessel or the city? Since we are now bonded, I should be able to travel through the barriers with you to your various islands, not just Castle Island.*

Oh, yes. We need to check on the palace and see if we can find Lord Oyenar for an update. We may need to drive stormers out of the city, as well.

I do enjoy driving out enemies. Almost as much as I enjoy hunting. Also, I seem to recall that bog bears proliferate on this island. Wreylith flew toward the river mouth. *Succulent and delicious bog bears that are nearly extinct on the mainlands.*

Did you rescue me to save me from certain death or because you wouldn't be able to get through the barrier to hunt those bears without me?

Your death would be inconvenient since it would leave nobody capable enough to heal me when I'm wounded.

So, you'd miss me as much as your belly would miss being filled with bog-bear meat? Syla sensed the barrier as they flew toward it, though it was as invisible as the one around Castle Island.

Equally so, I'd think. I—

Wreylith struck the invisible barrier instead of flying through, and she screeched as sparks flew and light flashed. Her back tilted, her wings flapping wildly, and her talons jerked and released Syla.

Startled, Syla barely managed to flatten her hand to her face to keep her spectacles on as she plunged twenty feet. Cold water enveloped her, and she almost swallowed a mouthful when she came up, a wave striking her in the face.

What happened? she blurted telepathically, though it had been obvious.

It seemed Wreylith misremembered the past, or something was different about her bond with Syla than it had been with Queen Erasbella., and the dragon could only fly through the shield on Castle Island.

The barrier kept me from approaching. Wreylith sounded puzzled. *I flew through it in the past when I carried your ancestor.*

Did Erasbella have to say or do something to allow it?

I do not recall. I will have to sort through my memories. Wreylith tried to fly down to pluck up Syla again, but the current had carried her through the barrier. *I cannot retrieve you.*

Guess I'm swimming. Syla grimaced, well aware that stormers remained alive on those ships. With her dragon ally unable to help her, she would have to pray that she could make it to the fleet vessels before an archer with a grudge spotted her.

13

At least one archer took note of Syla swimming through the waves toward the *Stormslicer*. Through the water droplets clinging to her spectacles, she could make out the big black dragon, Ozlemar, circling near the barrier and General Jhiton, his bow across his lap, gazing down at her.

Wreylith remained close and roared at them. Jhiton looked blandly at her, not appearing concerned, probably because a half dozen stormer dragons remained in the area. Syla wished her aunt had been firing the weapons platform at *them* instead of Vorik. Since Wreylith was stuck out there by herself, the stormer-allied dragons might go after her.

Though Ozlemar might have been close enough for his rider to loose an arrow, Jhiton surprised Syla by not doing so. Nor did he order his dragons to attack Wreylith. His gaze shifted to the water between the Kingdom ships and the mouth of the river. Was he, also, looking for Vorik to come up?

Whatever his reason for not firing at her, Syla took advantage of it. Fighting the waves, she kept swimming toward her ship.

Bogberry Island didn't have a protected harbor created by

natural terrain, only a couple of rock jetties that extended outward near the mouth of the river, and swimming wasn't easy. Fortunately, when Major Hixun spotted Syla fighting the currents, water splashing her face and threatening to rip her spectacles free, he sent a dinghy toward her. Every time a wave lifted her high enough to see to shore and all around, Syla looked for Vorik, refusing to believe that he'd died. He was so strong and resilient that he could have survived even a *death launcher* crafted by the gods. She was sure of it.

Besides, with water clinging to her lenses, it wasn't as if she could see well. He might have been swimming along twenty yards to her right, and she wouldn't have known him from a dolphin.

I am being threatened by these domesticated dragons who are made brave by their numbers, Wreylith said. *I will go perch on the Island of Eliok and contemplate my memories. I am* certain *that our bond should allow me access to the protected islands as long as you are on my back.*

Or dangling from your talons?

That should suffice.

I hope you can remember. I would appreciate having you here with me.

Naturally. A dragon is a powerful ally.

Undoubtedly. Thank you for plucking me up before Jhiton got me.

I will expect horn hogs and other delicacies in exchange for my assistance this morning.

As soon as I get back to Castle Island, I'll arrange it.

I am also interested in acquiring the rights to create a suitable cave.

A cave? On Castle Island?

Yes. It is not comfortable to perch for long periods of time on the roof of a castle, and it rains frequently on your island.

It's good for the crops.

My scales are moldering.

That's dreadful. When we get back, I'll get out a map and figure out what land that belongs to the royal family has caves.

My cave should have a view of the sea but be protected from the elements. North-facing isn't ideal. Too many storms roll in from that direction. I do enjoy an east-facing cave so that I might bask in the early-morning sunlight when it's not hidden behind the clouds. As I grow older, I find a sunbeam quite delicious when it seeps through my scales to warm my bones.

A wave splashed Syla in the face, and she tried to swipe water out of her eyes without knocking off her spectacles. *You've been contemplating this a while.*

It's important to look toward one's future.

Of course. I'll help you find a good home.

Syla owed Wreylith whatever she wished. The dragon may have saved her life. *Vorik* might want to kidnap Syla, but his brother clearly wanted her dead. Had Jhiton been angling for that all along? Merely humoring Vorik by suggesting a kidnapping would be acceptable? Or had something changed recently? Maybe Captain Lesva had been whining to Jhiton about how odious Syla was. She had no idea if they had any kind of relationship beyond junior officer to superior officer, and she didn't care. She hoped she never came face to face with either of them again.

"Wishful thinking," she muttered as the dinghy reached her.

Two pairs of strong arms reached down, lifting her out of the water and onto a wooden bench.

"Thank you."

"You're welcome, Your Majesty," both soldiers said.

A young one added, "We won the battle. Did you see? That was brilliant. I *love* that weapons platform."

"I've grown quite fond of it too." Syla slumped down on a wooden bench.

As the dinghy approached the *Stormslicer*, Aunt Tibby and Fel watched from the railing. Fel held a torn piece of cloth to his head and needed a healer's attention. Tibby was watching Syla warily. Because she had fired the round that might have killed— that had gone *after* Vorik? Syla wouldn't believe him dead until she saw a body.

She stirred at the realization that, yes, she *should* have seen his body if he'd been struck. He wouldn't have sunk, right? He was lean and muscular so probably didn't float *easily*, but salt water was so buoyant. She'd seen *other* bodies, after all, including those of dragons. Albeit, dragons, she was fairly certain, had some attributes of birds, such as hollow bones to make them lighter for flying. They might naturally float.

"I'm sorry, Syla." Tibby greeted her at the railing as soon as she climbed aboard. "But I had to do it. He's not... I know you like him, but he's an enemy. They all are. You have to know that."

Fel nodded firmly. "He tried to destroy the weapons platform."

"I know." Syla couldn't bring herself to say it was all right. It wasn't. Nor did she say that she more than *liked* Vorik. She hadn't admitted that to anyone, not even him. Not even herself.

A soldier came up with two coarse gray towels and offered them to her.

"Thank you." Syla bundled herself in one and draped the other over her shoulder.

"I only got a kerchief," Tibby said.

"You didn't douse yourself in the sea," Fel told her.

"It feels like I did." Tibby wiped her face and the back of her neck. "Engineers aren't meant to go into battle."

"You did well, Aunt Tibby."

Except for that last shot...

Syla didn't speak the thought aloud. Major Hixun was walking up.

"I wasn't plucked up by a dragon at least." Tibby shuddered. "I swear, if not for the scales of your red one, I wouldn't be able to tell it from the others. That wasn't the first time it plucked you up by its talons."

"*She*. Wreylith is a she. And she saved me from enemy archers."

"*She* then flung you into the ocean." Tibby clapped her hands together in a *splat* motion. "Your allies treat you similarly to your enemies."

"Wreylith can't fly through the barrier right now, so there wasn't much else she could have done."

"Flying down and placing you gently in the waves, or even on a floating bed of kelp, would have been more acceptable."

Syla didn't respond, envisioning herself hopelessly mired in kelp and drowning. Instead, she nodded to Hixun, who looked like he wanted to report.

Fel and Tibby moved away, talking about the dubious merits of dragon allies.

"Your Majesty," Hixun said. "The fleet commander wants our ship to dock and find out if the island lord and his family are safe."

"Yes. I want to know that too. And… I should speak with him." After her meeting with Lord Ravoran, Syla didn't *want* to speak with Lord Oyenar, but he shouldn't loathe her as much. She hadn't, after all, taken his island's shielder. Still, he might blame her for the attack on his city and his smoldering palace. She grimaced.

"After we ensure the area is secure, Your Majesty." Hixun looked toward the stormer ships. There was little sign of the crews. "There were men and women aboard those ships. We've seen some swimming to shore instead of out to be picked up by their dragon-rider allies." He scowled in disapproval.

"I've been told in the past that dragons can only carry two humans," Syla said, "at least for an extended distance. There were a lot more crewmen than seats available on those dragons. And…"

"They might not yet be done attacking Bogberry Island."

Syla had been thinking the same and nodded. "Especially since they haven't achieved their goal."

"Do you *know* their goal? I haven't had an opportunity to ask what you learned from questioning Captain Vorik."

Er, what *had* she learned? That tentacles rhymed with spectacles? She could have figured that out on her own, if she'd been inclined to contemplate it.

"They want the shielder here down," Syla said, as if Hixun couldn't have guessed that already. "They must have believed Lord Oyenar or maybe his wife, Abrya, know the location and could get them in. She's a moon-marked relative of mine."

"Do they? Can they? Do *you* know where it is?"

"I do, yes, and I think Abrya does. Her husband may or may not. Yes, send your men in to secure the area, please." Syla wished she could go with the troops right away, not wait. Given time, the stormers would regroup and might attack again. For all she knew, they might already *have* Oyenar and Abrya. Syla needed to find out. But it wasn't as if she could grab a sword or bow and be of assistance. "Please prioritize finding Lord Oyenar and Lady Abrya."

"Yes, Your Majesty."

Igliana reports that the Freeborn Faction dragons are being forced to leave the Island of Eliok, Wreylith said, her telepathic voice distant. She had probably already reached its shores. *While those stormer dragons battled your fleet, others were here lurking, waiting to attack as soon as that weapon was no longer close enough to protect the harbor.*

Syla slumped, feeling overwhelmed. She'd been afraid of that. Even with the weapons platform, she feared she and her people were in water far, far too deep.

~

Vorik came ashore on a rocky beach on the outskirts of the city, more than a mile from the mouth of the river. He'd retained his weapons but lost the bag of candles and drugs he'd taken from

Syla's cabin. That didn't bother him since he'd mostly wanted to ensure she couldn't use them on him if she recaptured him. Something told him she wouldn't hesitate to do so given a second opportunity.

On the beach, the air smelled of salt, seaweed, and berries he couldn't identify, something that relished growing near the ocean. Clumps of them sprouted from low bushes between buildings and dangled from the top of a bluff farther down the beach.

Body aching, Vorik made himself jog in that direction. He doubted the citizens were out clamming or searching for seashells when a battle had taken place in front of their homes, but curious eyes might be observing through windows. When he glanced back, he spotted Syla's ship tacking with the wind to zigzag up the river, fighting the current to reach the docks. Towpaths lined the waterway, but there wasn't anyone manning them at the moment.

Even from his distance, the large marble weapons platform was visible, gleaming undamaged under the afternoon sunlight. If he'd succeeded in even chipping a corner of the thing, he couldn't tell.

At least he'd survived the projectile that the aunt had tried to annihilate him with. In his mind, he'd sensed a warning from Syla, not words, but she'd somehow conveyed that he needed to dive. Immediately. If not for the warning, he wouldn't have seen the attack coming in time. It *almost* hadn't mattered. The blazing silver sphere had dived into the water right behind him. Only luck had sent him swimming past a white sturgeon as large as he. The projectile had slammed into *it* and exploded. The underwater shockwave had disoriented him, but he'd managed to stay below, holding his breath and swimming as far as he could before surfacing. He'd worried the aunt would be watching, ready to take a second shot, and had managed to come up behind one of his people's ships.

When Vorik passed the last of the homes edging the beach, he stopped with a hand on the rocky bluff to look back and debate his next move. He hadn't succeeded in kidnapping Syla, but Jhiton's choice to *shoot* at her made him reconsider the wisdom of doing so. Vorik wouldn't take her to their camp only to have the general slay her.

Storm god's wrath, why had Jhiton chosen to shoot at her anyway? Vorik had thought... Well, Jhiton had said he would protect Syla if Vorik brought her to their camp.

He spotted a dead dragon floating out beyond the barrier and answered his own question. Jhiton rarely lost his temper, but he had to be furious at how many allies—dragons and riders—they'd lost these past two days to that weapons platform.

Vorik, Jhiton spoke into his mind, as if he'd sensed Vorik wondering about him.

At first, Vorik didn't answer. Frustrated with the situation, he didn't want to speak with his brother.

Did you retrieve the queen? Jhiton added.

Her name is Syla, Vorik snapped, indignation making him answer. *You said you wouldn't let Lesva kill her if I kidnapped her, so I didn't expect* you *to loose a dozen arrows at her.*

It was four, and you had, at that point—and apparently still—failed to acquire her, so she was manning that storm-cursed giant weapon. Do you know how many dragons we've lost to it?

One arrow is all it takes to kill someone, and our dragons are invading her kingdom.

Jhiton didn't answer immediately, and Vorik expected his brother to question his allegiance, to suggest his loyalties couldn't be trusted. At that moment, Vorik didn't care.

That is true, Jhiton surprised him by saying, *and I don't fault her for defending her islands, however obnoxious it is that she's acquired that device. If I hadn't, however, kept her busy dodging arrows, she would have killed Ozlemar. She's targeted us before and was looking at us again.*

That's your fault for having a striking dragon that draws the eye.

Clearly. I'll inform Ozlemar that you find him so.

You were trying to kill *her, not make her dodge.* Vorik refused to be drawn into banter by Jhiton's dryness. He was pissed and would have punched Jhiton if he'd been on the beach.

To knock her off the weapon, Jhiton said, *and hurt her so she would be unable to continue using it, but not deliver a fatal blow. I believe I would lose my brother if I succeeded in slaying his queen.*

Vorik clenched his jaw. *She would have kept using it even if she were injured. And now the aunt knows how to use it as well.*

Yes, but she's more prone to hide underneath it.

Syla isn't.

Agreed. Her self-preservation instinct isn't as honed.

She'll risk herself for her people.

Yes. Dry again, Jhiton said, *As I stated before, I see why you like her.*

If she tries to kill you again, you'll deserve it.

I won't argue with that. Earlier, our incursion team failed to acquire the moon-marked Lady Abrya. I need you to try again to get the queen. To get Syla. We've regained Harvest Island. If we can acquire this one as well, we'll be well on our way to carving out a portion of the Kingdom for ourselves. And more. Once we have the three islands in the northern end of the chain, it'll be easier to keep them and use them to stage our troops and gain more.

You've a singular focus, Jhiton.

It's what makes me a capable military leader. I'm not distracted.

I enjoy my distractions, thank you. Vorik almost mentioned how much he'd enjoyed Syla's company the night before, but Jhiton would be underwhelmed if Vorik admitted he'd been having sex instead of putting all effort into kidnapping Syla and sabotaging the weapons platform. Or at least learning that the thing *couldn't* be sabotaged. They would have to sink the ship it was aboard.

That was doubtless what Vorik should have been doing instead of enjoying Syla's company.

"And, yet, I have no regrets," he said to a seagull eyeing him from a piece of driftwood.

Vorik pushed a hand through his wet hair, feeling bedraggled and hungry. Usually, he didn't mind the hardships of hunting, battle, and defending his people against the world, but today... today he wished he were with Syla instead of against her, with few cares in the world. Then they could relax and share a meal together, one involving a gardener dessert made with fresh fruit.

Groaning, Vorik leaned back against the rocks. The seagull squawked at him and took off.

Ozlemar and I are with the dragons back on Harvest Island, helping secure it. I'll check in with you at midnight to see if you've captured your queen. If so, we'll meet up with Agrevlari and pick you up.

Where will you—we—take her afterward?

Lesva's face floated into his mind, hard and cold. Vorik didn't want to take Syla to the new camp where the two women would be more likely to encounter each other.

To find the shielder for that island and claim it, Jhiton said.

Where is Captain Lesva?

She is also on Bogberry Island. She volunteered to take your duty of acquiring the lady to question.

Vorik's fingers curled into a fist, annoyed that Lesva always sprang in to show him up but mostly frustrated that her path might yet cross Syla's. *Has she achieved that task?*

Not yet. One of her overly exuberant troops found explosives and lit them off, causing portions of the palace in which Lady Abrya and her husband live in and govern from to collapse prematurely.

Is there a mature *time for a palace to collapse?*

After one's desired prisoner is captured and one's squadron is out.

I would hope we're not wantonly destroying things. Concerned his comment would be taken as censure for his brother's plans, Vorik added, *Especially if we intend to occupy these islands ourselves once we've won the Kingdom.*

We're more concerned about occupying the agricultural fields than the palaces. *I understand it has heated baths the size of lakes as well as underfloor pipes that warm the tiles one walks upon. Can you imagine anyone from our tribes living in such a place?*

Agrevlari would bask like a recently gorged mountain lion on a sunny ledge.

In the heated bath? Or on the floor tiles?

Both, I should think. Alternating.

So you suggest we give the palace to our dragon allies?

They've worked hard for us and made sacrifices. Especially today. They deserve heated floor tiles.

If they wish a palace, I'll gladly give it to them.

Is Lesva going to try again to get the lady? Vorik found himself walking back toward the city, urgency tightening his shoulders. Syla's ship had docked, and it made sense that she would go to see the lord and lady who ruled this island under the crown.

Yes.

What if I kidnap her first?

You're going to acquire both *women? And tote them over your shoulders like trussed hogs?*

Please, Jhiton. We've discussed my smile and its effect on women. There'll be no need for trussing. Vorik might truss *Lesva*. If only that would work.

I don't care who gets whom. I just want directions to the shielder and someone to open the magical door to whatever chamber it's stashed in.

I'll handle it, Vorik vowed. *You can call off Lesva.*

Jhiton didn't answer. He'd either been distracted or he simply wouldn't say what Vorik feared, that he *wouldn't* call off Lesva. Vorik would have to make sure he got to Syla first.

14

A KNOCK AT THE DOOR WOKE SYLA FROM THE DOZE SHE'D ALLOWED herself after the *Stormslicer* had docked. The soldiers who hadn't been sent ashore were repairing the vessel, and with bangs and thumps reverberating through the walls, she hadn't expected to fall asleep, but she'd been exhausted after using the weapons platform.

"One moment," she called after a second knock.

She opened the door to find Fel and Hixun standing in the corridor, burn marks blackening the wall behind them. Portions of the deck and hull were in bad shape as well. At least the vessel remained seaworthy.

"Your Majesty." Hixun bowed to her.

Fel peered past Syla's shoulder and into the cabin, as if he expected to find someone else. Who? Vorik?

"You never know," he grumbled, interpreting her question from the look on her face.

"I think Tibby got him," Syla said, though she didn't want it to be true.

"I *hope* she did, but I never saw him come up."

"No." Syla probably shouldn't have brightened. She did manage to keep from smiling with hope. "I thought you weren't that determined to see him dead after all the times he's helped us."

"He didn't help anything today. If he'd succeeded in blowing up the weapons platform, we would again be defenseless against dragons."

"True."

"And you said he wants to *kidnap* you."

"Yes, but that doesn't seem as bad as his brother wanting to kill me."

"You should avoid that whole family."

"I'd argue, but I suspect you're right."

"Of course I am."

Hixun cleared his throat. "Your Majesty?"

Fel stepped back, waving for the officer to speak. Meanwhile, he leaned his hands against a wall and stuck his foot out to stretch one of his calves. The battle had probably left him stiff.

"Have your men reported back, Major?" Syla guessed.

"Yes, the party we sent to the palace returned. They found Lord Oyenar, but he wouldn't go with them. His wife is injured with a broken leg and possibly other wounds, and he wouldn't leave her side."

"That's understandable."

"Yes, but our men offered to carry them both back if needed, and he told them to suck dragon balls."

"I… don't believe dragons have that anatomical feature."

"They don't, but he was pissed. From what the men gathered, a team of stormers invaded the palace while buildings in the city were being blown up, including one of the military barracks, as a distraction. They were trying to kidnap not Oyenar but his wife, Lady Abrya. He said they would have gotten her, but, during the fighting, part of the palace collapsed. The two of them were together and buried under the roof. He clawed a way out for them and said the only luck the gods sent his way was that the incursion team left when our fleet arrived." Hixun waved toward the sea where they'd battled the dragons.

"I'll get my first-aid kit so your men can take me to them." Syla turned to retrieve it from the desk.

Hixun lifted a hand. "We're working to secure the city, but our men already had a skirmish with two stormers, and we suspect there are more."

"If Lady Abrya is injured, I need to go now. It sounds like she has grievous wounds. I can promise you from past experience that having a roof fall on you isn't pleasant."

"Especially if said roof was knocked down by a dragon flicking its tail at it." Fel switched the leg he was stretching and sent a baleful look around her cabin.

"He's *not* in there," Syla told him. "And neither is his dragon."

Fel only grunted.

Hixun scratched his head but didn't comment on their exchange, other than to say, "If you wait until morning, we could have the city secure and—"

"No. I'll heal Lady Abrya and anyone else in the palace that needs it. Gather men to keep me safe as we walk there."

"Walk? I'll find men *and* a carriage."

"Queens are capable of walking," Syla said, but Hixun was already jogging off. At least he hadn't tried to lock her in her cabin to keep her aboard.

"Make it an *armored* carriage," Fel called after him. "That general could still be out there with his bow," he added to Syla.

"Ah, yes. I won't object to armor."

"Good."

I believe, Wreylith spoke into Syla's mind from afar, her telepathic voice faint, *that Queen Erasbella may have spoken a prayer to the gods or made a formal invitation while near the barrier the first time we flew to an island together. After that, it wasn't necessary, so that is why I'd forgotten, but I had to be welcomed the first time.*

How come you didn't need to be welcomed to Castle Island? Syla packed a bag as they conversed, not sure how long she would end up staying on Bogberry Island. Judging by all the smoke and destroyed buildings they'd seen, many people would need healing.

Perhaps because it is your home and that barrier knows you well.

That's not the original Castle Island barrier though. We just replaced it.

I am uncertain, then, but perhaps, crafted by the gods, the artifacts are ken to more than a mere human can understand.

Are ken? I'd never thought of the shielder artifacts as having intelligence and awareness, Syla said before recalling that the weapons platform had spoken to her, seemingly using the voice of one of the gods. She'd thought it might have been the moon god himself, but maybe it had been the artifact.

They can determine which enemies to keep out and when something dangerous is being cast through your barriers. They've some *kind of awareness.*

True. Syla knew from the historical texts that, in addition to aerial predators, the barriers had kept out the attempts of enemies to, after the invention of black powder, hurl explosives through them from their dragon mounts. Unfortunately, people *carrying* explosives were allowed through. Humans were supposed to belong on the islands. All humans.

If you cannot allow me access, I may need to leave the area completely, Wreylith said. *The stormer dragons are attempting to drive me away from the Island of Eliok.*

That's rude.

As I informed them.

If you come back over here, we can experiment, Syla said as someone knocked again.

"Your carriage is ready, Your Majesty," Fel reported through the door.

Very well, Wreylith said.

Syla secured her pack over her shoulders, but she had to double-check that she had the right one, because it seemed lighter than she expected.

"Because I didn't pack any books," she decided after confirming it held her clothing and toiletries.

After also slinging her medical kit over a shoulder, Syla stepped into the corridor. Several Royal Protectors waited to escort her, and she almost winced, feeling guilty about the men who'd died protecting her. If she hadn't been out in the open, they wouldn't have had to guard her from such a challenging position, but... what other choice had there been? Someone with a moonmark had to operate the weapons platform.

"May I carry your bags, Your Majesty?" A corporal pointed to her kit and pack.

"That's all right. Just be ready to attack enemies if anyone jumps out at me."

"Oh. Yes, Your Majesty."

"Queen Lia never let anyone carry her things either," one of the soldiers whispered to the corporal as the group headed above decks, Fel walking behind Syla.

That prompted a couple of approving nods, but one man eyed Syla and her pack with a darker expression in his eyes. She didn't know how to interpret it but reminded herself of the captain's warning about assassins.

The wooden docks along the shoreline had allowed several fleet ships space to tie up, and a couple more of their ships guarded the city from the mouth of the river. A gangplank had been extended from the *Stormslicer*, and Syla descended after the troops but paused on the dock to consider the *carriage* they directed her to.

Four horses were hitched to a wooden wagon with purple and red stains all over the interior. There weren't any benches, unless one counted the driver's seat. Pieces of metal siding—one was a sign that read *Farm Fresh*—leaned together, forming a tent in the wagon bed. A soldier waited to give her a boost inside.

"Is that a hay wagon?" Syla eyed the stains. "Or a *berry* wagon?"

"We couldn't find anything better, Your Majesty," the soldier said. "The carriage houses in the palace and also by the barracks were destroyed when the stormers attacked last night. We found this and cleaned it out the best we could and, er, armored it." He pointed at the pieces of metal leaning together.

"Yes, I can see how those would stop cannonballs and dragons."

"The dragons can't get through the barrier, and the cannons are all pointed toward the sea."

Syla debated whether the slender sheets of metal would even stop crossbow quarrels or arrows.

The soldier waved toward the mouth of the river. "Our fleet has also ensured that the stormer ships are secured, so nobody will be firing weapons. Though I understand there wasn't anyone left aboard those ships when our troops got there."

"Meaning the survivors all swam to shore and are milling about in the city?"

"Wherever they are, we'll defend you against them if they attack." The soldier lowered the tailgate with a clunk. Several cranberries rolled out and onto the dock.

"You were planning to walk," Fel pointed out when she hesitated to climb aboard.

"A fair point." Syla reached for the tailgate but paused as the soldier peered at the sky.

High above, Wreylith flew, surveying the island from beyond the barrier.

"That's your dragon ally, right, Your Majesty?" the soldier asked with a twinge of uncertainty.

"Yes. She won't bother us. She's probably scouting for us. Maybe *she* can find the missing stormers."

I've returned to this island and am nearby if you wish to experiment, Wreylith informed her. *Also, I believe I've spotted a bog bear snuffling for berries.*

I thought you might be scouting the island for our enemies.

Two bog bears! Wreylith added with excitement. *Oh, and that one is quite plump and succulent-looking. Their kind must be fattening up for the winter.*

Syla resisted the urge to suggest that a certain dragon might long to do the same thing.

"She's scouting?" Fel must have guessed from Syla's expression that she was communicating with Wreylith.

"Definitely scouting." Syla climbed into the wagon and sat cross-legged with her medical kit in her lap.

Fel and two soldiers joined her inside while the rest walked beside them as the horses pulled the wagon into the city.

While they bumped along cobblestone streets, Syla rested her palm on her moon-marked hand. *I would like to invite my dragon ally, Wreylith, to pass through the barrier,* she thought at it. She also tried to direct the thought toward the barrier above.

If anything happened, she couldn't tell. The quarter-moon birthmark didn't glow or tingle as it sometimes did when she drew upon her magic. She repeated the words, this time envisioning them being sent across the island and deep underground to where the shielder was mounted in a hidden chamber. Many years had passed since her parents had taken her to see it, but she remembered it was accessible through an abandoned section of the salt mine in Prominence Hill.

Since the mine lay miles inland, Syla didn't expect anything to come of her attempt, but her moon-mark surprised her by warming. An image of Wreylith formed in her mind, as if sent by someone—or something—and a sense of a question also formed, though she didn't hear any words.

Yes, that's my ally, Syla thought. *A dragon who is helping me keep the Kingdom safe. I believe she was here before, long ago.*

An image of a young bespectacled woman with dark hair and gray eyes formed in her mind, a roguish smirk on her lips and a sword in her hand. It took Syla a moment to recognize Queen Erasbella who, in all of her portraits, always sat demurely with needlepoint or knitting in her lap, and never with spectacles on. After reading *The Secret Life of Queen Erasbella*, Syla knew the historians had left out a lot about the queen and fudged the truth to create a figure with an appropriately royal and mature mien.

Yes, Wreylith would have been with Queen Erasbella when she came. Syla kept trying to direct her thoughts inland to the shielder, though, for all she knew, she could have been communicating with a magical toadstool.

A sense of acceptance came to her, and her moon-mark pulsed once, tingling warmly, before returning to normal.

Wreylith? I'm not positive, but I think you may be able to come through the barrier now.

I will attempt to do so.

Syla couldn't see the red dragon in the sky any longer—having a metal tent over her wagon didn't help—but she imagined Wreylith diving toward a bog bear with her fangs ready.

"As long as she shows up if we need help," Syla murmured.

Fel was peering into the streets with his hand on his mace, but he glanced at her.

"We'll find out soon, I suspect, if Wreylith is able to fly down to assist us." Syla wondered if the stormers who couldn't be found were gathered somewhere, planning a second attack. Since she knew where the shielder was, she would be a target.

"That would be helpful," Fel said.

As the wagon continued across the city and uphill from the river, Syla gazed into alleys and onto rooftops visible out the back. The wide waterway was also visible as they climbed in elevation, their surroundings changing from industrial factories and warehouses to residences that either looked toward the river or the sea. Perched on top of one of the last warehouses, a lone figure peered down at them. A lone figure in black riding leathers with tousled black hair.

Syla straightened. Was that Vorik?

Across the distance, his sharp emerald eyes met hers. She grinned. It *was* Vorik.

Relieved that the weapon hadn't gotten him, she almost waved, but she didn't want to draw attention to him. Besides, she reminded herself, he was trying to *kidnap* her. He was her enemy.

As if he could guess her thoughts, he smiled and blew her a kiss.

She stuck her tongue out at him.

Fel noticed and followed her gaze, but Vorik had ducked out of view. "What are you doing?"

"Wreylith may be hunting bog bears instead of joining us promptly," Syla said, though that probably wasn't a suitable explanation for her tongue gesture.

Fel squinted at her, but someone called out for the wagon to halt, and it rolled over something that made the wheels wobble, then pulled to a stop. They had reached the gates for the palace. One of those gates had been ripped off and lay in the street. It was what they'd rolled over.

"It looks like *dragons* helped with this attack," Syla said as she climbed out and eyed the destruction, "but that's not possible, right? The barrier was up."

"The dragon *riders* are formidable foes," a soldier said from the side. "Welcome, Your Majesty."

The soldier wasn't one of hers. He wore the maroon uniform of the palace guard. Abrasions and bruises darkened his face, and his hair was matted with blood, but he stood in the gateway, weapons in hand.

"Last night, I was on duty when a female with silver hair ripped the gate off, as if the hinges were made from twine instead of iron. And she did *that*." The guard pointed across the courtyard toward what should have been the grand entryway of the palace, but the carved doors had been torn from their hinges and smashed against the marble stairs. Those stairs were cracked, as if the gods had hurled lightning bolts at them. Or an irritated rider with a gargoyle-bone sword had employed all her strength and magic on them…

"I've witnessed the power of the riders bonded with dragons," Syla said, remembering Vorik's broken shackles.

Silver hair—that had to be Captain Lesva. Her dragon was dead, but maybe the magic from her bond would linger for a time.

The guard shuddered, then whispered, "That woman threw me across the courtyard as if I were a toddler."

"Dragon!" someone called in alarm from one of two towers framing the palace rooftop.

A magnificent red dragon with what looked like purple berry stains on her belly soared over the city, heading in Syla's direction.

"She's an ally!" she called to the guards in the yard and in the towers. Silently, she asked Wreylith, *Did you visit a bog on your way here? One full of ripe berries?*

I visited the bog bears *on my way. The fat one I caught ran through the brambles, flinging berries everywhere, but I caught it, and it was as delicious as I'd hoped. Hunting here will be glorious. Will you stay many days? Perhaps weeks?*

Probably not weeks. Syla still had shielder components to acquire.

But days.

We'll see. I'm honored that you took time away from your hunt to come check on me.

I ate my fill. For now. Should you need assistance, I will provide it. Wreylith alighted on the roof of one of the towers.

"That's probably not an architectural ornament the island lord ever wanted on his palace," Fel muttered.

"She's magnificent and beautiful, and she's helping us with our problems," Syla said. "He should have an ornamental carving made in her likeness. Many carvings. They could go all over the roof and improve the aesthetic."

"Is that berry juice staining your dragon's scales?"

Syla hadn't thought the purple splotches that noticeable, but her bodyguard had keener eyes than she.

She shrugged. "I understand there are bog bears on this island and that they're delicious."

"Her dinner must have put up a fight in the middle of berry-covered brambles."

"Dragons like a challenge, I understand."

A guard jogged out of the palace, using a side door instead of coming across the battered main threshold. "Your Majesty! You've come."

She didn't recall having met the guard before, but few people had ever looked at her with such relief.

"And you're a healer. A gods-gifted healer." The guard looked at her moon-mark. "The lord and lady need your help."

Syla nodded. "Take me to them, please."

"Yes, Your Majesty."

Will you wait here and keep watch? Syla asked Wreylith as she followed the guard toward the palace entrance, Fel and several Royal Protectors surrounding her.

Yes, but you must be careful.

Syla had already reached the doorway but paused. *Do you sense a threat in the palace?*

She remembered Vorik crouching on the rooftop and had no doubt the stormers planned to strike again.

I sense several humans with the power of dragon bonds in underground warrens beneath the city.

You mean the stormwater runoff tunnels? And you said several?

Several.

That was more than Vorik then. Or was Vorik being counted at all? Maybe Wreylith sensed Lesva and the team that had decimated the palace.

How far away are they? Syla looked around the courtyard, glad she didn't see any stormwater drains among the flagstones and gardens insides its walls, but with the gate broken down and only mundane men out here to fight the powerful riders, it wouldn't matter if Lesva's team came up outside of the palace grounds.

Perhaps two miles. You should hurry.

Grim, Syla hurried through the doorway. *I will.*

~

Vorik crouched on a rooftop as troops marched past below in the gray uniforms of Kingdom Enforcers. He'd also spotted men and women from the Royal Fleet searching the streets for intruders. Intruders like him.

So far, Vorik had been able to avoid the troops, but he doubted he would be able to slip into the palace and find Syla and Lady Abrya before nightfall. He was glad he'd spotted Syla heading in that direction so he knew where she was, but he'd been bemused to see her riding in a rickety fruit wagon. He'd also been surprised when she'd noticed him—or maybe she'd *sensed* him with her power—hidden on the rooftop. Nobody else had picked him out yet.

Maybe we're now inextricably linked because of our growing feelings for each other, Vorik mused to Agrevlari.

With nowhere to perch, the dragon had flown back to Harvest Island, but the distance wasn't so great that they couldn't communicate. *Are you speaking of the queen you attempted to kidnap? Do you not believe her feelings might be on the* wane?

Probably not because of that. She might be irked that I tried to blow up her weapons platform.

On behalf of all dragons, I regret that you did not succeed.

Me too.

I long to link with and share growing feelings with Wreylith, but with Wingleader Saleetha yelling into my mind and roaring at me, I was forced to attack her.

I saw that, Vorik said. *You even drew blood.*

That was because she attacked back, and my instincts took over. I am relieved she escaped the confrontation though she battled superior numbers. She remains magnificent.

But unwilling to speak with you?

A faint clink reached Vorik's ears, distracting him from Agrevlari's response. With troops marching about, there were many noises in the city, but that had come from the ground nearby, a narrow cobblestone alley beside the building he perched upon. He hadn't thought anyone was in it and crept to the edge of the roof to peek down, half-expecting to find a stray dog nosing at garbage bins.

But the alley was devoid of animals. Aside from a few scraps of rubbish, nothing occupied it except a metal grate over an opening that stormwater presumably ran into to be diverted to the river. Since his people didn't build permanent towns, Vorik knew little of such infrastructure, but stormer spies sometimes moved about Kingdom cities via the underground passageways. Might there be tunnels leading to that palace? Maybe he could reach Syla more easily using a subterranean route.

Agrevlari's words about his actions possibly making her feelings wane made Vorik hesitate to check out the grate. He worried there was truth to them. How many times could he impede Syla or outright act against her and expect that she would continue to care for him? When their gazes had met, her initial expression of delight had warmed his heart, but it had quickly faded to suspicion and wariness.

Another clink sounded, followed by a scrape-clunk. The grate moved aside, and a man stuck his head out.

Vorik blinked. That was Yevlor from Moonhunt Tribe. And he waved to someone back down in the darkness. Gavartash from Vorik's tribe, from his own wing, rose up and peered out. Had they been sent in as part of the incursion team that had lit fires and destroyed buildings? What were they up to now?

They ducked back into the darkness below the cobblestones, but they didn't replace the grate.

Vorik made sure no guards were tramping through the street out front, then hopped down into the alley.

"Hello?" he called softly through the opening, not wanting to startle armed men and capable warriors.

"Hello?" came a curious reply. It sounded like Yevlor.

"Is it a soldier?" Gavartash whispered.

"They don't call down *hello* before they attack us," Yevlor whispered back.

"Your faces don't inspire cozy warmth in people the way mine does," Vorik said.

After a long pause, Gavartash asked, "Captain Vorik?"

Vorik grabbed the edge and swung down into a dark tunnel, landing with a splash in six inches of water. The air was close, dark, and dank, with the only light coming through the opening above. It provided enough illumination for Vorik to make out the two men, and did he hear more mutterings farther back in the tunnel? Around a bend that he spotted? Yes, and he even sensed someone with magic back there. Someone familiar.

He sighed. Captain Lesva hadn't yet lost any power from the

death of her dragon. She might retain it for months. If another dragon deigned to link with her—after all, dragons *liked* ruthless ambition, and she had plenty of that—she might never lose her power.

"My mother likes my face all right." Gavartash looked Vorik up and down, his expression more wary than inviting, and there wasn't any humor in his eyes.

His gaze shifted toward the opening, as if he expected someone else to follow Vorik down. Who else would be with him? Syla?

Not yet...

"I'm alone," Vorik said, "with only my mission to keep me warm."

"What mission is that, sir?" Gavartash rested a hand on the sword in a scabbard hanging from his belt. "You attacked Captain Lesva in front of everyone, and she was trying to destroy that terrible weapon."

"She was trying to kill Queen Syla. Since I have orders to kidnap her, I had to stop Lesva." Vorik glanced toward the dark bend, but the sounds from that direction had quieted, and Lesva, though he still sensed her, hadn't come forward.

"We needed to sink that ship, sir," Gavartash said. "Destroy that weapon. The queen... Storm god's wrath, we can't *kidnap* her. She's dangerous. Remember what Devron said? She almost *choked* him to death. Just by touching him."

Vorik grimaced at the reminder that Syla had the power to hurt—to kill. She'd done more than constrict the airway of the assassin who'd tried to slay her in the wheelhouse of that whaling ship. The man had been dead at her feet. It was hard for Vorik to imagine sweet Syla the healer hurting anyone, but she could. Abruptly, he felt presumptuous about saying, when they'd been in bed, that she had been *his* captive instead of the other way around.

She hadn't minded, but he couldn't pretend that was true, that he had the upper hand with her.

"The queen should be killed and that ship sunk," Gavartash said when Vorik didn't answer right away. "That's what Captain Lesva wants to do."

"I have orders to kidnap the queen. She has a moon-mark and knows where the shielders are." Yes, those *were* the reasons Vorik had given to change his brother's mind on what to do with Syla...

"Others have moon-marks. She's too dangerous."

"I didn't ask your opinion, Gavartash. Take me to Lesva, and I'll discuss it with her." With his sword drawn, most likely. Vorik braced himself to face her.

But Gavartash didn't walk off. Instead, his hand strayed again to *his* sword. "She doesn't want to see you, sir. Earlier, she was suggesting that your wing should have a new leader."

"Are you going to challenge me for command of it?" Vorik wondered if Lesva had put Gavartash up to this confrontation. The kid had only been a rider for two years and wasn't bonded with a dragon. He was a talented fighter, but he hadn't previously said or done anything to suggest he wanted to challenge Vorik.

"We don't think you're making good decisions for the tribe or our people." Gavartash looked at Yevlor.

"Don't include me in this," Yevlor whispered. "Lesva wasn't rubbing *my* shoulder and getting me excited and ambitious."

"It wasn't my *shoulder* that she rubbed." Gavartash stepped back and drew his sword.

Despite saying he didn't want to be involved, Yevlor also drew his sword and faced Vorik.

"You're not offering a duel or a proper challenge?" Vorik rolled onto the balls of his feet, prepared for a fight, though he didn't want it and didn't yet draw his blades. "By the code, only one man may challenge another at a time."

"We'd be foolish to challenge you solo," Gavartash said. "And this isn't about the code. It's about doing what's right for our people."

"And satisfying the woman who's rubbing something of yours?" Vorik didn't want to fight his own men, and it bothered him that their concern about his leadership wasn't unfounded. But he hadn't yet gone against Jhiton, and that was who they should be looking to for guidance, not Lesva. *Lesva* should have come forward to challenge Vorik personally if she wanted to get rid of him.

"I'm doing this for our people," Gavartash said firmly.

Yevlor rolled his eyes but didn't correct his comrade. He was the first to move, flicking his sword in a feint toward the side of Vorik's neck.

Mindful of the tight confines of the tunnel and a wall behind him, Vorik leaped sideways, the water splashing under his feet, and drew his sword and dagger. He recognized the feint for what it was and didn't bother deflecting it, suspecting that Gavartash was the main threat.

Yes, the man lunged in while his comrade sent a second feint toward Vorik's hip. Vorik deflected both attacks, his eyes sharp enough to see the blades in the dim lighting. Further, after so many battles in his life, he sensed and anticipated the men's attacks. It helped that they were his own people, fighting with familiar combinations and patterns of stabs and slashes, attacks that Vorik had helped ingrain in them.

Weapons clashed, echoing loudly in the enclosed space. Not wanting the noise to draw the city's guards, and aware of others around the bend, Vorik summoned his magic to give him greater speed so that he could end the confrontation quickly. With a sweep of his dagger, he deflected an attack from Yevlor, then stabbed him in the back of the hand. The man cried out, dropping his sword into the water.

Gavartash tried to take advantage of the distraction, but Vorik parried his combination of thrusts and slashes without taking his eyes from the man's face. Movement in his peripheral vision warned Vorik of others coming, and he launched a rapid series of attacks of his own.

Since Yevlor was close to finding his sword in the water, Vorik kicked him back even as he focused his blades on Gavartash. The man managed to parry two blows but stumbled back and bumped into the tunnel wall, and the third attack slid in, knocking his sword away to disarm him. Before Gavartash could scramble away, Vorik pressed his dagger to the man's throat, using it to pin him against the wall. He turned his sword toward the oncoming troops.

Captain Lesva, her own sword drawn, slowed to a stop, but a female rider at her side fired a crossbow. Without removing his dagger from Gavartash's throat, Vorik ducked. The quarrel whizzed over his head and landed with a fleshy thud. Yevlor grabbed his shoulder as he spun away, stumbling and splashing in the water again.

"Idiot," Lesva snarled, pushing the woman's arm down.

"You said—"

"To kill him, yes," Lesva said, her icy eyes locked on Vorik, "but not to shoot in an enclosed space with our men nearby."

"To kill me, Lesva? After all we've been through? I'm wounded. Though not as wounded as some." Vorik glanced at Yevlor, not wanting an angry and injured man at his back, but Yevlor had abandoned trying to find his sword and backed to the storm-drain entrance. He slumped against the wall with his hand to his wounded shoulder.

"I'm sorry, sir," Yevlor ground out through clenched teeth. "I didn't want to."

Sword clenched in a hard and frustrated grip, Lesva stopped a few paces from Vorik. She didn't look surprised to see him. Had she seen him on the rooftop earlier and intentionally brought her team close? Yes, this probably hadn't been a chance meeting. But what had she intended? To attack Vorik while he'd been distracted fighting the other two men? She must have known Gavartash wasn't a match for him, but she had a lot of troops with her. Did they *all* want Vorik dead?

Other than the rider at Lesva's side, a lieutenant from Moonhunt Tribe who'd probably been loyal to the captain for years, the others hung back. Soldiers and riders from a number of tribes, they hadn't yet drawn weapons. But when Vorik's gaze skimmed over them, few met his eyes.

"You should be executed for the choices you've made," Lesva said. *She* had no trouble meeting his eyes. "The choices you've let your *penis* make." She looked in disgust at his crotch.

Vorik sighed, not interested in getting into that with her again. "As I was telling our riders, I've orders to kidnap Queen Syla and Lady Abrya."

"So do I," Lesva said. "The queen is here in the city, isn't she? We know she left her ship. Is she going to the palace?"

If Lesva didn't know that, Vorik wouldn't tell her. "She and Lady Abrya apparently both know where this island's shielder is and have moon-marks," was what he said. "If we can capture them both, Jhiton believes we can get past the mental defenses of at least one and learn its location." His brother hadn't *exactly* said that, but using his name might help Vorik get through to Lesva. "If we work together instead of against each other, it'll be easier."

"You've been working against me ever since you met *her*," Lesva growled.

"You've chosen to be obsessed with her. You're not obeying Jhiton's orders."

"Your *brother* is giving you far too much lenience in these matters. The queen must be killed."

"The *queen* has a moon-mark and knows where the shielders are."

"That's *not* what you care about, Vorik. You want to keep her alive so you can keep sinking your cock into her."

The soldiers glanced at each other or studied the ceiling and the walls, all looking like they wanted to be elsewhere. Anywhere else.

Vorik caught himself clenching his fist around his sword hilt. It wasn't appropriate to argue and be disrespectful in front of the troops, and he didn't allow himself to respond in kind.

"She's too valuable to kill," he stated. "I'm going to kidnap her and Lady Abrya. Per my orders. You can help me or work against me."

"I'm not helping you get laid and endanger our people, and you can find your own tunnel to the palace. You're not invited along with us."

Lesva eyed his sword, as if she was tempted to attack him even though her distraction had failed, but maybe she'd had enough of battling him. Thus far, she hadn't managed to come out on top. She turned her back and strode toward the bend in the tunnel, presumably having been in the city long enough to know a route that would take her to the palace.

The female rider walked at her side, not hesitating, but many of the other troops exchanged uncertain looks. Hopefully, that meant they hadn't all passed a similar judgment on Vorik.

He looked at them and raised his chin. "I'm following the general's orders instead of wandering off on my own self-imposed mission. If any of you want to come with me, I'll gladly accept you. There's a lot of work to be done."

"A lot of women to be kidnapped?" Gavartash muttered.

"It'll be dangerous, and there's a dragon and that weapons platform to contend with as well. For those involved in succeeding at this mission, it'll be glorious. And it'll help our people."

Lesva paused to scowl back at him. "Nobody's going with you, traitor. Come on, men."

Vorik spread his arms. He wouldn't mind skulking about the city and trying to accomplish his goals alone—it might be easier that way—so he wouldn't push hard to lure the men to his side. Besides, if nobody came with him, he would discover with unsettling clarity how his people felt about him, what his reputation had become. But it would be better to know than not know.

Surprisingly, Yevlor moved first, coming to stand beside Vorik. With a crossbow quarrel in his shoulder, he wouldn't be much help, but this was less about gaining men to employ in battle and more about... figuring out where the tribe stood.

After glancing warily at Vorik, Gavartash walked after Lesva. Several other men, however, slipped past her to join Vorik. She glared daggers at them.

In the end, two-thirds of her forces joined him. Yevlor was the only one from Lesva's tribe who left her, and it was probably more because his ally had *shot* him, but, aside from Gavartash, none from Vorik's tribe abandoned him, and he gathered most of the people from the other tribes.

Lesva hissed in disgust and punched Gavartash in the shoulder instead of welcoming him with open arms, then stalked off down the tunnel.

"He's not going to get as much rubbed tonight as he thinks," Yevlor said.

"He might have if he'd succeeded," someone said.

"Killing Captain Vorik isn't easy," another man said. "Only a dummy would try."

"Are we going to the palace, sir? There might be another tunnel that goes that way."

Vorik imagined two teams of stormers trying to sneak separately into a palace full of guards and with a dragon perched on the roof. Given Lesva's tension, the stormers would be as likely to end up fighting each other. All Vorik *really* wanted was Syla. Yes, he'd promised Jhiton that he would also retrieve the lady, but if he got Syla, wouldn't that be enough? She knew not only about this island's shielder but the locations of *all* the shielders.

But Syla was heading in the same direction as Lesva. Unless... Vorik scratched his jaw. Maybe he could lure her back to her fleet. To the ship with the weapons platform. She would come to defend it if it was under attack, wouldn't she? And if she returned to the docks, she wouldn't be there when Lesva arrived in the palace.

"I have another plan," Vorik said.

"What's that, sir?" a man asked warily. Thinking of Lesva's comments about why Vorik wanted to get Syla and worried he'd made the wrong choice?

"Who wants to help me sink that weapons platform?" he asked, sure none of them would object, not after they'd lost friends and dragons.

"Oh, yes," came a relieved statement. More than one.

Vorik nodded. "Follow me, men."

15

The island lord's palace was almost as large and sprawling as the castle back home, and Syla brimmed with impatience as the guard led her, Fel, and the Royal Protectors through marble-floored hallways laid with blue runners. They passed destroyed statues and busts, as well as artwork that had been ripped from the walls, the work of annihilation-loving humans rather than dragons. It was a reminder that people could be as savage as the ruthless predators.

Though the sights distressed Syla, it wasn't until they reached an infirmary that she lost her temper. The door had been blown open, and tools, beds, and equipment were strewn about, many destroyed and all covered in soot.

"Those animals!" Syla stumbled and gripped the doorjamb. "Did they hurl an *explosive* in here?"

"You didn't mind the rest of the destruction, but a slight to the infirmary is worth an outcry?" Fel poked her in the shoulder and pointed after the guard, who hadn't stopped his trek.

"A *slight*? It looks like drunken yetis swatting at wasps rampaged through there."

"This way, Your Majesty." The guard had reached stairs heading upward and waved for them to come.

Syla forced aside her affront and hurried to catch up. "We're taking a long way, aren't we?"

It had been more than a decade since she'd visited the palace, so her memory of it was fuzzy.

"Yes. My apologies for the circuitous route," the guard said as they climbed. "The main stairs collapsed under the roof. One of their explosives dropped on it. Or was intentionally *set* in that spot. That's where the lord and lady were when the roof came down."

"We're lucky the stormers don't use explosives more often," Syla said.

"They don't have the capacity to make them," Fel said. "If they've got them now, it's because someone gave them to them."

"Or they took them from one of our armories? They've had access to Harvest Island for weeks."

"True. We're lucky they haven't thought to hurl them through the barriers."

"That's been tried in the past, at least according to the history books. I don't know if black powder had been discovered yet when the gods walked the world, but they probably anticipated attempts to get dangerous weapons through. Explosives apparently blow up on contact." Syla slowed when the guard stopped in front of another uniformed man standing in front of double doors that were *leaned* closed instead of truly closed. No doubt because the hinges were warped or gone completely. Soot covered the wall opposite the doors.

"How come *arrows* can get through the barrier?" Fel touched his hip. Had one of his own wounds come in that manner?

"Maybe the gods thought you would be fast enough to move out of the way if you saw an arrow coming from a mile up in the sky."

Fel looked sourly at her. "It's the arrows you *don't* see coming that you have to worry about."

A woman's pained moan came from within the suite as the guards moved one of the heavy doors aside.

"She's here," the guard called into the room before stepping inside.

There were probably more armed guards inside protecting the lord and lady.

"The healer?" a man asked. "Send her in."

Syla hadn't spoken with Lord Oyenar for several years but recognized his voice. Though he was in his sixties, it remained firm and authoritative. She recalled that he'd been a high-ranking Fleet officer before retiring to serve.

"Yes, my lord. It's the healer who came in person with a fleet of ships and stood on a great weapon of the gods to fire magical projectiles that struck and killed *dragons*." The surprisingly enthusiastic guard curled his fingers into a thank-the-gods circle in front of his heart and waved for Syla to go in.

"That... doesn't sound like any of our usual healers," Oyenar said.

"I believe she's from Castle Island," one of the guards inside said, smiling.

Lord Oyenar, a white-haired man with a broad jaw and eyebrows like caterpillars, sat in a chair beside a four-poster bed and held his wife's hand. She lay under a blanket, dyed red hair sprawled around her face on a pillow, and a pair of spectacles on the bedside table. Her eyes didn't open, but Oyenar's bushy brows rose in surprise when Syla entered.

"Princess Syla," he blurted. "*Queen* Syla. I'd heard..." He waved to the guard who'd done the introduction. "That's what I heard, but I didn't expect you to come personally into the city. It's dangerous right now." He grimaced, as if its state represented a failing on his part. "You shouldn't have risked— I don't even understand why you're sailing about with the fleet. I am grateful that you brought the ships, and I suppose your mother would have come with them too, but you're..."

"Here to heal Lady Abrya." With her medical kit in hand, Syla walked to the bed.

"I do appreciate that. Gessa—the healer who usually handles injuries and ailments among the palace staff—was also injured. Even if she hadn't been, she doesn't have the gods-gift." He waved at Syla's hand.

"Few healers do. Since your wife isn't fully conscious, I'll ask your permission to use my magic to heal her."

"You have it."

"You're aware that it may leave her feeling kindly inclined and possibly beholden to me for a time?"

"That's fine. She's rarely beholden to me so it'll be good for her to be beholden to someone." Oyenar smiled, though his brow creased with concern as he glanced at his wife.

"I'll take care of her," Syla promised.

He nodded and relinquished his seat, letting Syla sit down to clasp Abrya's hand. She appeared unconscious but moaned softly at the touch. Oyenar winced and walked to a window, limping and rubbing his thigh. Two of his guards joined him, their view over the courtyard walls and toward the river. From the palace's elevated position in the city, they could probably see to the docks and maybe out to sea.

More concerned about her patient than the view, Syla set down her medical kit and closed her eyes to use her magic to examine Lady Abrya.

I'll be distracted while I heal this woman, she told Wreylith, sensing the dragon remained on the rooftop, *but let me know if the stormers get into the palace, please. If you have to yell into my brain to get my attention, that's fine.*

A dragon has no trouble speaking in a firm tone. Yes, when

Wreylith was this close, her telepathic voice had a tendency to boom.

I have noticed that.

One does not want a soft-spoken or meek ally.

Certainly not.

Abrya had the broken leg that had been reported, as well as a concussion and numerous other fractures and blunt traumas. Choosing the most dire injury to start on, Syla willed tendrils of magic into her patient to repair flesh and bone. She was glad to use her power on what it was meant for, healing not harming.

Though she sometimes fell into a trance to heal, the peril hanging in the air must have made her awareness want to remain present, for she found herself able to hear the men conversing at the window while she worked.

"I didn't expect Syla to come herself," Oyenar said softly.

"From what I've heard," one of his men said, "she's the one who retrieved that weapon from the desert and knows how to use it."

"Yes," another said. "She was always so quiet when she came with the family. I didn't realize. Well, I'm glad she's here."

"*I'm* glad she brought ships and drove the stormers away," Oyenar said. "They're up to something. More than a few random attacks. They have to be after our shielder. They want Bogberry Island, the same as Harvest."

"Oh, no doubt, my lord. Do you know where... Er, it's safe, right? The shielder? The stormers couldn't have learned..."

"Only my wife knows the location, yes. And I suppose Queen Syla must. The stormers shouldn't have a clue."

The men fell silent, and Syla focused on her task. She had no idea when the stormers would breach the palace and if Captain Lesva would be with them, but she expected to have to face that awful woman again, and she dreaded it.

Healing, fortunately, came easily to her, and she managed to work, despite the intrusion of distracting thoughts. She'd finished healing Abrya's concussion and broken femur and was focusing on cracked ribs, the lady stirring a little and her sighs less pained now, when a new voice spoke from the door.

"Erm, Lord Oyenar? Did you know... Well, there's a dragon on the roof."

"That's Queen Syla's dragon," Fel said, as if Syla could claim or *control* Wreylith.

She hoped Wreylith wasn't threatening anyone. Of course, if the red dragon ate a few stormers trying to sneak in, that would be acceptable.

"I'd heard about that," Oyenar said from the window, "when minor lord Axton sent a message from Castle Island full of gossip and asking if I planned to support her appointment as queen or if I was interested in backing someone more *experienced*."

"Yes, my lord," the man in the doorway said, "but he didn't mention—er, I don't think anyone mentioned—that this dragon of hers can pass through barriers. *Our* barrier."

"We knew she was able to on Castle Island," Oyenar said.

"But here, my lord? Is she a threat? She's, uh, looming."

"Let her loom. Maybe she'll keep the stormers away."

Syla hoped so.

A roar floated through the closed window. That had to be Wreylith.

Problem? Syla asked telepathically.

A crossbowman touched his weapon while looking at me.

And you let him know that's unacceptable?

Precisely.

Did he move his hand away from the weapon?

He ran into a stable. I believe after he wet himself.

If he's in that state, I guess it doesn't matter if his hand is on his crossbow or not.

Likely not, Wreylith said. *The rider I sensed with the power of a dragon bond is nearby now. She seems to be underground. I left to fly circles and attempt to locate her and was unable to see her in the area where I sensed her.*

It's Captain Lesva, I trust? Syla's dread returned.

I do not know the names of insignificant humans, but I can tell she is female and, when compared to the other puny members of your kind, powerful. I believe she is the one who attacked you on the deck of your ship. With the death launcher, you slew her dragon ally.

Yes, she won't be happy with me.

Indeed not. The slaying of a dragon ally is an unforgivable crime. Something about Wreylith's tone suggested that a human slaying *any* dragon was unforgivable.

I would prefer not to attack your kind. You're magnificent and beautiful and not a threat to the Kingdom when our shields are in place. But I must defend my islands.

I am aware. And we are *beautiful and magnificent but not so shallow as to favor humans simply because they flatter us.*

I would never think to do so to win your favor, Syla said.

That is wise.

I would deliver delicious livestock instead.

I approve of the plan to create a horn-hog farm. Perhaps it can be located near the cave lair I desire to establish.

That does seem the logical location for one, though it may be difficult to keep it populated with horn hogs.

Abrya stirred, her eyelids flickering for the first time. Her bleary gray-blue eyes fixed on Syla without recognition.

"Do you need your spectacles?" Syla asked, though enough years had passed since her last visit that she wasn't surprised that Abrya didn't remember her right away.

"Usually," she rasped.

Syla handed them to her and also offered a cup of water.

"Lord Oyenar?" She waved for him to come over. "Your wife is awake."

Oyenar joined them, sitting on the edge of the bed. "You look beleaguered and disheveled, my lady."

"Yes, but after I heal, I at least won't be haggard and pot-bellied."

"As I've informed you on many occasions, I like to store fat in my belly in case famine ever comes to the islands."

"As of last night's dinner, you were storing cranberry tarts and hazelnut cookies in there."

"I'm relieved the blow to your head didn't affect your memory," Oyenar said. "A roof fell on you, you know."

"I did see it coming down, yes. It was rude of you not to fling yourself atop me to nobly protect me."

"I did try, but age is catching up with me, and I'm not as fast as I used to be."

"It could be cranberry tarts slowing you down."

"I suppose that's possible." Oyenar reached over to Syla and clasped her hand. "Thank you. It's been dreadful not having anyone to tease and torment me this past day and night." His words were warm, and his eyes twinkled as he looked at his wife.

"He must have been terribly bereft," Abrya said, then squinted thoughtfully at Syla, a hint of recognition kindling in her eyes. "You're Princess Syla."

"*Queen* Syla," Oyenar said, though he'd also forgotten her title at first.

With the coronation so recent, it would take people time to grow familiar with it. And not everyone *wanted* to become familiar with it. Syla hadn't missed Oyenar's comment about one of the minor lords back home hesitating to accept the succession, and she remembered Relvin skulking around the castle with his aristocratic dice-playing comrades.

"Oh, yes. I'm sorry I didn't recognize you right away, especially since we're relatives." Abrya smiled, but it faded as she considered

Syla. "You've changed though. And you're not wearing a healer's robe, like you usually do."

"No, though maybe I *should* be wearing one. Fewer people and dragons might try to kill me."

No dragon has any concern about what garments a human wears. Back to perching on the rooftop, Wreylith was monitoring the conversation.

"Kill you?" Abrya asked.

"Even as we speak. A stormer invasion force including at least one bonded rider with enhanced abilities is in the tunnels under the palace and could attack at any moment."

Oyenar blinked and looked at Syla. "How do you know that?"

"A powerful ally with keen eyes and senses told me."

Abrya looked at Fel.

"Not him," Syla said and pointed upward. "Though his eyes are keen compared to mine."

Oyenar looked at her thick lenses but didn't say what he was probably thinking, that *most* people's eyes were keener than hers. Alas, true.

"Wreylith, the red dragon up there, is working with me," Syla told Abrya, who'd been unconscious when the guard had reported Wreylith's presence.

"Someday, you'll have to explain to us how you managed to wrangle the assistance of a dragon. They generally like to *eat* people." Oyenar rose and waved for his guards to come into the room.

"They're predators and enjoy a little wanton destruction here and there, but Wreylith assures me that humans aren't tasty," Syla said. "She prefers eliok, sheep, and horn hogs, the latter of which I believe I've promised to populate a farm with."

"Horn hogs aren't easily domesticated," Abrya said. "They don't get along well with humans or other animals, and those horns are sharp."

"Yes, but I understand they're delicious so I'll have to find a way to make it work."

Near the cave lair I will claim, Wreylith said.

Certainly. Then if there's trouble at the horn-hog farm, you'll be nearby to put an end to it. To them.

Oh, yes. If a dragon could telepathically purr into a person's mind, Wreylith did.

Oyenar had turned his attention to the guards. "Silor, Hilks, tell everyone to be alert, and check the storm drain grates in the courtyard. That's the only way people could get into the palace from below. They're very strong and locked to ensure that doesn't happen, but if someone were enhanced..."

"Yes, my lord."

Two guards remained after the pair ran off to relay Oyenar's orders.

As Abrya eased her legs out of bed and looked around for clothes, Oyenar considered Syla.

"Do you know what the stormers want? When they came last night, they didn't make any requests or take anything. They seemed happy just to destroy things." Frowning, Oyenar looked toward Abrya. "Including our *roof*."

"I believe it was an *anyone* they were trying to take." Syla extended a hand toward his wife. "You may have thwarted their plans by being buried under the roof."

"How fortunate for us," Abrya murmured, her hand straying to her leg.

"The invaders in the city disappeared when your ships were sighted and started shooting silver balls at their dragons." Oyenar pointed toward the sea.

"Unfortunately, the weapon isn't ideal for attacking people, and it would have done damage if I'd tried to send rounds into the city," Syla said. "More damage than the stormers had already done."

"Oh, I didn't expect you'd turn it toward us, any more than you would a cannon, but I was glad you came and used it on the stormers. Any blows we can strike to those bastards..." Oyenar nodded firmly at her.

"Yes." Syla found herself liking the man—and that he'd sounded disapproving when he'd spoken of minor lord Axton mentioning the possibility of other candidates for the throne.

A boom came from the courtyard. Fel came to stand beside Syla, his mace in hand as he placed himself where he could monitor the doorway and the windows.

"If any of your men need healing, Lord Oyenar," Syla said, "bring them in here. I'm not a combatant, but I'll do my best to help."

He nodded at her.

Syla debated what she would do if Lesva charged in to kill her. She didn't know, but she grabbed her medical kit and pulled out a scalpel and a couple of vials of astringent substances that she could throw in a person's eyes. She would at least try to do *something* to the rider captain.

Fel watched her but didn't tease her about the tiny weapons. He nodded, as if he agreed with the sentiment, then rotated his shoulder and lifted his leg to stretch his quadriceps. One never wanted to go into battle stiff, after all.

Another boom sounded, this time from the grounds at the back of the palace. Syla had a feeling the supposedly strong and locked storm grates were no longer secured.

"Brace yourself," she murmured to Fel.

Fel lowered his leg. "Always."

16

Vorik, with almost two dozen trained warriors crouched around him, stood in the shadows of a house upriver from the docks and most of the city. In addition to the *Stormslicer* and a few other Kingdom ships tied up along the dock, four were anchored out at sea near the remains of the stormer vessels. His people's already-destroyed ships looked like they'd received a few more cannonballs to the hulls since Vorik had seen them last, and he doubted anyone remained aboard. The men and women with him would have to figure out another way home, but if Jhiton was successful and lowered the shield and claimed the island, it would be easy for dragons to pick up people—or assist them in gathering more winter provisions from the bogs and fields.

"What's the plan, sir?" Yevlor crouched beside him, a makeshift bandage around his shoulder and the crossbow quarrel removed.

Another man pointed at a corner of the weapons platform visible from their vantage point.

Vorik nodded. "We're going to sink that ship and that thing with it."

"Isn't there a way to destroy it?"

"I dropped an explosive on it earlier, and it didn't even nick it, but if it's on the bottom of the river, the Kingdom won't be able to use it."

Probably. Vorik envisioned the determined Syla swimming down to plant her hands on the posts and fire at enemies while holding her breath. He probably shouldn't have smiled at the notion.

"What a weapon," Yevlor said. "Too bad *we* don't have one."

"We have dragons," Vorik said.

"Not in here." Yevlor waved toward the sky above, though they couldn't see the translucent barrier.

"We'll get them here eventually." Vorik eyed a couple of kayaks on a gravel beach in front of the house. He'd chosen to reconnoiter from the spot because there'd been no sign of anyone home, but now he wondered if he might borrow one of those craft. "In the meantime, I want that ship sunk. In fact, let's attack all the ships docked there. Take brands and set them aflame. I want there to be a lot of smoke."

Yevlor looked curiously at him.

Vorik didn't explain that he hoped Syla would see the smoke from the palace and hurry back so he could kidnap her. Besides, Vorik hadn't yet figured out how he would slip away with her while Wreylith was flying around the area. Bloody daggers, Syla might even return on the dragon's back.

Since none of that was what the men cared about, Vorik said, "To draw the attention of their troops and split their forces. Lesva and I may be... at odds—" what an understatement, "—but we have the same ultimate goal. If we can make things easier on her team in the palace by diverting some of the defenders, all the better."

His men nodded, satisfied with the answer.

"Lots of smoke," Vorik urged them. "That'll help me too. I'm going to swim downriver and sabotage the hull of that ship to make *sure* it sinks. If I can figure out a way to untether it from the dock, I might do that too. Better for the weapons platform to disappear in deeper water."

"Oh, yes, sir." Yevlor's eyes gleamed with approval.

Everyone's eyes did. They'd all lost friends to that thing.

"You're in charge, Lieutenant Doxinlur." Vorik nodded to the senior man, then headed to the beach for a kayak.

He didn't leave right away, figuring he would be less likely to be sighted coming downriver if the crew was engaged in defending their ship. If he hadn't been worried about Lesva reaching Syla at any moment, he would have waited until the middle of the night for this attack.

Are you in the area, Agrevlari? Vorik asked as he took the kayak to the water.

I am on the Island of Eliok.

Will you head this way? If my plan works and I'm able to capture Syla, I'll need you to pick me up once I get beyond the barrier.

You will swim out with your queen in tow?

I thought I'd paddle out. I have a kayak.

Will she not have Wreylith?

Are you suggesting the red dragon is a more useful tool than a kayak?

Undoubtedly. You are at a great disadvantage.

I'm going to make it work anyway. Once in the kayak, Vorik pushed off from the beach. A few ducks floating near clumps of grass quacked at him. *If I don't get Syla away from this island, I'm afraid Lesva will ensure she* never *leaves.*

That would be unfortunate. I have not minded her company. And Wreylith likes her, so she must be a worthy soul.

I *like her. Isn't that enough of an endorsement?*

It is not. You are overly distracted by her sex orifices.

It's more her curves than her orifices, and I like her character too.

Vorik paddled the kayak near the grasses along the bank, so he wouldn't be easily spotted, but kept his pace slow to give his men time to reach the docks. *Her determination and fortitude too.*

Because of your adoration, you are naturally trying to kidnap her.

To save her life.

Human relationships are strange.

Didn't you bite Wreylith the last time you saw her?

I did. That is not that strange, though I admit it is not ideal that she has declared herself an enemy. I still covet her.

Of course you do.

The river curved slightly, giving Vorik a full view of Syla's ship. It wasn't on fire yet, but the clangs of weapons rang out on the docks. He couldn't see his men but trusted they were the cause.

Are you heading in this direction? Vorik asked Agrevlari.

With great eagerness to assist in your mission.

You're either being sarcastic or hope that, despite your earlier clash, Wreylith will speak with you.

I long for her to do more *than speak with me.*

Like growling and hissing?

And roaring as she envisions us putting aside our differences to come together for a joining. Did I tell you how magnificent she was in the desert?

More times than I'd like to remember.

Such athleticism! Such stamina!

Not wanting to encourage further details—details which he'd already received—Vorik didn't reply. All he needed to know was that Agrevlari would be there when he kayaked or swam through the barrier.

Vorik eyed the crew visible on the deck of Syla's ship and decided they weren't yet distracted enough to miss a stormer in a kayak floating toward them. He gripped a half-submerged log sticking out from the bank to stop his progress.

More clangs rang out on the dock, and someone had reached

the deck of the ship. The crewmen who'd been in view near the railing ran toward the sounds of fighting.

To be careful, Vorik decided to slither over the edge of the kayak and into the cold river water. The current tugged at his clothes and sheathed weapons, but he'd swum in far more difficult conditions. He pushed the kayak away from the log and, using it for cover, hung on to the back while keeping most of his body submerged.

It floated down the river with him kicking behind it. Distant booms reached his ears. They didn't come from the docks but farther inland. Was Lesva attacking the palace? Cursed storms, where had his people come across so many explosives? They must have raided an armory here in the city.

Vorik kicked harder, willing his men to set the ships afire, whatever it took to draw Syla back in this direction before it was too late.

If anyone had spotted the empty kayak, they didn't shout out about it. In the chaos, maybe they wouldn't think anything of such a craft slipping free and floating down the river. That was his hope.

When Vorik neared the ship, he pushed the kayak so that it would float under the dock, hoping it would be caught in the pilings or the brush and that he could reclaim it after his sabotage. After he had Syla.

As the shouts and clangs of battle came from the docks and the deck of the ship, Vorik swam underwater until he reached the hull. He hugged it, hoping its curve would keep him out of view from the crew above, then maneuvered around it until he neared the weapons platform. Hoping its great weight would make the ship easier to sink, he started his sabotage.

"My apologies for trying to destroy your vessel, Syla," Vorik murmured, thinking of the lovely night they'd spent in her cabin.

He applied his gargoyle-bone dagger and sword to the hull,

regardless. Soon, the ship—and the weapons platform—would be on the bottom of the river.

The smell of smoke reached Syla's nose as more booms thundered from the courtyard. Shouts, clanks, and thuds from the bottom floor of the palace promised the intruders had gotten in.

"Hide in the closet, Abrya," Lord Oyenar urged, waving his wife toward a spacious room with chairs and trunks as well as racks of clothing and shoes. He'd found a sword and looked like he would stand with the guards if the enemy reached the suite.

"Is the roof more secure in there?" Abrya murmured and headed that way.

"If it helps, my dragon ally is nearby," Syla said. "Right above us."

"I don't know if that means the roof is more or less likely to cave in on our heads," Abrya said.

Wreylith roared. She sounded vexed. Because most of the fighting was going on inside, and she couldn't assist unless she destroyed portions of the palace?

"I don't either," Syla admitted.

"Comforting." Abrya, who'd probably had enough of being in the thick of the chaos, didn't object further and stepped into the closet. "You should come in here too, Lord Oyenar," she called.

"You must be sufficiently healed if you want me to join you for a closet tryst," he called back.

"That's *not* what I have on my mind. You're not as fast with a sword as you used to be. A stormer rider will slice out your tonsils and toss them to the dragon."

"It's lovely to have the staunch support of one's spouse," Oyenar told Fel.

"I imagine so," Fel said.

"They're on the stairs!" someone in the hallway cried.

"Keep them down there! No, get them *out* of here."

Wreylith roared again. Syla gripped a bedpost with one hand while she clutched her scalpel with the other. It wasn't an adequate weapon, but she knew how to use it better than real ones.

Fel eyed her, as if he might consider tossing her into the closet with Abrya. But then the clangs of swords and a cry of pain came from the hallway outside. The fighting had reached them.

Fel and Oyenar braced themselves inside the doorway while the guards fired crossbows and wielded swords in the hallway.

Glass shattered, and something flew through the window, a sphere that bounced across the floor and almost hit Syla in the foot. An explosive?

She sprang across the bed, hoping it could provide cover. Fel whirled, eyes wide, and snatched up the explosive. He threw it back out the window. At the same time, a gout of fire streamed down from the rooftop. It caught the explosive as well as whoever the dragon had been aiming at in the courtyard below, and a great boom shook the floor and rattled paintings on the walls. The windows shattered and broke, hurling glass into the room, pieces skidding all the way to the closet. Lady Abrya let out an exclamation of dismay.

Your enemy approaches, Wreylith warned.

I guessed that from the explosives. Thank you.

A cheeky archer is firing at me. Two of them!

Scraping noises came from the roof above. Dragon talons? There weren't windows facing the other side of the palace, but a scream erupted from the courtyard in that direction, and Syla imagined an archer going up in flames.

In the hallway, clatters and bangs sounded, and the guards in front of the doorway surged out of view to meet the threat. Oyenar stepped out to assist his men.

Syla pushed herself to her feet, expecting Lesva and her riders to come from that direction. She looked at her puny scalpel and wished she had some of her aunt's booby traps to throw. Anything that might prove effective against the rider captain.

Lesva didn't charge in from the hallway. Silent as death, the black-clad rider sprang in through one of the broken windows. If she hadn't landed on shattered glass that crunched softly, Syla might not have noticed, though as soon as she swung her head to look, she sensed the power of the woman. Silver braids bouncing on her shoulders, Lesva spotted Syla and ran straight toward her.

"Fel!" Syla cried as she threw one of her vials.

It arched accurately toward Lesva's face, but she batted it away with her sword. The vial shattered in the air, but if any of the astringent droplets struck her skin, they didn't disturb her.

Fel sprang at Lesva from the side, trying to keep her from reaching Syla. In an inhuman feat of strength, Lesva leaped high, her head brushing the coffered ceiling as she pulled her knees up to her chest. Fel almost lost his balance as he passed under her instead of colliding with her, but he caught himself and spun, swinging his mace at her.

Almost casually, Lesva deflected it with her sword as she landed. Not hesitating, she continued toward Syla.

Syla threw another vial, this time aiming for the corner of one of the bed posts. It clipped the edge and shattered, a few droplets flying toward Lesva's eyes as she approached. She closed them in time, but the liquid struck her cheeks and lips.

It wouldn't deter the great warrior, and Syla considered running into the closet and slamming the door shut. But that also wouldn't impede this foe. Worse, it would alert Lesva to Abrya's location. Instead, against her survival instincts, Syla lunged forward and grabbed Lesva's arm.

Fel tried to knock Lesva's sword away and grip her from

behind, but she deflected his mace while locking her gaze on Syla, her lip curling with anger and loathing.

Though Syla hadn't been able to best her the last time they'd battled with magic, she willed her power into the captain, hoping Lesva was more distracted this time. If the rider let her guard down, Fel would brain her. Too bad Oyenar and his guards were engaged in the hallway and couldn't help.

With startling ease, Syla's power flowed into Lesva. She sensed the woman bringing her own magic to bear, trying to form a shield to block Syla, as she had before. But something had changed. The moon-mark on Syla's hand flared, but the dragon tattoo on her other hand also activated. It tingled with power, so much that it almost hurt as it also sent magic through Syla and into her foe. The dragon power twined and mingled with that from Syla's godsgift, and Lesva gasped in surprise as she struggled to deflect it all.

She lifted her sword toward Syla, but Fel growled and swung his mace toward her head. Once again, she had to deflect his attack. Meanwhile, Syla sent a tendril of power to Lesva's trachea to cut off her air supply and another to her heart in case she had the strength to stop its beats, to end the threat forever.

Fire and smoke come from the ships in your fleet, Wreylith said.

I'm busy right now, Syla replied, sensing Lesva was far from defeated.

Her blue eyes burning with fury and determination, Lesva roared as she summoned more power and strength. She ripped her arm from Syla's grip and kicked her in the stomach, knocking her back into the nightstand.

As Syla lost her connection, her ability to harm Lesva evaporated. For a moment, Lesva spun and focused fully on Fel. Her blade blurred as she slipped it past his mace, stabbing him in the shoulder, then kicking him and sending him tumbling back.

He hit the floor, rolled, and came to his feet, his mace still in his hand, though he couldn't bring it up fully, not with the puncture in his shoulder. Lesva crouched to spring after him, but Syla ran forward, intending to grab her—to *touch* her—again.

A shadow fell over the windows, startling them all. Red scales flashed.

Wreylith's head was too large to fit through a window, but that didn't keep her from lowering her horns and ramming into the exterior of the building. Her great head came through *two* windows—and knocked out the wall between them.

Before Lesva could spin toward the dragon and strike with her sword, Wreylith snapped her jaws around her. Lesva was fast enough to bring her sword up and jam the point into the roof of the dragon's mouth, preventing the maw from closing, from crushing her to death.

Wreylith roared in pain but didn't let go of the captain. With a flexing of her long neck, Wreylith pulled Lesva out of the suite. Twisting the sword, the captain tried to drive it higher into the vulnerable flesh at the top of the dragon's mouth.

Syla winced in sympathy and lifted a hand, but there was nothing she could do.

Roaring again, Wreylith used her long neck like a whip and flung Lesva away from the palace. The captain flew over the courtyard wall and into the streets beyond, disappearing from view. Her sword went with her, but Wreylith roared again. It had probably hurt as much coming out as going in.

Thank you, and I'll heal you as soon as I can, Syla promised.

Wreylith roared again and shook her head like a dog flinging water after coming in from the rain.

"Fel, are you all right? We have to go after Lesva." Syla ran past him to the giant hole in the destroyed wall. "Make sure she doesn't come back to—" Spotting smoke in the distance made her trail off, and she gaped, then swore, remembering Wreylith's warning. "The fleet!"

The docked ships were burning, including the one carrying the weapons platform.

Syla swore again.

Climb on, Wreylith said. *I will take you there.*

Can you manage? How is your maw?

Dreadful, but dragons can survive many indignities. Wreylith lowered her head to the wall.

Syla rushed forward without hesitation. *A sword in the roof of your mouth is more than an indignity.*

"Your Majesty!" Fel blurted.

"Stay and protect the lord and lady!" As Syla climbed over Wreylith's snout and past her horns to slide down her neck to her back, Fel tried to follow her.

"*You* are my charge!" he bellowed, but Wreylith faced him and bared her fangs, denying him the same route to her back. He looked like he would try to follow Syla anyway, despite the fangs and the smoke wafting from the red dragon's nostrils.

"Protect Abrya!" Syla repeated as Wreylith drew away from the palace and crouched to spring into the air. "Lesva is still alive, and Lady Abrya is moon-marked."

Fel scowled but, as Wreylith flew away, turned back to guard the closet.

With the sounds of battle still raging in the palace, Syla hoped it would be enough. It was *possible* Lesva had died or at least been incapacitated after that landing, but Syla doubted it. She'd seen the woman survive too much to dare believe that.

Indeed, when Wreylith flew over the palace wall, and they looked down to the area where Lesva should have landed, Syla didn't spot the woman.

"Too bad she's not crumpled in a pile, having fallen on something pointy," Syla said.

Such as her own foul sword. The taste of my own blood fills my mouth.

"Don't worry. I have an ointment for that." Syla patted the dragon on the back.

Wreylith's rumble sounded more suspicious than anticipatory.

As the dragon flew toward the docks, Syla couldn't help but look back, afraid she was making a mistake by leaving the palace, that Fel and the other defenders would be overwhelmed and that Oyenar and Abrya would be taken. Or killed. But Aunt Tibby was on the *Stormslicer*, and Syla couldn't abandon her to the stormers. More, if the Kingdom lost their weapons platform, they lost their ability to take the fight to the stormers and defeat dragons. This might be the most important battle of the war.

17

For at least the twentieth time, Vorik plunged below the water's surface to hack and rip at the hull of the ship. As strong as his magical gargoyle-bone blades were, they were not adequate tools for carpentry. A trained saboteur, he was not, but when he thought of all the dragons that had died to the weapons platform—as well as riders he'd known his whole life—he found the wherewithal to keep going. Finally, he created a large enough hole in the side of the ship that he believed it would sink.

As he came up for air, it occurred to him to wonder how deep the river was in that spot. He imagined the vessel sinking only a couple of feet before landing in the silty ground below.

"We're taking on water!" someone yelled.

Vorik pushed his hair out of his eyes, not surprised it had taken people time to notice. With the entire crew on deck, fighting his men, he'd had as good an opportunity for sabotage as he could have wanted.

Sticking close to the hull so he wouldn't be spotted, he maneuvered around the ship, the air now hazy with smoke. Flames burned on the deck and also the docks.

Vorik peered upward, wondering if Syla had seen and was on her way. But what if Lesva had already gotten her? His gut churned at the thought, and he second-guessed letting Lesva and her team continue unopposed to the palace. Maybe he should have fought her, but that would have assured their men that what she'd claimed was true, that he was a traitor. And he was not that, damn it.

"There's a team in the water!" someone on the deck yelled over the chaos.

A team? Vorik was hardly that and didn't think anyone had yet seen him, but he angled under the dock for cover. He spotted the kayak, farther downriver and caught against the grassy bank.

"Now I just need Syla to make my escape," he murmured.

Except that he couldn't leave while his men were fighting above. They'd willingly stepped up to his side to assist him, and he couldn't abandon them.

Vorik sheathed his weapons and grabbed an algae-slick piling, intending to climb up to help them, but paused when he sensed a dragon approaching. Wreylith. Was Syla on her back?

He was tempted to remain in the water and hidden so he could choose a time to pounce, but with the dragon on the way, his men were in more danger. He pulled himself onto the dock and into the midst of the chaos. Fires burned around him and also on the nearby ships. One was sailing away from the docks. Trying to escape the stormers? Syla's vessel remained in place and sat low in the water.

"We're sinking fast!" someone cried.

"There's the one who did it!" A crossbowman spotted Vorik and raised his weapon.

Vorik dove behind a post, a quarrel buzzing through the air where he'd been. As he drew his own weapons, he spotted the red dragon soaring toward them. Yes, that was Wreylith, and Syla did indeed ride on her back, the sunlight glinting off her spectacles.

Her face was set with grim determination. He hated that they were on opposing sides, but when one of his men cried out in pain from the deck of her ship, Vorik didn't hesitate to run and leap over the railing to assist.

The crossbowman had reloaded and pointed his weapon at him again. With so many skirmishes ongoing, and the deck slanted, the straps that held the weapons platform in place groaning, nobody had come to help the Kingdom man. He fired, but Vorik anticipated it and threw himself into a roll, somersaulting across the tilted deck and springing up in front of his foe. His attacker tried to skitter back but realized he didn't have time to reload or escape and hurled the crossbow at Vorik.

Concerned far more about Wreylith than the man, Vorik calmly slashed with his sword, slicing the stock in half. Surging forward, he grabbed the startled soldier and spun, throwing him into the railing. Weakened by fire, the wood snapped, and he tumbled into the water.

"We're winning, sir!" a stormer blurted, spotting Vorik and charging up beside him, his sword bloody and his eyes gleaming.

If only Vorik felt that they were. But he nodded. "Yes, good work, Tems. As soon as the ship sinks, take the men and get out of here, all right?" Smoke tickled his throat, and he struggled not to cough as he glanced around, ensuring no enemies were sneaking up on them. Several crewmen leaped off the vessel, realizing its fate was inevitable. "Hide in the forest until we can get ships in to retrieve you."

"Yes, sir, but what about you?"

"I have another mission."

A roar came from the sky. The wind had shifted, blowing smoke across the deck and the docks, so Vorik couldn't see the dragon's descent, but he sensed it. And he sensed his danger. Syla might hesitate to kill him, but he doubted *Wreylith* would.

"Go." Vorik pushed Tems away, not wanting him to be taken out because he'd been standing too close to the dragon's target.

Agrevlari, Vorik asked silently, sensing his dragon ally flying out at sea, not far from the barrier. *I'm going to come to you soon.*

I do pine in your absence.

We might have to get out of here quickly.

Fleeing enemies?

One big red enemy.

Ah. The mighty Wreylith.

"You!" called a familiar female voice. The engineer aunt. Tibby.

Eyes watering behind her spectacles, she'd come up from belowdecks and was running through the smoke toward the weapons platform as she glared at Vorik. She reached it before he could stop her, climbed up, and grabbed the posts. By now, Vorik knew that was how the platform was operated, and he ran, intending to spring and knock her away, but Wreylith appeared through the smoke, her fanged maw opening right behind him.

Vorik dove *under* the weapons platform. Jaws snapped, fangs clinking off the corner of the marble device, and Tibby cried out, as alarmed as anyone.

"Sorry, Aunt Tibby!" Syla called from Wreylith's back as the dragon landed on top of the weapons platform.

Bloody daggers, how was Vorik supposed to kidnap Syla when her *dragon* was right there?

Two pairs of boots—all he could see from below—ran toward him. He started to roll out on the other side, but Wreylith's red maw came down, and hot steamy breath mingled with the smoke and flowed under the weapons platform.

He'd managed to get himself trapped and almost laughed at the foolishness of his choice to climb out of the river. He might end up captured by Syla again.

Then a snap sounded. Fabric? A buckle? Both? One of the

straps that held the weapons platform in place had broken, and the great marble structure skidded across the slanted deck toward the railing.

"Lift it off!" Syla called from above.

Was she talking to Wreylith? Vorik, rolling to stay underneath the platform, doubted even the powerful dragon could lift it by herself.

Another strap snapped, and flapping sounds erupted from above. Wings beating and stirring smoke, the dragon leaped into the air as her perch skidded toward the railing.

"Aunt Tibby!" Syla cried.

Was she still on the platform? Afraid he would be crushed, Vorik risked scrambling out from underneath. He rose in time to see a blazing silver ball shoot from the top of the platform. At first, he thought himself the target, but the aunt must not have wanted to hit the ship. The projectile slammed into a man—one of Vorik's men—in the middle of a sword fight with a Kingdom soldier on the dock. The magical sphere incinerated him with a blinding flash of silver light.

Horrified, Vorik turned toward the platform, his sword raised. Tibby hung on to one of the posts, her hand planted on the mark on its side, her gaze as determined as her niece's as she looked at Vorik. He had no doubt that he was her next target. Aware of the way those projectiles could follow a dragon—or a person—he was sure he wouldn't escape a second attack.

But thunderous snaps came from below, and the deck quaked under Vorik. It *more* than quaked. It gave way, and the weapons platform lurched, then plummeted downward. More wood snapped as it fell, and Tibby disappeared along with the entire structure. The deck also gave way under Vorik. Though the purchase under his feet dropped, he managed to leap away before it disappeared entirely. Using his dagger like a climbing pick, he caught a portion of the deck that remained intact.

As more people fled the sinking ship, Vorik pulled his way up the slanted deck and grabbed on to a solid portion of the railing. Flames burned all around him, black smoke choking him, but he could see that the weapons platform had disappeared and water bubbled up from below. Most of what deck remained was covered in water, and even as he watched, a mast snapped, wood and sail falling to cover the giant hole the weapons platform had fallen through. Vorik had a feeling it had broken through the hull and now lay on the bottom of the river, where the ship would soon join it.

He should have felt triumphant at accomplishing his mission, but a distressed cry came from above.

"Aunt Tibby!" Syla still rode Wreylith's back as the dragon circled.

Wings flapping so hard that smoke swirled and Vorik felt their wind from the railing, Wreylith hovered, briefly more like a hummingbird than a dragon, and snapped up the broken mast, tossing it aside. Then Wreylith plunged her head through the hole. But dragons were not hummingbirds, and her belly slammed against the wheelhouse. When she landed, unable to find a solid perch, more deck gave way. Wreylith lifted her head without finding the aunt and roared in frustration. As more of the ship broke underneath her, the dragon roared again and flapped her wings to fly upward.

Syla flattened her hand to her spectacles and surprised Vorik by diving off Wreylith's back and into the hole.

"Shouldn't be surprised," he muttered to himself, but would Syla have a chance at finding her aunt? Even with normal vision, it was hard to see underwater, and how would she swim without losing her spectacles?

Vorik released the railing, letting gravity take him toward the hole, and sheathed his weapons before he plunged into the water.

He'd only meant to sink the marble structure, not kill the aunt, and what if *Syla* died?

As the chilly water enveloped him, the thought horrifying him, he swam downward. Wood from the hull or broken deck snagged him, and he struggled to see through the wreckage. Something with more give brushed his hand, the material from Syla's dress. She was right beside him, clinging to a beam and trying to make her way deeper, but a pack strapped over her shoulder must have made it more difficult to maneuver. It had caught, and she couldn't pull it free.

As Vorik unfastened it for her, he spotted the white marble of the platform, half blocked by the broken hull. Leaving Syla, he swam downward. Even with daylight above and fires burning all around the ship, the water was murky, full of disturbed silt. If the marble had been black, he never would have seen it, but he reached it, his fingers brushing the cold stone. But where was Tibby?

He swam under the canopy of the weapons platform, checking the posts, but she wasn't clinging to them. His lungs started to burn, and he expected Syla must have returned to the surface for air, but she showed up beside him, hands groping, her face twisted in distress.

He patted her arm, having no idea if she recognized him or knew he was helping, and tried to point her upward. Movement to the side caught his attention, and he didn't wait to see if Syla took his suggestion. He spun and peered through the cloudy silt, glimpsing the movement again. There was Aunt Tibby, still alive and trying to pull herself out from under a section of the hull. The wrecked ship had settled on the bottom of the river.

With powerful strokes, Vorik arrowed toward her. If his lungs were burning, Tibby had to be close to drowning. He reached her, gripped her under the armpits, and pulled. But the entire weight of the ship seemed to be on top of her. Losing precious air bubbles, he pulled again, but even he wasn't strong enough.

Lungs now crying out for air, he drew his sword and hacked into the wood around her. He'd created this awful situation, and he had to save Syla's aunt. If he didn't... Syla wouldn't forgive him. She might not forgive him for this anyway, but sinking the weapon had been understandable. Sinking a fifty-something woman who wasn't even a combatant? No.

After sawing pieces from the hull, he was able to pull chunks away. Muscles heaving, he finally freed Tibby. Again, he grabbed her under the armpits. He kicked as powerfully as he could, angling away from the ship and the docks, hoping to come up away from the fighting. And hoping Tibby was all right. She kicked feebly, trying to assist him, so at least she was still conscious.

When they broke the surface, she gulped in so much air that she inhaled water too and coughed and coughed. Vorik swam toward a beach upriver from the fiery docks. Smoke bathed the surface, and he hoped no enemies would spot him, but the sounds of fighting had dwindled anyway. If Tems had obeyed his order, the stormers were departing.

As Vorik paddled Tibby to the bank, he peered back through the smoke, trying to spot Syla. He sensed Wreylith in the air, but she was flying toward the palace. Distant booms came from there. Had Syla found a safe spot and sent the dragon to help there? Lesva might be making her move at that very moment.

As soon as Vorik made sure Tibby was secure on land, he ran back into the river, diving and swimming toward the hull. He had to make sure Syla was all right. And the thought crossed his mind that, with the dragon distracted elsewhere, this might be his opportunity to kidnap her.

He swam around the wreck and burning wood in the water until he sensed... yes, there she was. Though a human's power wasn't as significant as a dragon's, hers was strong enough—bright enough—for him to detect. And then she coughed, guiding him further, and he swam around the wreck to spot her clinging to a burning piece of a mast tangled in a torn sail.

"Syla," he called, swimming toward her.

Her spectacles hung around her neck on a strap, and she peered blearily at him but rasped with recognition, "Vorik."

She sounded like she'd inhaled half the river, and she coughed again, but there was relief in her voice. Given that he'd caused all this, there *shouldn't* have been.

"I'm here." Vorik swam toward her and pulled her from the log, kicking to angle them toward the bank.

Syla struggled weakly, as if not certain she should go with him. The pack remained slung over her shoulder and impeded her, but she didn't peel it off. Oh, was that her medical kit? She wouldn't want to lose that.

"Your aunt is safe," Vorik added.

Syla slumped, letting him tow her. "Thank the gods."

She coughed again, dragging a wet sleeve over her face to dash water and maybe tears from her eyes.

The current carried them downriver as Vorik swam, and he spotted the kayak, tangled in grass at the bank. He almost laughed that it had remained close for him.

"Over here." Vorik paddled toward it, Syla not resisting him.

With her spectacles still around her neck, and her lungs busy expelling water with coughs, she probably wasn't thinking about how *he* might have started all this. And he had. Feeling like an absolute jerk, he reached the kayak and held it steady.

"Climb in." He gave Syla a boost.

Had there been a beach nearby, she might have left him to swim toward that, but the channel was deep downriver from the docks, the banks steep, and it would have been hard for her to pull herself out through the reeds and grass that grew to the edge. Not struggling, Syla let him push her into the kayak, even grabbing the side to pull herself in.

Eyeing the sky as he tracked Wreylith with his senses, Vorik slithered in after Syla and grabbed the paddle. Since the kayak only had one seat, it was awkward, with him kneeling behind her, but they didn't have to go far. He hunched low as he paddled, afraid archers would spot him and pepper him. But when he glanced back, it appeared that most of the soldiers had been turned into firefighters to keep the flames from spreading into the city. Since he didn't see any of his own people, he hoped they'd gotten away. Most of them.

Vorik winced as he remembered the man who'd been enveloped and instantly killed by that weapon. And he'd dived down and saved the life of the woman who'd launched it. He shook his head but couldn't regret that. He hadn't meant to kill Tibby, and the fact that he'd retrieved her was probably the only reason Syla wasn't struggling against him. She *had* to know he'd been involved in sinking the ship, and she might suspect he'd been completely responsible.

As the kayak arrowed down the river, Syla recovered enough to stop coughing and put her spectacles on.

"Vorik?" She looked at the bank as they passed it by. "Where are we going?"

"Would you believe I'd like to take you on a nature expedition to seek out rare birds and animals that inhabit this island's lowlands?"

"You're trying again to kidnap me." She looked back upriver, her mouth drooping as she saw the black smoke and flames of her fleet from the water. The other ships blocked the view of hers—all that remained above the water was one of the masts—but she had to know it had sunk.

"It's... my mission." Vorik didn't point out that it had been a self-appointed one. The alternative... hadn't been acceptable.

Syla shifted on the seat and gripped the edges of the kayak. He tensed, expecting her to push herself overboard and try to swim away. But she looked toward the skyline instead.

"Wreylith is coming," she said a second before he sensed the dragon on her way back. "When she said there were more explosions taking place at the palace, I sent her to check on Fel and Lady Abrya and her husband, but maybe that was a mistake." Syla frowned back at him.

"Likely so," Vorik said, sympathetic even if it had been advantageous for him.

It might not matter if Wreylith caught him before he escaped the barrier and reached Agrevlari. He paddled faster.

Syla didn't try to fling herself out of the kayak. Vorik was glad, since it would have slowed him down if he had to pause to grab her, but it surprised him. Maybe she was certain Wreylith would catch them and could easily pluck her up. She wasn't wrong about that…

Be ready, Agrevlari. Floating on the river's current, with Vorik's rapid paddling helping to speed them along, the kayak flowed out into the sea, but it would take time to reach the barrier and the green dragon flying back and forth outside it. *We're going to need to leave in a hurry.*

A great roar came from above the rooftops of the city.

A big hurry. Vorik didn't look back. He sensed Wreylith flapping her wings hard, coming for Syla—or coming to kill *him*.

I see that. You know I won't be able to outfly her while I carry two and she has no rider, right?

I… was hoping you'd have a burst of adrenaline if you feared for your life. Why didn't you bring any winged friends along?

You didn't ask for any. I have asked Zandelek and Yelorindash to come quickly from the Island of Eliok.

How soon can they be here? Breathing hard as he paddled through the choppy waves beyond the river's influence, Vorik peered across the sea, hoping to spot allies. As of yet, only Agrevlari was visible.

Not before Wreylith catches you and crushes you between her jaws.

That's disappointing.

Another roar sounded. By the gods, the red dragon was scant yards behind them. Syla's presence had to be the only reason Wreylith hadn't spewed flames and roasted him. But she wouldn't have any trouble snapping him up in her jaws.

He kept paddling but lowered himself and scooted closer to Syla, hoping Wreylith would have to be careful and that would make her slower. A hot wind blew across the back of his neck. Or was that *dragon breath*?

He'd almost reached Agrevlari, but they weren't going to make it. He could tell.

He was on the verge of lifting the paddle and his hands to give up, but a screech of anger and frustration erupted right behind them.

Startled, Vorik looked back in time to see Wreylith fly backward, as if she'd hit a wall at top speed. No, he realized. She'd hit the *barrier*.

Syla gaped as Wreylith splashed down into the water, her expression promising that she hadn't expected that any more than Vorik had. Though confused—the barrier had let the dragon *in,* after all—Vorik reacted quickly, balancing on his feet on the kayak as Agrevlari soared overhead. He leaped up, catching Agrevlari's leg, then swinging himself onto the dragon's back.

Syla shifted to lunge out of the kayak, but she'd waited too long. Agrevlari snapped her up in his jaws and tossed her into the air. She cursed and flailed, but Vorik leaned out and caught her, pulling her onto Agrevlari's back with him.

Wreylith screeched again, but she was trapped inside the barrier as Agrevlari flew away.

18

For the first couple of hours of their journey, Syla didn't speak, and Vorik didn't try to draw her into a conversation, certain she was fuming as she thought about how he'd masterminded the destruction of her ship and the sinking of the weapons platform. As they flew over the Sea of Storms and away from the Garden Kingdom islands, she didn't look back at him, merely sitting tensely astride Agrevlari in front of him.

The wind whipped at their clothes and hair, drying them, and she'd shifted her medical kit to rest in her lap, as if she worried he would take it from her. Or maybe she was contemplating pulling out a sharp surgical tool with which to stab him. He would deserve it.

This is harder than I expected it to be, Agrevlari, Vorik said.

It's been easier *than I expected since Wreylith has not been able to follow.*

I know, but I have to take Syla to Jhiton, and he's going to question her on the location of the shielders.

That was your goal all along, wasn't it?

I've just been trying to save her life. This feels like a betrayal. Is it?

Certainly not, Agrevlari said. *She will reveal the location of the shielder for the Island of Bogs, and dragons will soon be able to hunt there.*

So, it's not a betrayal to dragons.

It is not.

Vorik sighed, doubting Agrevlari would understand. He was probably distracted by fantasizing about whatever delicious prey lived among the bogs on that island.

Syla looked back, not at Vorik but to peer past him in the direction of her islands. By now, they were no longer in sight, but her expression suggested she hoped Wreylith had found a way through the barrier and would catch up and save her. And maybe the dragon would eviscerate Vorik in the process.

After the wonderful night they'd spent together, it disturbed him to have Syla feel she *needed* saving from him.

"I'm sorry," he said over the wind. "I wish there had been another way."

Syla eyed him over her shoulder. "I'm glad Aunt Tibby is alive, but I'm distressed that Wreylith is trapped."

Vorik was *relieved* that the dragon was. As Agrevlari had mentioned, he hadn't expected that, and it was making their getaway a simple matter. How helpful that Syla and Wreylith were still figuring out what their bond did and did not allow when it came to the islands' shields.

"That's what's disturbing you?" Vorik asked lightly, encouraged that she'd spoken to him. "Not my kidnapping you?"

"That was loathsome. So was sinking my weapons platform." She scowled at him and faced forward again.

"I know," he said without argument.

"But you had orders," she said.

"I did."

"You always have orders."

"I'm an officer in the Sixteen Talons," he said, "and sworn to do my duty, yes."

Oh, but that duty had come to chafe of late. And Vorik hated saying the words to her, explaining why he'd had to betray her. Especially when she'd never betrayed him. Nor had she tried to manipulate him into betraying himself. All the opportunities she'd had… and she hadn't.

"I'm sorry," he repeated, though he knew it wasn't enough.

She looked back again. "Where are you taking me?"

Vorik grimaced, reminded that the unpleasant part for her hadn't yet begun. "To General Jhiton in our new camp. He… has questions for you."

"I'll bet," she said sourly, fear flashing in her eyes before she hid it by looking away from him.

It was a dagger to his heart. He wanted to tell her that Jhiton wouldn't physically hurt her, but… what he planned wasn't much better. Was it *any* better?

While you were busy sabotaging that ship, Agrevlari said, *I heard from our dragon allies that the camp has been moved.*

Oh? We're still heading to the coast of Froha, right?

Yes, but fifty miles to the south. The Skillpoint Caves were flooded during the recent storm. Chieftess Shi ordered the camp moved to Nookfar until the waters recede.

Is there still a lake kraken living under the cave? Vorik asked dryly.

Reputedly, the lake is empty, save for cave crawlers, but they are not much of a threat to your people. And they are delicious when skewered and roasted.

They're all right. The Kingdom isn't aware of Nookfar, so it should be a decent place to camp for a while.

Quite.

When Syla had composed herself, she looked back at Vorik again. "If you return me to my people and my dragon instead of taking me to your camp, I'll drop to my knees and thank you the same way I did in my cabin."

The promise aroused his body in an instant, making him aware of what he'd been trying not to acknowledge, the warm weight of her between his legs as they rode, the spectacular curves of her backside against his thighs. The memory of their night in her cabin filled his thoughts, of her mouth around his shaft, so expertly drawing him toward a triumphant climax.

"Unfortunately, I can't do that," Vorik made himself say, though she'd gotten him hard with the mere suggestion of intimacy. Their time together was always amazing. Why couldn't they be lovers instead of enemies?

"Are you sure?" Syla's eyebrows rose. "We're all alone out here. Who would know?"

"Not quite alone." Vorik patted Agrevlari's scales.

"Does your dragon object to us having sex?"

"I think he would only object if we did it on his *back*."

"Then you'll definitely need to return me to my people. You were probably too busy sabotaging things to notice, but there are comfortable beds on Bogberry Island."

"I wish we could have spent time in one."

"Me too." She gazed at him, her lips parted, and the comment seemed genuine.

Oh, he knew she wanted to escape the fate he'd promised her, but he also believed she would have liked to spend more time with him. When they were together, her body came alive to his touch. That was real. He knew it was.

When he didn't answer, Syla looked forward again, but she also leaned back into him, letting her weight settle fully against his chest. Not hesitating, he wrapped his arms around her. As her warm body molded to him, his groin stiffened with eager anticipation.

Nothing is going to happen, he told it with an eye roll. But with

Syla so close, he couldn't resist kissing her on the side of her neck, then resting his chin on her shoulder. He wished he could ask Agrevlari to change routes. Maybe he couldn't take her back to her islands, but did he *have* to take her to the stormer camp? For an interrogation? What if they went somewhere else? Anywhere else?

As if she knew his thoughts, Syla leaned her head back onto his shoulder, her hair tickling his neck, the curve of her breasts drawing his eyes.

"Your offer *is* tempting," he admitted, his voice husky now. Bloody daggers, she could affect his libido instantly.

"But you won't take me up on it. Instead, you're taking me to your odious brother to be questioned."

"He's not odious," Vorik said, though his gaze lingered on her chest. He wanted to lift a hand to hold her, to stroke her. "He's sworn to do as our chiefs order and try to achieve what's best for our people."

"He tried to kill me."

If Jhiton could be believed, he hadn't been shooting to kill Syla, but Vorik doubted she would care.

"You've tried to kill him too," he offered instead. Maybe she would be reasonable and consider Jhiton's reaction fair. "Three—no, four times, I believe. He's been counting."

"I regret that I've missed him every time."

"Would you really want to deprive me of my only remaining brother?"

"In a heartbeat. I hope you'll forgive me if I try to stick a dagger in his chest while I'm a prisoner in your camp."

"Oh, he expects it. I regret to inform you that I'll have to do my best to keep you from acquiring such a weapon." He eyed the medical kit that she clutched in her lap, the strap loose over her shoulder. He'd seen her draw scalpels, scissors, and other edged tools out of it, as well as concoctions that she'd flung at the giant bugs that had tried to kill her. He smiled at the memory.

"I'll cheerfully claw his eyes out with my bare hands."

"I can't believe you're saying such things while you're snuggled in my arms, and I..." Vorik was aroused. Maybe he shouldn't admit that when she was his prisoner, but they were close enough that she could tell anyway.

"Keep looking at my chest?" she offered when he didn't finish.

"It is magnificent."

And it arrested his attention, especially a pert nipple pressed against the fabric of her dress. He didn't think she could be aroused, but...

Head still leaning back on his shoulder, Syla took his hand and guided it up to cup her breast. She watched him with rapt eyes, her full lips parted, as if she wanted nothing more than to kiss him.

A surge of hot desire swept into his groin, and he didn't hesitate to hold her and stroke her while wishing he could remove her dress. Her eyes closed as she shifted into his touch, as if she didn't care that they were enemies and wanted nothing more than for him to pleasure her. He couldn't resist lowering his mouth to hers, kissing her eager lips. And she responded with such passion that it startled him even as it aroused him further.

"Are you trying to seduce me, Syla?" he asked between kisses. "I know you can't be happy with me."

"I'm not," she said agreeably, lifting her fingers to trace his jaw, her delicate touch as arousing as her steamy kiss. "But I might get over being perturbed with you if you took me somewhere besides your camp to be interrogated."

By the eyes of the moon, he wanted to do exactly that. Especially when she shifted her weight, wriggling back into him, making him painfully hard with desire. With *lust*.

"Where would you like to go?" he whispered, that husky rasp in his voice again.

"Anywhere that we can be together," she said.

She arched her breast more fully into his hand and watched him over her shoulder, her magnificent stormy eyes finding him through her spectacles. The wind tugged at the hem of her dress, and he lowered his hand to the bare thigh it revealed, sliding the fabric upward. He trailed his fingers along her exquisite flesh, her softness a contrast to his rough callouses.

She moved her medical kit aside and shifted her legs apart in invitation. He slid them along her inner thigh, finding the heat of her core, stroking her through her underwear.

She gasped and pushed into his hand. Her naked desire for him excited him, as it always did. As *she* always did, and he rubbed her even as he debated where he could take her so that they could join. Where they could enjoy each other's company in private and then... afterward, maybe he would allow her to escape. That was what she wanted, and he knew she was using her body to try to get exactly that, but he didn't blame her, not for a second. He had only kidnapped her to save her life. He'd never wanted to deliver her to an interrogation session. Let his brother find the shielder chamber on his own.

But they were flying over the ocean toward the coast of Froha, toward a stormer camp where the Sixteen Talons and all of his tribe waited. Unless he redirected Agrevlari to the north or south, to land elsewhere on the coast, there was no place where they could *join*.

"Vorik," Syla moaned with longing, moving against his hand, damp through her underwear.

Her breasts shifted as she writhed, and he had to close his eyes to keep a modicum of control, to keep from tearing off her dress so he could have full access to her. With each passing second, he longed more and more to pull her into his lap and take her right there, while they flew a thousand feet above the sea.

With his lust flaring, he growled, the notion filling his mind.

He rocked into her, his cock so eager that it might tear through his trousers.

She turned her head to meet his heated gaze. "Take me back to Bogberry Island, Vorik."

There was power in her voice, a command. A mortal man without magic of his own might have jumped to obey, but he had his own power and the ability to resist. But did he truly *want* to? He wanted… *her.*

"I will," he caught himself saying, "but I need you *now.*"

He expected her to object, to try again to command him, but he slipped his fingers into her depths, and she nodded eagerly and kissed him again. She shifted her ass against his cock, and he couldn't restrain his desire any longer. He had to—

Three dragons approach from behind, Agrevlari stated without commenting on anything else.

Irritation flashed in Vorik, and he guessed who they were even before Agrevlari expounded.

Ozlemar is in the lead with Jhiton.

Vorik groaned, realizing he couldn't do anything now but continue on to the camp and hand Syla over to be a prisoner. To be interrogated.

How far back are they? Vorik asked, wondering if he at least had time to bring Syla to a climax, even if he couldn't sate himself. Maybe if he left her trembling with pleasure, she would be less likely to hate him over whatever happened in the camp.

Not far. The other dragons carry only one rider each, so they are catching up.

Damn it, Agrevlari. I'm trying to—

Effect a mating session on my back, which, as I've informed you before, is not permitted.

We weren't going to mate. Only—

You are stimulating her sex orifice, and you are intensely aroused. That leads to mating.

Oh, how Vorik wished it would. That it *could*.

But when he looked back, he saw Ozlemar and two blue dragons with riders flying after them. With Syla breathing heavily in his arms, pushing into his hand and rocking back against him, Vorik was tempted to satisfy her before the others caught up, but she wouldn't appreciate it if Jhiton flew up beside them and looked over while her dress was hiked up, her cheeks were flushed, and she was groaning with desire as she writhed in Vorik's grip.

She may have sensed their approach, regardless, because she lifted her head from Vorik's shoulder and looked behind them.

"We're about to have company." Struggling to cool his desire, Vorik made himself push her dress down.

Syla groaned when she spotted the dragons. This time, it had nothing to do with desire.

"Is that your general?" she asked.

"Yes."

She bared her teeth.

"I'm sure he's delighted to see you too." Vorik lifted a hand toward Jhiton, who nodded back at him. They were far enough apart that Jhiton's face was hard to read—though that was often the case when they were three feet apart too. Vorik hoped his brother hadn't gotten the gist of what was going on but worried his lack of a telepathic greeting before arriving meant he had.

"I suppose it's not regal to hiss at one's foe." Syla glanced down and must have noticed the laces on her dress were loosened for she cursed and shrank back into Vorik to use him to block Jhiton's view as she tied them more tightly. "Or to writhe in the hands of one's enemies," she added in a mutter, her cheeks flushed.

"You're newly coronated," Vorik said gently, wishing he could set her at ease but mostly regretting his choice to bring her. At the least, maybe he could use a touch of humor to distract her from her discomfort. "You can't be expected to know all the rules, traditions, and customs right away. I bet your elders haven't had time to instruct you on everything."

"I was *born* into the monarchy. I know all the bylaws, and we have a constitution. I've read it before."

"And it covers hissing and writhing?"

"It does not."

"Then I think *you* get to decide which actions are regal or not. Set the standard, if you will."

The sour look she slanted him didn't suggest she appreciated his humor.

"You can hiss at Jhiton if you like," Vorik offered, "and know it won't affect your regalness. You're a wonderful queen. Your people are lucky to have you."

She scowled over at Jhiton as Ozlemar drew even with them and slowed down to match Agrevlari's pace. It was a languid pace, and Vorik suspected his dragon had deliberately flown slowly so that the others would catch up, thus to ensure *mating* didn't occur on his back. Vorik couldn't blame Agrevlari for that.

"Have you learned the location of the shielder yet?" Jhiton asked, speaking aloud instead of telepathically. That meant he wanted Syla to hear for some reason.

"We haven't discussed it," Vorik said.

"What *did* you discuss?" Jhiton's flat tone suggested he *had* gotten the gist of what had been going on—and didn't approve.

"That Syla is a magnificent and fearless queen who's faced down more enemies than any one person should have to deal with in a lifetime." Vorik refused to look away from Jhiton or feel chagrined about his feelings for Syla. "She deserves our respect."

"Is that what you were doing on your flight? Respecting her?"

"Yes."

"She killed Lesva's dragon." Jhiton sounded exasperated. "*Many* people's dragons. I don't know how you can—" He flung a hand toward them, as if Vorik had been doing something reprehensible by kissing her and giving her pleasure.

"You and your *dragons* invaded my Kingdom, you bastard." Syla's fingers curled into a fist. "*I've* done nothing wrong."

Jhiton gazed at her with little expression before saying, "Bring her to camp, Vorik. I will handle the questioning." He waved toward Ozlemar's horns, and the black dragon surged ahead.

Syla slumped back against Vorik's chest. "It's not too late to turn around and take me back to the islands."

Vorik wished that were true, but the two other dragons flew behind Agrevlari, effectively hemming him in between them and Ozlemar.

"Yes, it is," he said sadly.

19

FOR THE REST OF THE FLIGHT TO FROHA, THE SECOND OF THE world's two major continents and a place Syla had never been, she glared between General Jhiton's shoulder blades. If he hadn't shown up...

Actually, Syla wasn't sure *what* would have happened if he hadn't shown up. When she'd tried to talk Vorik into taking her home—and offered sex if he did—she hadn't believed he would do so. All she'd wanted was to act as she thought he would expect her to. If she *hadn't* tried to talk her way out of her fate, he might have realized the truth, that she hadn't fought being kidnapped as much as she could have. She'd been *planning* for this possibility and was delighted that she had, so far, managed to retain her medical kit. One of Jhiton's people would doubtless think to search it—or take it from her—but at least it would be in the camp, and she might find a way to reach it when she needed it.

Though she'd almost dropped it when Vorik had slid his talented fingers under the hem of her dress and left her gasping. Her cheeks flared with heat and embarrassment, and she hated that the general had probably witnessed at least some of her writhing. Yes, that was the precise word, and she rubbed her face at the memory. The general probably thought her an idiot, not the magnificent and fearless queen that Vorik had described.

Syla told herself that she *wanted* Jhiton to underestimate her. It would be best if all the stormers in their camp did. If they believed her crafty and dangerous, they would watch her closely and never give her an opportunity to escape with the shielder components.

She sat up with interest when a lush green coastline came into view above vertical white cliffs that faced the sea, rising hundreds of feet, save for gaps where it looked like the gods had smashed their great fists down to break them away. From maps, Syla knew the terrain was varied and stretched inland for more than a thousand miles, with all manner of interesting geological features. One day, if she survived the war, she would ask Wreylith to take her on a trip to see the world.

Unease sank into her gut at the thought of the red dragon. Oh, Wreylith would doubtless be fine on Bogberry Island by herself—she'd probably only waited five seconds after realizing she couldn't fly after Syla to start hunting berry-loving bears. But Syla had thought her dragon ally could play a role in her escape with the shielder components. More, she'd counted on it. If Syla managed to steal the components and sneak out of the stormer camp, how would she cross the sea by herself to return to the Kingdom? She didn't see any signs of civilization along the cliffs ahead—certainly nothing like a dock with a whaling ship and a friendly captain willing to help.

She looked skyward, away from storm clouds gathering on the northern horizon, and toward the position where the moon would rise, then sent a silent prayer to the moon god. *If there's any way you can send Chieftess Atilya or another Freeborn Faction rider a vision about where I am and how I could use a ride back to the Kingdom, I would appreciate it.*

She didn't expect an answer or any kind of acknowledgment—

aside from a couple of times when it had seemed like she might have received a little divine assistance, she hadn't seen much to suggest that the gods remained present in the world. But lightning flashed to the north, bright against the darkening clouds. It was probably a coincidence, and she vowed to exhaust all possible ways to escape on her own, but she chose to see it as a hopeful omen.

Still flying ahead on the black dragon, Jhiton looked back at her. Had he seen the lightning? Storms were common over the sea, so he couldn't think much of it, unless he had the ability to read minds and had somehow heard her prayer.

When his gaze lingered, Syla lifted her hand to give him a rude gesture.

Vorik snorted. Jhiton's expression didn't change. After a moment, he turned forward and pointed, directing the small wing of dragons to descend toward one of the gaps in the white cliffs.

Maybe Syla shouldn't have, but she leaned back into Vorik, wanting to draw whatever support he would offer before they arrived and she had to deal with Jhiton one-on-one for the first time. Vorik was the last one she should have sought support from, but… he always gave it. It might have been her imagination earlier, but he'd seemed on the verge of doing what she'd asked, taking her somewhere else besides his camp.

Not hesitating, Vorik wrapped his arms around her.

"I'll keep anyone from hurting you," he said quietly.

Jhiton was the main person Syla worried about, and she wondered if Vorik would step between her and his brother if she were in danger. In the shielder chamber, in the heat of battle, he'd done just that. But, if there had been more time then, if Kingdom troops hadn't been on the way, would he have truly faced off against his brother? What if Jhiton had forced the issue and attacked Vorik?

"Any chance your general will leave promptly on another mission, and you'll be in charge of questioning me?" Syla asked.

"*I* haven't had much luck getting information out of you. It's been the other way around. I've babbled more to you than I should have, due to my enrapturement." He glanced at her chest before smiling at her.

"Your enrapturement with my boobs?"

"With *all* of you, in truth, but they are especially fine."

She was on her way to be interrogated in an enemy camp; she shouldn't have been flattered and pleased by the statement. And yet...

"You're fine too, Vorik," she said softly.

"If that were true, I would be helping you escape, not delivering you to my people."

And he wouldn't have sunk her weapons platform.

"I agree," she said.

Vorik sighed, brushed her cheek, and leaned forward as Agrevlari spread his wings to glide in for a landing on a beach tucked into a gap between the cliffs. Broken branches, driftwood, and pinecones littered the sand, and she guessed the same storm that had hit her islands recently had reached these shores.

A few seals lounging in the area scattered at the dragons' approach, hurrying to escape into the water. From the head of the beach, a steep grassy slope stretched inland with an animal trail meandering upward until it drew level with the top of the bluff. From there, it disappeared into a forest of towering evergreen trees.

Jhiton and his black dragon had already landed, and he'd slid off to examine large footprints in the sand. Even though the high walls of the cliffs left the beach in shadow, Syla could make out the marks well due to their depth and size. They hadn't been left by the seals. Something large and heavy had visited recently, and, as Agrevlari alighted on the beach, she thought of books she'd read on the dangerous creatures that made Froha their home.

When the two blue dragons landed beside Agrevlari, who growled and nipped at one he must have felt was too close, Jhiton beckoned to the pair of riders. He didn't look at Vorik or Syla, instead pointing his men toward the tracks.

"Not a kraken at least," Vorik called to the general.

Judging by the baleful look that Jhiton gave him, he wasn't in the mood for humor. Or *was* it humor?

"Kraken?" Syla asked quietly.

"Let's just say that the camp we're visiting wasn't our *first* choice." Vorik winked, slid off Agrevlari's back, and offered her a hand down.

She accepted it and landed in the sand, making note of their surroundings in case she had to come back to this spot for... she didn't know what for. It wasn't as if anyone would come to pick her up.

Wreylith? She sent the word out to sea, though they'd crossed hundreds of miles, and she doubted she had the power to communicate telepathically that far away. But wasn't the krendala supposed to allow riders and dragons to speak from a much greater distance than typical? She always carried the little red figurine along with her these days.

I remain entrapped on this island, came Wreylith's reply, her voice very soft but distinct enough to understand.

I'm sure you're traumatized.

Dragons are born to be free, not caged.

How many bog bears have you joyously hunted down and eaten since I left?

Only two.

The stormers have brought me to the coast of Froha. Will you ask one of the Freeborn Faction dragons if they'll come and retrieve me?

Syla thought wistfully of the cheerful Igliana. She would be delighted if the orange dragon showed up.

One? How many stormer dragons are there?

I'm not sure. At least four.

It will take more than one Freedom Faction dragon to rescue you from so many. And there are probably more than you've seen.

Yes, but I intend to rescue myself. I'll only need to be picked up.

She braced herself for Wreylith to reply that she was a puny human and could never escape a camp guarded by dragons. Or a camp guarded by humans for that matter.

You will suborn the rider who services you sexually? was what Wreylith asked.

Syla's cheeks heated, though it wasn't as if anyone would overhear their telepathic conversation. Even if Jhiton had the ability to spy, he was busy checking out the tracks.

He appears most devoted to you, Wreylith added. *He may indeed be willing to assist you in escaping.*

He's the one who kidnapped me.

Did you not desire to be kidnapped?

Well... sort of.

You sent me to check on your allies in the large human dwelling when I could have remained close.

I know, and I am *hoping to use this opportunity to find the shielder components. I have a medical kit full of drugs that can help me get away from the camp, but I'll need someone to pick me up and take me back to the Kingdom. Promise however many livestock you need to, please.*

Will the livestock be for the dragon who comes to get you or the dragon who arranges the rescue?

Syla resisted the urge to roll her eyes. Wasn't Wreylith sated from all those bog bears?

Both, was what she thought back to the dragon.

Hm, very well.

"They're heading toward the camp," one of the riders

observed, pointing toward the tracks and the trail leading to the bluff.

"Yes." Jhiton straightened. "And dire wolves are often accompanied by dire vultures, which have a propensity to carry off our children if we're not vigilant." His people had to already know that, so Syla suspected the words were for her. Jhiton glanced at her before continuing to speak to his men. "Ask your dragons to stay in the area. We left many of our winged allies in the Kingdom to reclaim Harvest Island and be ready in case we get another opportunity at Bogberry, but we lost many of them—and several of our skilled riders—to that gods-forsaken weapon."

"It's a gods-crafted *wondrous* weapon," Syla stated.

Vorik gave her a warning look that probably meant she would be wise not to talk back to Jhiton or ruffle his feathers. She lifted her chin, having no intention of being cowed by the general or any of his riders.

"Either way, it's in the river now," Vorik said cheerfully.

"Not a deep enough burial for it," Jhiton murmured, looking at Syla again, as if that were *her* fault.

Syla bared her teeth at him and fantasized about driving magical daggers into his heart. If she got close enough to touch him at any point, she wouldn't hesitate to use her power to kill him, and she eyed his chest now, wishing she could press her palm flat to it and send her magic straight into his heart.

The general's eyes narrowed as he watched her face, and, for the second time that day, she wondered if he could read her thoughts. She hadn't heard of a human with that ability, but who knew what powers he derived from that great black dragon?

Vorik rested a hand on her shoulder. "Let's head to camp, General. The dire wolves are more active at night, and it's getting dark."

"Agreed," Jhiton said. "And it'll be easier to question our captive there. Healer Yavaron has the powder."

"Powder?" Syla looked to Vorik, remembering that he'd taken items, including the hydra-scale powder, from her cabin, but he didn't have a pack with him now, nothing but his weapons and clothes.

He didn't look surprised by Jhiton's comment but didn't explain.

Jhiton smiled tightly and led the way up the trail.

Agrevlari, Ozlemar, and the blue dragons flapped away, heading out to sea and down the coast. To hunt? Since the trees and bushes grew densely atop the bluff, reminding Syla of the rainforest they'd visited along the coast of Droha, the dragons might struggle to find places to land. This was probably as close to the stormer camp as they'd been able to bring their riders.

Vorik followed Jhiton up the trail, making sure Syla came with him. She adjusted her spectacles and stayed close to Vorik. The two riders who walked behind them gave her cool looks, and she suspected everyone in the stormer camp except Vorik would hate her instantly for having used the weapons platform to kill their comrades. What were the odds that Vorik would truly be able to keep anyone from hurting her? Or worse?

The blades of waist-high grass along the path had razor edges, making her wish she wore trousers instead of a dress. At least the hem fell past her calves. A couple of stunted trees they passed had thorns along their narrow, bent trunks. Even though the green foliage above looked lush, Syla was sure a lot of the flora here could open a wound on a person. The predators would be even more likely to do so.

Jhiton looked up, and Syla followed his gaze. Against the dark sky, the storm clouds having drifted closer, a huge black vulture with a white spot on its chest sailed overhead. She'd never seen a bird so large, not on her islands, and, with talons almost as long as those of a dragon, she believed it was far more than a scavenger. Its size promised Jhiton's statement about the vultures here stealing away children was likely true. *Large* children.

As they reached the top of the bluff, screeches, roars, and blood-curdling shrieks drifted out of the forest. Again, it reminded Syla of the rainforest on Droha, though the salty air wasn't as warm or humid.

Instead of heading inland, the trail turned to follow the coastline, meandering through a mixture of conifers and deciduous trees, some of the leaves already turning yellow, orange, and red for the year. A squirrel with fangs chattered at them from the branches. A huge pinecone dropped between Jhiton and Vorik. Too bad it hadn't hit the general on the head, though he probably would have reacted in time to swat it aside with one of the two swords sheathed at his waist, as he'd done with her explosives in the shielder chamber on Castle Island.

Again, she dreaded the idea of spending time alone with the man. Though she didn't want to be questioned by Vorik either, she would prefer a friendly face, especially if she was to be drugged. He would be far less likely to take advantage of her. Though he would do his duty, as he always did, and ask the questions his general wanted answers to.

She grimaced and hoped she could find the shielder components and figure out how to escape *before* the questioning.

Jhiton turned off the path, padding across mossy rocks, and toward the mouth of a cave that Syla didn't notice until they were almost upon it. Though the entrance was wide and higher than their heads, jumbled boulders around the front helped hide the dark opening. Further, stalactites inside leered down from above like jagged dragon's teeth. She'd only read about such rock features. Thanks to the volcanos that had formed most of the Kingdom islands, the majority of the caves back home had been carved out by magma and were tubular in nature.

Before entering, Jhiton lifted a hand toward the top of the cave.

Syla jumped. In the fading light, she hadn't seen the man perched up there among the moss-covered boulders. As well as he blended in—he wore fur-trimmed animal-hide clothing rather than black rider garments—she might not have spotted him under any circumstances.

"We always have a sky watcher on duty around our camps," Vorik said, reminding her of the term the stormers had. "Wyverns aren't that prevalent in this area, but there are plenty of other aerial predators we have to watch out for."

"Ground predators as well," one of the riders behind them muttered.

"Don't forget about the cave crawlers," his comrade said.

Jhiton gazed coolly back at them. What, were his men not allowed to chatter?

"When we bring prisoners to camp," he said, "the idea is to learn from them, not volunteer information about our people."

"You're being grumpy this evening, General," Vorik said. "Prisoners prefer it if you question them with good-natured cheer."

Jhiton didn't respond, only leading them into the spacious cave. Without cheer.

At first, stalactites and rock formations kept Syla from seeing how many people resided inside, but the lights from fires promised dozens of inhabitants, and the air was thick with the scents of burning wood and roasting meat.

As numerous sets of eyes turned toward them, Syla braced herself for hatred and vitriol. And many of the gazes were cool or outright hostile when they landed on her, but some were curious. Some belonged to children, and a band of boys and girls ran past, kicking a ball made from stitched leather in a game that involved bouncing it off the rock formations and bopping it with elbows, chests, and heads but not hands.

"Hi, Vorik!" One kid waved at him. "Will you play with us later? Is that a gardener? Oh, hullo, General." The wave turned to a salute for Jhiton, whose cold aloofness probably didn't endear him to children. Or anyone.

The ball bounced off a stalactite and flew toward Syla's head. She ducked, seeing it angling at her from the side more easily than she usually would have, but Vorik stepped in to catch it before it could reach her. He looked curiously at her as he tossed the ball toward the group.

"No hands, Vorik!" one admonished him.

"I didn't think the queen would be impressed with me head-butting a ball like a mountain goat," he replied.

That comment prompted the kids to issue goat-like bleats as they ran along the edges of the camp, kicking the ball and being yelled at by mothers and grandmothers. A white-haired woman smiled while also waving a menacing wooden spoon at them.

Syla was struck by the homeyness of the setting. Though a couple of armed men patrolled the area, some wandering into view from the depths of the cave, she realized she was, for the first time in her life, seeing stormers in the natural state in which they lived their lives, not as invaders or potential troublemakers visiting her islands. There were more aged men and women than she'd expected. Their reputation would have led her to guess they sent their elders out to die in order to preserve winter food stores for those still of an age to bear children and protect the tribe. Even if they didn't do that, she would have thought that, simply due to the harshness of their environment, not many people made it to old age.

"Come," Jhiton said to Syla.

"The questioning is going to start right away?" Vorik asked. "Can't we give her a meal first? Queens are more garrulous and cheerful on full stomachs."

"That's not mentioned in the history lores." Jhiton twitched his fingers toward Syla, then walked off, assuming she would obey.

She clenched her jaw, longing to see the kids' ball sail across the cave to club him in the back of his head.

Vorik rested his hand on the small of her back and nodded for her to follow, making it clear that he would walk beside her. Maybe he meant the gesture to be supportive, but he was her captor as much as Jhiton was. *More.* He'd been the one to kidnap her after all, and even if he would protect her from harm—and flying balls—he wouldn't stop the questioning.

Though she walked where he indicated—he could easily hoist her over his shoulder if she resisted—nerves jittered in her stomach, and she gazed carefully about the cave. This time, instead of looking at the inhabitants, she tried to spot the shielder components. Vorik hadn't said anything to suggest his people had destroyed them, so they ought to be there. They *had* to be there, otherwise there was no point in Syla having allowed her capture. Not that she could necessarily have stopped it. But, as Wreylith had pointed out, she could have fought harder against it.

She spotted Chieftess Shi sitting with a group of adults in a corner of the cave sectioned off from the others by rock formations. Jhiton nodded at her over the heads of those around her. She nodded back.

All going to plan, was it? Syla grimaced.

"Isn't it dinnertime yet?" a girl of five or six asked plaintively. "We have food now, don't we? I'm hungry."

"We have food, but you still have to wait for it to cook." A gaunt woman with sparse white hair and a hunched spine stirred soup in one of several giant shells the size of metal stock pots back home. A rich broth that smelled wonderful simmered over one of several fires burning close together in what one might have called a kitchen area. Meat also roasted on spits, dripping juices down into the flames. "Hunt Night Soup is a delicacy that must be nursed along so that the flavors develop." The woman scattered rosemary, thyme, and a few less easily identifiable herbs atop the liquid in the shells.

"It's been cooking *forever.*"

"If you whine, the cave crawlers will get you," another woman said, a baby snuggled in her arms swaddled in a soft hide wrap. It gurgled happily while swatting at a braid of the woman's hair.

"Or the dire vultures!" one of the boys who'd been playing in the ball game said. "I saw two earlier. One almost ate Tamuel."

"Did not," a boy who might have been his twin said. "Anyway, I can run faster than you. They'd pluck you up before me."

"No chance."

As Jhiton led Syla deeper into the cave, the conversation faded from her awareness, but she glanced thoughtfully back a couple of times. The powdered dayvak buds in her medical kit came to mind. Usually, the sedative wasn't delivered en masse, but she knew it could be diluted in a liquid. Also, if it were mixed into a flavorful dish, the bitter taste might be masked, and *Hunt Night Soup* sounded like something that might have a ritual aspect and be shared with all.

If she could figure out how to sprinkle her powder into those shells...

Aware of Vorik watching her as they walked, she looked forward again and attempted to mask her thoughts. More than once, she'd thought he might also have a slight knack for mind reading. He probably didn't, but he was, at the least, attentive and intuitive.

The rock formations had made it difficult to see how far back the cave stretched, and they walked farther than Syla expected as it narrowed into a wide tunnel. The group passed the last of the campfires, but a few lanterns had been jammed into nooks in the rocks to provide light enough to see into side chambers. Some were empty, some had people sleeping in them—those who stood *sky watcher* duty at night, perhaps?—and some held sacks of food or haunches of curing meat that hung from racks or were tied to stalactites to dangle.

Syla missed a step when she spotted crates of fruit and squashes sitting beside kegs of beer and ale with Kingdom labels painted on the fronts. She ground her teeth, though of course she'd known the stormers were taking food—*stealing* it—from Harvest Island. It was, after all, the reason they'd invaded and started a war.

She couldn't keep from shooting an accusing look at Vorik. She expected it to result in a defiant or determined expression from him, but his green eyes were chagrined, maybe even regretful. He didn't look away from her but might have wanted to. Of course, he was, as he'd told her and demonstrated, honorable. He probably agreed that his people needed to do *something* to ensure they had food for the winter but wouldn't support stealing from farmers who'd spent all season cultivating their crops and protecting them from pest insects and animals. His people might consider that less heroic than *sky watching* but surely as necessary.

A single soldier with a dagger and mace stood guard in front of a dark nook, yellow light from a lantern across the tunnel highlighting his lean, stoic face. There weren't any sources of illumination in the nook, so whatever was back there was hidden by darkness.

Syla didn't give it more than the passing perusal that she'd granted the other nooks, because she didn't want her captors to notice her interest, but her heart beat faster. A man wouldn't stand guard in front of a chamber with nothing of importance in it. He had to be protecting the shielder components. He'd probably been placed there because of her arrival.

Jhiton turned into the next side nook. The tunnel continued deeper into the darkness, descending downward as it narrowed, but there weren't any more lanterns in that direction. Nothing about it suggested it might lead to another exit. If Syla was to escape, she would have to go through the camp and out the front.

They clambered over uneven ground and past a few columns and stalagmites to find a small campfire with an aged woman sitting cross-legged in front of it. An older man lay on a blanket near her, but he departed when the group approached. Was the woman the healer that Jhiton had mentioned? Tending a patient? There were a few sacks near the side of the cave and jars made from pieces of horn or shell or carved from wood.

A tiny blue jar rested on the ground next to the healer, and Syla's gut churned. She didn't know how Vorik had gotten it here ahead of her, but it was the container that held hydra-scale powder. Or it was one identical to the jar Teyla had found. She supposed the stormers might also have hunted for treasures in the storm god's laboratory before leaving the desert.

However the powder had arrived, it was here, and the stormers were ready to question her.

As soon as Syla walked in, the healer nodded and reached for a gourd of liquid. She swished it, opened the lid, and picked up the blue jar.

"You may go, Vorik," Jhiton said.

Vorik stopped beside Syla, his shoulder brushing hers, and met his brother's gaze. "I'm staying."

Jhiton walked toward them, and Syla tensed. The general reached for her medical kit. She tensed further, her grip on it tightening. Though she didn't know when she would find an opportunity to drop the Dayvak buds in the soup, it would never come if she didn't have access to the kit.

"Release this," Jhiton said. "Vorik will put it somewhere safe."

"It's my medical kit," Syla said.

"I'm aware." The cool look that Jhiton gave Vorik suggested he thought Vorik should already have relieved her of it. Maybe he had an inkling of the sharp tools—and drugs—inside.

"I'm not leaving her," Vorik said quietly, the words not meant to carry to the healer. If he defied his brother occasionally, he probably didn't do so in front of witnesses. "I promised her I wouldn't let her be hurt."

"And I told you that she won't be hurt." Jhiton stepped closer, his chest less than a foot from Syla.

Taller than his brother and just as lean and muscular, despite being at least ten years older, Jhiton exuded the power granted by his dragon bond. Even though Vorik exuded similar power, Jhiton was more intimidating. *He* didn't smile at Syla with warm eyes, and she believed that if Vorik hadn't been there, Jhiton would already have his hand around her throat, choking her as he used his magic to torture and question her in a similar manner to that Lesva had used. Maybe a more effective manner…

Though Syla reminded herself that she had power of her own that she could draw upon, that didn't reassure her. She had to fight down the urge to step behind Vorik. Like dragons, stormers probably had more respect for people who faced them without fear. Or at least without giving in to their fear.

Behind Jhiton, the healer poured a large dose of powder into the gourd and swished it about. Syla found the preparations ominous. She'd managed to keep from sharing her secrets during Lesva's interrogation, but if her mind was addled or weakened from a drug… By the eyes of the moon, what if her desire to get the magical components back turned into her betraying her people by giving up the locations of the shielders? She not only knew where the Bogberry Island artifact was but where they *all* were.

Dear gods, what had she been thinking? She was the *last* person who should have allowed herself to be captured by the enemy.

"I'm not leaving her, Jhiton," Vorik said, his voice as cold as Syla had ever heard it.

"There's no reason for you to stay." Jhiton was just as cold, his taut body radiating dangerous energy.

Beside her, Vorik was the same way. A part of her wondered if she should encourage them to fight, but Vorik had once suggested that his brother had taught him everything he knew and might best him. If Syla lost Vorik, she would be all alone and surrounded by enemies without a protector. And, with a hundred people or more camped out front, it wasn't as if she would be able to slip away while they fought.

"There is," Vorik said. "You'll be less ruthless if I'm watching."

"This task may require a lack of *ruth*."

"She deserves ruth," Vorik said, his voice softening as he gazed into his brother's eyes. "You've already taken her whole family from her."

Syla didn't expect the heartless general to do anything but scoff, but Jhiton looked from Vorik to her for a long moment, then stepped back. His eyes, the same emerald as Vorik's, were much harder to read, but maybe they grew slightly less cold.

"Very well," Jhiton said. "You may stay."

Syla didn't feel like she'd won a victory, not when Vorik was *also* her captor, but she did believe that if he was present, he wouldn't let Jhiton be as monstrous. Would it be enough? When the healer rose, her concoction prepared, Syla doubted it.

"It must be drunk?" Jhiton asked the woman.

"That would be the simplest way to get it into her."

"She won't voluntarily drink." Jhiton eyed Syla again, then his brother.

To see if Vorik would stop him if he tried to force it down her throat?

Syla clenched her jaw and lifted her chin. The healer watched Jhiton, a doubtful expression on her face. Syla hoped that the woman, like her, was sworn to help people, not harm them, and would object to someone being hurt by having her jaw pried open so that she had no choice but to gulp that liquid. But… she doubted the woman would disobey any order Jhiton gave. Even if he wasn't one of the tribal chiefs, everyone in the camp had shown deference to him as he walked past.

"We'll have to force it down her throat," Jhiton told Vorik.

"What's the *less* simple way to get it into her?" Vorik asked, though he sounded wary.

Syla could guess but doubted nomadic people who used shells for cook pots would have syringes with needles.

The healer gazed thoughtfully at her. "Bring her medical kit to me."

Syla almost groaned. Just because they didn't have forges and glassworks and couldn't *make* syringes didn't mean the healer wouldn't know how to use one from the Kingdom. And Syla, who'd been so pleased that she'd managed to bring her medical kit along, had inadvertently delivered one into the enemy's hands.

20

VORIK HAD MADE A MISTAKE. HE SHOULDN'T HAVE CAPTURED SYLA and brought her here. Yes, those had been his orders; bloody daggers, he'd even suggested—no, *requested*—them, but that had been out of desperation to save her life. He hadn't thought it through, hadn't realized what a betrayal it would seem to him. What a betrayal it *was*. Escorting her into the depths of the cave had made him feel like a villain. Maybe this would help his people, but at what cost? His heart? His soul?

Wasn't there another way? One that wouldn't have the stormers and the gardeners killing each other over those islands for the rest of his life? And beyond? It wasn't what the gods had wanted when they'd placed humanity on the protected islands. And this... this betrayal of Syla wasn't what *he* wanted.

At his side, she stood straight, her usually expressive face masked, her eyes grim behind her spectacles.

Vorik watched bleakly as Jhiton reached for her medical kit. Her hand tightened reflexively around the strap, as if she would fight him for it, but she must have determined that she wouldn't win that battle because she let go. She did flex her fingers and eye

Jhiton as he took the kit to the healer. Thinking about how she'd once used the power of her touch to kill?

Since they'd landed, Vorik had been watching for signs that she would try that. Normally, he would trust that Jhiton could take care of himself against any foe, but he didn't know how fast Syla could work her magic to kill. He wasn't even positive that touch was required.

Healer Yavaron delved into the kit and pulled out a long, slender cylinder with a small reservoir and a needle. The thing looked ominous. Vorik hadn't seen such a device before, but, as Yavaron poured some of her concoction into the reservoir, he got the gist of what it would do, deliver the drug directly into Syla's bloodstream.

"That's not sterile," Syla said. "You can't just stick it in someone's vein."

In *her* vein.

"Your magic will keep you from becoming infected," Yavaron said with certainty.

Syla looked like she would object further but didn't. Maybe she knew the statement to be true.

"Hold her," Jhiton said.

Vorik hesitated. The word *betrayal* floated through his mind again. Especially when Syla looked at him, her mask slipping to reveal fear and concern in her beautiful gray eyes. Less for herself, he knew, and more for her people. She feared letting their secrets slip, the secrets that kept them safe on their islands.

"Hold her," Jhiton repeated, "or I will."

The words seemed to promise that his grip would be anything but gentle. Yet Vorik still hesitated, keenly feeling the difference between passively watching something dreadful happen and being an active participant.

No, he amended. There wasn't a difference. Either way, he was guilty.

It was the speculative gleam that entered Syla's eyes that propelled Vorik to step closer. If Jhiton were the one to grip Syla, she would try to kill him.

In these circumstances, Vorik wasn't confident that she wouldn't kill *him*. Or at least attack him.

Regardless, he stepped behind Syla and gripped her arms to keep her from fighting the application of the needle. She clenched her jaw, her back going rigid, her muscles tense. She glanced at Vorik and closed her eyes, as if struggling with an internal debate. He had no trouble guessing what it was and braced to use his own magic to defend himself if need be.

As Healer Yavaron stepped closer, Vorik sensed Syla's power coiling within her. The moon-mark on the back of her hand glowed silver. Would she lash out at Yavaron?

Though Yavaron wasn't bonded with a dragon and didn't have any magic, she must have seen the silver glow and sensed the danger. Stopping a few feet from Syla, she looked at Jhiton, a question in her eyes.

Jhiton lifted a hand toward Syla, and Vorik tensed. He didn't think his brother would strike Syla, but he readied himself to defend her if need be.

Jhiton paused, his head tilting as he looked toward the cave entrance.

Four dragons allied with the Freeborn Faction are flying along the coast, Agrevlari spoke into Vorik's mind.

Ozlemar must have been giving a similar warning to Jhiton.

How far away? Vorik asked. *Do they seem to know where our camp is?*

They are yet dozens of miles away.

It doesn't take dragons long to cover such a distance.

Of course not. Dragons are magnificent.

Concerned with Syla's fate, Vorik didn't offer a typical snarky reply. Instead, he watched Jhiton to see how he would react.

His eyes narrowed, and he looked at Syla. "Did you speak to the Freeborn Faction dragons and tell them where you are? How far away can you communicate with their kind?"

Syla glared at him without answering.

Ozlemar has ordered us to fly down the coast to intercept the dragons and keep them from finding the new camp, Agrevlari said. *We are four to their four. We can keep them from encroaching.*

Good, Vorik replied. *Thank you.*

"Or is it Wreylith that you can communicate with from afar?" Jhiton asked Syla. "That would make more sense." His gaze shifted to Vorik. "You said there's a krendala?"

"Yes," Vorik said.

"Did you take it from her? I trust you searched her thoroughly while you were riding together." Jhiton's eyebrow twitched.

"A gentleman doesn't touch a lady's... krendala."

Jhiton gave him a baleful look, then turned back to Syla and opened his mouth but must have realized she wouldn't answer his questions voluntarily. He flicked a finger toward the healer.

After glancing uneasily at the glowing mark again, Yavaron told him, "Push up her sleeve, and hold her arm still."

Vorik could have shifted his grip to do that, but Jhiton glanced at him and reached for Syla himself.

"Careful," Vorik said to remind his brother of her power, though he was sure Jhiton hadn't forgotten Devron's report.

The withering look Syla gave Vorik when she glanced back made the word *betrayal* come to his mind again. But he had to protect his brother as surely as he wanted to protect her.

Jhiton pushed up the sleeve of Syla's dress, then held her by the wrist and elbow, turning her arm so that a vein would be accessible.

Syla didn't move, but Vorik sensed her summoning her power. He squeezed her arms and whispered, "Don't," but he couldn't bring himself to tighten his grip enough that it would be painful. Not even for Jhiton.

It didn't matter. Jhiton had power of his own and created a shield around himself that blocked the tendrils of magic that Syla tried to send into him. As Yavaron lifted the needle to Syla's arm, Jhiton held Syla's gaze. She summoned more power as she glanced at the needle, a surprising amount of power.

From the outside, it was hard for Vorik to sense exactly what was happening, but she seemed to draw from the dragon tattoo as well as her birthmark, the different types of magic mingling inside of her. Then she created a spear of energy that she thrust toward Jhiton.

His eyes widened in surprise at her power, but he didn't release her arm. Though his jaw tightened from the effort, he managed to fend off her attack. Then he must have countered it, sending his magic into her, because she rocked back slightly, fear flashing in her eyes. She recovered, hardening her defenses, and masked her features, not letting him see her concern. His eyes closed to slits, but he didn't seem to push his attack further, merely keeping his own defenses up.

When the sharp tip of the needle touched her skin, Syla tried to pull away physically and threw more magic at Jhiton. Vorik's heart ached, and he wanted to release her, to let her run away, but with his entire tribe camped between here and the exit to the cave, there was nowhere for her to go. Someone who didn't care for her would tackle her and hurt her. If she could even escape Jhiton. His grip hadn't shifted, and he deflected her second spear of power. No, Jhiton wouldn't let go. Even if Vorik did.

Syla snarled, straining from her effort, but she couldn't keep the needle from sliding into her vein. Yavaron emptied the reservoir into her, then skittered back.

Jhiton released Syla's arm and also stepped away. With nobody else touching her, Syla shifted her attention—her *power*—to Vorik. To strike?

Again, he braced himself, though a trickle of doubt crept into him. He was strong, but did he have as much power as his brother? Agrevlari was a strong dragon, but he wasn't Ozlemar's match. Maybe…

Though she seemed on the verge of attacking him, Syla didn't. She slumped, the magic within her growing still. She swallowed, and looking over her shoulder from behind, Vorik could see tears glisten within her eyes. It was not, he was certain, from the pain of the needle, and he closed his own eyes, regret filling his heart. He'd made a mistake. He shouldn't have helped with this. He should simply have walked away from this war, from his brother and his people. Going into exile would have been better than this, than betraying someone who kept helping him—who always refrained from hurting him—even though they'd been destined from the beginning to be enemies.

"How long will it be before the drug takes effect?" Jhiton asked Yavaron.

He had no regrets. This was exactly what he wanted.

"It might have been up to an hour if she'd ingested the liquid," Yavaron said, "but this will be faster. It might take only a few minutes before it acts upon her and lessens her inhibitions about answering questions."

Jhiton nodded and looked at Vorik. *Agrevlari told you about the Freeborn dragons?*

Vorik didn't want to answer his brother, didn't even want to look at him, but this was about the safety of their people. *Yes.*

They're here for her. It wasn't a question.

Probably.

This was supposed to be our hidden camp and base of operations for the next few months. Jhiton glanced at Syla, but her chin was still to her chest. She'd blinked away the moisture in her eyes, but her cheek ticked, as if she was struggling with herself. No, she was struggling with the effects of the drug.

I shouldn't have brought her here, Vorik said.

Another locale would have been safer. Jhiton misunderstood what Vorik had meant, that he shouldn't have kidnapped her at all. *But if you'd remained on Bogberry Island, her dragon would have eviscerated you.*

That is true.

Jhiton stepped closer to Syla, drawing her gaze upward. "Where is the shielder on Bogberry Island?"

The muscle in Syla's cheek ticked again. She shook her head.

"Have you moved the shielder on Castle Island?" Jhiton asked.

She opened her mouth, as if she wanted to answer, but managed to close it again without speaking.

"She's losing her resolve," Yavaron said. "Any moment now…"

Jhiton's eyebrow twitched, and he glanced in the direction of the cave entrance again. Concerned about the Freeborn Faction dragons? Vorik thought Agrevlari and the others could keep them from finding this place, but a part of him wanted the dragons to arrive. Then maybe, Syla *could* escape. Before being the instrument of her people's ultimate demise. How would she live with that?

"Where is the shielder on Bogberry Island?" Jhiton repeated.

"I hope you fall into the deepest chasm in the storm god's twisted lair and burn for all eternity," Syla told him.

Jhiton slanted a long look at Yavaron, who could only spread her arms.

"Her moon-mark may defend her from this as much as it does from physical and magical interrogation," Jhiton mused.

Hope crept into Syla's eyes, but she looked like she didn't know. She was feeling the effects of the drug in some way. Vorik could tell.

"Maybe try asking her something she has less built-in reticence about answering," Yavaron suggested. "It may help along the process. Ask her something like her name or favorite color."

Jhiton gazed at Syla. "Do you love Vorik?"

Syla blinked. So did Vorik, and he felt like he should punch Jhiton. But… he also caught himself leaning forward, wanting to know the answer.

"I…" Syla said. "Maybe," she whispered, glancing back at him.

"That's *not* her favorite color, General," Yavaron said dryly.

Ignoring her, Jhiton glanced at Vorik. It crossed his mind that his brother might have thought to use Syla's love to his advantage, if she'd admitted to it. Vorik scowled at him, glad she'd given a vague answer.

Unfazed, Jhiton asked Syla, "What's your name?"

"Syla Moonmark." As soon as the words came out, she frowned at him. Realizing she was answering the questions and not liking it?

Jhiton nodded. "Your favorite color?"

"Periwinkle. Did you know that I lobbied to have the healers' robes for the Kingdom temples changed to that color? The dark-blue ones are *so* drab. Our patients must think we're personifications of death when we walk in. That *can't* put them in a good healing mood. Periwinkle is so much perkier. Admittedly, it would be harder to clean. People bleed on you sometimes, you know. It's not their fault, of course. The dark colors hide stains, I suppose. Did you know that one of my second cousins is a chemist? She uses the power of her moon-mark to study existing substances and combine them into new ones. She wrote to me about a bleaching powder derived from… I believe it was chlorine, yes, and said it could be used to get stains out of white materials, like sheets. Maybe our robes could also be turned to white."

Jhiton hardly ever looked surprised, and that wasn't the precise expression he wore now, but his mouth drooped farther and farther open as Syla continued. Vorik smiled, having heard her go on about something she was passionate about a couple of times, though this was probably induced by the drug. Maybe lowering her inhibitions also made her chatty.

"What's your favorite hobby?" Jhiton looked wary as he asked the question and glanced at Yavaron.

She could only shrug back.

"Oh, I adore all things related to herbalism, pharmacology, and the history of healing. I collect old books and antique medical tools, you know. My cousin Teyla studies ancient civilizations, but I'm mostly interested in the practices of healing they had and the tools they made. I love that which is related to healing and helping people."

Yavaron sighed, looking wistfully at Syla, and Vorik suspected she also felt regret about being a part of this. She was as dedicated to helping people as anyone and probably didn't care for any of this.

"I had collected so many wondrous specimens from past times," Syla continued, "but then the stormers invaded the capital and destroyed the temple and my room. I lost almost everything and so many friends and my whole family too." She hiccuped, tears filling her eyes. This time, with the drug impacting her, she didn't blink them away.

Vorik had to blink away tears of his own as sympathy welled within him.

Syla seemed to remember that Jhiton was *one* of those stormers, and she squinted at him, a hint of suspicion entering her eyes.

"Any other hobbies?" Jhiton doubtless wanted to ask about the shielders, but he had to be waiting until he knew the drug would prompt her to answer.

"I like to read about all manner of topics, and in the summer I adore swimming. I've always been such a klutz on land, but everything is smoother in the water. I almost feel graceful sometimes." Her suspicion faded, and she brightened when she said,

"Oh, and Vorik has said he'll teach me to juggle. I'm sure I'll have no aptitude for it, but I think he would like it if I tried. He gave me some balls. He thinks it'll help my eyesight. Well, not exactly that, but my peripheral vision. Yes, that's what it was. He's nice to care, isn't he? And when he smiles at me, and his eyes are warm, I get all mushy inside." She giggled. "Mushy isn't a very good word, is it?"

That giggle startled Vorik. Poor Syla had been in mourning since he'd met her, and he'd never heard her giggle. But the drug...

"It's a fine word. Vorik is mushy too." Jhiton arched an eyebrow at Vorik.

Vorik scowled at him.

"He was wondering," Jhiton said to Syla, "where the shielder for Bogberry Island is."

Vorik's scowl deepened. This was the whole point of capturing and questioning Syla, but Vorik hated that his brother was trying to use her feelings for him against her. And dread rather than triumph filled him when she answered.

"Oh, it's in the salt mine at the core of the island. In the back of the original tunnel, behind a relief carved of the sea god."

"Excellent," Jhiton said.

"You need a moon-mark to access it," Syla warned.

"That won't be a problem. Did you say you've moved the shielder artifact on Castle Island or that it's still in the same spot?"

"I..." Syla's suspicion returned, and was that knowing dread creeping into her eyes?

It was hard to tell from behind her, but Vorik believed she'd realized she'd made a mistake.

"Where is the shielder on Vineyard Island?" Jhiton asked.

"I don't think—"

A shout came from the depths of the cave system. "Trouble coming! Cave crawlers rushing up this way in a hurry."

Jhiton stepped back and drew his swords. Vorik released Syla, intending to go with his brother—if the cave crawlers were on the move, something deep in the tunnels had disturbed them.

"Stay here," Jhiton said. "Keep your prisoner safe. And in place."

As Jhiton jogged out, several armed men and women from the front of the camp appeared outside their nook. Together, they ran deeper into the cave complex.

Scant seconds passed before the person who'd shouted the first warning yelled, "A kraken moved into the underground lake!"

Vorik cursed. He'd been joking when he and Jhiton had spoken about the possibility, but such threats were real in their world and always had to be expected.

We've engaged with the Freeborn dragons, Agrevlari told Vorik. *They've claimed to be hunting and seeking shelter from a storm that's starting to batter the coastline, but we believe they're looking for your queen.*

"When the mad god sends a storm, he sends a hurricane," Vorik muttered the old saying.

Yavaron shook her head, returned the needle to Syla's medical kit, and picked up her own healing supplies. "I'm going to be needed out there."

More warriors ran through the tunnel as cries of engagement came from the underground lake. Pig-like squeals accompanied the shouts of men. The cave crawlers. They would be fleeing the kraken, but they had claws and sharp teeth, making them threats on their own, and if they saw the stormers as obstacles to escape, they would be vicious. The cave kraken, of course, made no sounds. Such creatures never did.

"Vorik?" Syla looked blearily at him as Yavaron stepped out of the nook, leaving them alone. "What's happening?"

"Nothing good." Vorik longed to go fight with his people, but Jhiton had ordered him to stay, and he would. A part of him, however, wondered if Syla was lucid enough to escape while his people were distracted. He shouldn't want her to do that, especially when the drug had been working, and they could gain even more intelligence from her, but the ignominy of it all disturbed him. Even if she hadn't been hurt, she'd been betrayed. When they'd been in the opposite situation, she hadn't drugged him—or let anyone else drug him. She'd respected him and his honor. "You're a better person than I am," he murmured to her.

The uncharacteristic confusion that furrowed her brow stung him, and he found himself hoping the drug wore off soon. And that he could figure out a way to keep Jhiton from applying it again.

"I'd have better luck reasoning with the cave kraken," he muttered.

21

A scream of pain echoed up from the depths of the cave. Syla struggled to clear her muzzy thoughts and figure out what was happening. She'd been taken prisoner, hadn't she? By the stormers. Yes. That awful General Jhiton had been questioning her, and she... She'd spoken to him. Why?

She almost found the answer, but then it escaped, her mind fogged, reality elusive. She grew aware of Vorik standing at the entrance of their section of the cave. His back was to her, his sword in his hand, as he looked into a tunnel illuminated by lanterns.

Another scream sounded along with dozens of unfamiliar animal noises. Something skittered into view beyond Vorik. It looked like a waist-high rat with grimy, curly fur and a long tail. If it had eyes, she couldn't see them, but it shrieked, somehow seeing or sensing Vorik as he sprang into the tunnel at it.

His sword slashed too rapidly for the creature to evade, but others followed the first. *Dozens* of others. Several bit at Vorik, but he danced out of reach, a blur of movement. He slashed to kill at the same time as he leaped and twisted to evade. A few more creatures tried to bite him, but others only sought to get past. He tried to stem the flow, but there were too many, even for him. Several skittered around the fight as he slew others, their bodies large enough that they got in the way after they fell.

"Cave crawlers coming!" Vorik called toward the entrance of the cave as he drove his blade into the skull of another creature.

Two more ran past before he could stop them. Snarling, he looked like he wanted to race after the ones that were getting by, but he glanced in Syla's direction and stayed where he was.

She vaguely remembered that there was a camp up there. A large camp of his people with elders and children.

One of the giant rats—cave crawlers, he'd called them—diverted into her nook. She scooted back, looking around for a weapon. There was her medical kit. Could she pull out a scalpel in time?

But Vorik caught the creature before it reached her. He leaped onto its back and plunged his blade into its neck. It let out a bone-rattling shriek before its legs collapsed underneath it.

Out in the tunnel, several more creatures ran past. Vorik spun, but two armed men, one limping but determined, chased after them.

"Defend the camp!" someone called.

Vorik glanced at Syla again. She nodded that she was fine. He nodded back and returned to crouching with his sword at the entrance to their nook. He wanted to help his people—she had no doubt—but he would make sure she wasn't in danger. At least not from the cave crawlers. She was in danger from something else, wasn't she? If only her mind weren't so fuzzy.

She went to her medical kit, trying to remember what drugs she'd brought along. Was there anything that could clear her thoughts? Had she hit her head?

No, she realized in a flash of clarity that came when she spotted one of her syringes. That cursed General Jhiton had drugged her. With hydra-scale powder. She didn't know the ancient substance as well as modern drugs, but maybe thelenium would help. That promoted wakefulness and clarity.

As she placed a bitter tablet under her tongue, willing it to dissolve and enter her body quickly, she brushed a small bag of powdered dayvak buds and paused. There was some significance to the sedative. She'd meant to use it, hadn't she?

She couldn't remember where or on who but tucked the bag into her pocket, hoping illumination would come soon. The bitterness of the tablet she'd slipped under her tongue made her want to spit, if not gag, and she looked around for water. There was a gourd with a cap, and she reached for it, but a memory flashed into her mind. That woman—a healer?—had put hydra-scale powder into it, and... her gaze strayed to her arm. A hint of dried blood smudged her skin next to a vein.

In the tunnel beyond Vorik, several more armed men passed by, having to climb over the bodies of the cave crawlers that he'd killed. Blood and ichor spattered their faces and clothing, promising they'd also battled a subterranean foe.

General Jhiton appeared, jumping lithely over one of the bodies.

"The kraken is dead," he said.

"Good," Vorik said.

Syla closed the medical kit and knelt back from it an instant before Jhiton looked into the nook. He squinted suspiciously at her and opened his mouth, but Vorik spoke again.

"Some of the crawlers got past."

A moan of pain drifted to them, promising people near the entrance had been injured.

Jhiton swore under his breath. "Keep watching her."

"We need a healer!" a woman called. "Yavaron is hurt. Where's her apprentice? Little Havalla?"

Syla touched her medical kit, intending to say that she could help, but her mind was starting to clear, and the puzzle pieces clicked together. She remembered being questioned. She remembered trying and failing to kill Jhiton with her power. She remembered everything. Curse of the storm god, she'd told them the location of the Bogberry Island shielder.

"Havalla is hurt too, but she's doing her best," someone called. "Chieftess, over here."

Vorik looked at Syla, a question in his eyes, but he didn't ask it.

"You look like... you," he said instead.

"Yeah. You look... like an enemy."

He shook his head sadly. "Yes."

The squalls of a baby accompanied the moans and groans of others in pain. The one she'd seen on the way in?

Syla closed her eyes, wrestled only briefly with a decision, then grabbed her medical kit and stood. "I can help those who are injured."

Vorik didn't look surprised. He lifted a hand in invitation and guided her into the tunnel and toward the main area.

"But if your brother is injured," she added, "I'm not healing him."

"He looked hale when he passed through," Vorik said.

"Fate never strikes fairly."

"No." He touched her shoulder.

~

Outside the cave, the wind railed, and branches broke as more bad weather swept in from the Sea of Storms. A loud crack-thump suggested an entire tree falling.

Inside, the cave remained dry and protected from the elements, and people rested after clearing away the corpses of the crawlers. Some had been injured, but nobody complained. Such events were common in the life of the stormers. After all, desirable lairs protected from storms and aerial predators were popular with more than just humans. At least nobody had died during the battle. A couple of people would have been in more dire straits if not for Syla.

Feeling indebted to her, Vorik stood close as she went from injured person to injured person, cleaning wounds and applying bandages as well as her healing magic when the wounded gave their permission for it. Several times, she let herself sink into a deep trance that left her vulnerable. Vorik kept his hand on the hilt of his sword, making sure everyone knew Syla was under his protection. But everyone saw that she was helping their people, and nobody even looked crossly at her. Early in the process, she healed Yavaron, who then started helping her, acting as an assistant more than the master the tribe had relied upon for decades. Yavaron, though she had a great deal of knowledge and experience, didn't have the gods-gift, the quarter-moon-shaped birthmark that glowed silver from Syla's hand as she worked.

We are chasing three of the faction dragons down the coast in the opposite direction of the cave, Agrevlari reported, his telepathic voice more distant than before. *We fought briefly, but the storm is unpleasant, even for mighty dragons, and both parties may break off to find shelter soon.*

Vorik had already told Agrevlari about the attack in the cave. Thanks to the dense canopy outside, and the size of the cave entrance itself, the dragons couldn't have done anything to help. It was probably only bad luck that both attacks had happened at the same time—it wasn't as if krakens communicated with dragons—but Vorik wondered, thoughts of the gods arranging things coming to mind again.

Weren't there four of them? Vorik asked. *Did you kill one?*

The orange dragon that we flew with to the desert disappeared inland.

She's probably the one Wreylith sent to find and retrieve Syla. The others are a distraction.

One of the others bit me in the shoulder.

Thus distracting you.

Agrevlari growled into his mind.

Thank you for the update, Vorik said. *I'll keep an eye out for the orange dragon. Igliana, wasn't it?*

Yes.

Hushed voices raised on the other side of the cave. For a while, Jhiton had been over there, speaking with Chieftess Shi, General Amalia, and a couple of tribal elders. More concerned about Syla and the injured, Vorik hadn't been trying to listen in on their conversation, but Shi sounded angry now. She folded her arms over her chest and glared at Jhiton. Jaw tight, he glared back. It took Vorik a moment to realize they must have switched to telepathy.

Syla leaned back from her current patient—Alecton, the boy who'd almost hit her with a ball—and patted him on the shoulder. "Rest for a time. You'll be back afflicting your game on passersby soon."

"All right." Alecton glanced around. To make sure there weren't many witnesses? "Thanks," he said in a whisper.

"You're welcome."

Without looking at Jhiton, Syla picked up her kit and moved to another patient, Fria, one of the women who'd been cooking dinner when this had all started. The campfires continued to burn, but someone had moved the soup shells away from the flames so the meal would stay warm but not scald.

As Syla knelt again, cutting away Fria's torn trousers to examine deep bites along her leg, Jhiton left the meeting. He picked his way past their resting kin and gestured for Vorik to step back a few paces from Syla. For a private word? They had telepathy for that.

Vorik almost objected to leaving Syla's side, but nobody had threatened her, and she would probably prefer *not* to have Jhiton looming over her while she worked. She hadn't even given any indication that she appreciated having *Vorik* close. If she remembered the answers she'd given under the influence of the drug—and he had a feeling she had—she might not want to speak with him again. Ever.

As soon as we've rested and recovered, Chieftess Shi wants us to return to Bogberry Island, Jhiton said telepathically.

I'll bet. Vorik couldn't help but feel sour.

Syla was here, *helping* their people, and the stormer leaders were still plotting to overthrow hers. Couldn't they take a break from their war?

As if Jhiton could guess Vorik's thoughts, he said, *We need to strike before the Kingdom queen returns to tell them that we know the shielder's location.*

Returns? Vorik arched his eyebrows. *Are you planning to let our prisoner go?*

In the morning, we'll question her again and learn the locations of the other shielders.

Syla wouldn't like that, but did Jhiton intend to take her home after that? Or have Vorik do it?

That didn't make a lot of sense since they needed someone with a moon-mark to open the shielder chambers. Syla would be the logical choice.

And then? Vorik asked.

Chieftess Shi agrees that it wouldn't be right to kill her after this. Jhiton extended a hand toward Syla, who'd settled between one of the fires and Fria, eyes closed as she rested a hand on the woman's leg.

Vorik could sense her drawing upon her power.

Shi wants her kept here while we get at least one more shielder, Jhiton added, *but has agreed to return her alive.*

When?

Eventually.

Like after we've taken over most of the islands?

Shi wants it to be after we've taken all *of their islands,* Jhiton said dryly, looking toward the chieftess's camp.

That might not be wise. The Freeborn dragons are out looking for Syla. I assume Ozlemar has kept you apprised.

He has. He's not concerned about them. They may have agreed to be allies of the Kingdom, but they're not going to risk their lives to get Syla. Wreylith might, but these dragons don't have a bond with her.

Vorik thought about Igliana, believing she might be an exception, but didn't point that out to Jhiton.

Fria sighed softly. In relief?

Syla continued to draw upon her power, but her eyes had opened partway, and she was gazing at the fire—no, at a giant shell of soup meant to feed everyone in the cave. Maybe she sensed Vorik's attention because her gaze shifted briefly to him, then toward the ceiling, as if she were concentrating and not looking at anything in particular. That was probably true, but as his brother spoke about plans to get the shielder, Vorik's instincts told him Syla was contemplating something. He turned slightly, as if Jhiton had his full attention, but he kept Syla in his peripheral vision.

Do you want to be involved? Jhiton asked, forcing Vorik to focus on him in truth. *In getting the shielder?*

If you think I can be of value, take me.

She would have to stay here, of course. Jhiton tilted his head toward Syla without looking at her.

You don't think she wants to come along to help us steal her people's precious artifact, huh?

She would be a hindrance if she were on the island.

She and Wreylith would kick our asses.

Jhiton snorted.

Our dragons won't be able to help us until after it's destroyed, Vorik reminded him.

Syla's eyes were open again. She slipped her hand into a

pocket and pulled out… What was that? A sack? Something wrapped in cloth? While keeping one hand on her patient, still healing her, Syla worked it open. The sack held some kind of powder.

I'm aware, Jhiton said. *I won't argue that Wreylith is a formidable opponent, but as long as we can use the moon-marked Lady Abrya, we don't need to take Syla.*

Syla *is becoming a formidable opponent too,* Vorik pointed out before the rest of his brother's words sank in. Was he implying that Lesva had succeeded in kidnapping Lady Abrya?

Syla looked over at Vorik and Jhiton. She must not have thought they could see her from their positions because, after peeking surreptitiously around the rest of the cave, she scooted closer to the soup.

Vorik froze, not looking directly at her, but watching nonetheless. Were the contents of the sack *poisonous*? No, Syla wouldn't poison the people she was healing. Vorik didn't believe that. She might poison *Jhiton* if she got the chance but not innocent people.

She has power, Jhiton agreed.

You barely kept her from squeezing your heart into pieces. Vorik debated what to do as Syla sat by the fire with the sack of powder in her lap. Was she going to put it in the soup? That had to be it. What would it do? Make those who ate it sick so she could get away while they were distracted with their discomfort? An understandable plan, but Vorik couldn't risk letting her do something that would harm his people.

I was able to thwart her, Jhiton said, *but I agree that she's strong and getting stronger. I think she was drawing upon the gods-gift as well as the power from her dragon tattoo. The power from her bond with Wreylith is probably just starting to blossom within her.*

Jhiton started to glance toward Syla, and Vorik reacted on instinct rather than doing what was wise. He stepped in the opposite direction and pointed at Shi to pull Jhiton's attention that way.

If we leave Syla here, will she be safe with our chieftess? Are you certain *that Shi agrees that it would be proper to let Syla live? Or was she saying that to mollify you? You're honorable, Jhiton, but I'm less certain about the honor of some of our leaders these days.*

While he asked the questions, Vorik lifted a hand in Syla's direction, hoping to catch her eye and silently convince her to stop. Vorik didn't want Jhiton to catch her sabotaging the soup, because he would react mercilessly, but Vorik also didn't want her to do anything to his people.

Jhiton surprised Vorik by gripping his arm. *I know you care about her, and I've been lenient about that, but you can't let your feelings for her be a distraction. Our victory is within reach. We must focus on getting the shielder and nothing more.*

Forgetting the powder, Vorik scowled at Jhiton. *Does that mean Shi* hasn't *promised that Syla would be safe here as a captive? Without me to keep an eye on things?*

She did not threaten the queen in any way.

So, no promise. Vorik extricated his arm from Jhiton's grip. *Let's take her with us. We can get the shielder and then drop her off with her people.*

You think she's going to let us get the shielder *while she's with us? With her dragon back in reach and our dragons stuck beyond the barrier?*

Our dragons will only be stuck until we accomplish our mission.

That'll take time, Vorik. And she has power beyond what the dragon lends her. As you pointed out, I felt it myself.

Vorik took a step back. *I'm not leaving her here.*

You will *leave her here, and you will obey your orders, or you can walk out of this camp and not return.* Back stiff, Jhiton strode toward the cave exit.

Jhiton... don't make me choose between you and her.

This is not about me. *You are choosing between her and your loyalty to our people.* Jhiton disappeared into the storm.

Vorik glanced at Syla, but her eyes were closed, her hand on Fria's leg, her chin drooped to her chest, as she'd been before. He almost wondered if he'd imagined her opening a sack. There was no sign of it.

He thought about confronting her and checking her pockets to see if the sack was in one—in one and empty. But he didn't want to pick another fight. And if she was effecting an escape... he wasn't that sure he wanted to stop her.

22

Syla lay on her back on a fur near the rear of the camp and stared at the stalactites hanging down from the ceiling. With the fires burning low, the shadows were deep between the rock features.

She'd removed her spectacles to sleep but doubted that would happen. Her mind was busy mulling over what she would do if she couldn't escape. She'd poured the sedative into the soup, but the communal meal she'd expected hadn't happened. Maybe it would have if the creatures hadn't attacked, but people had been coming by the shells of simmering liquid a couple at a time, and some had chosen the roasted meat as well or instead. Even among those who'd consumed the soup, they might not have received enough of the sedative to make a difference.

Vorik hadn't taken any soup, and Jhiton hadn't even returned to the cave. He was out there in the storm, sulking or doing whatever his tiff with Vorik had inspired. She hadn't heard their telepathic words, but their body language had made it clear they'd been arguing. About her, she knew.

Outside, the storm continued to rail, branches—if not entire trunks—snapping under the gales. Maybe she would get lucky, and a tree would fall on Jhiton. If not… she would encounter him if she tried to escape. An unpleasant thought. Without Vorik's watchful eye on him, Jhiton might take the opportunity to remove the source of the conflict between him and his brother.

No, not might. He absolutely *would* do that. It would be logical, and he seemed the logical sort.

Syla grimaced and looked toward Vorik. He lay nearby, ostensibly sleeping, but he shifted now and then, so she doubted he was doing more than dozing intermittently. He probably felt he had to keep an eye on her so nobody would bother her—and she wouldn't bother anyone. Earlier, he'd tried to keep her from dropping the powdered dayvak buds into the soup, but he'd also shifted Jhiton's attention when she'd been doing exactly that. He was as conflicted about their relationship as she.

After revealing the location of the Bogberry Island shielder, she should have hated Vorik for capturing her and restraining her so the hydra-scale concoction could be administered, but… hadn't she done this to herself? She could have tried harder to escape his kidnapping attempt. But she'd wanted this opportunity.

And she had to use it. She had to gain *something* from this misadventure.

Syla put her spectacles on, sat up, and looked toward the back of the cave. In the depths of night, it was hard to see much, but a couple of lanterns continued to burn in that tunnel, and she didn't see anyone standing guard in front of the nook she'd noted earlier, the nook she believed held the shielder components.

The camp was quiet, with nobody moving about, but dawn probably wasn't far off. She would have to make her attempt now… or never.

Fortunately, the stormers hadn't tied her up before she'd lain down to rest. Chieftess Shi had come over, demanding it, but Vorik had said he would watch her. He'd also pointed out that Syla had healed their people and that she should be treated well. They'd gotten what they'd wanted from her.

Shi had argued that Syla had only helped people to soften their attitude toward her and had reminded Vorik that there would be further interrogations in the morning, that the tribal leaders wanted the locations of *all* the shielders. Syla shuddered at the idea of divulging more Kingdom secrets. She couldn't stick around for that.

Wreylith? she called telepathically, hoping the dragon wasn't deep in slumber and would hear her.

She had to touch the krendala and reach out twice more before she received a response.

Is there not a storm there? Wreylith asked, not sounding appreciative of being woken. *The type of storm that prompts wise creatures to den up and sleep through? From what I've heard, it stretches across the entire Sea of Storms right now.*

There is a storm, but I need to escape. I... Syla hated to admit that she'd failed to keep her secrets. *The stormers will be a threat again as soon as the weather clears. I need to get away from them and beat them back to Bogberry Island.*

If she did, maybe she could grab Aunt Tibby and have her unmount the shielder so they could move it to another location. At the least, she could get troops to the salt mine to guard the entrance. Maybe she would get lucky, and her allies were even now retrieving the weapons platform from the bottom of the river. Too bad the salt mine was more than five miles inland—beyond its range.

You should have told me your precise location earlier. The Freeborn Faction dragons searched all along the coast where they believed a stormer camp might be.

I don't know where we are on a map, but they were close when they encountered the stormer dragons.

So they assumed. Those dragons drove most of them far away, and they've dared not return with the storm raging. Only Igliana managed to evade them and nest on the mainland, but she had to travel far down the coast so her enemies wouldn't sense her.

Can Igliana sense me?

Your magic makes you easier to sense than most humans but not from great distances. Tell me when you escape, and I'll ask her to look for you after the storm abates.

Syla frowned. She had to escape *before* the storm abated.

I'll do so, she said, hoping Igliana could find her in time once she did.

Since nobody had reacted when she sat up, Syla dared ease away from the fur.

Vorik didn't stir at her movement. Nobody did. A man who'd been ordered to stand guard near the entrance was slumped down across a rock mound. At least *someone* had eaten enough soup to be affected; she assumed the vigilant stormers wouldn't otherwise take naps while on guard duty.

Syla picked up her medical kit and rose to her feet. If someone confronted her, she would claim to need to pee. With no toilet facilities in the cave, the stormers went outside for that. Earlier, she'd seen a few venture out into the storm, but it had been some time since anyone had gone.

As she picked her way past camps and toward the back of the cave, she expected someone to yell at her at any moment. She kept glancing back, certain Vorik would rise and stop her. But nobody stirred, and she made it to the tunnel. The guard who should have been alertly keeping anyone from reaching the shielder components lay slumped across a rock, similar to the one out front. She squeezed past, careful not to brush him.

Little lantern light penetrated the nook, and it went back farther than she would have guessed, but she soon sensed the components. They were all magical, after all. She could detect all three, the teal ore, the desiccated moss-bulb powder, and the orb from the storm god's laboratory.

Unable to see anything, she groped and prodded her way toward them. When last she'd seen the items, the ore and orb had glowed, but someone must have wrapped them up.

When she reached them, fingers brushing fabric, she realized the orb and ore were still in the pack she'd put them in. She was tempted to untie the flap and look inside to verify with her eyes that they were there, but she didn't want the light to wake the guard. She slid the pack over her shoulders, then patted around and found the ceramic amphora, the lid secured. She hefted it with one arm and shifted the medical kit on its shoulder strap so that it rested against her hip, then headed out, wondering how by the eyes of the moon she would run and hide while carrying so much. She certainly couldn't fight. Would she even be able to ride on a dragon?

Praying that she would somehow slip away without anyone noticing, she returned to the main portion of the cave. Reminded that Vorik hadn't consumed any of the soup, she picked a route that stayed away from him. He lay on his back, the same as he had when she'd departed, but she couldn't tell if his eyes were open or closed.

Closed, surely. If he'd been awake, he would have stopped her.

Heart beating in her ears, Syla reached the entrance and stepped past the sleeping guard. She resisted the urge to quicken her pace. If she tripped and dropped one of the items—or made any noise at all—someone who hadn't consumed the soup would hear her and waken.

A gust of wind nearly knocked her into the wall before she reached the mouth of the cave. Rain blew sideways, cold even though it was only the beginning of fall, and spattered her spectacles.

I'm out, Wreylith, she thought. *Will you tell Igliana to look for me?*

More wind blew, and Syla could hear the roar of the sea, waves crashing into the cliff under the bluff.

I will tell her, but if it yet storms there, she may not be able to search for you.

You might mention that I'm thinking of starting a horn-hog farm so that I can always have delicious livestock for my dragon allies.

You wish me to bribe her? Wreylith asked dryly.

Yeah, will it work?

Probably. She is young and naive.

I'll reserve some horn hogs for you too.

I *am not young or naive.*

But you'd accept offerings of horn hogs if they happened to come your way.

Certainly. Sheep and goats as well. And the pesky but delicious venomous sword iglets that hug the sea floor and are difficult for dragons to catch.

I'll keep your tastes in mind.

Outside the cave, Syla looked left and right through the trees, their leaf- and needle-filled branches swaying in the wind, the dark night making it hard to see anything. No moon would guide her way, and a wise traveler would hunker down and wait for day. But she dared not wait.

She picked her way along the animal path that had led the stormers up to the cave. It would be easier and safer to return to the beach where they'd arrived, but people would look there first for her. Instead she went in the opposite direction, hoping to find an open spot along the bluff where a dragon might land.

Igliana, Syla tried calling, in case her power might reach to where the orange dragon had nested for the night. *I've escaped from the stormers and am badly in need of a ride. Are you out there? Can you hear me?*

Only the wailing wind and the roar of the sea answered her.

Soon sodden from the rain, the amphora slipping in her grip,

Syla bumped against a log and fell over it, almost losing everything. Weary and miserable, she wanted to stop to rest, but… she sensed someone out there with her. A person with power.

Jhiton?

It might be that Vorik had noticed she'd left and come to look for her, but her instincts told her it was Jhiton even before she could identify him for certain. She pushed herself to her feet and turned in the direction of the sea.

Igliana, she called again. *If you can hear me, I'm angling for the bluff. I'll try to find a spot where you can reach me.*

No dragons will fly in this weather, spoke a cold telepathic voice from nearby.

Jhiton.

Fear blasted her, and her heart slammed against her ribcage. Jhiton had never spoken into her mind before—and she'd never wanted him to.

Syla picked up her pace. Had it grown slightly lighter? Was dawn approaching? With the heavy cloud cover, it was hard to tell, but she had to hope daylight would come, that the storm would abate, and Igliana would be able to reach her. But she worried all that would take hours, and Jhiton…

Where was he? She'd first sensed him behind her, but he'd disappeared from her awareness. Could he mask his presence somehow? Was he even now creeping closer?

Syla glanced back but didn't see anyone. Ahead, the trees were less dense. She went in that direction until she could make out the ocean in the distance, beyond an open rocky space on the top of the bluff. The cliff underneath dropped away a hundred feet or more before reaching the sea, and she stopped instead of going out onto the bare rock. She remembered Captain Lesva falling off a cliff after lightning struck and didn't want to tempt fate. *She* would never survive plummeting that far.

Igliana is searching for you, Wreylith spoke into Syla's mind.

Thank the gods. Syla peered into the dark sky over the sea, hoping the dragon would fly into view soon. Before Jhiton crept up and plunged a dagger into her back.

You may thank me. *She was sleeping, but I woke her with the promise of your upcoming horn-hog compound.*

Excellent, and I do thank you.

Syla looked behind her again, certain she hadn't imagined sensing the general. She definitely hadn't imagined his voice in her head.

Vorik? She tried to call back to him. They'd never spoken telepathically, but he'd seemed to sense her when she'd shouted a silent warning when he'd been swimming away from the weapons platform.

Vorik has not left the cave. Jhiton's voice came from behind her and to the right, and she spun in that direction. He stood between two trees, the wind whipping his cloak and riffling his short dark hair.

She could again sense his power. His magic.

He gripped a longsword in each hand and stared at her with steady cold eyes. *What did you do to my people?*

They're fine. Just sleeping.

Sleeping.

Yeah.

As silent and inevitable as death, Jhiton strode toward her.

Not wanting to be maneuvered toward the edge of the bluff, Syla tried to shift sideways through the trees. But when she went left, he leaped lightly over ferns and logs to block her route. When she attempted to go in the other direction, he did the same, hardly expending any effort, though he moved as fast as a cheetah to intercept her. To deliberately try to maneuver her out onto the bare rock near the edge of the bluff.

She had little choice but to back in that direction and hope Igliana would swoop down and grab her before Jhiton reached her. But, if he wanted, he could reach her in an instant. It wasn't as if she could run as fast as he, especially not with her arms full.

"Let me guess." Syla glanced back to check her distance to the edge—and the gray sky for dragons. "If you cut my throat with a sword, you'll have to explain yourself to Vorik, but if I fall off the cliff, accidents happen, now, don't they?"

Vorik answers to me.

Yeah, and that was the problem, wasn't it?

I would not prevaricate with him. Put down the shielder components.

Ah, maybe that was the only reason he hadn't attacked. For whatever reason, Jhiton wanted them for his people. If she stumbled and dropped the amphora, it might break, and the moss-bulb powder could be ruined by the storm. If she fell off the cliff and into the ocean, all three components might be lost.

"No, thanks. I'd like to keep them."

Jhiton kept walking closer, slowly now, like a stalking predator, and she was drawing precariously close to the edge. She had to delay him somehow, long enough for Igliana to find her.

"Why don't you take a break from being dreadful and go back to your camp? I haven't done anything to you." Frustration crept into Syla, and she ended up shouting over the wind with more passion than she'd intended. "I haven't even done anything to your people except defend my Kingdom. Meanwhile, you've taken almost *everyone* from me. Everyone I loved. This wasn't how it was supposed to be." She caught herself, the emotions too raw, too real. She wanted to buy time but not by exposing her vulnerabilities to Jhiton.

His face remained cold and dispassionate, and she had little doubt that he would do it all again. As he strode closer, scant feet away now, she believed he would take this opportunity to kill her, to end the source of the friction between him and his brother.

A glance back revealed that she could go no farther. She'd

reached the edge of the cliff, and stormy white water frothed and churned below, battering rock formations that thrust up from the sea like fingers. If she jumped—or was pushed and fell—she wouldn't survive the drop.

On impulse, she spun and held the amphora out over the edge. Jhiton halted.

The components might not mean as much to the stormers as to her people, but he had ordered them collected, and he'd been protecting them. He'd likely realized that destroying the islands' protection completely would leave them exposed to the elements and winged predators. After his people took over, he might want the shields to be returned to duty.

Syla bared her teeth at the thought of that.

You won't drop it, Jhiton said, but he had paused his advance. *You need that more than I do.*

"Yes, I do, but if the Kingdom can't have a shield, then neither can you. Bastard." So many raindrops spattered her spectacles that she struggled to read his expression, but she didn't have a hand free to wipe the lenses. She almost didn't notice his head turning back in the direction of the cave. Then she sensed what had drawn his attention.

Vorik sprinted out of the trees with his sword in one hand and a dagger in the other. Without hesitation, he ran straight at Jhiton.

Jhiton had time to spring away from Syla and the edge of the bluff, raising his blades to defend himself. Then Vorik was upon him.

Their gargoyle-bone swords clanged like metal, throwing blue sparks when they met. And they met too swiftly for her to track. Those sparks rained in all directions, landing on the damp rock at their feet.

As fast as the cheetahs she'd likened Jhiton to earlier, the men sprang about, dancing in and out, dodging and parrying. They never lost their balance on the wet and uneven ground. They were far too sure-footed for that.

Aside from the clangs of their weapons, they didn't make a sound, neither shouting at the other nor even grunting or groaning as their blows were deflected. If they conversed at all, it had to be telepathically, but maybe they each knew where the other stood, and there was no need to speak.

Syla needed to creep away, to get as far from them as she could in case Jhiton won the confrontation. But they were mesmerizing, so nimble and athletic, so powerful; it was almost impossible to look away. Besides, if Vorik lost, he might need a healer. Would Jhiton allow her to help him before he returned to killing her?

She wished she could tell who was more likely to win. Before, Vorik had said his brother had trained him and that he wouldn't want to fight him, implying Jhiton would win. But Jhiton had flecks of gray in his black hair. Vorik was still young and in the prime of his life. Wouldn't he have a slight advantage?

Unfortunately, Jhiton didn't look aged or slow in the least. Never had she seen someone wield two longswords, and it was incredible that he did so without bumping them against each other, without any hint of awkwardness, each hand as gifted as the other. But Vorik also used his sword and dagger without any hint that one side was less capable than the other.

As they leaped about, their dragon bonds giving them the power to somersault over each other's heads and leap up to swing from tree branches to avoid attacks, Syla couldn't tell if they were holding back. She didn't believe either of them wanted to kill the other, but they didn't hesitate to slash with those deadly blades. If all they'd wanted to do was settle an argument, they would have used fists, not swords.

For the first time, Jhiton growled, and he picked up the speed of his attack. As a blade whistled toward Vorik's thigh, he bumped against a tree and couldn't keep it from slicing in. But he didn't cry out, didn't make a sound at all, only digging in and renewing his attack on Jhiton. He glanced at Syla, as if drawing strength from her concerned face, and pushed his brother back. He even tried to angle Jhiton toward the edge. But the general didn't allow himself to be so maneuvered. With the two longer blades, he seemed to have the advantage, forming a wall of moving magical bone. Vorik couldn't get close enough to draw blood.

I see you, human friend!

Never had Syla been so delighted to have a dragon speak into her mind. And when she looked south, she spotted the orange dragon flapping her wings against the wind, arrowing up the coast toward the bluff.

I'm relieved to see you, Syla said. *I need a ride.*

Oh, that is most apparent.

Syla inched closer to the edge. The thought of leaving Vorik when he was in trouble, when he needed healing, distressed her, but she reminded herself that the stormers knew where the Bogberry Island shielder was now. She had to return and prepare for another invasion. Besides, once she was gone, Jhiton and Vorik wouldn't have a reason to continue their battle. The way they were trying to kill each other now made her question that assumption, but she hoped it was true.

The men glanced toward the dragon as Igliana swooped down, talons extended, and plucked Syla from the edge of the bluff. Though Syla had expected it, it was still terrifying when those talons tossed her, and she barely kept hold of the amphora. The pack with the ore and orb slumped to one side, and she almost lost her medical kit as she fought to keep everything else. It was far more Igliana's magic than any graceful maneuvering in the air on Syla's part that allowed her to land on the dragon's back. Before she could use her power to anchor herself, Igliana's magic wrapped around her, holding her in place, and they flew away from the cliff.

Syla looked back toward land, toward the battle, but too much rain spattered her spectacles for her to see well. With the dragon flying swiftly out to sea, the men were already indistinct against the trees.

I love you, Vorik, she thought as Igliana carried her away.

Even if he couldn't hear the words, she hoped he knew.

~

Vorik kept an eye on his brother as they watched the orange dragon depart with Syla on her back. As strong gusts of wind battered them, Igliana's wingbeats faltered, but she didn't hesitate to continue out to sea, determined to carry her rider away, whatever the weather.

Vorik and Jhiton had stopped fighting when she'd swooped down, Jhiton spinning toward the dragon and raising his blades, probably not certain if Igliana would pluck up Syla or try to end his life. Vorik had taken the opportunity to back away. With sweat and rain running down his face and making his hands slick, he wanted no more of the battle. Further, his leg throbbed where his brother had cut him. But Syla had gotten away. That was all that mattered.

Jhiton shook his head, looked at Vorik, and lowered but didn't put away his swords. "Are we done?"

"You tell me." Vorik wiped his face with the back of his sleeve but also didn't sheathe his weapons. He hadn't been fighting with everything he had, but it had seemed like Jhiton had been, that his brother might have killed him, the ultimate punishment for going astray.

Jhiton looked hard at him for a long moment, then wiped his blades and sheathed them. "I don't know what to do with you, Vorik."

"You could demote me."

"How would *that* help anything?"

"Well, I wouldn't be directly under your command."

"No, you'd be tormenting some poor captain who would then report all your shenanigans to me."

"Were you going to kill Syla?" Vorik asked.

Surely, *Jhiton* was the one in the wrong here.

Jhiton eyed him. Vorik realized he hadn't yet sheathed his own weapons.

"If I say, yes, will you run me through?"

"If I tried, I doubt I would succeed." Vorik sheathed his blades. He'd never had any intention of killing his brother. All he'd known was that he had to stop Jhiton. "You're still as fast and deadly as you always were."

"You're a strong fighter as well." Wind gusted, managing to snap Jhiton's cloak even though it was sodden. He looked out to sea, but Syla and the orange dragon had disappeared. "I intended to recapture her and return her to the cave."

"So Chieftess Shi could arrange her death while we were back in the Kingdom." It didn't come out sounding like a question, and Vorik realized he believed the words. It wasn't so much that he thought their tribal leader a heinous criminal. It was more that Shi had less reason to care about Vorik and his potential broken heart than Jhiton did.

"I don't know what Shi would have done. Neither do you."

"It was a risk Syla wasn't willing to take."

Jhiton snorted and walked into the trees. He flexed his hip, rotated it, then unbuckled his weapons belt so that he could sit on the ground, a boulder somewhat sheltering him. Vorik might not have drawn blood in their battle, but he felt a modicum of satisfaction that he'd at least caused his brother to develop a twinge in his hip. A small victory.

"You're not going to chase after her?" Vorik asked.

"I already asked Ozlemar to come get me. He said he's not going to fly in this weather."

"Dragons. So persnickety."

"Indeed."

Weary himself, Vorik joined Jhiton in the shelter of the boulder. Reminded of a time after their father had passed when they'd sat back-to-back, alternately watching the sky and looking out at a stormy beach while grieving, he assumed that position now.

"How'd she get past the guards and out of the cave?" Jhiton asked.

"I don't know." Vorik shrugged, though he'd seen the men sleeping atypically hard when he'd passed.

"Truly?"

Vorik hesitated. "She might have drugged the soup."

"With a sedative?"

"Yes."

"You saw and allowed it? What if it had been a poison that killed everyone?"

"I knew it wasn't."

When his brother didn't answer, Vorik didn't know if it was because Jhiton thought he was an idiot, or if his silence meant agreement. By now, Jhiton had to also be getting a feel for Syla's character.

"You don't expend that much energy healing people you're going to kill later," Vorik added, in case it was the former.

"You know her well," Jhiton said.

"Yeah." Maybe he shouldn't have said more, but he wanted his brother to understand. "I think I'm falling in love with her."

"I know."

"Are you going to kick me out of the Sixteen Talons?"

According to the age-old rules, one could challenge a superior officer to a duel, but one couldn't leap out of the woods and try to cut him or her down without warning.

"Do you want me to?" Jhiton asked softly.

The wind was dying down, and Vorik didn't have any trouble catching the words. "No."

"I can't have you working against us."

"It's only where Syla is concerned."

"*Syla* is the queen of the kingdom we're trying to take over. She's going to be *concerned* with every aspect of every mission." Jhiton gave him an exasperated look over his shoulder.

"That's not *my* fault. She's noble and wants to personally help defend her kingdom."

Jhiton grunted. It might have been more like a growl.

"You're the one who first sent me to seduce her," Vorik pointed out. "You really have only yourself to blame for this."

Jhiton scoffed. "I didn't know she had magical lips and that her kiss would ensorcel you."

"Her lips are very nice. Other parts are even nicer."

"You've always been into boobs."

"Oh, yes." Maybe Vorik shouldn't have grinned, since his brother sounded more disgusted than understanding, but he couldn't help himself. Even if the world was chaos, Syla had gotten away, and his mood was lighter. "Maybe we can find you a nice well-endowed Kingdom woman with magical body parts capable of ensorcelling you."

"That's not going to happen."

"Too bad. You need a woman."

"I had one," Jhiton said softly. "She left me."

"That's not your fault." Vorik couldn't bring himself to speak poorly about his brother's ex-wife. She'd been a good woman, and they'd been a solid match for many years. It had just been too hard for them after all the miscarriages and then the loss of their only son who'd lived into boyhood.

"Are we going to have to fight again if we encounter Syla on Bogberry Island?" Jhiton asked.

It sounded like a serious question. Vorik didn't want to give an honest answer and opted for a playful one.

"I hope not. You stabbed me in the leg."

"You held your own." Jhiton touched his hip. "You've grown into a good fighter."

Was there some pride mixed in with Jhiton's ongoing exasperation? Since he'd been responsible for most of Vorik's training, it might make sense.

"Yes, you'd better watch out," Vorik said. "I'll have my eye on your other hip next time."

Jhiton didn't answer the quip, and Vorik hoped he knew he was joking.

"It's natural for the son to one day surpass the father," Jhiton eventually said. "Father told me that when he was training me, and I was doing my best to be as good as he—and mostly being frustrated because I wasn't. He said it would be a bittersweet moment when it finally happened but that he would be disappointed if it *didn't* happen."

"Is that true for older and younger brothers too? Am I destined to surpass you?"

"No."

Vorik laughed.

"Not when the younger brother is fattening himself with berry desserts every chance he gets."

"Sadly, I haven't had the opportunity to get enough of those for that to happen. I wouldn't mind having a little fat though."

"General Jhiton!" came a woman's voice from the direction of the cave.

Jhiton sighed and pushed himself to his feet. "Chieftess Shi must not have eaten much of the soup."

"Are you going to get in trouble over this?" Vorik asked.

"She'll be irked with me, but I'm not worried about any consequences she or the other chiefs might dole out."

No, he had as much sway among the tribes and the elders and soldiers as any of them did. Maybe more. If only Jhiton would push for leadership of the tribe. But that wouldn't change anything, would it? He wanted to conquer the Kingdom and take their islands as much as the chiefs did.

"That said, you need to figure this out, Vorik." Jhiton frowned down at him. "You can't be at odds with the tribe and the Sixteen Talons and remain with us. If you love her, go join her in the Kingdom."

"And turn against you and all our people?" Vorik grimaced. As he'd been contemplating earlier, he would choose exile over that.

"I wouldn't care to fight against you in a real battle, but..." Jhiton spread a hand. His head tilted before he finished the thought. He gazed to the north. "Ozlemar has received a message."

"From whom?"

"Something is going our way, at least."

Vorik, who thought quite a bit was going Jhiton's way, raised his eyebrows.

His brother clasped him on the shoulder. "Lesva got Lady Abrya."

"Ah." Vorik couldn't feel triumphant.

Shi called again, and Jhiton released him, buckled on his sword belt, and strode back toward their people, toward his duty. As he always had and always would. If one of them was going to change, it would have to be Vorik.

23

Full daylight came, and the wind abated as Igliana flew Syla across the Sea of Storms. As the gray clouds grew less dense, a few beams of sunlight crept through, sending down rays from the heavens. It should have been a scene of promise and hope, but Syla, wet and shivering and clutching the amphora in her lap, kept looking back, expecting to spot a black dragon in the sky. Jhiton's black dragon. If he caught up, he would keep Syla from returning to Bogberry Island to warn her people of the new threat.

I do not sense dragons behind us, Igliana said telepathically.

How far do dragon senses extend?

Many miles. Tens of miles. Much farther than the senses of humans.

We are a puny species.

So Auntie Wreylith informs me. I think you are fun. Igliana tilted her wings and sashayed left and right.

Her protective magic ensured Syla would stay on her back, though Syla now habitually used her own power to anchor herself to dragons. It was safer that way.

Did you know that Teyla read to me when she rode upon my back? Igliana added.

I did not.

The text was a nonfictional historical accounting of the storm god's laboratories and the minions he created—she was attempting to learn everything she could before our visit to the Dire Desert—and it was a touch dry—and by dry I mean boring—*but she added stories from her memory. Historical stories of adventure, and she was certain to highlight the magnificence of dragons and how we were the storm god's greatest creation.*

It's wise to highlight the magnificence of dragons when one is riding on one.

Oh, certainly. I was most entertained.

I'm glad. And I'm glad you came to get me and dared the storm. Reminded that Igliana was quite young by dragon standards, Syla decided it wouldn't hurt to bolster her ego—especially since it sounded like Wreylith quashed it often. *That was very brave of you.*

It was, wasn't it?

It must be the reason the stormers aren't giving chase. Clearly, their *dragons are unwilling to come after us. They likely fear the storm.*

Even the great black? Would he fear a little wind?

Ozlemar? He may be too grouchy to want to get his wings wet.

Igliana made a chuffing sound that Syla had heard a couple of times before from Wreylith and thought was the equivalent of laughter.

Elders can be grumps, Igliana said. *They are always certain they are right and dismissive of youths.*

I've noticed that myself, but as queen, I probably should have a dragon that others respect and who challenges me. Wreylith will keep me from getting too full of myself. Syla, who'd yet to feel she was appropriate and experienced enough for the throne, couldn't imagine ever adopting such an attitude, but one never knew.

Yes. You are fortunate that she claimed you.

She what? Syla blinked at the terminology.

I believe humans call it being bonded, having a magical connection to the dragon who...

Claims me?

Yes.

Since Syla had been prone to calling Agrevlari *Vorik's* dragon, she supposed it was fair that the dragons thought of their linked humans as *theirs. As a claimed human, it must be my duty to prepare a suitable lair and horn-hog farm for my dragon.*

Oh, that sounds lovely. May I visit the horn-hog farm too?

I... think it'll be protected under the Castle Island shield, and only dragons bonded to moon-marked residents would be permitted through the barrier. Since Wreylith was presumably still stuck under the Bogberry Island barrier, Syla couldn't pretend to know all the rules and added, *I'm uncertain though. Perhaps Wreylith will bring you a horn hog now and then.*

That would be delightful but seems unlikely. Elders think youths should scrap and scramble and get their own food. Even my parents, who are quite lovely by dragon standards, nudged me out of the nest before I scarcely knew how to open my wings and fly.

Dragon parents sound like they might be challenging to please.

Yes, but they adore me, due to my verve.

More rays of sunlight shone through the clouds ahead, turning the sea from a drab gray to a deep blue where they touched down. And was that Bogberry Island in the distance?

Syla blew out a slow breath, trying to still the nerves squirming in her belly. Though she was glad to have escaped, and mollified that she'd gotten the magical components, she'd failed to keep the shielder location a secret. Dread filled her at the knowledge that she would have to admit that to Lord Oyenar, that the already beleaguered residents of Bogberry Island would have to deal with another stormer incursion. And this time, their enemies would bring all the forces they could.

"I've betrayed my people as surely as Venia did," she whispered, remembering her sister's body on the floor of the shielder chamber under the castle. Venia's betrayal had been inadvertent, a byproduct of falling for a stormer with a handsome face, but General Dolok hadn't been sympathetic in the least. Because of Venia's failing, he hadn't given Syla a chance to prove herself. And now... when he heard about Syla's blunder, he would know he'd been right.

What happened? Igliana asked.

I let the stormers give me a drug that loosened my tongue, and I told them where the Bogberry shielder can be found.

You let *them? Were there not many, many of them? And you were alone?*

Yes, I don't think I could have escaped my fate, but... Syla wrestled with the knowledge that she hadn't tried as hard to escape Vorik's kidnapping as she could have, that she'd thought it might be a good idea to be swept off to the stormer cave. She looked down at the amphora. She'd accomplished what she'd hoped, but at what cost? With the components, Aunt Tibby might be able to repair the Harvest Island shielder, but the stormers were about to do their best to destroy another one. *If it hadn't been Vorik, I would have fought harder to escape.*

You are not a dragon. You are not even a warrior among the two-legs.

I'm not completely helpless though. Syla couldn't imagine using her power on Vorik, but if Jhiton had been in that kayak, dragging her out to sea, she wouldn't have hesitated to use her magic on him. Or any other stormer, for that matter. Instead, because Vorik had been involved, she'd believed... She supposed she'd believed she could use their relationship to come out ahead. And he *had* helped her escape. But he'd also held her while the healer stabbed that needle into her. She sighed, as conflicted about him and their relationship as she'd ever been. *I think the problem is that I tried to be clever so that I could redeem myself for past failings. I want to protect my people, Igliana, but I also want to be... worthy of the throne. Worthy enough that others won't scheme and try to kill me to take it for themselves. Instead, I've put my people in greater danger than they were in before.*

The stormers have not taken your artifact yet!

No, you're right. Syla straightened her back. She would speak with her fleet commander and Lord Oyenar and whatever military leaders he could summon, and they would come up with a plan. It wasn't as if the stormers could ride their dragons to the salt mine and use them to extract the shielder. For the time being, the barrier was up, so they would have to bring ships or swim to land themselves. Even if some of the stormers were enhanced by magic, they were still human. *We'll find a way to stop them,* she said with determination.

Certainly. You can accomplish this.

Syla rested a hand on Igliana's cool scales. *You're a good dragon. A very good ally.*

Better than Wreylith?

Syla managed a smile at the youthful tone. *You're certainly more encouraging than she is.*

Yes, very much so. Igliana sashayed again.

As they flew closer to Bogberry Island, Wreylith came into view, sunbeams gleaming on her brilliant red scales. Syla didn't yet know for certain why Wreylith hadn't been able to leave the island and watched to see if she, as Syla drew closer, would be able to soar through the barrier. Wreylith didn't try. Once she was out over the coastline, she did the aerial equivalent of pacing back and forth and waiting for them.

You've finally returned to free me from this imprisonment! Wreylith boomed into Syla's head.

Sorry my escape took longer than you would have liked. Were there not delicious bog bears here for you to hunt? And were you not comfort-

able knowing that no stormer dragons could reach and threaten you while you relaxed and swam in the many lakes?

No matter how vast the comforts of a cage, it still confines you. Dragons must fly free.

I understand the sentiment.

We are not bonded, so I cannot fly through the barrier. When Igliana reached the invisible shield, she flew alongside it, matching speed and altitude with Wreylith on the other side. *Hold on to your items.*

Syla frowned at the thought of another dousing in the ocean, but she had little choice. *If you fly low and drop me, I can paddle over to—*

Igliana startled her by twisting her neck in the air, her fangs reaching for Syla. As friendly and *encouraging* as the orange dragon was, having that deadly maw lunge close was alarming, and Syla barely had the presence of mind to guess her intent and grab the amphora and grip the straps of her pack and medical kit. She'd no sooner clutched everything than Igliana picked her up and tossed her like one of Vorik's juggling balls.

Fear almost made Syla scream as she soared through the barrier hundreds of feet in the air. Reminded that Wreylith was less inclined to use her magic to guide a rider into place and keep her on, Syla struggled to arrange herself to land on the red dragon's back without bouncing off. Even so, when she thumped onto her hard red scales, she lost her grip on the amphora as she tried to flatten a hand to Wreylith to use her magic as an anchor.

Surprisingly, power flowed from the red dragon, righting Syla and securing her in place. But the amphora tumbled toward the ocean.

"That's a shielder component," she blurted.

Wreylith dove after it, and Syla remembered the newspaper that the dragon had incinerated.

"I need that! Don't toast it, please!"

Reaching the amphora scant feet before it would have disappeared into the water, Wreylith opened her jaws. Syla closed her eyes and winced, afraid she would hear the snapping of ceramic and watch the precious moss-bulb powder fly out to land on the waves. But with surprising gentleness, Wreylith caught the amphora in her jaws. Her belly skimmed the water as she spread her wings, then flapped them to regain altitude. Once she was high enough, her neck twisted, and her head came back, allowing Syla to take the amphora from her grip.

"Thank you, Wreylith." Syla slumped in relief. If, after everything, she'd lost one of the rare shielder components, she didn't think she could have faced Lord Oyenar or Aunt Tibby. The only thing that would make explaining the impending stormer incursion less difficult was that she'd at least achieved one small victory.

Igliana roared and somersaulted in apparent approval for Wreylith's athletic maneuver.

The young are so easily impressed, Wreylith said, flying inland. They were on the far side of the island from the city and the palace.

On the way here, we discussed that Igliana is pleasantly encouraging. Syla lifted a hand toward the orange dragon, disappointed that there was no way for her to fly to the island to help. Syla would need all the help she could get against the stormers.

Easily impressed, Wreylith repeated. It seemed she had no interest in being encouraging. *Your enemy pronged her sword into the roof of my mouth.*

Oh! Syla had been so distracted by her own problems that she'd forgotten. *Let me see if I can heal the wound for you while we're flying.*

Mighty dragons do not need the assistance of puny human healers.

Certainly not. I'll get started right away.

Do so.

Fortunately, the magic of dragons helped them to heal quickly from most wounds, and it didn't take long for Syla to send tendrils of power through Wreylith's body and to the roof of her great maw. She knitted bone and flesh back together as they flew inland.

You might want to refrain from breathing fire for a while, she advised. *I imagine that would irritate a wound.*

Thus I discovered. In the aftermath, I almost wished for one of your foul slimy concoctions.

You mean my soothing salves.

Slimy.

Since Syla didn't want to apply a salve, slimy or otherwise, to the roof of a dragon's mouth, she didn't argue further on the merits of her medicines. By the time Wreylith flew over Prominence Hill, Syla had finished her task, trusting nature—and the dragon's inherent magic—would ensure she would soon be able to breathe fire again without trouble.

Before heading to the capital, Syla had Wreylith circle the hill so she could study the bogs, lakes, and forests below. She'd seen maps and once traveled to the salt mine via a road that led up its slopes, but she'd never seen the area from above and tried to conjure tactical thoughts.

Lake Talindar took up a large portion of the flat, forested top of the hill, and several fishing boats had dared to venture out after the storm. A half mile from the body of water, a couple of wooden buildings marked the mine entrance, one holding a lift cage that descended into the earth. Rail tracks led from the double doors of that building and followed the road as it meandered down the hill.

The ground-level portion of the operation was unassuming, especially considering it had existed and been in continuous use for centuries, but Syla knew from her previous visit that the mine was anything but. With multiple levels spread over hundreds of vertical feet, each level dozens of feet high, any one of them could have held an entire army. What if that was what the stormers brought? Great armies that would march through the forests and bogs to the top of the hill where they could force their way into the mine? Only a handful of people could go down via the lift cage at a time, but even small numbers of stormers were challenging opponents, especially if riders were among them. Even their ground troops, the Storm Guard, were better warriors than most Kingdom soldiers.

"We'll have to start sending people to the mine right away," Syla murmured to herself. "It'll take time for our troops to descend too. Though I suppose we could plant soldiers all around the mine entrance and try to keep the stormers out."

Hypothetically, that might work. The Bogberry natives ought to be able to summon more people than the stormers could bring by ship, but she couldn't help thinking of the amazing power and athleticism of the riders and worry that greater numbers wouldn't be enough.

As they flew along the main road heading to the coast, they spotted wagons carrying uniformed troops. Other men were on foot searching the bogs and forests.

At first, Syla thought they might have somehow learned the stormers would be after the artifact and were preparing, but not many wagons were heading toward Lake Talindar. They were spread out all over the place, as if they were searching the island for something.

Or… someone?

Unease crept into Syla.

"Will you take me to the ship or wherever Aunt Tibby is, please, Wreylith? I think we're going to need booby-traps. If not an engineering miracle."

After Syla spoke, she realized she didn't know if Tibby was safe. Vorik had said he'd helped her to shore, but what had happened after that? What if *she* was who the troops were searching for? The fleet ships had been sinking and in flames when Vorik had stolen Syla away, and she'd been so preoccupied with her own fate since then that she hadn't thought to worry about her aunt. And what of Lord Oyenar and Lady Abrya and the palace? Lesva, she feared, had survived the battle and probably gathered her troops to try again to reach them.

"*Is* Aunt Tibby all right? Do you know?"

The last time I flew over the city, she was on the remains of the docks with your bodyguard and local humans, directing the bringing of lifting equipment. Only the mast of the vessel you rode here is visible above the surface of the river. It and the weapons platform are underwater, sunk to the bottom.

Syla had suspected that and assumed they wouldn't have a way to use the gods' weapon to keep stormers out of the mine, but she groaned anyway.

"Vorik, why couldn't you have kidnapped me *without* sinking my ship?" She had little doubt that he'd deliberately chosen that target. After all, he'd been trying to destroy the weapons platform earlier. He might even have known she would come if he lit her ship on fire. "I need to end the relationship I never should have had with him, don't I, Wreylith?"

You find him a stimulating sexual partner.

"Yeah, I enjoy our encounters way too much, and it's not only sex. It's... he's..." Syla huffed out a frustrated breath as they flew closer to the city. "He's my enemy, and I don't think that's going to change. He's too loyal to his people and his brother. I understand that, but it's why we can't be a we. I never should have allowed myself to fall for him."

Stimulating partners aren't always easy to find. Perhaps you should suborn him.

"Have you managed to suborn Agrevlari?"

I have not tried. Up until recently, I did not think I found him the least bit intriguing.

"But then you had that engaging encounter on the rock formation?"

That was vigorous and appealing, but he grew more interesting when he showed me his mettle as a fighter and even dove past my defenses to bite me. Wreylith let out a roar before descending toward the docks, a wooden crane visible. Aunt Tibby and a couple of men stood near it, working or maybe, judging by their gesticulations, arguing.

"That doesn't look sturdy enough to pull the heavy marble platform off the bottom of the river," Syla said dubiously.

Back in the capital, they'd had access to a lot of high-quality machinery, and it had still been a laborious process to get the weapons platform from the courtyard of the castle down to the docks and onto the *Stormslicer*. Prying it away from the wreckage of the ship and lifting it onto land would be even more challenging. Especially since that crane looked like something that might have been state-of-the-art a few centuries past.

It took four strong dragons to carry it across the ocean, Wreylith said.

Yeah, and they only had access to one dragon.

"I hope Aunt Tibby can work a miracle."

Even if she could, as Syla had just been thinking, the weapons platform wasn't the answer to the current problem.

"We're going to have to figure something else out." She looked back to the lingering clouds on the horizon and wondered if the stormers would give them time. What if they were already on the way?

24

VORIK AND JHITON RETURNED TO THE CAVE AS THE STORM ABATED outside and people inside started to wake from their drugged slumber. Jhiton didn't say anything about Vorik attacking him, only reporting to Chieftess Shi that Syla had gotten away.

"I'm surprised she slipped past you." Shi eyed Jhiton's wet clothing. "Hardly anything ever does."

Her gaze shifted to Vorik, and he wondered if she'd somehow gotten the gist or guessed what had happened. Had a scout been out there who'd witnessed the fight and reported to her?

"I am not infallible," Jhiton said without looking at Vorik.

Vorik didn't regret helping Syla get away, but he hated that he so often had to feel guilty now. No, *dishonorable*. That was the word that kept coming to mind. His feelings for Syla were putting him in conflict with his people, and he didn't like it.

"What matters is that we know the location of another shielder," Jhiton said as General Amalia joined their group. "Bogberry Island can soon be ours, especially if the Kingdom troops haven't pulled the weapons platform off the bottom of the river yet."

Jhiton looked at Vorik, as if he had insight into how quickly that might be done.

"I sank it and the ship it was on, and it's a tangled mess under the water. I'm sure they'll figure out how to get it out eventually, but we might have a day or two."

"It would have been better if it had sunk out at sea where the water is deep enough that they would never retrieve it," Shi said.

Vorik wanted to grind his teeth and glare at her but made himself smile and bow instead. He didn't need to make an enemy of the leader of his tribe, and she already had reasons to doubt him. "My apologies, Chieftess. I had limited resources at my disposal. Captain Lesva was busy with her own mission."

"Captain Lesva *accomplished* her mission." Shi looked at Jhiton. For confirmation?

He nodded. "According to our dragon allies, Lesva has Lady Abrya and is hiding out in the bogs, waiting for us."

Vorik was tempted to say that he'd accomplished his mission too, but the Kingdom troops could have already fished the platform off the river bottom. And nobody had wanted him to kidnap Syla, though it *had* proven fruitful.

"I asked Zandelek, our dragon ally with the longest telepathic range," Jhiton said, "to send word to Harvest Island to the dragons there to see if any can swiftly fly to Bogberry and intercept the queen, but the orange dragon she rides is young and fast and might be able to avoid them."

Vorik kept his face neutral, but he *hoped* Igliana avoided the other dragons. After all he'd fought for, he didn't want Syla to die out at sea to an enemy she didn't even know.

"We should assume, however," Jhiton continued, "that the queen will return in time to warn her people that we know about the shielder's location. It would behoove us to move as quickly as possible to invade and take it before they have time to position a great number of forces to block us—especially since we won't have our dragon allies until we can lower the barrier."

"Moving quickly will be important, but we should also gather more troops than we have here." Amalia waved to indicate the fighters in the cave. "*Many* more troops. All those on Harvest Island will join in, but, as you pointed out, our dragons won't be able to help. We'd better contact the tribes that aren't too distant so we can get more soldiers and riders to help with the attack."

"We do already have many ships in the area, poised for this very opportunity." Jhiton surprised Vorik by looking at him. "You've come to know these people—and their queen—better than the rest of us. Would you suggest attacking as soon as possible with the troops near the area or taking a few days to gather everyone we can?"

"We don't need *his* opinion on their military tactics," Shi said. "Especially not based on what he knows about the woman he's having sex with."

"She is their ruler and will have a say in the military matters, especially since she'll likely remain on that island if she knows we're coming." Jhiton smiled faintly.

What, did he *approve* that Syla would keep herself in danger?

Vorik did respect that about her, but he also wished she would go back to her comfortable throne on Castle Island and leave the defense of the Kingdom to her soldiers. Then he wouldn't have any qualms about joining an invasion force going after the Bogberry shielder. Well, not *many* qualms. That niggling part of him that worried about the fate some of his leaders wanted for the Kingdom subjects made him hesitate to throw his heart into this.

"She's not going to command troop movements, I assure you," Shi said, glancing at Amalia.

The general hesitated, but then nodded at her. "I wouldn't think so, no. She's a healer with no military experience."

Jhiton looked thoughtfully at Vorik again.

"I... wouldn't underestimate her." Vorik didn't know what else to say. Especially in front of Shi, he didn't want to mention that Syla had gotten the best of *him* more than once. As he reflected on the past couple of days, he wondered, not for the first time, if Syla had *let* him kidnap her so that she could do exactly what she'd done: retrieve her shielder components. After all, she'd come prepared with that sleeping drug. Her only miscalculation had been that *they* had drugs as well and had been capable of fishing information out of her.

"No," Jhiton said softly. "And they'll be working to get the weapons platform out of the river."

"Yes." Vorik nodded.

"We'll gather all the troops we can," Amalia said, "but it sounds like we should attack as swiftly as possible too."

Shi nodded. "And I order you to do so, generals. Take the battle swiftly to them so that we have the element of surprise and can catch them unprepared."

After Amalia and Jhiton agreed to the command, the women departed.

"They're not going to be surprised as long as Syla gets there first," Vorik said when he and his brother were alone.

"Agreed," Jhiton said. "We'll have to be crafty."

Did he already have a plan for that? Vorik wouldn't be surprised. He didn't know whether to hope Syla and her people came up with something equally crafty or not.

~

"Abrya is gone," Lord Oyenar said as soon as Syla walked into what the soldiers had dubbed the war room, a spacious office in a barracks near the palace grounds. Unlike most of the military installations in the city, it had survived the stormer attacks unscathed.

"Gone?" Syla looked at Fel and Aunt Tibby, who'd accompanied her, along with several Royal Protectors.

"Gone," Oyenar said. "That terrifying woman with the silver hair returned and got Abrya. The last I saw, she's alive, but I don't know for how long."

"Until the stormers have gained access to the shielder chamber." Fel waved to the back of Syla's moon-marked hand.

"They don't know where the shielder chamber is though. What good would Abrya be to them, unless..." Oyenar's shoulders slumped. "Storm-cursed bastards, they're going to interrogate her. Of course. *She* knows the location."

It occurred to Syla that it might not matter that she'd told Jhiton where to find the shielder. The stormers might already know. Of course, the gods-gift usually granted a degree of mental fortitude that made those with moon-marks better than average at resisting blurting secrets during interrogation. She hoped Abrya could endure Lesva's questions, as Syla herself had when she'd been the woman's prisoner.

An officer in uniform came up to Oyenar and drew him aside. He was one of many high-ranking officers standing or sitting around a huge table made from a single slab of wood. A younger soldier was tacking maps of the island to the wall while a bespectacled man with a pen had a tally going labeled *Dragons and Their Last Known Locations*.

As strange as it seemed, the dragons might be the least of their problems. Syla rubbed the back of her neck, tired and wondering when the last time was that she'd slept, other than briefly dozing on Igliana's back on the way across the Sea of Storms. She'd been worried about pursuit, but exhaustion had forced a few short naps upon her.

As Oyenar conferred with his officer, the dread that had been lurking in Syla's belly all day remained. She hadn't yet informed him that she'd told the stormers about the shielder, and she didn't look forward to it. Thus far, only Tibby and Fel knew, and they'd been grim since they'd received the news. It had been a struggle to pull Tibby away from assisting with setting up machinery to retrieve the weapons platform, but since she'd once done work in the mine, she might have useful input during this meeting.

"She hasn't been found yet," Oyenar said, turning back to Syla as his officer joined the others at the table. "We've got search parties out, but… it's a big island."

"I'm hoping the stormers won't interrogate her. They… don't technically need to." Syla would have preferred not to explain why she knew that, but she couldn't withhold crucial information. "They already know the location of the shielder."

"What? How?" Oyenar blinked slowly. "Oh. My men said you were captured. I've been so distraught and sending troops all over the island to search for my wife that I… I didn't forget, Your Majesty, but I didn't think there was anything we could do to help you."

"There wasn't."

"Did they interrogate *you*?"

"General Jhiton did, unfortunately, yes. Unbeknownst to me, he'd gotten his hands on hydra-scale powder, a drug that lowers your inhibitions and leaves you inclined to answer questions." She pushed up her sleeve, though the needle had slipped in and out without leaving a mark. She almost wished it *had* marked her so Oyenar would be more sympathetic.

His jaw was clenched, his eyes frosting over. She didn't know if his feelings were directed at her or toward the stormers and didn't ask, afraid of the answer.

"They only got the location of one shielder out of me," Syla said, "but it's the one that matters most to your people."

Oyenar closed his eyes. "Yes."

"Are you sure they didn't get more?" one of his officers asked.

"I'm sure. After the questioning, I remembered what we discussed."

"I'm relieved, but..." The officer frowned at Syla. "How come they didn't take advantage of the situation to extract the locations of all of the shielders?"

"I got lucky and escaped."

"You escaped General Jhiton? And however many of his riders were with him? How? Your dragon ally was stuck here. Or... were you questioned here? On our island? And we didn't know it?"

"No, they took me to a camp on the mainland. As I said, I got lucky, and cave crawlers and, apparently, a lake kraken—though I never saw that—attacked their camp from within." Of course, *that* hadn't been what ultimately allowed her to escape, but she didn't want to mention Vorik, much less explain their atypical relationship in front of all these men, most of whom she'd yet to meet formally.

The officers stared at her. In disbelief? She wasn't sure.

"The gods must favor you," one said.

"That would be nice," Syla said, "but from what the stormers say, the world out there is dangerous, and terrible predators attack their camps often."

"That is true. There's a reason they want our protected islands. If they're coming here, we're going to need assistance. General Larek." Oyenar looked at one of the officers. "Find a fast ship—multiple fast ships—and deliver messages to Castle, Frost, and Vineyard Islands. Ask them to send their fleets to help us. If Bogberry Island falls, it'll cause trouble for the whole Kingdom. *More* trouble."

"Yes, my lord."

As the general left to set the request in motion, Oyenar looked back to Syla. "Your Majesty." Before continuing, he gazed around the room. "Actually, I need everyone to take a break."

"My lord?" the senior officer remaining asked.

"We're going to have a discussion that includes the secret location of the shielder," Oyenar explained.

"The secret location that the *stormers* now know? Does it matter if we learn it?"

Oyenar hesitated, probably realizing it was true that there might be little point in withholding it from his men now, but he ultimately waved toward the door. "Just take a break."

"Yes, my lord."

After the men stepped out, Oyenar looked pointedly at Fel, Tibby, and the Royal Protectors. Syla waved for Fel to lead those men out. The protectors were probably used to being dismissed for important meetings, but Fel frowned. Syla was tempted to let him stay, but Oyenar would object. After all, the island lords had all been sworn to secrecy regarding the artifacts. Not all of them even knew the locations of the shielders on their own islands.

"You can stand outside the door," Syla told Fel.

He grumbled, started for the hall, but noticed that nobody had asked Tibby to leave. "Is *she* staying?"

"She already knows the location," Syla said.

"Ah." Tibby lifted a finger. "Actually, I don't."

Syla waited for Fel to leave and close the door before saying, "You worked in the salt mine, and you don't know?"

"I worked on repairing and building magically enhanced machinery *for* the salt mines," Tibby said. "I didn't wield a pickaxe and shovel in them."

Syla didn't point out that the Kingdom valued the salt and that there was nothing ignoble about that profession, especially since Oyenar distracted her by saying in a startled tone, "It's in the salt mine?"

"You didn't know?" Syla almost berated herself for speaking of its location openly, but what did it matter at this point? Everyone would get the gist as soon as the stormers appeared at the mine. Besides, she needed Oyenar in on the planning. As a former general, he had a lot of military experience to offer, and she had nothing.

You have the assistance of a dragon, Wreylith pointed out from her rooftop perch, apparently monitoring Syla's thoughts—and the conversation.

I'm most appreciative of that, Syla replied silently.

"I'd guessed it might be on the hill somewhere," Oyenar said. "But in a tiny hidden cave, not a mine where dozens of people work. *Hundreds* if you count everyone in the area involved in the packaging and transportation as well as the extraction."

"When the shielder artifact was placed many centuries ago, the mine was relatively minor and only one level deep," Syla said. "People used to climb in and out via a rope. They used the same rope to pull out buckets of salt. It's always been a precious commodity for humans, but until the gods moved most of humanity to these islands, the population in this area wasn't significant. At the time, there were a couple of miners with artistic streaks who carved some of the original statues and reliefs as they removed the salt, and the shielder is behind one of the sea god, which I unfortunately divulged to the stormers. They don't know which level it's on, but they'll probably figure out that all the deeper levels would have been carved out in later centuries."

"Let's hope they're not bright enough to guess that," Oyenar said. "And spend their time wandering lost on the lower levels. Don't they get their salt from salt licks? Like animals? They might not know anything about mines."

"I wouldn't assume they're dim," Syla said dryly.

"I suppose you're right. As far as I know, there's only one access point to the mine. That's advantageous and will make guarding it simpler." Oyenar touched one of the maps attached to the wall. It showed an aerial view of the lake and the nearby processing and entrance buildings. Another map offered a cross-section of the mine itself with five levels, all extending horizontally outward from the central shaft with the lift cage.

"The passages are longer than I would have guessed." When Syla had visited the mine before, it had only been on the top level with the ancient carvings and the shielder chamber. "It looks like they extend out under the lake. Is that right?" She eyed the direction marker in the corner, then looked at Tibby.

"You might need a geologist for a detailed consultation, but the lake is presumably supported by solid caprock above the salt dome that created Prominence Hill as it formed long ago." Perhaps guessing the reason for Syla's surprise, Tibby added, "The lake is long and wide but shallow, only about ten feet deep in most spots, and the first level of the mine has more than fifty feet between its ceiling and the surface."

"So, none of the water has even gotten into the mines?" Syla asked.

"Not that I've heard of. That would be disastrous. Salt, after all, dissolves in water, and the pyramid-shaped pillars that hold up the ceilings on each level are made from salt that the miners left behind to act as supports."

Syla bent forward and gripped her knees, a thought trickling into her mind, though she almost rejected it outright. If she created irreparable damage, it would be more devastating for the Kingdom than for the stormers.

"The magically protected chamber isn't made out of salt, right?" Syla asked. "They were all designed to be impervious."

"That's right." Tibby squinted at her. A notion of what Syla was thinking? "The artifacts themselves are nearly indestructible too, save for from other magical items, such as gargoyle-bone blades. As we've unfortunately recently learned."

"So even if a shielder were immersed in water, it would keep working?"

"Oh, most assuredly. If you remember your history on the

matter, the Harvest Island volcano erupted even as the gods were establishing our kingdom. The original chamber was breached and first flooded with seawater and then magma, but the shield around the island remained up. When the gods extracted the artifact to move it to a new location, it was, at least according to the scribe detailing the event, fine. After that, the gods put more magic into the chambers to further ensure their safety from geological events."

Oyenar frowned. "Why would our artifact chamber be *immersed* in water? What are you thinking, Your Majesty?"

Syla straightened but held up a finger and looked at Aunt Tibby instead of answering. Oyenar wouldn't like her idea, and if it wasn't feasible, there was no point in pursuing it anyway. "When you were talking about your work here, you said you used your magic to make drills, right?"

"Among other tools, yes." Tibby sounded wary. Yes, she'd already twigged to Syla's idea.

"How fast could it cut through... did you say fifty feet of rock? Rock and salt, I guess."

"It could vary a lot, depending on the material, and, of course, the width of the hole, but it could drill anywhere from one to twenty feet an hour."

"That's... quite a range." But, if the stormers gave them enough time, it could be doable, especially if a team started right away. The deed might be done before the enemy even arrived.

"Operating machinery is in line with my talents, so with the help of my power, it could go faster." Tibby waved her moon-marked hand. "But I don't know how we'd set up to drill down *through* the lake, if that's what you're thinking. You'd need a stable platform. You couldn't set up a drill on a barge."

Syla scratched her cheek, feeling her engineering knowledge inadequate for this plan, but Tibby hadn't yet suggested it wouldn't be possible. "What if you set it up below and drilled upward? There must be various types of excavating equipment already down there, right?"

Each level, she recalled, was cavernous. Wouldn't there be plenty of room to set up machinery?

Tibby hesitated, then nodded. "Drilling upward… might be possible, and it would be easier to hide what we were doing. But Syla, this could destroy the mine completely. Forever."

"Would it also protect the shielder forever?"

"Until someone invented a technology or magic for swimming underwater, I suppose."

"A new mine could be started elsewhere on the hill, couldn't it?" Syla didn't know if the salt dome Tibby had spoken of filled all of Prominence Hill, but if it accounted for a great deal of it, wouldn't there still be salt left down there untouched?

"I suppose." Tibby didn't sound enthused by the plan, and her gaze had shifted to the maps.

"Wait." As they'd spoken, Oyenar's expression had shifted from one of confusion to one of enlightenment. Stunned and horrified enlightenment. "Are you talking about flooding the mine?"

Oyenar shook his head, though another thought must have occurred to him because he abruptly frowned down at the floor instead of objecting.

"Maybe it could be a last resort," Syla suggested, "though if we didn't start *before* the stormers came, it would be hard to get it done in time after they arrived. Maybe Tibby could set up the drill and just go partway to the lake?"

Tibby, her chin in her hand, continued studying the maps and didn't reply.

"I'm horrified at the thought of losing the mine," Oyenar said, "but if we could lure enough high-ranking stormers, especially their damned riders, into it and trap them in the flood, that could be a hard enough blow to end the war."

It was Syla's turn for stunned horror, and she gripped the table for support. She hadn't been thinking of trying to trap anyone—to *drown* anyone. Just flood the mine so that the shielder chamber would be inaccessible when the stormers arrived. Even with enhanced magic, their riders surely couldn't hold their breath long enough to swim far enough to reach it. Besides, if the salt pillars dissolved, the water would collapse the mine after flooding it. This would deny access to the shielder for generations to come—if not forever—and it could continue to operate, undisturbed by enemies.

"General Jhiton leads most of the battles personally," Oyenar mused, "and I bet he'll have Captain Vorik with him and a number of other high-ranking riders. Maybe some of their Storm Guard leaders too. I don't think they'll have a map, so they won't know where to search. They might bring numerous parties down there. And the silver-haired woman. Captain Lesva. If *she's* caught down there, all the better. Of course, I need to get Abrya back *before* the stormers drag her down there. Gods." Oyenar swore and sat in a chair. "We can't start this until… There can't be any chance of my wife being trapped down there."

Syla had felt the warmth drain from her face—maybe her entire body—at the mention of Vorik, and she immediately thought she would have to find a way to warn him. But she couldn't, could she? If she did, he would warn Jhiton and the rest of the stormers. He would have to. They were his people.

"I think we should just flood the mine to deny access to the shielder," Syla said. "It would be a permanent way to keep it safe. That's better than moving it to another locale where it could be found."

"*I* think we should lure as many of the bastards down there as we can," Oyenar said, "and drown them like rats in a monsoon."

"Perhaps," Tibby said, raising a finger, "we should determine if either scenario is feasible. I need to do some calculations on the volume of space in the mines based on these maps and how much water is likely in the lake. The water would flow down to the deepest levels first. It might leave the stormers in a dry tunnel. At the least, they would see the water flowing past and have time to escape while it fills the lower levels."

"We could seal access to the lower levels. The lift cage shaft is the only way down to them." Oyenar's eyes lit.

"The walls, floors, and ceilings are made from salt," Tibby reminded him. "The water would eventually erode it all away."

"*Eventually*," Oyenar said. "Like a snow melt after a great Frost Island storm, it wouldn't happen right away."

"No."

"It doesn't take men long to drown." Oyenar pointed at the top of the cross-section map. "We could set explosives at the entrance of that shaft as well. Bury it once the stormers are down there. The only way out would be through the hole you drilled, and with the water coming down, they wouldn't be able to climb out against the current, right?"

"That's... right." Tibby's face had gone pale. Tibby, who'd once suggested poisoning Vorik and had informed Syla how rational she was, didn't have the stomach for his plan.

Syla shook her head, not liking it either and regretted that she'd planted the seed.

But Oyenar pumped his fist. "I'll get those bastards back for killing my people, destroying my palace, and kidnapping *my wife*. I'll send teams to prepare the explosives and load materials to block off the lower levels, and Lady Tibaytha, we'll take you to the mine to set up your drill. Syla—will you look for Abrya? From your dragon's back, please? We have to get her away from that stormer woman before we can do any of this."

Since her nemesis, Captain Lesva, would be *with* Abrya, Syla wanted to shake her head and say *no*, but they had to get her back.

Tactically speaking, it would also be ideal to deny the stormers a prisoner with a moon-mark to open the chamber.

"I will search for her, yes." Maybe Syla should have felt guilt, not relief, that she wouldn't have to set up what might be, if it came to pass, the largest—and potentially most deadly—booby-trap in history, but she didn't want to help with that. If they found Abrya and dealt with Lesva, she told herself, it might not be necessary. Or they could go with her original idea of drowning only the impervious shielder artifact. "Yes," she repeated, nodding to herself.

Next to her, Tibby, who *did* need to participate in the set-up, did not nod. She was still pale. Even she must not have been able to summon the desire to kill stormers en masse.

But Oyenar, so freshly angered and affronted, had no quibbles. He gripped Tibby's shoulder and pointed her toward the door.

"Come," he told them both. "The stormers already have spies—saboteurs and *kidnappers*—on this island. We'll have to move carefully and quickly. *Very* quickly."

25

An hour before the Sixteen Talons would fly to Bogberry Island for the invasion, in a small clearing near the cave, Vorik sparred with a couple of riders in his squadron. He needed to burn off nervous energy and also wanted to make sure his skills were at their sharpest.

When Jhiton walked over, having finished a run and exercise routine of his own, Vorik thought little of it, assuming his brother also wanted to spar. And Jhiton saluted him with his swords, an invitation to practice, but only a few minutes into their match—a less heated battle than they'd shared on the top of the bluff—Jhiton spoke telepathically to him.

We need to discuss something.

Vorik paused and lowered his sword and dagger. *Unless it's about blueberries, blackberries, or cobblers made from the fruit, I doubt I want to partake.*

It is about your role in the upcoming battle.

So, no berries.

Once we've claimed Bogberry Island, they will be aplenty.

I look forward to it.

Jhiton sheathed his weapons and gazed at him. *Do you?*

Look forward to eating fruit and desserts made from fruit? Always.

You know what I mean. You've expressed concerns about the chiefs' intent and whenever the queen is involved...

Their intents are questionable.

And the rest? Jhiton raised his eyebrows.

Vorik shrugged. *You know I have feelings for her. It's not my fault she keeps involving herself in our war.*

Jhiton gazed toward the sea, the roar of the waves audible through the trees. Bracing himself for something he wouldn't like, Vorik waited, though he also sensed Agrevlari approaching, and was that Ozlemar and Chieftess Shi's blue dragon, Uxtar, with him?

Where have you been? Vorik asked Agrevlari. *Those aren't your usual hunting companions.*

Ozlemar ordered me to accompany him to scout the Island of Bogs from above the shield and locate with certainty the entrance to the human salt mine. Your leaders also hoped to find that there might be other older entrances that are less well known and would allow stealthy access by your people.

Were there?

Not that we were able to determine. Even the main entrance is not obvious from high above. Only rail tracks leading away from a building suggest its locale. Mining activities ceased while we were in the area, and Wreylith came to glare up at us.

From under the shield? Is she still trapped there? Vorik wondered if the dragon and Syla had figured that out yet.

She did not answer my questions, saying only that she would mercilessly remove my every scale and roast me alive if I partook in an invasion.

So, her love for you continues to deepen.

We exchanged some spirited insults. I believe she has grown to appreciate me.

Undoubtedly. Will you compose another ballad for her? Vorik watched Jhiton, still waiting for whatever he intended to say, but his steady gaze toward the sea suggested he was communicating telepathically with Ozlemar.

I believe I may challenge her to a rigorous but nonlethal duel instead. She's not proven as enraptured by my singing as I would have believed based on my success with other females.

She's a special dragon.

Most assuredly. Let me share what I saw from above as Ozlemar is doing with Jhiton. We were supposed to take careful note of terrain features that might allow you to approach stealthily, something that will be difficult when the enemy anticipates your arrival.

Definitely.

Imagery of the sprawling Bogberry Island, as seen from high above, filled Vorik's mind. He'd flown over it before and was familiar with its many lakes, meandering waterways, and shallow bogs with greenery between.

That's the lake near the mine entrance, Vorik said when Agrevlari's attention focused on a wide body of water with numerous fishing boats and barges trolling about. Freshwater fish tended to be less challenging to acquire than the dangerous and often razor-fanged, tentacled, electrified, or venomous creatures that survived and thrived in the Sea of Storms. *And the mine entrance?* Vorik added as Agrevlari shared a couple of unassuming wooden buildings a half mile from the end of the lake. The tracks Agrevlari had mentioned were the only thing suggesting their purpose.

We believe so, yes.

"Those boats and barges are interesting," Jhiton murmured.

"They are?" Vorik asked. "I thought they looked remarkably uninteresting."

"The only road leading up to the mine passes that lake. If we could get people there first and perhaps station them on the boats, we could use range weapons to attack Kingdom troops being transported to the mine. That would give our parties more time to search without interruption."

"Syla has to be telling them all about our plans. They'll get people there before we arrive."

"She doesn't know about our plans." Jhiton raised frank eyebrows. "Correct?"

"I didn't tell her anything, but she *knows* our destination and can figure out where to put troops."

"We'll see. Armies don't move swiftly, and I've also ordered that the city be attacked again as a diversion. It's unfortunate that we don't have a map of the mine. Since we've never thought to target it before, our spies didn't attempt to obtain information on the facility. I've sent word to Captain Lesva to try to find a map."

Vorik snorted. "She'll probably tote the kidnapped lady over her shoulder and go to the mine herself ahead of time to complete the mission without us."

"That isn't what I ordered, but it would be acceptable. Once the shielder is down and our dragons can access the island, it'll be much easier to capture."

Vorik bristled at the idea of Lesva assigning herself yet another mission, and he worried about Syla perhaps being in the area, maybe asking her engineer aunt to make booby traps to place. But with Jhiton watching him again, all Vorik said was, "True."

He sensed more dragons approaching, flying up the coastline from the south. At first, he thought the Freeborn Faction allies were returning, but Jhiton nodded, as if he'd expected visitors.

"Swordhawk Tribe," he said, "and Chiefs Lyzart and Velesh are also on the way with wings of dragons. They should have ships heading to Bogberry Island too."

"Ah. Maybe you should send word for Lesva to wait for our arrival. There's little reason for her to risk her life when backup is on the way."

Jhiton gazed blandly at him. "Are you worried for her or worried your queen will cross her path?"

"I don't think that confrontation would go well for either of them. Syla is likely to be with Wreylith, who may be perched right atop one of those mine buildings. After all, she *knows* we're coming."

"Lesva would sneak past them."

"You don't think Wreylith would sense her? Or spot her? With a kidnapped woman slung kicking and screaming over her shoulder?"

Jhiton conceded that with a hand tilted upward. "We'll plan to divert Wreylith and the queen, if she's with her dragon. As I said, unless Lesva handles everything before we arrive, we'll need time to search the mine."

"Do you want me to lead one of the parties that will do that?" Vorik asked.

Jhiton didn't answer right away, instead giving him the thoughtful gaze that had become frequent. He glanced toward people walking in and out of the cave and switched to telepathy. *Chieftess Shi has suggested that I assign you to stay here while we invade the island and claim the shielder.*

Vorik rocked back on his heels. *You don't want me to come?*

She mentioned that another lake kraken might find its way into the pool below and threaten the non-combatants that remain here. The dire vultures have been lurking in the area as well. We can't leave our people in danger while we take all our fighters on this venture.

Vorik folded his arms over his chest. *Vultures aren't the reason Shi doesn't want me to come.*

No. She doesn't want you involved because you are conflicted when it comes to Queen Syla.

Vorik opened his mouth to protest, but how could he? He'd admitted as much himself.

Many people don't want you involved for that reason, Jhiton continued. *Even those who didn't have an opinion before or weren't aware of your relationship previously noted that you stood protectively close to her when you brought her here, that you seemed more like her bodyguard than kidnapper. Many people see the way you look at her, Vorik.*

Again, Vorik wanted to protest but didn't have a believable argument to issue.

You will stay here and protect the camp, Jhiton said.

From vultures.

And krakens.

You know full well that krakens are rare. If we'd expected even one to visit that lake, we wouldn't have camped here. It'll probably be a decade before another one enters the water down there, especially since they can smell the stink of death of their own kind long after the corpse decomposes.

Yes, but you'll stay here regardless. Jhiton inclined his head toward him and walked into the cave.

You may regret not taking me along. I'm a good warrior, and you know it. And Syla... You can't underestimate her. She has that power, but she won't use it on me. I want to be there.

To ensure she's not killed?

To watch your back, Jhiton. She'll go after you. She hates you. If I'm there, I can...

What? What could he do except be conflicted? Vorik closed his eyes and sighed. As much as he hated that the tribe didn't trust him, did he *really* want to destroy Syla's shielder? And doubtless kill a bunch of her people in the process? No, he'd already had his fill of this war.

Stay here, Vorik. It'll be for the best.

Vorik sighed again, something telling him that it *wouldn't* be for the best.

Vorik sensed Agrevlari fly inland until the dragon found an outcropping on which to perch. *Did you catch our conversation?*

We are to be denied the glory of battle and given the modest duty of sky watchers.

Yeah.

You will obey your brother's wishes?

He's my superior officer, and I'm honor bound to do so.

Hm.

Though perhaps after they depart, after we've ensured there are no threats to the camp from above or below, we could visit Harvest Island to go hunting. After all, if Syla gets the shielder for that island repaired, it won't be accessible to dragons for long. You'd naturally want to visit the hunting grounds one last time, right?

The most delicious prey has mostly been consumed by all the dragons visiting, but perhaps a small eliok might yet be found.

I'm glad you're in agreement with me on this. Vorik wouldn't disobey his brother, but Jhiton hadn't told him that he couldn't go hunting, and if something dire happened on Bogberry Island, and his people needed his help, he wouldn't be far away.

~

Vorik waited until well after Jhiton and Chieftess Shi left with the main forces before asking Agrevlari to meet him in an open area so they could head out. He didn't feel like he was disobeying his brother—besides, it was Chieftess Shi who'd specifically not wanted him along—but... he also didn't want to flout that he wasn't going to stay behind. He'd checked the depths of the cave for threats, even killing a couple of aggressive crawlers that had moved back into the area, before packing his bag and letting a couple of the elders know that he was going hunting.

We will *hunt while we're there,* he told Agrevlari as he walked toward the bluff where he'd attacked Jhiton. *I'm not being dishonest.*

I do enjoy a good hunt. I'm quite envious of Wreylith for gaining access to the Island of Bogs. I understand the bears that proliferate there, feasting and fattening themselves on all manner of berries, are extremely delicious.

Are you also envious that she was trapped *on that island?* Vorik assumed that the dragon could leave now that Syla had returned —as long as *she* left—but imagined Wreylith had been irked.

I can think of many less appealing places to be trapped. There are all those lakes for swimming, and are there not also hot springs on the western end? I do enjoy a mineral soak after a good hunt and feast. Perhaps you can arrange for me to be trapped there later, Vorik.

I think you'd have to bond with someone with a moon-mark for that.

Hm.

I hope you're not contemplating leaving me for Syla's aunt.

Oh, not the aunt. Certainly not. She's not a warrior.

She tried to shoot you when we first met. Vorik stepped out of the trees and found Agrevlari perched on the bluff, waiting for him. All signs of the previous day's storm had passed, and an inviting blue sky stretched out over the sea.

That is true, but I believe I would prefer to remain with you. If you succeed in destroying the shielder there, I will soon be able to hunt the bears.

And the mineral soaks?

Oh, yes. A dragon's scales are rejuvenated, with their natural oils restored, by time spent in hot springs. In the aftermath, you will admire my healthy sheen.

As much as I care about the shininess of your scales, I feel compelled to remind you that destroying the shielder isn't my mission. Vorik jumped up to land astride Agrevlari's back. *I don't* have *a mission.*

Why am I certain you will find a way to insert yourself into the midst regardless?

Because we've been bonded for many years, and I want you to do your hunting on the adjacent island.

Quite.

Agrevlari set off across the sea at a leisurely pace, probably guessing correctly that Vorik had no desire to catch up with the others. Eventually, some of the stormer dragons flying around the islands would sense them, but Vorik didn't need to invite a challenge.

On the way, they passed over stormer warships sailing toward the Kingdom. Soldiers on deck among the crews looked up and waved to the green dragon flying overhead. Of course. They thought Vorik and Agrevlari were joining them for the mission. Vorik lifted a hand in return though with each ship they passed—had his leaders called for troops from *every* tribe?—he grew more worried that Syla wouldn't escape the confrontation alive. Even if she stayed in the palace and directed the action from afar, she would be in danger. Jhiton had already said he would order troops to attack the city again, to provide a diversion. And, knowing Syla the way he did now, Vorik doubted she *would* stay behind to direct events from afar. She might be waiting for the invasion force in the shielder chamber with explosives and other booby-traps placed all around.

He smiled and shook his head. *I suppose we can't kidnap her again.*

Your queen? Do you again have the urge to mate with her?

I always have the urge to mate with her, but I'm more concerned about keeping her alive.

So you can mate with her.

Vorik frowned at the back of Agrevlari's horned head. *That's not* all *I think about.*

Last time you kidnapped her, scant hours passed before you were stimulating her sex orifices.

I had no idea you were keeping track of the time or our activities so assiduously.

It was a long flight.

Vorik sighed as they passed over another stormer ship. *This is just about saving her life, Agrevlari. She wouldn't appreciate me swooping in and stealing her from her troops while they're engaged in battle, but... I'm afraid she's in danger again.*

So, you wouldn't mate until the next day?

I'm not talking to you anymore.

Very well.

They didn't remain silent for long. Dragons on the horizon made Agrevlari bank and fly farther east instead of more directly southeast toward Harvest Island.

Was that the wing from Icecarver Tribe? Vorik hadn't realized they'd been called from the far north.

Yes.

Jhiton is going to make damn sure he doesn't fail, isn't he?

Your brother is a determined human. To avoid notice, I will fly over to Castle Island before swinging south toward the Island of Eliok.

Good idea, Vorik said, though they would inevitably be spotted, regardless. If he *did* want to kidnap Syla, how would he get close without his people seeing?

Vorik shook his head. There was no way. He would have to prevaricate and hope Jhiton and Shi hadn't told many people that they'd ordered Vorik to stay home, and he would have to hope he didn't run into them specifically. His stomach twisted at the idea of defying his brother openly, but he'd attacked Jhiton the day before. Maybe... maybe Vorik had already made his choice to leave his people, and he hadn't yet realized it. Maybe neither of them had.

Agrevlari, why don't you just fly straight toward... Vorik trailed off as a fleet of warships below drew his attention. They were Kingdom ships, which would have made sense, but they weren't sailing toward Bogberry Island. *That's strange.*

They weren't sailing toward Harvest Island either. They looked like they'd come from islands farther south and were heading toward Castle Island.

But the Kingdom capital was shielded and not, as far as Vorik knew, being targeted by any of Jhiton's troops. It was coming into view now, and there weren't any dragons in the sky around it. Nor did any stormer ships lurk off its shores.

Do you sense any dragons around Castle Island, Agrevlari?

I do not.

Then why are all those ships heading there?

I do not know, but it appears that vessels that should be loyal to the queen are not sailing to assist her on the Island of Bogs.

It was silly, since Vorik shouldn't have *wanted* more warships to challenge his people's forces, but he felt affronted on Syla's behalf.

Fly as close to Castle Island as you can, Vorik said. *I want to see... if there's anything to see.*

As Agrevlari soared closer, Vorik didn't know what he expected to find, especially since they wouldn't be able to see much detail from beyond the barrier, but he leaned to the side and looked intently down.

There are many warships already in the harbor, Agrevlari observed. *More than there were the day of our invasion, and we destroyed a great number of the island's craft then.*

Meaning these are from elsewhere in the Kingdom. The Castle Island locals haven't had time to rebuild a fleet.

I have little knowledge of shipbuilding but would assume not.

It takes a while. Vorik pointed at the vessels in the harbor, so many that there wasn't room at the docks for them all. *The islands are far enough apart, especially those in the southern half of the chain, that those ships had to start sailing a while ago to reach this port. Whatever this is about, it was set in motion* before *Syla returned with word that we'd learned the location of the Bogberry shielder.*

That seems likely.

They might have set sail before we even kidnapped her. Did she *summon them for some reason? Before she left? And she hasn't been able to get a message out to change where she wanted them to go?* That seemed possible since so many stormer dragons had been in the area these past days. His people might have intercepted messages.

Even as he started to believe that reasonable, his sharp eyes picked up on something below. Agrevlari was flying above the castle, and the royal blue flag that usually hung on the wall, that which signified the Moonmark royal family was in control, had changed. He had no idea what gardener family or faction was represented by a yellow flag, but the meaning sank in right away.

Someone else has taken power while Syla has been away. Urgency filling him, Vorik flattened a hand to Agrevlari's scales. *Take me straight to Bogberry Island.*

You will attempt to kidnap her immediately?

I... don't know what I'll do, but I'll bet she doesn't know about this yet. She may be in danger from even more than our people. I have to warn her.

Your queen has many enemies. Agrevlari banked to fly toward Bogberry Island.

Enemies she doesn't deserve. She needs... Me, Vorik thought but didn't say, reminded that Agrevlari, despite their bond, was loyal to his wing and those he served with. And those dragons had long ago promised themselves to be allies to the stormers since they all had the same goal of gaining access to the Kingdom islands. If Vorik left his people to stand at Syla's side, he might be walking away from Agrevlari, his friendship and his bond.

As he urged, *Hurry, please*, Vorik accepted that, but he also didn't announce his intentions. First, he had to make sure he could find Syla and, if she needed it, save her. Then... then he could figure out the rest.

~

Syla rode on Wreylith's back with Fel perched behind her. He'd been unwilling to be left behind. Since they were looking for a deadly enemy who could kill Syla with a swipe of her sword, she hadn't rejected his offer of help.

Fel gazed indifferently down at the bogs and eventually Lake Talindar as they flew around the top of Prominence Hill. *He* was unaware of the plan that Syla had proposed and Lord Oyenar had expanded greatly upon, so he probably thought nothing of the wagons of troops winding up the road that led past the lake on their way to the mine buildings. She hoped someone warned the fishermen to bring their boats in so they wouldn't be casualties if fighting broke out, but she could imagine Oyenar not wanting to clue the stormers in that anything was amiss by doing so.

Do you sense anyone with magical power? Syla asked Wreylith.

Not yet, but that is what I'm seeking. If we fly close enough, I should be able to detect through their inherent power the female rider captain and also your moon-marked relative.

You'd think Lesva would start losing *some of her power since her dragon is gone.*

It will linger for some time. It's even possible for a dragon, knowing its end nears, to transfer more of its power into a bonded human before its death.

Oh, great. A more powerful Lesva. Exactly what I hoped for. Syla told herself she'd already faced Lesva in Oyenar's suite, and it hadn't been any worse than before. If anything, she'd done better than the first time they'd pitted their powers against each other.

"With the trees so dense between the bogs in this area," Fel said, watching the ground below, "it'll be difficult to see stormers sneaking up the hill. They won't use the roads or the river. They'll stay under cover."

"Wreylith is attempting to *sense* our enemies."

True, she'd only spoken of Abrya and Lesva, but she would sense other riders if they skulked about below.

"Through magic, I assume," Fel said.

"Yes, though I understand dragons also have keen eyes and ears and a strong sense of smell."

"They've effectively seen and smelled enough elioks to nearly make them extinct on Harvest Island," he grumbled.

"I didn't know that species meant something to you," Syla said, though she also lamented that so many dragons had enjoyed free rein to hunt on the island these past weeks. And, if she failed here, another island would be laid bare to them.

"I enjoyed the steak we had in the castle."

"The steak from the haunch that Wreylith delivered to us? You can't bemoan dragons hunting and also enjoy what they've caught and shared with you."

Wreylith didn't comment, but a rumble reverberating through her body might have indicated agreement.

Fel grunted an acknowledgment. "Is Tibby going to be able to work on building a new shielder from the components you returned with? Even if that one is destined for Harvest Island, we could use it if some stormers manage to take down the one here. Plant it right in one of the palace towers and activate it."

"Aunt Tibby is... working on another project right now." Syla spotted the first wagons arriving at the mining buildings, troops unloading with a woman in a dress among them. Tibby. Several armed men accompanied her past a shallow bog and to the building with the lift cage inside. At least she was well protected.

"What project could be more important than fixing the shielder?" Fel asked.

Even though she trusted him fully, Syla was reluctant to explain the plan, as if voicing details might make it more likely to come to pass. "I think she needs the outside shell and components from the destroyed shielder back at the castle," she said, though she had no idea if that was true. At the least, Tibby probably hadn't brought along the magical tools she would need.

"We should send her on a ship heading back as soon as possible, then." After a moment, Fel added, "There's no reason for an engineer to be trapped in a war zone. Because of her moon-mark, she might be targeted."

There was a reason, but Syla kept it to herself. Instead, she lightly asked, "Goodness, Fel, do you care about her fate?"

"She's gruff, insulting, and thinks I'm a warmongering idiot."

"So, you like that she challenges you."

Fel's grunt sounded like denial, but it wasn't as vehement as Syla would have expected.

"I think you're growing on her too. Maybe you two can go to a nice diner for a meal after this is all over." Realizing there were numerous ways the war could end up being *over*, Syla amended her words. "After we've driven out the stormers and secured the Kingdom."

"If we succeed at doing that, I'll go to a meal with anyone. Even your dragon."

"Wreylith is a delightful dining companion." Syla thought of the intestines that Wreylith had flung upon the stone wall.

Dragons do not seek to be delightful, Wreylith said. *Certainly not in the eyes of puny humans. Hold. Others are speaking with me.*

Wreylith flew around the lake, her presence making the fishermen look up. Even though they'd probably heard by now that the red dragon was an ally, and Wreylith's flight was low enough that they would be able to see Syla on her back, the men skittered under cover.

Igliana and other Freeborn Faction-aligned dragons are informing me that many new dragons have entered the area.

Stormer dragons.

Yes. Some are alighting on the Island of Eliok. Others are approaching this *island.*

With riders that they intend to drop off so they can swim in and invade?

Perhaps, but there are also many ships in the sea—stormer ships—that are full of troops, and they are also approaching this island.

Full of troops means... what? Dozens of men? Hundreds?

At least. Igliana has counted twenty ships so far.

Syla grimaced, though it was what she'd expected would happen. "I guess they're sending more than a team."

Fel's next grunt was one of inquiry.

"Wreylith says a lot of stormer ships and dragons are close." Syla hadn't seen any vessels in the waters near that cave, nor had it housed hundreds of men. Jhiton must have called for troops from all of their tribes to join in on this.

As Wreylith flapped her wings to carry them from the lake to the buildings again, Syla glimpsed someone in the trees. It had looked like a man rather than Lesva, but had those been black riding leathers the person had worn?

"I saw someone in the trees," Fel said, but he pointed at least a hundred yards farther up the bank than where Syla had glimpsed someone.

"There may already be stormers on the island moving into the area." Syla couldn't see any ships anchored in the waters beyond the shield yet, but stormers had helped Lesva attack the palace—and Vorik attack the docked ships—so there were people here already. "We'd better go down and warn the military leaders that Oyenar sent on those wagons. We may have less time to prepare than we thought."

When the road, railroad tracks, and buildings came into view again, the wagons she'd mentioned were already on their way back. Returning to the barracks in the city to fetch more troops most likely. Syla didn't see any of the men left in the area. Had they all gone down into the mine with Tibby? Someone should have been placed on guard around the buildings, surely.

I sense them, Wreylith said.

Lesva and Lady Abrya? Syla asked silently as Fel asked, "The female dragon rider and Oyenar's wife?"

Apparently, Wreylith was including him in the conversation now.

A bonded rider and a moon-marked human, yes. Wreylith descended toward one of the buildings.

"Are they already inside?" Syla groaned.

Lesva might run into Tibby right away and attack her out of principle. Or try questioning her for information on the shielder chamber's location in the mine. Or did she already know that? As Syla had worried about before, Lesva had been with Abrya long enough to extract that information.

Your mine shaft is too narrow for a large and magnificent dragon to enter, Wreylith said.

Even small and modest dragons would struggle.

Indeed. We are not exiguous creatures.

"What's exiguous?" Fel asked, though he'd probably gotten the gist.

"Ask Aunt Tibby. She's well-read."

He snorted. "She'd probably use it to describe my genitals."

"She's classier than that."

"My intellect?"

"That sounds right."

I will land on the roof, Wreylith said.

Perfect. Thank you. We need to go down there and make sure Tibby and the shielder are safe. Syla dreaded entering the mine with only Fel as an ally. It had made sense for her to scout the area and search for Abrya from the safety of the sky with the powerful Wreylith along. But without the dragon...

Hopefully, Syla could find the troops already in the mine and requisition a squad to help her.

As they landed on the rooftop, Fel pointed to a man near the rail tracks. A *dead* man.

Syla slumped. "Lesva must have *just* come through."

How had this unraveled so quickly? Syla had thought they'd have time to put their plan in place.

"Yes." Fel slid off Wreylith's back and jumped to the ground, his mace in hand, his crossbow slung across his back.

More gracefully than usual, Syla also slid off the dragon's back. Typically, she would very carefully and awkwardly maneuver herself if she had to climb down from something, but a strange sense of vigor prompted her to jump off the roof. She landed on her feet beside Fel, feeling as if she'd dropped two feet instead of more than ten, and he blinked, looking surprised as he belatedly held out a hand to steady her if she needed it. She did not.

You are coming into the power that my magic grants, Wreylith stated, sounding smug.

Handy timing.

Too bad it wouldn't be enough to allow her to defeat Lesva in a confrontation.

"Let's find Tibby and the rest of the troops that went in." Syla eyed the body on the tracks. "Before it's too late."

26

The lift cage rattled as it descended on chains, a magical engine in the building up top powering it, linked to simple glowing buttons for up, down, and stop. It was possible Aunt Tibby had played a role in creating it, but something told Syla the lift had been built in a much earlier era. With a worn wooden floor and metal bars for the ceiling and walls, it hadn't changed an iota since she had visited more than fifteen years earlier. It might not have changed in centuries. A dented and pockmarked iron cart resting inside with them also might have been original to the mine. A few chunks of salt and fine powder coated the bottom of it.

Though large enough to fit eight or ten people, the lift cage felt claustrophobic, the ride down a lot less safe than it had seemed all those years ago with her parents and siblings and a couple of bodyguards cozily crowded in with her. Venia had complained, she recalled, that their brother, Gylonar, had been deliberately sneezing on the girls and blaming it on the dust. Syla shook her head bleakly, missing them all.

"How deep does this go?" Fel's knuckles were tight, both

around the haft of his mace and the handle of one of the two lanterns they'd grabbed from the building.

Through their many adventures, her bodyguard had been fearless, but it was with wary eyes that he looked at the shaft as the sides changed from dark grayish-brown rock to off-white salt with pinkish striations. He hadn't seemed disturbed by the cave they'd found the teal ore in, but this felt tighter. More ominous.

"According to the map," Syla said, "the deepest levels are hundreds of feet down, but I've only been in the topmost one, and that's as far as we should need to go. We should be almost there."

Fel's *hm* wasn't that heartened.

"If it helps, the levels of the mine themselves are spacious. *Cavernous.* Wreylith could have fit down there with us—if she'd had a way in."

The shaft around the cage disappeared as they entered the first level, the space as vast as she'd promised. Syla lifted a hand to the *stop* button but waited to press it. As she'd recalled, it was thirty or forty feet, it not more, from the ceiling to the floor, and the first level stretched into the darkness in all directions. Great pyramid-shaped pillars of salt had been left untouched, the mine carved out around them, to support the high ceiling.

Lanterns burned on some of the pillars, with a couple of carts full of salt lined up on tracks near the lift cage. It almost appeared as if the place were engaged in its normal operations, but Syla spotted a body next to one of the carts, and her heart sank. There was nothing normal about this situation.

The body belonged to a uniformed soldier, not a miner, and she hoped Oyenar had sent word ahead and cleared the place of workers. Military casualties were bad enough. Syla didn't want to worry about simple laborers being turned into additional victims.

When the lift cage drew even with the floor, Syla reached for the *stop* button. But a boom and a flash ahead and to the left startled her, and she almost didn't halt them. For an instant, the entire mine was lit from the brilliance of the explosive, revealing pyramid supports stretching back in wide rows for what seemed like miles, and she got a glimpse of shadows—people—hundreds of yards in the distance before the darkness returned.

Fel stepped in front of her. "It's not safe to get out here."

"I've got more explosives, and I'm not afraid to throw them!" Aunt Tibby yelled.

Syla hit the button. "We *have* to get out here."

She tried to push Fel aside so she could open the gate, but he threw the latch himself and ran out first. A crossbow quarrel zipped away from the direction that Aunt Tibby's voice had come. Then another boom followed the first. Tibby was aiming at something—someone—deeper in the mine.

Syla ran after Fel as he rounded one of the pyramid supports. Lanterns flickered on it and yellow light glinted off the metal of equipment-laden wagons and large wheeled machines, a few of which hummed with magic. It took Syla a moment to spot Tibby and two guards with crossbows.

There were no lanterns lit in the depths that they faced, but the flashes of light had revealed people in black, a few with white gargoyle-bone blades.

"There are stormers already down here," one of the soldiers told Fel when he walked up, as if he were the senior person present that they needed to report to, not Syla.

"We saw the bodies," Syla said.

"The stormers were waiting down here for us. How did they get here so quickly? I know there were reports of ships on the way, but—"

"These are the same people who attacked the palace and the docks—the weapons platform."

Tibby frowned at Syla as she lowered a flat square-shaped package identical to the explosives she'd made weeks earlier to defend the shielder chamber under the castle. "Is *he* with them?"

"Vorik?" Syla asked. "The last I saw, he was back on the mainland, but I'm sure he's coming."

Tibby bared her teeth.

"He fished you out of the river," Syla pointed out.

"He's the one who put me *in* the river," she said.

Since Syla couldn't argue with that, she only spread her arms.

"If this must be discussed with enemies about, at least stand behind cover." Surprisingly, Fel gripped Tibby's arm first, guiding her into a nook between a machine and a pillar.

Syla joined them while the guards stood behind the wagons and pointed their weapons over them and into the darkness. The stormers had to remain in the area, shrouded by the shadows, but they weren't doing anything at the moment. And they didn't make a sound. Syla sensed someone with power but didn't think it was Lesva.

"You shouldn't have come down here," Tibby told her.

"Neither should you, but we have missions." Syla raised her marked hand, then glanced from the wagons and machinery to the lift cage. "How did the miners get all this big stuff down here?"

"The things I worked on were brought in pieces and assembled down here." Tibby wiggled her fingers.

"We need to get more men down here," one of the soldiers said, glancing at the cage lift for a different reason. "Have more troops arrived?"

"The wagons were going back to the city to get more when I came via dragon," Syla said.

The soldier mouthed *via dragon*, apparently not parsing that as a normal mode of transportation.

"But… we shouldn't bring more people down here." Syla gave her aunt a significant look and waved at the machinery, silently asking if what she needed to drill with was in the machine-storage area with them.

"We *have* to, Your Majesty," the man said as Tibby nodded back to Syla. "The stormers outnumber us and have *magic*."

"I know, but we'll have to try to avoid them."

"They're after the shielder, aren't they? How are we going to *avoid* them?"

"They don't know exactly where it is. Or they shouldn't." Syla remembered that Lesva had Abrya, who might have divulged that information. Abrya might even now be leading Lesva to the chamber with a sword pressed into the back of her neck. "Have you seen Lady Abrya or Captain Lesva? The silver-haired woman?"

"I know which one that storm-cursed scion of the mad god is." Tibby climbed into the cab of a giant wagon with machinery in the back. "No, I haven't seen her, and I hope not to."

Fel lifted his hand, as if to pull her back down where she wouldn't be visible to someone in the distance. "Are you *going* somewhere?"

"The mission that Syla mentioned must be completed." Tibby waved toward the machinery in the wagon, which included numerous sections of long, thick helical bits.

Were there enough to be assembled to reach the surface? The drill machine itself looked complicated with a glowing bulb and panel of switches and levers that presumably powered and controlled everything.

"You two, go with Lady Tibaytha." Syla pointed at the soldiers. "Sergeant Fel and I will find Lesva and deal with her."

"You can't deal with her, Your Majesty," one soldier blurted. "She took out half a squadron by herself in the palace. I was there. And there are archers down here that took out the rest of our team just minutes ago. There are only one or two riders with them, but they're deadly too."

"We'll get some more men down here," Fel said firmly, giving Syla a defiant look.

Aware of the possibility that the mines would later be flooded, Syla didn't want to bring any more people down than necessary, especially since the lift cage was slow and couldn't hold many occupants. But… she had to be reasonable. She and Fel wouldn't defeat Lesva and a horde of stormers without help.

"Get reinforcements, Syla. If we do this—" Tibby waved at the drill bits, "—it won't happen quickly. And once we get through, anyone down here will see what's happening and have time to get out."

"All right." Syla had envisioned the lake rushing in like a huge waterfall, but the drill wasn't so wide that the hole would be huge, and the mine was vast. Even if Oyenar got a team down here to seal off the lower levels, she supposed it would take hours for this one to flood. Her aunt must have done some math to figure it out. Knowing that made Syla's muscles loosen. She'd been imagining Oyenar's scenario, of armies of stormers being drowned, but Tibby's vision had to be more accurate. The goal was as Syla had wished, to deny access to the shielder chamber, not drown the enemy. "All right," she repeated. "Tibby, would any of these machines be useful to us as… er, weapons?"

Syla waved at the other wagons with equipment built into them or loaded on the backs. A couple of them looked like digging and boring devices, while others were simply large carts for hauling salt and maybe men. None of them looked like an armored carriage. *That* was what she needed.

"You might run over a slow stormer with one," Tibby said.

"*Slow* is not an appropriate adjective for describing those people."

"Unfortunately not." Tibby pointed at the front of a wagon with a shovel-like device on the back. "That one has a covered cab and can move faster than a person can run, probably even an enhanced person, and you'd be somewhat protected from quarrels. Put your hand on the panel there. It'll activate for you without a foreman's key."

"All right."

Fast was what they would need to catch up with Lesva.

"Here." Tibby leaned down from the cab of her wagon and handed a bag to Syla. "There are numerous explosives in there."

"I… when did you make all these?"

"I've been preparing to end up in trouble with you for *days*. I was lucky to get them off the ship before your lecherous rider sank it. The bag almost blew up with all those fires around."

"He's delightful, not lecherous."

"He looks at your boobs every time we meet."

"Yeah, but I like that."

Tibby rolled her eyes and pointed at the bag. "Be careful. Remember, those detonate on impact."

"Throwing explosives in a mine doesn't seem wise," Fel grumbled, eyeing the dark depths above them. If not for the earlier explosions with the flashes of light, they wouldn't even know where the ceiling was up there.

"Don't aim for the pillars." Tibby put her wagon into gear, and it rolled forward. "Aim for the rider captain's chest."

"Go with her," Fel reminded the soldiers.

They glanced at Syla, as if torn between defending their queen and obeying orders.

"We'll get more people down here," Syla told them. "It'll be fine."

They hesitated, but Fel growled, and the men hurried to catch up and climb onto the wagon with Tibby. It heartened Syla that her aunt headed in the opposite direction from the shielder chamber—and the stormers lurking out there. But that might mean that Lesva knew exactly where the chamber was and had already gone that way, leaving these men behind to guard her back.

"I don't think we have *time* to go up for reinforcements, Fel." Syla no longer sensed the rider she had earlier and suspected all of the stormers had moved deeper into the mine. Closer to the hidden chamber. "If they get to the shielder and destroy it, the whole island will be lost. We have to stop them." They also had to buy time for Tibby to drill.

"Let's see how fast this wagon goes." Fel surprised her by climbing into the cab, then leaning out the side to find something to prop his crossbow on so he could fire to the front.

Syla climbed in beside him, carefully tucking the bag of explosives under the control panel, then laid her hand on it. A couple of gauges and a small blue bulb flared to life, causing the wagon to hum with power. There were two levers to operate it, and Syla moved them experimentally. She'd never driven anything more magically or technologically advanced than a horse-drawn carriage and lamented that she hadn't asked Tibby for a lesson. But her aunt's wagon had already passed the lift cage, disappearing into the darkness on its way to a section of the mine under the lake.

"Do you know how to operate this, Fel?" Syla would gladly have moved over if he did.

"As your aunt would be quick to point out, my specialty is more destroying machinery than using it." Despite the words, he pointed at a pedal on the floor. "Step on that?"

Syla did so, and the wagon surged forward with a *ker-thunk* that tipped it sideways for a moment, nearly throwing her into Fel. She glanced out the side of the cab and spotted a triangle of wood that had been under one of the tires to keep it in place.

"You're more dangerous than the stormers." Fel gripped the frame of the cab with his free hand without lowering his crossbow.

"Let's hope that's true." Heart pounding, Syla figured out the steering and headed them in the direction the stormers had gone.

"Does it go faster?" Fel asked.

She experimented with the foot pedal, pressing it harder. The bulb flared brighter, and the wagon surged forward, carrying them rapidly between the great pillars and into the dark depths.

"Excellent," Fel said. "We'll run those bastards over."

Syla knew Lesva would never be caught by machinery rolling toward her but whispered, "Let's hope," anyway.

Sodden from yet another swim in the sea, Vorik jogged through trees and brush, skirting bogs and creeks while trying to remain hidden from possible aerial observers. Agrevlari had flown him in from the eastern side of the island, where they'd passed numerous stormer dragons with riders, but neither Jhiton nor the chiefs had been among them, and nobody had questioned Vorik. Of course not. He was a captain and the general's right-hand man.

"For now," he murmured as he ran, leaping over logs and ferns, urgency making him a touch reckless. An intuition told him that he didn't have much time, that Syla was in danger from more than whoever had taken over her castle—her kingdom.

A few eyebrows might have raised when Vorik had leaped from Agrevlari's back and into the sea with only his weapons, but he hadn't been the sole rider leaving a dragon to swim through the barrier. Now and then, he sensed others with magical power and knew that more of his people were somewhere on the island, already on their mission. Several times, he ran in another direction to avoid them, and he lost his bearings somewhat since he'd never been to the area. Also, night had fallen, enshrouding the forest and hiding the bogs, many invisible beneath lily-like plants that covered inches of water. Since he was already wet, it hardly mattered when his boots sank in, other than that it slowed him down and irritated him.

A part of him wondered if he'd made a mistake in not heading to the city and the palace. Maybe he should have first checked there for Syla. But Agrevlari had said he sensed Wreylith inland, and Vorik's gut told him that Syla would be with her dragon tonight.

He came to a wide lake that he'd only seen from above before and exhaled in relief, certain it was the body of water near the mine entrance. Yes, there were the fishing boats he'd seen in Agrevlari's memory, not yet drawn in for the night. Was that odd? Vorik didn't know. The freshwater lake appeared calm. Maybe the fishermen lived on their boats.

He'd only taken a few steps along the shoreline when he realized there were people swimming in the water, the night shrouding them but movement drawing his eye. And he sensed someone with magic among them. Was that Grilovar, one of the bonded riders from his squadron?

Vorik paused, trying to figure out why so many of his people—there had to be dozens—were swimming out to the boats. Then he remembered Jhiton contemplating stationing people on them to attack troops coming up the road.

A grunt and a cry of pain carried over the water from one of the boats. The noise was quickly squelched, save for a splash. Someone being thrown overboard?

Yes, stormers were swarming out of the water and onto the boats. More splashes followed. Grim, Vorik had a feeling that *bodies* were being thrown overboard, not men. Jhiton wouldn't want anyone to survive who could shout warnings that enemies had taken the lake.

Vorik continued along the shoreline until he reached a path angling toward the mine buildings. The lights from numerous lanterns were visible between the trees ahead, and he suspected some troops had arrived before the boat takeover. Sticking to the shadows, he walked toward the buildings. Voices sounded, and horses attached to wagons whinnied.

Hearing troops checking the woods not far from him, Vorik had to slow down as he approached one of the wooden buildings. A wide door was open with rail tracks coming out of it. The access point to the mine had to be inside of the building. Unfortunately, numerous soldiers were stationed in front of it, and it did indeed look like wagons of more men had just arrived. Even as Vorik watched, troops jumped out, adding to the numbers he would have to somehow get past if he meant to enter the mine. But was Syla down there? Or up above? He didn't know.

The soldiers were calm, ready to do battle. They didn't seem to yet know what was going on at the lake. Many looked toward the forest, as if they expected Jhiton's forces to rush straight out of the woods and toward the mine entrance. Eventually, maybe the stormers would if that was the only way down.

Sensing a dragon—Wreylith—Vorik looked up at the night sky. He frowned, aware that if he could sense her, she would also be able to sense him, thanks to the magic of his bond.

The red dragon alighted on the roof of the main building. Several soldiers jumped, but none drew weapons. By now, they had to know the dragon was Syla's ally.

But where was Syla? She wasn't on Wreylith's back.

Vorik's shoulders slumped. Had she already gone into the mine?

Vorik stretched his senses downward, trying to detect her. Like him, she didn't have a magical aura as great as that of a dragon, but he was attuned to her, and he thought…

Yes, he sensed her down there, in the opposite direction from the lake. And was that Lesva that he also sensed? He groaned silently at how close they were. If he didn't get down there now, it would soon be too late.

Vorik was tempted to surge out of the trees, even if it meant fighting his way past all those soldiers to reach the building. Why weren't they down there with Syla, anyway?

There probably were some in the mine, he reasoned, but Lesva would cut her way through such men without much trouble. Vorik needed to get down there.

As he crept closer, reaching the edge of the trees, the clip-clop of hooves sounded, another wagon being hauled up the road. Or multiple wagons? If Jhiton's boat teams attacked them, that might provide the distraction Vorik needed.

Many of your ships have maneuvered into position along the northern shoreline of this island, Agrevlari said from outside the barrier, *and others approach the mouth of the river on the southern side with men at the weapons, ready to fire at the city.*

Jhiton's diversion. Have Syla's people gotten the weapons platform off the bottom of the river yet?

When I flew in that direction, I observed them using large machines with many chains in an attempt to do so, but it was not yet out of the water.

Let's hope they don't pull it up in time. Given all the forces Jhiton and the chiefs were bringing to bear, Vorik didn't think the weapons platform would defeat them, but it could destroy ships as easily as dragons.

Or ever. The thing is foul and despicable.

Wreylith's tail flexed, and Vorik didn't answer. The dragon's head turned on her long neck, and glowing golden eyes peered through the trees at Vorik. She'd sensed him.

His first instinct was to run into the woods, but he needed to go down into the mine. Besides, he didn't want to lure the dragon toward the lake. If she'd sensed him, she would also sense the other stormers with magic. The dragon might then fly around, torching those boats and alerting the Kingdom soldiers to Jhiton's plan.

What are you doing here, rider? Wreylith's voice was suspicious, and a trickle of smoke wafted from one of her nostrils.

Meanwhile, two wagons stopped in front of the buildings, and tailgates clanged as they were thrown down.

"Hurry up and get that lumber into the lift," someone called. "And where's Teetan, the engineer?"

I came to help Syla. Vorik forced himself to meet Wreylith's gaze, though he also wondered if he might sneak in and manage to get himself ported down with that lumber, whatever it was for. Building defenses in the mines? *She's in danger,* he added. *Captain Lesva is down there with her. Can you help me get down into the mine?*

Wreylith gazed at him so steadily it was unnerving. Worse, a couple of the soldiers had noticed her look and were peering in Vorik's direction.

You care for her and serve her needs sexually, Wreylith said, *but you remain a part of the enemy nation.*

Yeah, it's an ongoing problem. I don't love her people, but... I do care about her. More *than care. Help me before it's too late. Please.*

You are likely here to steal that which protects this island and she seeks to keep hidden.

I'm not. I admit that my people are, but I only came because I care about Syla.

Just visible in the light from the soldiers' lanterns, another trickle of smoke wafted up from Wreylith's nostrils. Wrath of the storm god, maybe she meant to roast him.

I also came to warn her! Vorik added quickly.

That she is in danger? She knows.

Does she know that someone replaced her family flag on her castle? And that a huge fleet of Kingdom ships has gathered in the harbor on Castle Island?

The dragon paused, but did she believe him? Her eyes continued to glow balefully, and another tendril of smoke wafted up. She looked like she wanted to set *something* on fire. Whether he would be the target, he didn't know.

I think someone is taking advantage of her being gone, Vorik continued. *They* already *took advantage. She may be in danger from more than my people. Can you assist me in getting down there to speak with her—to help her?*

When the dragon sprang into the air, wings flapping, Vorik expected her to send a gout of fire at him. He drew his swords and backed away. But Wreylith flew in the other direction, crossing a bog and streaming flames into the forest. Men shouted, some backing up, but others drew weapons and ran in that direction.

"It must be the stormers!" someone shouted.

Vorik stared, certain it was exactly that. Wreylith must have sensed a rider approaching. Maybe an entire squadron, and she was—

Why do you stand still, human? Wreylith asked into his mind as she flew a circle over the trees, pouring more flames into the forest. *Do you not know a distraction when you see it?*

Oh! Vorik left his hiding spot to find a way to slip past the troops. Many remained, including the newcomers with the wagons, but those who hadn't run to check were looking toward Wreylith and the flames. Moving silently, Vorik managed to reach the building and dart through the doorway unnoticed. *Thank you,* he thought to Wreylith as he ran through the shadows to a square hole in the wooden floor.

You will protect Syla from the dangerous female.

Yes, I will.

She is worthy of a dragon bond, but she is not yet a great fighter.

She's a great healer and smart and loyal. Vorik peered into the hole. He'd expected a lift for descending, but it must have been at the bottom because only chains dangled down into the depths.

She has great potential, the dragon said. *Later, you will serve her as she wishes.*

Smiling, Vorik grabbed one of the chains and started climbing down. *I look forward to it.*

Booms came from the direction of the road, and Vorik lost his smile and paused in his descent. Had Wreylith inadvertently blown up kegs of black powder or something else explosive? No, she hadn't been sending her fire toward the road, only into the forest.

Your people have taken over the fishing boats and are attacking wagons bringing troops, Wreylith coolly informed him.

I'm… not with them.

I will help the queen by slaying all those who seek access to the mine and that which is within.

I wish you wouldn't, Vorik said, *but I understand.*

And so did Jhiton. He'd known what he was getting into.

As another boom sounded, this time answered by a dragon's roar, Vorik continued his descent. The one who needed his help most was down there.

27

As large as the mine was, it didn't take much time to travel through it on the fast-moving magical wagon. Twice, Syla sensed a rider or glimpsed movement in the shadows, but the stormers must not have known what to make of them. They didn't put themselves in front of the wagon, and they didn't attack, save for an arrow that shot out of the dark, glancing off the roof of the cab. Fel promptly fired back, but they couldn't see into the shadows to know if his quarrel struck. They'd passed out of the area where lanterns were lit, probably because this level wasn't being mined anymore.

A scrape on the roof of the cab made Syla jump. As they'd traveled deeper into the original mine that had been carved out with nothing more than chisels and pickaxes, the ceiling had become significantly lower. Ahead lay the last of the pillars before a maze of tunnels stretched, the walls carved with elaborate pictures of the gods as well as of favored livestock and stalks of wheat and other grains that had been paramount in the early days of agriculture.

"We're not going to be able to drive all the way back to the shielder chamber in this." Syla slowed the wagon down.

"The early miners must have had a lot of time on their hands," Fel grumbled, eyeing the carvings. "And a lenient foreman."

"I think some of these were commissioned. The mine was treasured in the early days of the Kingdom since salt was vital and something non-perishable that our ancestors could trade all over the world." Syla peered into the gloom around them. A single magic-powered lamp on the front of the wagon allowed them to see in the direction they'd been driving, but darkness obscured everything to the sides—and behind.

The corner of the wagon bumped against a salt pillar, and she stopped it, doubting they could make it deeper into the mine. It wouldn't have been a good idea to drive straight up to the hidden chamber door regardless. If Lesva *hadn't* learned exactly where it was, Syla didn't want to show her.

Faint thuds started up behind them, from the direction of the lift cage and beyond. Since they echoed from the pillars, Syla would have struggled to guess the exact origins if she hadn't known. Clanks and rumbles also reverberated through the floor.

"People are going to hear that," Fel said. "Maybe up above as well as down here."

"Yes." When Syla had envisioned her plan, she'd thought they could do the drilling *before* the stormer army arrived. She'd had no idea that some were already lurking in the area. Some or a lot.

Enemies have arrived, and the battle is engaged, Wreylith spoke into her mind.

Up there? Syla almost said that she'd already found lots of enemies in the mine.

Yes. Some have taken over the boats in the lake and are firing upon your troops coming up the road. Others are in the forest and advancing toward these buildings.

I thought we would have more time. Can you keep them from coming down into the mine?

Certainly. No humans will pass underneath me without notice. Should they attempt to do so, they will not fail to experience the incendiary flames of my wrath.

Dragon wrath is a terrible thing.

Yes.

Syla's instincts tingled with a warning, and she whispered, "Down."

Without question, Fel obeyed, pushing her low as he also ducked. An arrow that had been fired with more accuracy than the first sailed through the top of the cab where their heads had been.

"We'll be easier targets now that we're stopped." Fel lifted his crossbow over Syla's head and fired into the darkness.

A soft clink sounded as his quarrel skipped off something hard. Probably one of the salt pillars.

"I'm not sure we should get out right away." Syla glanced toward the route ahead, wanting to check on the chamber but also aware of the witnesses watching them. "This is decent cover, and we've got ammunition." She opened Tibby's bag, revealing a surprising number of the flat, square packages—her explosives.

Fel eyed them. "I'm starting to appreciate that woman."

"Even though she insults you often?"

"I get insulted by a lot of people, but *they* don't give me explosives." Fel picked up a couple of the packets.

Another arrow arced out of the darkness, sailing over the wagon and clinking off a pillar behind them, chipping away a chunk of salt.

"Stormers are usually more accurate than this." Fel gave her a significant look. "They may be trying to delay us."

"If they want to keep us away from the shielder chamber, they could kill us," Syla said, but she agreed that the stormers seemed to be shooting to keep them busy rather than actively trying to slay them.

"You might be their backup plan for getting in." Fel pointed at her hand.

"Or... something happened to Lady Abrya." Syla hoped not, but what if Lesva had accidentally *killed* her captive?

"There also might be only one archer."

She looked sharply at him. She hadn't sensed the bonded rider for a while. Had most of the stormers run ahead to beat the wagon to the chamber?

No sooner had the thought occurred than four shadowy figures appeared in the darkness. Three men and one woman, all wearing fur-trimmed Storm Guard chainmail, ran toward the wagon. They'd put away their bows and drawn swords.

Fel raised his crossbow to shoot. Syla grabbed one of the explosives and eased out of the cab so she had room to throw it, careful to avoid the support pillars.

These stormers weren't as fast as Jhiton, the last person she'd thrown explosives at, but they knew to avoid them. One warrior ducked and kept coming, and the other three ran or rolled to the sides. Two sprang behind pillars for cover as an explosive struck down, blowing up with a great boom. The other two were knocked down by the shockwave. Syla also felt it and staggered back, bumping into the wagon. Fel remained rock steady and fired another quarrel. It slammed into a man's shoulder. The female stormer was already down, rolling and grabbing her side.

Before Fel could reload or Syla grab a second explosive, one of the men who'd run behind the pillar came out on the other side and charged at her. She jumped back into the cab, thinking she might drive the wagon away and escape the stormers—or use it as a weapon to try to run them over. But he was on her before she could start it again.

He stabbed at her with his sword, and she dodged, surprised

by her speed. She easily evaded the blow, then kicked the man in the chest to knock him back. He went flying, as startled by her strength as she was.

Before he could recover, she flattened her palm to the control panel and put the wagon into reverse, backing away from Fel, who'd jumped out on the other side and was wielding his mace against a stormer who'd reached him.

The man she'd kicked recovered quickly and leaped into the cab before Syla could get far enough away. Lunging, he grabbed her with one hand as he swung his sword with the other. But it caught on the frame with a loud clank.

As he shifted, maneuvering to turn his sweeping blow into a stab, Syla called upon her power. Her moon-mark flared silver as a tendril of magic extended into him, then wrapped around his trachea. As the tendril tightened, she leaned back and raised her leg to kick him again. If he hadn't been startled—and scared—with his eyes bulging as he reached for his throat, she wouldn't have gotten the best of him, but she caught him off balance, and he tumbled out of the cab.

She shifted the levers and backed the wagon away from her foe. Since they were no longer touching, her magic didn't remain in him, and he jumped to his feet, his airway returning to normal. She shifted the wagon's direction and drove straight at him.

As he crouched to spring aside, Syla pulled another explosive from the bag. He was fast enough to escape being run over, but she hurled Tibby's weapon after him.

Distracted by dodging the wagon, he didn't see it in time to escape. It exploded, light flashing, and he screamed as he was hurled across the mine. When Syla glimpsed limbs torn off and flying free, she looked away, her stomach churning. It would have been kinder to kill him with her magic.

"I don't want to kill *anyone*," she said with frustration, but her feelings didn't keep her from driving toward Fel to make sure he would survive his encounter.

One of the stormers he'd shot lay still—probably dead—but the man with the shoulder wound rose and ran toward Fel with a sword. Syla steered right, putting him in her sights.

Like the other stormer, he was agile enough to time a leap to escape being hit. And, as soon as the wagon passed, he jumped toward Syla in the cab. She ducked low, pulling her foot from the acceleration pedal, but there wasn't room to dodge. He slammed into her, knocking her onto her side, his weight crushing down on her. Metal rasped as he drew a dagger, but she once again summoned her power, the magic eager to spring forth. Silver light bathed the cab and his face as he lowered the dagger toward her throat. She struck first, tendrils of power tightening around his heart and his trachea.

This enemy seemed to expect her attack and didn't stop. His dagger continued its inexorable descent toward her throat. Terrified, she squeezed his heart with all her power. The dagger grazed her skin but didn't cut deep, and she got a hand up to knock it aside as the man tipped off her, grabbing his chest.

"Syla!" Fel blurted, leaping into the cab and grabbing the stormer. He hurled the man outside and to the ground, but their enemy was dead before he landed. Fel raised his mace as he faced the stormer but must have seen the man's eyes frozen open in death.

Panting, Syla pushed herself to her knees and gingerly touched her throat. The cut hurt, and blood trickled down her neck, but it wasn't serious.

"I forgot you're not as helpless as you look." Fel gave her an expression somewhere between reverence and fear, but at least he didn't make any superstitious gestures this time.

"I'm more helpless than I'd like." Syla rose to her feet and vowed to find someone to teach her self-defense if not how to fight the way her great-great grandmother Queen Erasbella had. With her new ability to hurl herself about with far more speed and strength than usual, she was as dangerous to herself as to others. Probably *more so* to herself. "And that one didn't get the word that I'm the backup moon-mark."

That was only a hypothesis she'd come up with, she reminded herself.

"I still think they were here to delay us. Which way to the chamber?"

There are many more stormers arriving than I expected, Wreylith said. *They are overwhelming your Kingdom troops. Since your enemy had taken over the fishing boats to fire upon your reinforcements, I flew over to light them on fire, but now the building through which you entered the mine is compromised. Stormers are climbing down the entrance shaft. Many stormers. I can light the building on fire to prevent more from slipping in, but...*

We have to take the lift cage out that way!

Yes, I believed you would desire the building to remain in an unburned state.

I do, yes.

I'm also having difficulty stopping your enemies now that they're so intermingled with your troops. Sounding frustrated, Wreylith added, *You should be up here with me.*

I'm sorry. I wish you were down here with me.

I will focus on the enemies on the lake. I believe that only stormers remain on the boats, so it is simpler to attack them.

Good.

"Syla?" Fel poked her arm. "Which way?"

"I got an update from Wreylith, and there are more stormers entering the mine. A lot of them. We need to hurry."

Fel cursed.

"Follow me." Syla stopped the wagon and climbed out of it,

stepping over the man Fel had downed. All four stormers were dead, but greater threats, she had no doubt, lay ahead.

As they hurried down an ancient passageway carved into pure salt, the distant thuds of Tibby's drill, relentless and impossible to miss, trailed them. Syla hoped that none of the stormers were drawn to investigate the source of the noise. The two soldiers with Tibby weren't enough, not to deal with such well-trained fighters.

A distant boom came from the same direction as the drill noises.

"Is she throwing explosives?" Fel looked over her shoulder, though darkness, distance, and the rows and rows of thick pyramid supports blocked the view.

"If she is, it's because she's in trouble again." Syla was half-tempted to take the wagon and drive back to check on her aunt, but magic flared ahead, something dormant suddenly coming to life. No, something that had been hidden behind an insulated door abruptly being revealed. "The shielder," she blurted, doubting Fel, who had no power of his own, would sense it.

She picked up the bag of explosives and hurried in the direction of the magic, trusting Fel would stick with her. The tunnel curved, and they came to an intersection marked by statues and carvings in the salt walls. Silver light seeped from the leftmost passageway, and Syla turned, Fel right behind her, mace and crossbow in hand.

Syla pulled out one of the explosives, but she realized, as she spotted the open door that had been hidden within the sea-god carving, that throwing one of Tibby's booby traps in the tight tunnel wouldn't be wise. Out in the open, with the ceilings high overhead, there hadn't been as much risk, but here... here, she could collapse the passageway.

Before reaching the doorway, the tunnel widened into an oval room. The silver light illuminated more statues and carvings, as well as a woman on the floor. Lady Abrya, bound and gagged, lay unmoving near the doorway.

A shadow stirred beyond it. Someone had already gone into the shielder chamber.

~

The cavernous salt mine was much more expansive than Vorik had envisioned, nothing like the tight low-ceilinged tunnels he'd seen in mountains where people had dug for ore. Even with his keen night vision, he could barely see the high ceiling, the light from the lanterns mounted on great pyramid-shaped pillars not reaching such a height. Nor did the weak flames do much to brighten the white floors of salt that stretched away in all directions, polished smooth by centuries of boots treading upon them.

Weapons in hand, Vorik walked toward a *thud, thud, thud* in the distance. When he'd arrived on the first level, he hadn't been able to sense Syla or Lesva, and he'd questioned if he was in the right place. But the lift cage had been there, suggesting someone had gotten out. Still, he'd questioned if the shielder, having been crafted by the gods so long ago, would be on the first level or, for its safety, deeper down in the mine.

When the thuds paused, he did too.

The deeper levels would have been added later, he reasoned. *Probably long after the gods made the special chamber for the shielder. This must be the right level.*

He'd been talking to himself, but Agrevlari responded. *You may want to make your visitation brief.*

This doesn't look like a place that one could explore in a brief period of time, but what prompts you to say that?

The rhythmic thuds started up again, and Vorik looked in that direction. The regularly spaced pyramid supports blocked his view, but he continued on. What was making that noise or what it indicated, he didn't know, but if some machinery was responsible, he assumed Syla's aunt was involved. And if her aunt was back there, Syla ought to be with her.

Ozlemar has discovered my presence and wants to know what I'm doing here.

Did you tell him about your desire to hunt elioks one more time?

It was your *desire to visit Harvest Island.*

Yeah, you can blame me for this. Tell him it's not your fault. I strong-armed you into bringing me here.

Even with your magic, your modest human arms could do nothing to force a dragon to go where a dragon did not desire to go.

Tell him I bribed you with promises of smoked salmon then.

That is more believable.

We're simple males, both driven by food. Vorik smiled, thinking of the blackberry cobbler Syla had made. For the rest of his days, he would cherish the memory of that dessert and her giving it to him without poison sprinkled in.

Indeed. He wants to know where my rider is.

Where's his *rider?* Vorik hoped Agrevlari would report that Jhiton was on Ozlemar's back and sending in troops while he orchestrated the battle from afar, but his brother was more likely to be here, leading men into the fray.

Ozlemar is suspicious and will tell me nothing, but I can see that Jhiton isn't with him.

I was afraid of that. Wary that he would run into his people, Vorik eyed the dark expanse in all directions as he continued toward the noise. Most likely, they would be as drawn by it as he. Just because he couldn't yet sense Lesva didn't mean she wasn't back there.

A whirring and clanking joined the thuds, and he picked up his pace. Even the floor reverberated with the power of the machinery. It felt like someone hammering at it with a giant battering ram, but he couldn't imagine what use that would be.

Unless someone wanted to knock down the support posts to bury this section of the mine? Could that be Syla's plan? To collapse the ceiling and block access to the shielder?

Vorik came to a wall before reaching the source of the noise. Back here, there were no lanterns lit, leaving little light by which to guide him, but he sensed a touch of magic nearby. The shielder? Could someone have already reached it and opened the chamber? Lesva might have gotten the location from Lady Abrya.

As Vorik followed the wall toward the magic and noise, the reverberations underfoot grew stronger. And did he sense *multiple* sources of magic ahead? The largest one seemed to be at floor level, but a couple others were higher. Closer to the ceiling? Again, he imagined Syla intentionally collapsing this section of the mine.

Though the thought made him want to turn in the other direction, Vorik forced himself to continue forward. Light was visible ahead now, an orange glow that seemed magical in nature.

When he eased around a pillar, lingering in its shadows, a wagon and a boxy machine came into view. The hammer he'd imagined wasn't correct. A long, thick drill extended upward, magic emanating from its length as it spun into the salt and rock of the ceiling, chunks thudding down around it. The orange glow came from a control station on the machine where Tibby stood, her hand on a lever. Two uniformed Kingdom soldiers crouched nearby, their backs to the wagon as they faced outward with crossbows in their hands.

Vorik didn't see Syla, but she had to be there, didn't she? Usually, he could sense her power when they were close, but there was so much magic in the area that it could have drowned out her aura. It did for the aunt. The moon-mark on the back of Tibby's hand glowed silver as she interacted with the machinery, and he remembered that she was an engineer. Whatever she was doing—drilling a hole in the ceiling, but why?—probably aligned with her gods-gift.

Other than the drill, there wasn't anything of significance in the area that Vorik could see. Hadn't Syla said the shielder chamber's door was hidden within a carving? There weren't any. Nothing indicated this was anything other than a back corner of the mine.

Vorik looked upward again, trying to match the ground he'd traveled over with where he was in the mine. Usually, he was a decent navigator, and he knew he could find his way back to the lift without trouble, but he wasn't sure which cardinal direction he'd taken when he'd left it.

Before he could ponder further, movement near another support pyramid drew his gaze. At the same time as he saw someone in the shadows, the person drew close enough for Vorik to sense. Jhiton.

As Vorik had feared, others had heard and been drawn by the noise of the drill. And Jhiton didn't pause to ponder it. He drew throwing knives from a belt sheath and stepped away from the support, trusting the darkness to hide him. The soldiers weren't looking in his direction, and the aunt's focus was on the ceiling and chunks of salt clunking down to the floor around her machinery.

Jhiton ran away from the support post and straight toward the drill, unconcerned about dodging crossbow quarrels the men might fire.

Still afraid Syla was in the area and would be his brother's next target, Vorik pulled out a throwing knife of his own. As he stepped away from his support post and lifted it, hoping to time his throw to strike Jhiton in the back of the head with the hilt, he glimpsed something high above in his peripheral vision. A tiny red glowing dot fifty feet up on the pyramid, right by the ceiling. It made him pause. That had to be something magical. A trap?

The distraction cost him. Jhiton had time to pump his arm

twice and throw his knives. They sped with deadly accuracy toward the guards, a blade lodging in each man's neck.

Tibby screamed and ducked behind the wagon.

Vorik tore his gaze from the dot and threw his own knife. He couldn't let Jhiton kill Syla's aunt.

The weapon spun end over end, not making a noise, but Jhiton sensed its approach regardless. He didn't evade it fully, and the blade clipped his ear instead of thudding into his skull.

"*Vorik*," he said in exasperation, drawing his twin longswords. He glanced toward the wagon—Tibby wisely remained hidden behind it—but held the blades toward Vorik. "Are you going to fight me *again*? Over *her*?" He waved one sword toward the wagon.

"Syla's down here too. You know it."

"If she stays out of the way, she doesn't need to die."

"She *won't* stay out of the way. Neither of them will." Vorik waved toward the aunt's position.

As Vorik groped for a way to convince his brother to promise not to hurt Syla, Tibby rose into view with something in her hand. One of her explosive booby traps.

"Look out," Vorik barked as Tibby hurled it at his brother.

Jhiton launched himself into a forward roll, avoiding the square flying through the air, and sprang to his feet as it landed. It boomed as light flashed, the shockwave pummeling him in the back and almost knocking him to the ground again. Jhiton recovered his balance and ran, not toward Tibby but toward Vorik with his swords in hand, frustration and determination in his eyes.

With gut-wrenching certainty, Vorik realized his brother had run out of patience with him. All he had time to do before Jhiton was upon him was draw his sword and a dagger and spring behind the wide support so they would have cover for their fight. After that, he could do nothing but defend himself.

Jhiton came at him with a flurry of blows that left Vorik on his heels, backing and backing again. Daunted, he realized he hadn't seen his brother come at him with full intent to hurt—or even to kill?—before.

Vorik struggled to relax his muscles, loosening them so he could deflect the lightning-fast slashes that came at him from both sides, the twin swords carving through the air with such precision that they never touched, never tangled. Pain erupted on the side of Vorik's thigh as a slash made it through. As he accepted the blow, another sword sped for his neck, a slash meant to decapitate him.

Yes, Jhiton had decided that, for the good of the people, Vorik needed to die.

Vorik didn't want to kill his brother, but what choice did he have? If he didn't defend himself, he *would* die. And *Syla* would die. Vorik couldn't allow that. He had to stop the threat not only to his life but to hers.

Oddly, that realization filled Vorik with the calm he needed to defend himself. The decision had been made, and his muscles loosened. The slashes of their blades rang out, drowning out the thuds of the machinery, and time seemed to slow, allowing Vorik to see each sword strike with clarity, to parry with the perfect stroke, to keep Jhiton from driving him back farther.

Vorik kept his awareness of his surroundings, knowing the aunt might throw another explosive, but she wasn't in view at the moment. There was only Jhiton and the frustration brimming in his usually calm green eyes, his face otherwise chiseled in stone.

He tried to back Vorik against a support to limit his maneuvering room, but Vorik sprang to the side and launched a kick to keep his brother back. A sword came down, almost catching his shin, but he was too fast and drew his foot down, then lunged in.

Jhiton whipped his sword across to halt his advance, but Vorik deflected it, then pushed in close, stabbing with his dagger. Jhiton caught it with his own blade, and for a moment, they stood in tableau, weapons locked together and muscles straining as each sought to push the other back, to overpower him. The dagger inched toward Jhiton's throat, surprising Vorik. When had he grown stronger than his brother?

Before the dagger reached him, Jhiton sprang back. He swept both his blades in, knocking Vorik's sword and dagger aside with such force that it affected Vorik's balance. When Jhiton kicked at his hip, Vorik was a fraction of a second too late recovering and getting out of the way. The blow knocked him back.

Vorik rolled away, crashing into the pillar, but he jumped up immediately, spinning in time to meet another rush from Jhiton. Swords rang out as they clashed again. Vorik slashed and thrust, feeling urgency building. If they didn't finish this soon, the aunt would throw explosives at them. Or Syla would die to Lesva's blade.

That fear made Vorik even faster and more determined. Though he threw everything he had into getting past his brother's defenses, he was startled when his sword sank deep into Jhiton's gut. Surprise widened Jhiton's eyes as well.

Horrified, Vorik pulled his blade out and jumped back.

"I'm sorry," he whispered as one of the swords dropped from Jhiton's hands.

It clattered to the floor. Jhiton pressed the tip of the other one down for support, leaning against it and grasping the deep wound in his gut. It would be a fatal wound, unless...

"I'll take you to Syla," Vorik blurted. "She can heal—"

A boom and a flash of red came from above them. Vorik's first thought was that Tibby had thrown another of the small explosives, but this was something else. He remembered the red dot as a second boom came from the top of a nearby support pyramid. Smoke filled the air, cracks sounded, and boulder-sized chunks of salt slammed down from above. One landed on Jhiton, knocking him flat. A smaller one clubbed Vorik on the shoulder, and he stumbled backward.

Tibby had set these explosives, not thrown them, placing them where they would bring down the ceiling. Vorik backpedaled as more of it came down, and the support post crumbled. Chunks of salt struck him, a cloud of fine white dust filling the air and hazing the view. That didn't keep Vorik from seeing mounds and mounds of rock forming. Only his speed and utter fear gave him the wherewithal to escape being buried.

In the end, three explosives blew, and three supports collapsed, bringing a huge portion of the ceiling down to form a mountain where Vorik and Jhiton had been fighting. Where Jhiton had been injured and hadn't escaped.

Vorik's gut twisted, and he didn't want to accept that. He wanted to believe that Jhiton had somehow rolled away from those boulders and that the sword wound hadn't been as fatal as it had looked, but the truth refused to be pushed aside. Vorik hadn't intended to, but he'd killed his brother.

As it grew quieter, the cloud of salt hanging in the air, half-shrouding the hills of boulders that blocked the view of Tibby and the wagon, Vorik grew aware of the thuds of the machinery continuing. Whatever that woman was doing, she was still doing it. He couldn't see all the way up to the dark ceiling—the *new* ceiling—but could tell she hadn't collapsed the entire section of the mine. Above the salt was probably solid rock—he'd seen the layers of it as he'd climbed down the shaft. Tibby had only dropped enough of the ceiling to protect herself from enemies as she worked. Enough to make a tomb for Jhiton.

Vorik gripped the hilt of his sword, angry with himself but frustrated with Tibby as well. He started toward the rock piles, intending to climb over them and put a stop to what she was doing, but Wreylith spoke into his mind, making him pause.

Whatever you are doing down there, it is not helping Queen Syla.

I haven't found her yet.

She is not near you, but another of your people is near her. The rider with the silver scales.

Silver hair. Lesva.

Yes. She threatens Syla at this very moment. The dragon shared imagery with him of a different section of the mine, of old low and narrow tunnels, of carvings and statues.

Trusting there wasn't much time if Lesva had already found Syla, Vorik ran off to look for her. He might be making a mistake—another one—in leaving Tibby and her machine, but Syla didn't have time for him to delay. He had to reach her before Lesva finally succeeded in her goal of killing her.

28

Syla could sense the artifact and see its silver light flowing through the open door of the chamber, so it hadn't been destroyed yet, but she hurried forward, afraid Lesva was poised in there with a gargoyle-bone blade capable of destroying the shielder.

"Wait." Fel shuffled his weapons so that he could grip Syla's shoulder.

Syla didn't *want* to wait. She needed to check on Abrya as well as the artifact but agreed that this felt like a trap. And then, she felt the familiar powerful presence of Lesva. Not inside the chamber but behind a statue. The silver-haired rider captain sprang toward them with a sword.

Fel rushed to intercept Lesva, blocking her from reaching Syla.

Though Syla wanted to help, she sensed that the shielder was in danger and, while Fel engaged with Lesva, ran toward the doorway. She forced herself to leave Abrya to check on later and rushed inside, her aunt's bag gripped in her hand and an explosive drawn to throw.

The shielder chamber, reinforced with magic, was the one place in this low-ceilinged section of the mine where she might get *away* with throwing one, but she would have to be careful not to detonate it near the shielder itself. As sturdy as the artifacts were, she didn't want to risk it.

A rider in black crouched with a gargoyle-bone blade raised, about to try to destroy the great silver orb mounted similarly to the shielder on Castle Island. Syla almost threw the explosive at him without hesitation, but he was so close to the artifact. Fortunately, he spun toward her instead of striking it. Unfortunately, he rushed toward her in the doorway and swept his blade at her throat.

Syla darted to the side, her new speed rather than any skill allowing her to escape what would have been a killing blow. That speed startled her though, and her shoulder clipped a wall. If not for the strap holding her spectacles on, they would have flown off.

If her enemy was surprised by her unexpected athleticism, he didn't show it. He simply sprang after her again.

She ran around the shielder and into the chamber but bumped a statue. Afraid she would detonate the explosives by accident, she took a heartbeat to lower the bag to the floor, then spun and threw the remaining booby trap at her pursuer. It caught him in the chest.

As it boomed, white light flashing, Syla half-leaped and half tumbled behind the shielder. She hit the ground hard and rolled to the back wall, stunned for a moment as she stared up at a depiction of the full moon carved into the salt, the eyes of its benevolent god clear in the craters.

Something landed with a wet thud beside her. A portion of the man's torso.

"Dear gods," Syla rasped, rolling away, tears stinging her eyes. The atrocities were too much. This was *all* too much.

Clangs came from right outside the door, and she made herself rise. She sensed that Lesva was out there, and Fel couldn't defeat her, not alone.

Syla ran around the shielder and toward the door, stepping over body parts while trying not to look too closely at them. She glanced back, remembering the bag she'd left behind, but the dead man's head had landed on it. Her gorge rose, and she wavered, telling herself she needed to go back and grab the explosives but horrified by the thought of rolling the bloody head aside.

Movement outside the doorway drew her attention. Lesva had turned to face Syla. There wasn't time to go back for the explosives. She had to keep Lesva from entering the chamber and striking at the shielder.

Syla sprang outside, almost tripping over Abrya, and flung her palm against a flat panel integrated into a carving near the door. Only because she'd visited the mine before did she know it was there. Even as Syla's palm touched it, activating the door closing mechanism, Lesva ran toward her. She jammed her boot against the door to keep it from shutting.

Syla grabbed Lesva's arm, sending power into her and hoping to push her back. But Lesva, too, had magic, and, as she had in all their other confrontations, she armored herself from within, using her power to push back against Syla's attempt to stop her.

"Fel!" Syla rasped, hoping that if she distracted Lesva he could rush up from behind and brain her with his mace.

But he only answered with a faint groan. He lay crumpled several yards away, blood staining the white ground beneath him, and neither his crossbow nor mace near him.

The shadows in the tunnel stirred, and a black-clad figure with a sword strode toward them from the darkness. Syla groaned, remembering that Lesva had allies down here with her. Many allies.

Then she realized she could sense the man, the powerful magic within him, and he was familiar.

Lesva groaned.

"Vorik!" Syla blurted.

Lesva snarled and reached for Syla's neck.

Syla jerked her arm up to block the grasp and managed to twist her hand to grip Lesva's wrist. Lesva grabbed her back with a snarl. Syla summoned all her strength to attack the woman with her power, to send a dozen tendrils of magic into her, to various parts of her body. Surely, Lesva couldn't deflect them all. And *Vorik* could brain her.

But would he? He'd come with his people for the shielder, hadn't he? He might care about Syla, but nothing had changed. He was a stormer, an enemy.

"Release her, Lesva," Vorik said coolly, stopping a few feet away and raising his sword.

Busy deflecting Syla's magical attacks, Lesva didn't glance at him, only snarling, "You act like *she's* the victim here. She's attacking *me*."

"You're trying to destroy her people's shielder."

"That's our mission, you *ass*. You betrayer!"

"If that's what you believe I am, come over here and challenge me."

Teeth bared, Lesva glared at Syla instead of Vorik. Lesva marshaled her power, letting her defenses lower so that she could counterattack. Syla found *herself* on the defensive, trying to do something she'd never, as a healer, learned to do: create a defensive wall of power around her body to block magical attacks meant to crush her organs, to kill her. She groped to learn on the fly, to push Lesva away, just as Lesva had been doing to her. A dagger of power got through, stabbing her like a knife to the gut, and she gasped, almost bending over, but she managed to strengthen the wall and push that magical dagger back.

"You will fight *me*, Lesva," Vorik commanded. "Face to face. Don't make me stab you in the back."

"Only a coward would do that," Lesva said, her icy eyes locked on Syla.

"No. A man defending the woman he loves would do that." Vorik looked squarely at Syla.

Later, she would treasure that statement—he'd never said before that he loved her—but it took all her mental and physical strength to keep Lesva from slaying her.

"All you love is her flabby body," Lesva said.

Tired of her insults—and of her—Syla growled as she drew upon both her moon-mark and her dragon tattoo for power. Sending more magical tendrils into her foe, she also used her weight and strength to thrust the woman back, wanting her foe away from her.

Surprisingly, Lesva flew backward. She was agile enough to catch her balance and keep from going down, but surprise widened her eyes. She lifted her sword, and Syla braced herself for another attack, but Lesva instead turned on Vorik.

"I challenge you," she said. "To a duel. You know the rules."

"I do, and I accept your challenge." Vorik looked at Syla. "You may not interfere."

Syla should have snorted and said she wasn't bound by their ways, but what came out was, "Oh, I'm fine with that."

She didn't want anything else to do with Lesva and hoped Vorik killed her, once and for all. Judging by the wary glance that Lesva threw at her before striding toward Vorik, she might not want anything else to do with Syla either.

"I sure hope that's true," Syla muttered.

As the duelists sprang for each other, Syla finished what she'd started, pressing her palm to the wall to close the door. It ground shut, and a faint hiss sounded as magic engaged, once again sealing the chamber.

Clangs and clashes rang out, drowning out the thuds from the distant drill. New bangs, sounding more like a hammer on nails, had joined in with the distant cacophony, and Syla had no idea what it signaled.

Exhausted, Syla wanted to slump against the door as Lesva and Vorik battled, but she knelt by Abrya instead. She was so still that Syla touched her throat, afraid Lesva had killed the lady after forcing her to open the door, but her heart was beating. Abrya didn't stir at the touch, however, and Syla worried she would be trampled by the combatants.

As they'd once done on a cliff in the rain, Lesva and Vorik fought, gargoyle-bone blades a blur as they clashed. The combatants threw in kicks as they danced about, dodging and lunging, mesmerizing. Before, Vorik had seemed the stronger fighter, but he'd also hesitated, not committed to killing the woman who'd once been his lover. Would he hesitate again? He knew Lesva was doing what his people wanted, and he... he was probably disobeying orders again.

"I love you too, Vorik," Syla called, in case it mattered, in case it would make him believe his sacrifice—his *betrayal*—was worth it.

He glanced at her but only for a second. Grunting and snarling, Lesva attacked him with unrelenting fury.

Movement to the side made Syla look away. Fel was pushing himself into a sitting position, looking blearily around for his weapons. Blood ran from the side of his head and a split lip. The tip of his ear was missing, but that didn't keep him from detecting a new threat, and he turned, squinting into the gloom.

Two men in Storm Guard uniforms were creeping down the tunnel toward them.

Syla circled the combatants and rushed to Fel's side, afraid she would need to protect him. Along the way, she glimpsed his mace and grabbed it.

"Captain Vorik!" a man cried in dismay.

"He's attacking Lesva," the other blurted. "Did he turn traitor?"

Vorik didn't respond, though a flash of pain that had nothing to do with wounds or the battle crossed his face. This time, his betrayal would have witnesses. He probably wouldn't be able to return to his people.

Syla crouched and pressed Fel's mace into his hand. Vorik had made his choice, and she had to hope he won. Otherwise, she and Fel would be in trouble.

Lesva glanced at the men, one cradling a crossbow in his arms as they approached, and she snarled, "Shoot him!"

"That's not allowed by the rules of the duel to which you challenged me," Vorik said, a little breathless but calm.

"It's allowed to kill *traitors*," Lesva panted. "Senzok, shoot him!"

"I can't get off a clear shot, Captain," the crossbowman called and glanced at his comrade. They'd stopped twenty paces down the tunnel, and neither looked like he wanted to rush forward and attack Vorik.

His fellow soldier pointed at Syla, and their expressions firmed. They would have no trouble attacking *her*.

From Fel's side, she rose to her feet, hands spread, wishing she hadn't lost the remaining explosives.

A gasp came from behind her, then a thump. Syla risked glancing back as Fel struggled to rise beside her, to defend her once more. Lesva had fallen, disarmed, her hand clasped to her gut and blood streaming between her fingers.

Those fingers twitched, and she groaned, so she wasn't dead, and Syla hated to worry about her coming after her again in the future, but... she couldn't blame Vorik for not slaying one of his own people. Nor could she stomach the idea of slipping over there and finishing her off. She could barely handle that she'd killed people in self-defense. Besides, she doubted Vorik would allow her to walk over there with the magical equivalent of a dagger in her hand. Nor did she think the two stormers who'd arrived would allow that.

Looking as exhausted as Syla felt, Vorik walked toward her, though his focus was on the two stormers. The man with the crossbow had it pointed at Syla but watched Vorik warily, not looking like he knew if he should shift his aim or not.

Vorik drew even with Syla, standing at her side, his sword lowered. Only then did Syla notice that it had grown quiet. The drill was no longer banging away in the distance, nor did she hear the hammer blows that she'd caught earlier.

Unease crept into her. Had stormers followed the drill noise back to Tibby and found her? And stopped her?

Or...

Vorik cocked his head, as if he heard something. More stormers coming?

No, it was water that flowed down the passageway toward them, curling around the legs of the two men and then reaching Syla and the others.

Confusion furrowed Vorik's brow. "What's happening?"

"We need to get out of here." Syla remembered her aunt saying it would take a while for the mine to fill, but panic and claustrophobia made her voice tight with fear when she added, "*Now.*"

Vorik didn't know where the cold water curling about his ankles had come from, but, even if he hadn't seen the worry in Syla's round eyes, he would have guessed the threat that it represented.

"What happened?" Tems, one of the two stormers who'd arrived, waved at the water.

"It's from the lake." Syla helped Fel to his feet, wrapping an arm around his waist to support him, but she looked to the unconscious lady with distress twisting her face.

"The *lake?* It's a mile away in the other direction."

"That noise..." Merimoth, the other stormer, said. "Were they *drilling* up into it?"

Leaving the musing to them, Vorik strode through the water to the chamber door, where Lesva and the Kingdom woman both lay barely conscious.

With blood streaming from Lesva's wounds, she tried to push herself up, but she struggled to support her weight. The lady issued a confused groan as the water washed her face, but she must have received a blow to the head or something to keep her from regaining full consciousness. There was a moon-mark on her hand, and Vorik realized she had to be Lady Abrya, the woman he'd originally been assigned to kidnap.

"Help me carry them," Vorik told the men, using his firm command voice, hoping they would forget that they'd witnessed Lesva calling him a traitor and him sliding his sword into her.

They glanced at Syla, then hurried past her to join him.

Vorik lifted the lady over his shoulder, leaving Lesva for them. He'd never met the lady but regretted that she'd been dragged down here so Lesva could force her way into the chamber. He was starting to hate this war, hate all of this.

"I can walk," Fel grumbled as Syla led him up the tunnel, but he had to lean heavily on her. He must have tangled with Lesva before Vorik arrived.

Ignoring him, Syla said, "Thank you," to Vorik as he joined her with Abrya slung over his shoulder. Tems and Merimoth came behind, carrying Lesva between them.

"You're welcome, my lady queen." For her sake, Vorik tried to make his tone light, though his heart was heavy. "It's always a pleasure to be in your presence, but do tell me. Is it my imagination, or has this water already risen in the forty seconds since its arrival?"

"It's been longer than that, but it may be rising, yes. I wonder if Lord Oyenar's men succeeded in sealing off the lower levels. That banging..." She peered into the darkness ahead and walked more quickly.

Vorik didn't usually fear much but caught himself eager to

match her pace if not start sprinting. If the tunnel filled completely, they would drown. Was that a possibility?

"You planned this?" he asked.

Syla hesitated. "We thought if we flooded the mine, the shielder wouldn't be accessible to your people."

"To *any* people, I'd think."

"We don't need it to be accessible for it to continue working."

"Better if it *isn't*," Fel said. "Will that wagon operate in the water?"

"I'm not sure." Syla glanced back.

Tems and Merimoth weren't injured and shared the burden of carrying Lesva, so they were keeping up easily, and Vorik could tote Lady Abrya without trouble. Syla and Fel were setting the pace, slower than they probably wished, but there was a hitch in the bodyguard's step as he leaned heavily on her. Vorik walked beside Syla in case they needed help. As they traveled farther up the tunnel, the water grew deeper, rising over their knees, and striding against it became more challenging.

When the wagon Vorik had passed earlier came into view, the mine opening up beyond it, Syla gaped. Though the wheeled contraption had to be heavy, it wobbled slightly, then shifted a few inches, bumping against a support.

"Is that thing *floating*?" Fel asked.

"I don't think we're driving it anywhere," Syla said glumly. "We'll have to walk."

"If the water gets much deeper, we'll have to *swim*."

"Maybe that'll be easier on your injuries," Syla said. "At the temple, we have—had—a pool for water therapy. It's gentler on the joints than land-based modalities."

Fel looked balefully at her. Vorik managed a smile, always glad that Syla didn't fall apart during calamities.

The thought that she might have intentionally *caused* this calamity alarmed him, though maybe it shouldn't have. She would do almost anything to protect her people. Except betray him. For whatever reason, she'd never done that. He'd meant the words about love he'd spoken when facing off against Lesva, and he'd been touched when she'd called the same to him. He would help Syla get her relative out of the mine and stand by her against the rest of his people if need be. Jhiton had said Vorik had to choose, and he chose Syla.

Syla slipped in the water and lost her footing, ending up clinging to Fel instead of assisting him. Taller and heavier, he remained on his feet and steady. Vorik shifted Abrya so he could reach out and help Syla back to her feet. With the water above his thighs now, he worried none of them would be able to keep their footing much longer. The distance to the cage lift felt farther and farther. At least, now that they were in the open part of the mine with the high ceilings and great pyramid pillars that supported them, Vorik felt they had time, that the cavernous space wouldn't flood that quickly.

But when he glanced at one of those pillars, water streaming past, an alarming thought popped into his mind.

"Salt dissolves," he blurted. "The water will erode it away, won't it?"

"Eventually, yes," Syla said without surprise. The thought must have already occurred to her.

He imagined her with her leaders in a conference room somewhere, calmly planning this. Just as Jhiton and Amalia and Shi had calmly planned the invasion. Gods.

The water lifted Vorik's feet from the ground, and he struggled to stay connected, to walk as long as he could. He was a strong swimmer, but he wouldn't be able to maneuver out of here that quickly while pulling the lady.

Are you underground? Agrevlari asked from beyond the island's barrier.

In the salt mine, yes. Vorik wondered how much of the battle the dragon could see from miles away. From a great enough height, the lake and road and buildings might be in view.

Something is happening to the lake.

Oh, I know.

First, Wreylith was merely lighting boats full of your people on fire. I and many of our ally dragons have been threatening her, promising a swift death to her once the barrier is down, but she hasn't been deterred.

Vorik thought of Syla's admission to coming up with the plan to flood the mine and eyed the water flowing past him. *I don't think the barrier is coming down. Ever.*

Yes, I see the problem. The water is draining *from the lake. Very... vehemently.*

What does that *mean?*

A whirlpool has formed at one end. It has great power, and portions of the shoreline are being pulled into the water. The burning ships are also being drawn toward it. Swiftly and inexorably. Anything in the water is being pulled toward the whirlpool, including people trying to swim away. I don't understand what's happening.

I do. It surprised Vorik that the water flowing through the mine around him was so calm. Calm but, as Agrevlari had said, inexorable.

Vorik's feet lost purchase on the ground again. Grim, he started paddling. The two men behind him did as well, pulling Lesva along. Fel was taller than the rest of them and still walking, but he was helping Syla as much as the other way around now, and that made their progress slow. Even carrying Abrya, Vorik pulled ahead when he started swimming.

As Fel gave up and also started swimming, an explosion boomed somewhere ahead.

"Was that your aunt?" Vorik asked, the cold water enveloping him fully, some splashing his lips, its taste salty. Of course. "Who else is down here?"

"Wreylith said *your* people have taken over the buildings and have been coming down."

Vorik groaned. He didn't want to hear that.

"They'd better not be blowing up the lift cage," Syla said. "That's the only way out."

Vorik had climbed down using the chains, but if he had to ascend that, carrying the lady over his shoulder, that would be challenging. And could Fel make the climb while injured? What about Syla? She didn't seem injured, but did she have the strength to pull herself up that far?

Growing grimmer by the moment, Vorik swam faster.

Another boom sounded. This time, they were close enough that he also saw a flash.

"That *could* be my aunt." Syla sputtered as a surge of water flowed past, maybe caused by the explosion. "But I really hope she's gotten out of here by now."

"Me too," Fel said.

With strong strokes and determination, the group kept swimming. The water had reached the level of the lanterns mounted on the pyramid supports, and they were starting to go out, leaving little light. Even with his keen night vision, Vorik was surprised when something bumped past his shoulder. Was that…

"A body," he said.

"Another one over here," Fel said.

"The explosions," Syla said, "must have gotten them. Or… fighting. I don't know."

Yes, over the last couple of minutes, a few clangs had reached Vorik's ears, but he hadn't known if they were from swords clashing or mining machinery or something else entirely.

Another body floated past, and they were near a lantern, so there was more light, enough to see the face, though Vorik had already recognized black rider leathers.

"Remarin," he said. "He is—was—in my squadron under my command."

He'd probably come down with Jhiton.

Syla glanced over. "I'm sorry. I didn't mean..."

"It's what they chose."

"It's not what *you* chose though?" Syla glanced at the men coming behind them, but they were probably too busy swimming and pulling Lesva to listen in.

"I'm not even supposed to be here. I came because— Oh." Vorik almost laughed that he hadn't had a chance to tell her what had changed things for him, making him disobey orders to come. But it wasn't funny, and he hesitated to give her more bad news now, but if they were separated... "I flew past your castle. There's a yellow flag hanging from the wall where your family's was. And there are dozens of Kingdom ships in the harbor, presumably to support whoever took over the castle."

Syla spat water. "Those ships are supposed to be coming *here*."

"Yellow," Fel said. "Is that the Fograth family?"

"Yes," Syla said. "They moved quickly. I didn't even know— I mean, I guess I knew, but I expected Relvin would be the one to take the throne. I thought he was angling for it."

"General Dolok wouldn't have supported him," Fel said.

Syla coughed as more water flooded her mouth, and she focused on swimming.

So did Vorik. The current was more agitated now, threatening to separate them, to send them floating into the depths of the mine to drown instead of letting them reach the exit.

You have not drowned yet, Agrevlari stated. *I sense through our bond that you live.*

I'm fine. Other than needing to swim *through what I walked over earlier.*

Interesting. Up here, what is unfolding is, even by dragon standards, epic. Agrevlari was flying above the barrier, directly overhead now, so he had a decent view of the island below and shared what he witnessed. Beneath the barrier, Wreylith was sailing about, sending gouts of flames into troops and leaving trees burning in her wake, but the lake was what was mesmerizing, with boats being sucked under near the huge whirlpool the dragon had described. Like a giant drain, it pulled down everything from wreckage to shrubs and trees that must have been growing close to the crumbling shoreline. *There is a hole, and the water is flowing into the mine, yes?* Agrevlari asked.

Oh, yes.

You had better escape while you still can.

We're working on it. Vorik shifted his grip on Abrya so that he could dash water out of his eyes. Nobody was talking now, their group all panting from the ongoing exertion. Only the shouts, clashes, and clangs from the direction of the lift floated to them, carrying far over the water and echoing from the salt pillars.

There is another complication, Agrevlari said.

What more could go wrong tonight? Vorik frowned as another body floated past, the woman's throat cut. It wasn't the *water* that was killing people, at least not yet.

During this time, the gardeners have continued to work to extract the weapons platform. It is now resting on the solid cobblestones of the street near the burned docks, and they are maneuvering an undamaged ship into place so that they can load it onto the deck.

Storm-cursed luck. Just when Vorik had thought things couldn't get any worse for his people.

The next body that floated past wore a Kingdom uniform. That didn't make him feel any better.

Wait, Syla is with me, and the aunt is down here too, Vorik said. *They're the only ones who can use the weapons platform, right?*

I am unaware of its operational parameters.

Yeah, me too.

Perhaps you should have discussed them during one of your many encounters with your queen.

We were busy discussing other things then.

It wasn't as if Syla would have told him all its secrets, anyway.

Sex orifices.

You're a pain in the ass, Agrevlari.

Yet, I still await you beyond the barrier. If you can escape.

Another boom sounded, so close that it hurt Vorik's ears. And light flashed, revealing… by the eyes of the moon, there were not only people ahead around the lift cage, but there were a *lot* of people. Swimming and wielding weapons, they battled each other and also shot wary glances toward a magical wagon larger than the one that had floated away. It was also floating but seemed under control, like a ship with a wheel. Tibby stood aboard, one hand on an orb that glowed with power and one… She was the one throwing explosives.

"Get away from the lift, you savages!" she called.

Two sodden Kingdom soldiers knelt on the wagon with her, a new pair that she must have acquired along the way after Jhiton killed the others. They gripped maces and kicked or swung at approaching swimmers—those were Vorik's people trying to climb aboard to destroy the wagon and stop Tibby.

"How do we get to the lift cage and out of here?" Fel swam close to a pillar, pulling Syla with him, and gripped it to pause their advance. "Don't call out," he warned Syla.

She'd lifted an arm, probably trying to get her aunt's attention, but they were in darkness and too far away. Besides, Tibby was getting ready to throw another explosive. The people treading water around the cage lift were fighting, as if not even aware of her threat. Were they trying to kill each other? Or just get into that cage and escape the mine?

Vorik stared bleakly, realizing that was it. They weren't fighting to kill each other; they were fighting for space. Four people had gotten into the lift cage, and they were pushing out enemies who tried to swarm in while simultaneously trying to pull in allies.

Though Vorik wanted to help his people—and also wanted to make sure Syla escaped—he followed Fel to the pillar and anchored himself on it, not sure what to do. He couldn't release Abrya, nor would he be as effective a combatant as usual while swimming. Meanwhile, the water kept rising. Whatever the solution was, he didn't think it was a *sword.*

Splashes came from behind him, and Tems cursed. Vorik turned in time to see someone swimming away, someone with silver hair. Lesva.

At first, he thought she'd woken enough to figure out what was going on and meant to take her chances fighting through the people around the cage and try to escape. But she swam back the way they'd come. Deeper into the mine.

Syla watched her go. "Is she going to try again to get into the shielder chamber? Those tunnels weren't very high. They'll be flooded by now. And she doesn't have a moon-mark."

"I don't know," Vorik said.

"Should we go after her, sir?" Merimoth asked.

"No."

"Some of the stormers are climbing up the chains." Fel pointed above the cage toward men slithering up into the darkness of the shaft.

Vorik nodded, encouraged. Everyone could escape that way if they worked together—or even simply ignored each other—for twenty minutes.

Syla wiped her face. "I think they'll get captured. I'm talking to Wreylith. With her help, Lord Oyenar's troops have reclaimed the area around the entrance up there."

Someone who'd disappeared into the lift shaft tumbled back into view, knocking another climber off the chain as he fell. With a heavy thump, the man landed on top of the lift cage, not moving. An arrow protruded from his neck. It was one of Vorik's people.

He closed his eyes. The Kingdom troops weren't going to let any stormers out. Even a strong and capable fighter couldn't spring out of a hole fast enough to defend against arrows from archers who stood all around it.

Another body fell into view, an arrow driven into the top of the man's skull.

Syla wiped her face again, a shake to her hand. She couldn't approve of such grisly means, but she probably couldn't stop them. Except through Wreylith, she couldn't communicate with anyone up there.

"Syla!" Tibby had spotted them, and she maneuvered her floating wagon toward them. A few stormers tried to intercept her, but she hurled another of her explosives. It struck one of the men in the head and blew up.

Vorik had never felt so helpless in his life. He was on the verge of leaving Abrya with Fel and Syla and swimming over to try to gather his people, to bring order to the chaos, but he didn't know how. Two more bodies fell out of the shaft. The cage lift started clanking upward, a surprising mix of stormers and Kingdom troops inside, their backs to the bars, their weapons pointing at each other, though they must have made a truce, whether spoken or not, because they didn't attack each other.

Those left behind shouted and splashed in dismay.

"Climb aboard," Tibby said when she'd maneuvered the wagon close.

Syla and Fel didn't hesitate to do so, and they reached over for Abrya. She'd woken at some point but hadn't fought to get away from Vorik, and she groped now for the wagon.

"What are *you* doing here?" Tibby asked Vorik in exasperation.

"Regretting that I disobeyed orders," Vorik said.

"We'll all have a lot of regrets after tonight," Syla said.

"That's the truth." Tibby grunted, then in a softer voice, the words meant for Syla, added, "That was the last of my explosives. Do you have anymore?"

"I'm afraid not." Syla reached for Vorik, waving for him to climb aboard with them.

He did and looked back to his two men, but they were swimming toward those around the bottom of the lift shaft instead.

A distant boom came from above. Cries of alarm and pain came from the shaft, and the lift cage tumbled back into view. Warped and no longer attached to the chains, it plunged into the water, landing on people who'd been swimming underneath.

"Wreylith said the archers up there have orders not to let any stormers out," Syla said.

"Some of our own people were in that cage." Tibby gawked at it.

"I think… they have orders not to let *anyone* out. Whoever is in command is willing to sacrifice his own people to ensure as many stormers as possible die." Syla shook her head and met Vorik's eyes, as if to apologize, to say she never would have given that order.

"The queen will *not* be sacrificed," Fel said.

"I'd prefer not to be either," Tibby said tartly, then eyed the orb that controlled and powered the wagon. In a softer tone, she murmured, "Maybe I can rig this to explode."

She'd turned the wagon toward the crowd of swimmers. A single chain still dangled down from above. Vorik could climb it, but if he would be shot at the top…

The moon-mark on Tibby's hand glowed silver as she rested it upon the orb, manipulating it with magic. How would making the wagon explode help them? Maybe Lesva hadn't been crazy to swim away from this group.

"How are *we* going to get out, Syla?" Fel asked, as if she had a plan.

Syla held up a finger.

Puny humans, Wreylith boomed, her voice directed to everyone. *Back away and allow the queen to arise from the water tomb, or I shall slay you.*

"That's how." Syla pointed at her aunt. "Get us over there. The lift is destroyed, so we're going to have to climb."

"Oh, of course," Tibby said. "We're so agile and lithe that it'll be easy."

"To get out of here with my life, *I* will carry you." Fel told her, waving at the ever-rising water.

"A minute ago, you were leaning on Syla," Vorik said.

"For this, I can summon reserves."

"Can you carry Lady Abrya, Vorik?" Syla asked. "I think I can climb out on my own."

The statement surprised him until he remembered that she ought to be gaining strength from her dragon link by now. She nodded, as if she knew his thoughts.

"I can, yes," Vorik said. "Especially if it means I'm allowed to depart without an arrow in my skull."

"I should be able to arrange that," Syla said. "Or *Wreylith* will."

"I'd rather depend on you. Wreylith doesn't adore my charm as much as I'd like. And she definitely doesn't adore my dragon."

"I think she's warmed up to him slightly since he bit her."

"Dragons are odd."

"Yes. Uhm, Aunt Tibby." Syla pointed toward the swimmers they were approaching, many still with weapons in their hands.

Faces contorted with anger, they looked like they wanted to take their frustrations out on the wagon and its occupants. If the stormers recognized Vorik, it wasn't apparent.

Tibby sent more of her power into the orb. It started throbbing, and a clunk sounded as she removed it from its mount.

Realizing what she would do, Vorik shouted to the stormers, "Swim away from there. Get out of the way!"

Tibby didn't object to his warning, and Syla didn't either.

She yelled, "Let us depart, and I'll arrange for everyone to get out without being shot."

The Kingdom people in the water obeyed, the ominously pulsing and glowing orb perhaps swaying them as much as her words, but Vorik's people… They raised their weapons in defiance and kept swimming toward the wagon.

"Get out of there!" he yelled again.

A few obeyed, but more glared at him, and someone shouted, "Traitor!"

Since he was riding with Kingdom people on their wagon, Vorik couldn't deny that the word applied, but he tried one more time. "She's about to throw an explosive!"

"A big one," Tibby murmured, holding the orb aloft with both hands. With its power source removed, the wagon was slowing, the current started to affect it, but it continued toward the shaft.

Someone pumped an arm to throw a knife. Not certain of the target, Vorik pulled Tibby *and* Syla down. The blade glanced off the top of the orb and didn't damage it. If anything, it pulsed faster, waves of magic that Vorik could sense rolling off it.

Tibby snarled like a tiger and hurled the orb. It landed in the water in the middle of the aggressors and blew up with such light and power that it dwarfed all the explosives that had been thrown before. The wagon rocked, throwing Vorik to his back and knocking Fel into the water. Nearby, one of the salt pillars crumbled. Chunks of the ceiling followed, tumbling into the water and floating like icebergs. Snaps and cracks sounded, promising more of the ceiling would come down. One chunk struck the wagon, diverting it from its course.

"We have to swim!" Tibby shouted.

Vorik grabbed Abrya and Tibby and leaped in, swimming on his back to more easily kick and pull them along with him. At his side, Fel and Syla also swam through water that churned in the aftermath of the explosion. Chunks of salt plummeting down didn't help the situation, and Fel cursed as a head-sized piece struck his shoulder.

Fortunately, the group made it to the shaft without anyone attacking them. Vorik didn't know if there was anyone left *to* attack. Body parts floated everywhere, and he couldn't help but feel he'd failed his people. He should have dueled Shi for the tribe and tried to turn the tides, tried to lead the stormers toward a truce and a peaceful way to obtain food. Instead, he'd let Jhiton and the others force them down this path.

"There's the chain," Fel said.

"I'll go up first," Syla said.

"Don't you dare." Fel reached for her.

"Nobody is going to shoot me." Surprisingly swift, she dodged his grasp and gripped the chain. Her spectacles had fallen around her neck, but she shimmied up the chain with the same determination as she did everything.

Vorik managed a smile as Fel cursed.

"Wreylith has cleared the way," Syla added. "Hurry up after me."

"Oh, we will," Tibby said.

Vorik waited, treading water and waving for Tibby and Fel to go ahead of him. He wanted to ensure that nobody else threw a knife. But nobody moved nearby. The explosion had been… far too effective. Mentally, he added "Aunt Tibby" to his list of women not to underestimate. That whole family was far more than they seemed.

"Who are you?" Abrya asked blearily as Vorik arranged her so that he could climb out with her in his grasp.

"Vorik, my lady." He left off *captain*. After this blatant defying of orders, he expected to lose his rank. "Just Vorik."

29

Before Syla reached the top of the shaft, her muscles quivering from the effort of pulling herself up on such a long climb, she could see flames above, as well as stars in the night sky. The beam the chain and pulley were attached to had survived the destruction, but the building as a whole might not have. Smoke wafted across the shaft, blocking the view of the stars.

Despite her firm assertion that nobody would shoot her, Syla told Wreylith no fewer than ten times that she was coming and to make sure soldiers didn't fire at her or anyone in her party.

Something stirred in the smoke, and Syla flinched. An enemy? No, a scaled red underbelly came into view, talons wrapping around the beam. Wreylith's great head lowered so she could peer into the shaft.

Queen Syla comes, she boomed to all around, *from the soggy depths of the destroyed mine, having vanquished her enemies, ready to lead her people again.*

Have I mentioned that dragons tend toward the dramatic? Syla asked.

And that you appreciate my many excellent qualities, yes.

That is true. I also appreciate that I don't see any archers.

They have backed away from the shaft, per my command, but many are here watching, quite curious, and a wagon carrying the island lord has arrived.

Good. Syla knew Oyenar would be relieved to see his wife and also hoped he could give them all a ride back. Well, maybe not *all* of them.

She didn't know what she would do with Vorik. Letting him sneak away to rejoin his people would be ideal, but she could already tell that the blazing flames lit the area as if it were noon on a sunny day. Sneaking anywhere would be difficult.

"Your Majesty?" came an uncertain voice that she didn't recognize.

Arms shaking, Syla pulled her head even with the top of the hole. Two soldiers with their bows on their backs reached down and helped her out.

"Thank you," she said with great sincerity.

Even though her new strength had helped her immensely—before, she would have struggled to climb even five feet up a rope—that had been an arduous way to depart a mine. But she couldn't complain. She'd escaped when many others hadn't.

As the soldiers helped her out of the shaft, Tibby and Fel reached the top. More men crept into the remains of the building. As she'd guessed, only one wall and a few support posts and beams remained. Outside, fires had scorched the earth and burned the other building completely, while flames danced in the forest all around. Before, the lake hadn't been visible, but enough trees had burned—or been knocked down by dragon ire—that Syla could see it and gape. The water line had dropped, though not as dramatically as she'd expected from her experience below, and the lake swirled, pulling everything toward the newly drilled hole. The boats... She didn't even *see* the boats. Had they been sucked down to the bottom? The hole wouldn't have been wide enough to draw them in, but Syla hadn't envisioned the water having such power as it emptied out of the lake.

Had the people on those boats been pulled under too? Unable to escape? Even though Wreylith had reported that stormers had taken over the vessels, maybe killing the fishermen they'd caught on board, she hoped everyone had been able to swim away. So many had already died. She hadn't wanted this. And the memories of people horribly dismembered by the explosives would haunt her. Everything about this night would.

One of the soldiers cursed. "Is that Captain *Vorik*?"

"Yes, but don't shoot." Syla lifted a hand.

Armed men were already surging toward the shaft.

"He's carrying Lady Abrya," Syla added, giving a more compelling reason for everyone to hold their fire.

"Stand down, men!" came a call from the road. Lord Oyenar strode toward them. He must have heard Syla's words because he switched to a dead run.

Vorik, face red from the effort of climbing with the weight of an extra person, pushed Abrya out ahead of him. Warily, he followed and stood beside Syla.

"Don't shoot," she said again. "He's..."

She looked at Vorik, as always, groping for an explanation for him.

He raised his eyebrows. Probably curious as to how he would be classified.

"My prisoner," she finished with an apologetic shrug.

As long as they didn't kill him, she could make sure he had a way to escape later. Not that he necessarily needed her to arrange anything for that.

Vorik smiled sadly but with acceptance. "I believe it *is* my turn to be the captive."

"Yeah."

Oyenar pushed soldiers back so he could embrace his wife. She'd recovered enough to wrap her arms around him and fall into his embrace. Her injuries aside, it looked romantic. Syla wished she could fall into Vorik's embrace, but dozens of eyes were watching. Maybe *hundreds*. Oyenar had sent wave after wave of troops up here, and he'd been right to do so. More stormers than she'd expected had arrived to be a part of this. Oyenar—and, whether Syla had wanted it or not, she and Aunt Tibby—had delivered the devastating defeat that he'd wanted.

"Your Majesty." Oyenar kept a grip on his wife's hand as he faced Syla. "Your weapons platform has been loaded onto one of our ships, the *Fanged Whale*. May I request that you use it to help drive off any stormer vessels or *dragons* remaining in the area?" He looked up.

Only one dragon was in the sky above the barrier, a familiar green-scaled one. Agrevlari. Good. That would make it easier for Vorik to escape.

"Yes, but..." Syla remembered Vorik's warning and grimaced. "I need to depart as soon as possible. I've received intelligence that, in my absence, someone from the Fograth family has taken over the castle and talked several islands' worth of ships into arriving in the harbor at Castle Island to support them." Realizing someone might wonder where she'd gotten such *intelligence,* especially with Vorik standing next to her, she waved up to Wreylith, doubting the dragon would mind receiving credit.

As Wreylith swished her tail, saying nothing to belie her, Syla watched Oyenar's face, wondering if he'd known. Might he also have been invited to send ships? But surprise lifted his eyebrows.

"I'd heard inklings of Lord Favrik Fograth's ambition, and of his sons openly considering opposing your rule, but I've been busy here lately. For all I know, there's a message on my desk requesting my help."

"I think," Abrya murmured, "we should support Queen Syla rather than opposing her."

Oyenar opened his mouth but paused.

Abrya added, "I insist."

"Yes, my love." Oyenar bowed ruefully at her, then faced Syla again. "Perhaps, the *Fanged Whale* could carry you back to Castle Island, and you could fire at any lingering stormer ships and dragons on the way."

"I..." Syla glanced at Wreylith. She could get back more quickly on the dragon's back, but what would she do with Vorik? If she left him here, someone might kill him. At least a dozen nocked bows were pointed at his chest right now, despite her assertion that he was to be her prisoner. If she took him to Castle Island, and nobody recognized her rule or obeyed her orders, he might be killed there too. They *both* might be.

"I'll send a suitable escort with the *Fanged Whale* with orders to support you once you arrive." Oyenar nodded to his wife, and she nodded back.

Given how many of his ships had been lost to the stormers, Syla doubted the escort would be enough to stand against all the vessels and allies the Fograths had gathered, but it would be something. Maybe between his fleet and Wreylith, it would be enough.

"I accept your offer, Lord Oyenar," Syla said. "Thank you."

Movement in the shaft made Vorik draw his sword and Syla spin to look. She grimaced with guilt. She should have realized others would make it to the chains and climb up after them.

As the archers aimed their bows, she lifted a hand. "Lord Oyenar, there are stormers as well as Kingdom troops down there that may have survived. After all that's happened, we shouldn't kill anyone else. Please let them out."

She watched Oyenar, who scowled at the word *stormers*, and Abrya's eyes were more vengeful than compassionate after what she'd endured.

Testing her power more than she should have, given what was going on back on Castle Island, Syla said, "I insist they be allowed to live."

Oyenar's jaw tightened, but he nodded. "Very well. We'll take the stormers prisoner." His face lightened as a new idea seemed to come to him. "We can keep them to barter with them in future negotiations. The stormers may also have some of *our* people."

Syla had envisioned taking anyone who crawled out of the flooded mine to an infirmary, not a prison, but the archers allowed Vorik to help a stormer out of the hole, so she didn't argue. The next survivor wore a Kingdom uniform, and she decided there might be some hope if their peoples had allowed each other to crawl away from certain death without fighting.

In total, only five people came up, and Syla shook her head with bleakness. Vorik's face was also bleak as he watched the shaft, then peered down into it.

So desolate was his expression that it made her wonder at the root of it. He'd lost men down there—friends, surely—but that had been going on all week. Was it just now all catching up with him? Or...

She rocked back with realization.

"Was your brother down there?" she asked softly.

Vorik sighed. "I fought him before coming to find you. He..." He looked toward Tibby. "The ceiling collapsed on him. Both of us. I clawed my way out, but he'd been injured." He winced. "*I* injured him." The stab to the gut he pantomimed suggested a wound that might have been deadly even if the recipient hadn't been buried afterward. "I'm sure he was dead before I left to find you."

"I'm sorry." For the sake of the Kingdom and the memory of her family, Syla had wanted Jhiton dead, and even tried to engineer it herself, but she regretted that Vorik had lost someone he loved. The only close family he had left, from what he'd told her. "Thank you for coming for me."

She had no doubt that Vorik had attacked his brother for her sake, and emotion filled her throat. What a sacrifice to make for her. How could she ever be worth that?

Vorik nodded but didn't say anything. Maybe his throat was also tight with emotion.

"How long until the mine fills completely?" Oyenar asked Tibby.

She considered the lake and looked thoughtfully into the shaft, though it was fully dark down there, the lanterns long since submerged. "Quite a few hours, I'd think. Though the pillars may erode and the ceiling collapse before then." Tibby gazed around at the troops and the wagons. "It *might* not affect the ground we're standing on, but that would be a gamble. I suggest evacuating the area."

"Agreed," Oyenar said. Maybe he'd already been wondering about the stability of the ground underneath them.

At a nod from him, men with weapons turned them toward Vorik again.

"We'll take your prisoner to a wagon, Your Majesty," one said.

Looking defeated, even though he'd saved her life, Vorik didn't so much as twitch an objection. As the men surrounded him, he didn't even seem to see the weapons. His gaze remained bleak.

"I'll come too," Syla said and walked beside Vorik. Deciding she didn't care what people thought, she clasped his hand.

Though his eyes were haunted, he returned the clasp.

~

Do you wish me to facilitate an escape? Agrevlari asked, flying a couple of miles to the side of the ship that Vorik sailed on with Syla, Tibby, Fel, and numerous Kingdom troops. And the weapons platform, which had been strapped ominously to the deck again before they'd boarded.

Vorik trusted it was only in his imagination that the ancient device knew what he'd done and emanated dark menace toward him. At least Wreylith, who perched in her customary spot on the wheelhouse, hadn't emanated such feelings toward him. She'd merely swished her tail when the troops had led him past her and belowdecks. Apparently, accompanying Syla on her vessel had satisfied the whims of the shielder artifact, and it had let the dragon pass through on the way out to sea.

Not at this time. I'm going to try to help Syla get her Kingdom back before going... Going where? Vorik didn't know. Back to his people? He doubted he would be welcome. The two men who'd seen him fight Lesva had likely survived. And *she* might have survived. As for Jhiton... Vorik didn't think anyone except Tibby had witnessed that battle, but he couldn't return and lie about what had happened. His honor wouldn't allow it. *I'm going to try to help Syla,* he repeated, deciding not to worry about his own future at the moment. *She has the support of the Bogberry Island lord, but she has a daunting mess to deal with at home.*

Quite. We saw many, many *more ships than she has now in the Castle Island harbor with more on the way.*

Yes.

Will her people allow you to assist her?

I don't know.

Are you in shackles currently? That might be a clue.

Vorik snorted softly. *She didn't let them shackle me. I am in a prison cell, but it's quite posh.*

A posh prison cell?

There's a bed, a chamber pot, a porthole, and someone brought me a meal as we sailed away. There were even apples and pears.

I will not be able to assist you on Castle Island.

I know. You should... I'm not sure what you should do, Agrevlari.

Vorik had to swallow a lump in this throat at the idea of sending his bonded dragon of many years back to his people, possibly never to see him again. But the stormer-allied dragons had always made it clear that they'd joined with his people because of their mutual goal to gain access to the bounteous Kingdom islands, and if Vorik wouldn't be working toward that end...

Currently, I am speaking with Wreylith, Agrevlari informed him.

Is she talking to you again?

She said she regretted that the barrier didn't give us an opportunity to engage in battle last night, as she would have enjoyed a vigorous engagement with a spirited foe. Though she is willing to assist the queen, she finds fighting only puny humans to be unsatisfying. I invited her to fly away from the death launcher and engage in a physical altercation with me now, but she says she must prepare to aid the queen in reclaiming her throne.

Is a physical altercation *what you want with her?*

As I learn more about her, I believe that a fierce and challenging battle might lead her to desire to mate—more so than my singing.

I think that's likely too.

A lock turned in the door, and Vorik sensed Syla in the corridor. A guard with a crossbow stepped in first, looking suspiciously at Vorik and waving for him to back to the wall before he would allow Syla to enter. Other guards, including some of her Royal Protectors, lurked in the corridor.

"Thank you, Sergeant," Syla murmured politely while shooing him back outside with one hand. She held a small circular pan in the other, something that smelled of apples and cinnamon and other spices he couldn't name.

Vorik's mouth watered.

"Are you *sure* you want to be alone with him, Your Majesty?" the guard asked. "We've heard that you have, uhm, powers now, but he's dangerous."

"Not when he has baked goods in his mouth." She showed the pan to the guard.

The man's brow furrowed as if he didn't know if that was a joke or not.

"It's true," Vorik offered. "I hardly ever threaten people who give me delicious food."

"I'll be fine." After succeeding in shooing the man out, Syla closed the door, then lifted the apple dessert toward Vorik. "The palace and barracks kitchens on Bogberry Island are in a shambles—most of the city is—so this isn't fresh, but I had a bite of another one. It's still tasty."

"It smells wonderful." Vorik accepted the dessert but set it aside so that he could envelop her in a hug. "You do too."

"I haven't bathed yet, except in salty lake water."

"It doesn't matter." Vorik rested his cheek against her hair, inhaling her scent and appreciating the warmth of her body against his. And that she returned his hug without reservation.

"I'm sorry that you lost so much," she whispered into his shoulder. "When I came up with the idea… I didn't think through all the ramifications. I certainly didn't realize half the shoreline and all those boats would be pulled under. And I meant to flood the mine *before* your people arrived." The distressed tightness in her voice didn't surprise him, and he knew that she wouldn't have willingly chosen a path that had killed so many. But he also knew she would always do what had to be done to protect her people. "And I'm sorry that you lost your brother."

"That was because of my choice, nothing you did." The aunt might be the reason Jhiton's wound had ultimately been fatal, but Vorik had run his brother through with his sword. That would haunt him for the rest of his life, but as he held Syla in his arms—warm, beautiful, and determined Syla—he couldn't bring himself to wish he hadn't done it. If Jhiton had been with Lesva at the shielder chamber, Syla wouldn't have survived the encounter. Jhiton may have humored Vorik more than he should have in regard to their relationship, and he might have even respected Syla, but he wouldn't have hesitated to kill her. Not if she stood between him and his goal.

"You only made that choice because of me," she said. "If I didn't exist, you never would have pitted yourself against your brother."

"Eyes of the moon, Syla, if you didn't exist, who would have brought me… what did you say that is?"

"A three-day-old apple tart."

"It's magnificent." Vorik gripped her shoulders and leaned back so he could look into her eyes, and the moisture in them touched him. The tears weren't for Jhiton—she was probably relieved he was gone—but born out of sympathy for him, for his distress. Of everyone onboard, nobody could know more than she what it was like to lose family. "*You're* magnificent," he added. "And I'm going to help you reclaim your throne."

"I really do love you," she whispered.

"As you should." Vorik smirked, then lifted her spectacles from her nose and set them on the table with the dessert. They could enjoy that later. But now…

Syla slid her arms up around his shoulders and kissed him, her thoughts seeming to match his.

Vorik returned the kiss more gently than he might otherwise have, but he was drained after the long night, after losing so much. He sensed the same in Syla, a need for comfort as much as sex. But he enjoyed the touch of their lips as he slid his hands over the curves of her body. He had lost so much, but he had her, and she loved him.

Maybe there shouldn't have been tears as they kissed, but their lips were salty, their regrets mingling with their passion. Mourning as much as love brought them together, a need for mutual support, something to remind them that they'd lost much, but *they* were still alive.

He trailed his fingers down her throat, then around to rub the back of her neck, to relax her even as he aroused her. And aroused himself. The heat of her body pressing against his made the memories—the horrors—of the last couple of days fade, at least for a time.

They undressed each other, hands roaming, desire growing. Her fingers threaded through his hair, nails grazing his scalp, and his entire body went taut with need.

"Oh, Syla," he whispered, cupping her with his hands, making sure to please her as he relished her touch on his body.

He slid his fingers from her breasts down her abdomen and lower, brushing her, wanting to thank her for all the times she could have worked against him—could have *killed* him—and hadn't. Her support meant so much. Now, it meant everything.

"Vorik," she gasped as he slid his fingers into her, making her twitch toward him, wanting more stimulation, more of him. That was exactly what he intended to give her. "I need—" She gripped his shoulders, fingers tight.

"Me?" He smiled, then lowered his mouth to her breast as he stroked her below, feeling her readiness. Even under the worst of circumstances, she always responded to him, always wanted him. He loved that. He loved her.

"You," she agreed, arching toward him.

His need growing more intense, Vorik lifted Syla onto the bed. As soon as he came down beside her, he shifted atop her to feel her wonderful curves against his chest, then returned to kissing her, stroking and tasting her mouth as his fingers explored her lower depths. Her heated core throbbed with eagerness, inviting him in. *Needing* him in.

Her fingers flexed and tightened on his shoulders as she

rocked into his touch. Already she panted, sweat glistening on her skin. It was so hot. *She* was hot.

A part of him wanted to linger, making the moment last, but he'd grown so hard. And when she lowered a hand, wrapping it around his thick shaft, her fingers were electric. He caught himself groaning and pushing into her touch.

"I need you," she whispered, breathless.

"You're so demanding, my queen," he said, realizing he was breathless as well. Her hand on his cock was so intensely arousing as she flexed her fingers around him. "Syla."

"Vorik." She spread her legs and drew him to her.

"Syla. My beautiful Syla." He drank her in with his eyes as he plunged into her, his desire to be gentle waning as lust flared within him. But she took him eagerly, as she always did, her passion-filled eyes saying his powerful thrusts were exactly what she wanted. She even cried out, begging for him to plunge into her again, faster, harder. For a fleeting second, he thought of what the guards in the corridor might hear, but as he sank into her, her hands gripping and rubbing his shoulders and arms as she arched up to meet his every plunge, he forgot them. He forgot his losses and his angst and regrets. He forgot everything but Syla for whom it was all worth it.

Her cry of ecstasy when she came made him so happy that he followed right after, pouring himself into her, wanting to claim her, wanting her to be his forever. Soon, they collapsed together, sated. Wondrously sated.

"Vorik," Syla whispered, her breathing still heavy, their chests pressed together, their arms wrapped around each other. "Thank you for coming."

He knew she meant in the mine, but he smiled and nuzzled the side of her neck. "I'll always come for you. I even come for you when you're not around."

"Really," she said, dryness in her tone as she ran her hands along his back, sliding them over his butt and squeezing him.

"Every night," he assured her. "Sometimes in the middle of the day as well. I love you."

He shifted to his side, pulling her over so they remained close upon the sheets, sweaty and spent and satisfied.

"I love you," he repeated, so she would know he meant it, that it wasn't his sated lust speaking.

"I love you too." She kissed him, her eyes glistening again. Not from sorrow this time, he thought, but because his love meant something to her. Maybe it meant a lot. He was glad. But she looked so serious that he had to lighten his tone for his next words.

"I especially love that you haven't let anyone shackle me this time. You're a wonderful captor."

"A much better one than you." Syla smiled and pushed her hand through his tangled hair.

"I didn't let anyone shackle you either."

"*You* shackled me. And let them poke drugs into me."

"I'm sorry. That was inconsiderate."

"It was. I don't know why I brought you a tart." Syla lifted the pan from the table with a smile that suggested she would, despite her suggestion that it was inferior because it had been baked a few days earlier, enjoy sharing it with him.

"Because you're a wonderful, forgiving, and magnanimous woman."

"I am."

They rearranged themselves in a sitting position in bed, leaning against the wall with her leg atop his, their shoulders touching, and they split the dessert in half. At the first bite of deliciously spiced baked apples with their buttery pastry topping, Vorik's eyes rolled upward.

"I really *do* love you." Vorik wrapped an arm around her shoulders.

She leaned into him. "Good. I need that. I need you."

"You absolutely do," he assured her with a kiss to her temple. "I look forward to helping you get your kingdom and your castle back. Especially the kitchen."

"It's an important room to control."

"Oh, absolutely."

Vorik had no idea what his future would hold, and if soldiers would throw them both into a dungeon cell as soon as they arrived, but they would be together. That was enough.

THE END

www.ingramcontent.com/pod-product-compliance
Lightning Source LLC
Chambersburg PA
CBHW020631020726
47494CB00001B/142
9781951367527